I0629577

SPARKS FLY UPWARD

ALSO BY KELSEY GIETL

HOPE OR HIGH WATER — OVER THE ATLANTIC
Across Oceans
Twisted River

HOPE OR HIGH WATER — WAR ACROSS WATERS
Broken Lines
Unsettled Shores

LARKSONG LEGACY
For a Noble Purpose
Dusk Shall Weep
Sparks Fly Upward

For updates and behind the scenes info, subscribe to the author's newsletter at: https://kelseygietl.com/newsletter

LARKSONG LEGACY • 3

Sparks FLY UPWARD

KELSEY GIETL

Purple Mask Publishing
Saint Charles, Missouri

+JMJ+AMDG+

Sparks Fly Upward
Copyright © 2024 by Kelsey Gietl.
All rights reserved.

No part of this book was generated by AI. No part of this book may be used or reproduced in any manner whatsoever, including integration with AI tools, without prior written permission of the author.
For information, contact:
Purple Mask Publishing
2025 Zumbehl Rd, Ste 33
St. Charles, MO 63303

This is a work of historical fiction. References to real events and locales are only intended to provide a sense of authenticity. All other characters, places, incidents, and dialogue are a product of the author's imagination. Any resemblance to actual events, locales, or persons, living or dead, is entirely coincidental.

Sparks Fly Upward and all previous and subsequent writings (both published and non) by Kelsey Gietl are intended to be read for entertainment purposes. Kelsey Gietl will be held harmless for any personal actions committed on the part of the reader resulting from the information included herein.

ISBN-13: 979-8-9856744-4-6
ebook ISBN: 979-8-9856744-3-9
Library of Congress Control Number: 2024906675
First Edition

Scripture quotations are taken from The New American Bible, St. Joseph Edition.

Lyrics from "What Happiness Can Equal Mine" sourced from *The Catholic Hymn Book* (1851).

Cover design by Kelsey Gietl (kelseygietl.com)
Cover photos: Face and Arms of Woman used under license by Envision Literary Photography. Red Curtains from "Las Vegas Vibes and Textures" by Mick Haupt and "Sparkler" by Ben Collins used under free license by Unsplash. Additional images from The Metropolitan Museum of Art, New York, Open Access Collection.
Back cover photos: "Brown Cardboard Box on White Table" by Dan-Cristian Păureţ and "Red Curtain" by Peter Herrmann used under free license by Unsplash.

For all those who endure human trafficking, our modern-day slavery.
May you find healing in God's arms.

*"For mischief comes not out of the earth, nor does trouble spring out
of the ground; But man himself begets mischief as
sparks fly upward."*
(Job 5:6-7)

KEY CHARACTERS

INCLUDED IN *SPARKS FLY UPWARD*

FAMILIES IN LARKSONG, WASHINGTON TERRITORY

Martha Louis — 36-year-old former Missouri house slave. After escaping with her mistress turned friend, Sarah, she now lives in Larksong in Washington Territory.

Roma and Lemuel — Martha's sister and brother, sold at the slave market twenty-six years ago. They haven't seen each other since.

Garrett Lark — 34-year-old former plantation son with a Gift for locating people. Originally from Charleston, South Carolina, he now resides in San Francisco, California.

Josiah — The Larks' former butler who is like a second father. He now lives with Garrett in San Francisco.

Daniel Lark — Garrett's 38-year-old brother in Charleston

Tobias Lark — Garrett's 36-year-old brother in Larksong

    Sarah Walcott Lark — Tobias's 34-year-old wife

    Philip Lark — Tobias and Sarah's 4-year-old son

Jamison Lark — Garrett's 32-year-old brother in Larksong

    Coraline Owens Shay Lark — Jamison's 29-year-old wife

    James Lark — Jamison and Coraline's 2-year-old son

Cade Lark — Garrett's 26-year-old brother in Larksong

    Alice Ann Owens Lark — Cade's 23-year-old estranged wife and Coraline's sister

    Julep Lark — Cade and Alice Ann's 4-year-old daughter

Alonzo and Geraldine Lark — The Lark brothers' parents (deceased)

Anwillik (*ann-will-ick*)— The 28-year-old Chinook leader in Larksong

    Tleyuk (*tay-yook*)— Anwillik's 9-year-old son

THE CIRCUS

Ashley Sterling — The 63-year-old owner of Sterling's Theatrical

Rella — Sterling's 34-year-old wife of four years, an equine acrobat

Clary — Sterling's 24-year-old daughter, a fire tender

Kayus — Sterling's right-hand man, a strongman

Julio — One of Sterling's guards

June, Nora, and Olo — Equine acrobats

Lissie and Rodrigo — Trapeze artists

Hubert and Benson – Jugglers

Moses – Stable hand

Louisa – Head Kitchen Cook

At the beginning of the eighteenth century,
in the first month of the year of our Lord,
the sailing ship Oblique
made her final stand against the sea.

After the earth moved and the waves crashed,
only seven of her crew remained.
Forever changed by God's great thunder,
their legacies carried on.

One-hundred-and-fifty-eight years later,
this is but one of their stories...

1

AUGUST 1858
LARKSONG, WASHINGTON TERRITORY

Postmark — Mr. Garrett Lark, San Francisco, California
Recipient — Miss Martha Louis, c/o Chenookville Post Office

My dearest Martha,

I have good news at last. As you know, the past year has been successful and the hotel's assets continue to climb. Mr. Sterling's investment has returned five-fold and I have almost saved enough to repay the final few hundred. Which means Josiah and I will be home by Christmas.

Will it be strange, do you think, coming home after so many years? I worry about my brothers most. You say there will be open arms, but I wonder if those arms are only open to strangle me more fully. Your letters assured forgiveness; then why is my soul so uneasy?

I still remember the night we sat together by the trail fire. You let me kiss your hand goodnight, and you can't imagine the conflict it caused me. Back then I wouldn't have admitted all the things I've written down and I doubt you'd have liked me much if you heard them in person either. This paper gives me a chance to lay it out right.

So, here's the truth we have resisted: I love you, Martha. I know you have doubts and you'd rather I not admit it, but six years of reflection is a long time. After chasing too much and finding too little, there's only one thing I want and that's you. If you don't feel the same, all I ask is you not tell me in a letter. I probably wouldn't come home, and for the first time, I think I want to.

I ask only that you consider it. Eight more months and we can decide everything then.

Yours,
Garrett

Martha tucked Garrett's letter into her apron pocket, turned her eyes upon the dusty-blue Pacific Northwest waves, and once again, questioned the good Lord's many graces. May they delight and confuse her forevermore.

After all these many years of correspondence, Garrett Lark had finally admitted he loved her. Garrett, the man who was all wrong for her and she for him. Six years ago, their friendship would never have had a chance to blossom and now, here they were, considering forever. Heaven help her, but the good Lord's will had never been more complicated. For a former plantation slave and a former plantation son in a country fiercely divided by race, it was a situation most precarious and insensible. For as many reasons as she told herself to remain distant, another several dozen encouraged her to fall headlong into the void. Garrett had never seemed to mind her skin's deep copper hue. To him, their friendship was like one of her mama's hymns—the same melody played in two separate keys. If only the entire world could sing such a song.

She inhaled the salty sea air and released her breath. Sand gritted her bare toes from upon the blanket where she sat, but her present company was enough to calm her anxious mind. One of her dearest friends, Coraline, shared the space on this Sunday afternoon, her nearly-two-year-old son, James, secure in her lap. The toddler threaded spruce-carved beads onto a piece of braided twine, laughing as he upended the finished creation and let the beads fall back into his lap.

Several paces down the shore, Coraline's four-year-old niece, Julep, played with one of her Chinook friends, nine-year-old Tleyuk, and her cousin Philip, Sarah and Tobias's son, who was also four. The town of Larksong continued to expand with their ever-burgeoning families and thankfully little of the trouble from years past. Compared to all Martha had left behind on Walcott Plantation and the Charleston plantation before that, there was little here to be ungrateful for.

Thank goodness for little miracles. Larksong was the only place she and Garrett stood any chance at happiness. Mixed marriages may be legal in some states, but none of them idealized it, let alone encouraged it. It was the only reason they had kept their intimate correspondence hidden from his brothers. Not that they wouldn't approve for they loved them both, but for the fact that it confined them quite completely to Larksong's boundaries. Until recently, Garrett had always been rather a free spirit. She supposed she wanted to make sure he had safely settled before they broke the news.

If, when he returned, there was even news to break.

"Auntie Marta!"

Martha opened her arms in time for the little dark-haired bundle of tussled limbs and bouncing curls to trip across the sand into her embrace. Sweet Julep took Martha's face between her four-year-old palms with serious eyes so reminiscent of her mother. "Auntie Marta, we need more wood for the house."

About twenty yards down the shore, Tleyuk laid a neat row of sticks atop a miniature Chinook lodge, the same type that made up the town's residences. After the Puget Sound battles of '56, around thirty native families had chosen to remain in the once-abandoned village, while the others rejoined the main tribe on Shoalwater Bay. Tleyuk's mother, Anwillik, had been appointed chief of the Larksong natives after Quea'Quim, her brother and the former chief, died during the war.

Martha raised both brows at Julep. "Why more wood? It seems as though your creation is almost complete."

The girl shook her head, curls flying. "Uh unh. It's too boring. It's a square. I wanna add another room. And some pretty flowers."

"I hope you are not becoming prideful." *Like your mother*, Martha thought but bit her tongue. Julep still didn't fully understand that her mother wasn't returning for her. She knew Mama Alice Ann went off on an adventure across the ocean and sometimes adventures took a long time. Like in the Bible stories her papa told.

After Alice Ann left two years past, Martha became Julep's primary caretaker while Cade, Julep's father, saw to the town's needs alongside Tobias and Jamison. Coraline, as Alice Ann's sister and Julep's aunt, should have been the one to carry the task, but such was impossible due to her failed eyesight. Which meant that caring for little James also fell to Martha's capable hands. Most days she didn't mind. She loved children and none more so than the son and daughter of her heart.

Thankfully, Coraline intervened this time. "Julep, I doubt your father would want you in the woods. It's easy to get lost. Remember the story of Little Red?"

"But Auntie Cora," Julep whined.

"I'll take her." Tleyuk hopped through the sand to their side. "I know these woods better than anybody. She'll be safe. Philip too."

Philip hardly glanced up before he went back to digging a trench around the lodge, probably to fill with sea water or seashells later. "I stay here."

Tleyuk shrugged. "One less to care for."

"One fewer," Coraline corrected.

Julep's arms tightened around Martha's neck. "Pease, pease, Auntie Marta? I be real good. I stay with Tleyuk, cross heart and hope to die." She unlinked her fingers enough to cross one index finger over her chest. Martha frowned. She had always hated that children's saying. Too many of their town had already died. If Julep heard some of the events of the westward trail, she'd probably be scared to death.

For today, Martha would let her innocence remain.

She squeezed Julep and let her go. "Yes, of course, my jewel, have your fun. Stay with Tleyuk!" she called as the pair slipped and slid through the sand and up the ridge to the tree line.

Little James tried to scramble off his mother's lap, fighting to follow. "Juju! Yukyuk! Me p'ay too!"

Coraline swung him around and held him close. "No, no, love. You're not old enough to wander just yet. If I have my way, you'll be right here forever." She finished the sentence on a whisper.

Martha knew that, given her friend's blindness, Coraline never expected to have a child and care for him. Yet, here they were, working as a community to provide her the motherhood she so deserved. During their walks along the shore, she often expressed the joy which filled her heart over the love of her surrogate sisters.

Neither had Martha expected to find such happiness and now—she pressed a hand to her apron pocket and the letter within—she waited on the edge of a life no slave ever dreamed about. How she wished her parents, her sister Roma, and her brother Lemuel, could be there to live this same life. Her parents, she'd left back in Charleston on the plantation which bore her. Her brother and sister had been taken to market with her when she was ten. Likely, she would never know where they ended up.

Part of her enjoyed the illusion that they were with families like the Walcotts, well cared for and relatively content. Other times, she daydreamed they were tucked away in a wilderness town like Larksong. If she were braver, she would ask Garrett—*should have* asked him long ago. All the Lark brothers bore exceptional Gifts, with Garrett's being able to find people, wherever they may be. But if she were honest with herself, it was better not to know than to discover they were dead.

A dreadful scream ripped her from her memories. A child's shriek then another, first a girl, the second clearly a boy. She leapt from the blanket, granules of sand scattering from her hemline. Coraline's head turned in all directions and she clutched little James to her chest until he began to wail. She loosened her grip minutely, but still he fought her.

"What is that?" she cried. "Martha, is that...?"

Another shriek sounded, farther away this time, but discernibly in the direction Julep and Tleyuk had taken.

"The children!" Coraline yelped. "Martha!" She jerked as though she planned to run after them while knowing she could not.

"Stay with James," Martha ordered. "Philip, you stay with your Auntie Cora, ya hear? I'll bring them back here. The screams were probably an eagle snatching some critter." The death screams of a rabbit did sound eerily similar to the screams of a child.

Lifting her skirts above the sand, she sprinted into the woods, shouting the children's names. She crashed through the underbrush, twigs scraping through her stockings and cedar branches against her face and neck. She winced at each lashing as she forged ahead.

The children are fine, she chanted. *They are well. It was a rabbit. They are well.*

She shoved her way through another thicket and a body slammed into her from the opposite side. Tleyuk's tanned arms wrapped her waist, his face pressed against her middle as his tears streaked her apron. Her sights swept the narrow clearing they stood in, past every tree and shrub, and over the needle-laden ground. No Julep in sight.

She knelt, prying **Tleyuk** away long enough to clasp his shoulders and stare into his deep brown eyes. "Where is Julep?"

He shook his head, eyes squeezed tight. "It's my fault. I shouldn't have taken her."

"It is not your fault, **Tleyuk**." No matter what happened, she would not blame him. He was but a child. "You must tell me where she is."

"They took her."

"Who?"

"Two big men. I didn't know them. I tried to stop them, but they hit me. I fell...I couldn't..." He heaved great breaths and she wrapped him again in her arms. "Martha, are they going to kill her?"

"No, no, of course not. Don't worry. We'll find her." She kissed his hair and took his hand. "But not alone. We're going to need some help." She would find Cade, then return for Coraline, James, and Philip.

As they half-ran, half-tripped their way to town, hand in hand, she sang one of her mother's long-ago songs to help calm them both. Mama used to sing it as a lullaby in those years before Martha and Roma were reassigned from the slave quarters to maids in the big house, when they were still young enough to dream up beautiful dreams. Before, in time, they, too, were stolen from their family without a trace.

> *"For da Son of Man come down to seek.*
> *To seek, to save. To save so we.*
> *So we may be da chil'dren saved,*
> *the chil'dren of the Savior.*
>
> *If it your Daddy's will, my Lord,*
> *The Lord who be in Heaven*
> *That He may seek, to seek and save.*
> *So none these lil ones shou' perish.*
> *So none these lil ones shou' perish."*

Please, Lord, she prayed. *Please, help me find her. I can't let that little girl perish.*

2

Martha shifted her carpet bag between gloved fingers as she waited at the end of the mail ship *Renton*'s debarkation line, her gaze fixed on Cade's ebony curls a respectable distance in front of her. For a month, the Larksong townsfolk had scoured the western half of Washington on down to Portland, Oregon, in hopes of retrieving even a whisper of Julep's whereabouts, but it was as if the child had turned to smoke. As hope wore thin, Garrett's Gift became their last prayer for her safe return.

Martha had been foolish to allow Julep and Tleyuk into the woods alone and perhaps more foolish to reveal the true depths of her relationship with Garrett to his brothers. Neither Tobias or Jamison thought it wise on her part but agreed that Cade wasn't known for his assertion. He couldn't be trusted to travel to California on his own. If he failed to convince Garrett to help, Martha was the only one their middle brother would listen to.

She dared a glance across the bay. San Francisco's clapboard structures and abandoned sailing fleet sat stoic, silent as to which one was Garrett's hotel. *Built it right into an old ship*, he had written once. *Lots of folks are doing the same with their businesses.*

According to his letters, the city used to receive dozens of new ships every day with thousands of money-hungry men ready to strike it rich. With gold dust flowing from the rocks like water, crews left their vessels where they moored, allowing them to pile up like kindling along the shore. As the city expanded, it had been built straight up to the water, surrounding the abandoned ships until they merged with the city itself. Vessels had been picked over, boards pried apart, sails stolen—hollow skeletons with gaping mouths and space between their ribs. Fires followed, sometimes set intentionally to rid the area of the ships by sinking them, other times out of carelessness from the miners who crowded the streets in makeshift tents and ramshackle huts. The last time she faced a city similar in breadth, she had been ten years old, standing on a St. Louis auction block.

"Next!" called the dock master. An ivory-skinned couple with five children stepped forward, each of their darlings dressed in miniature sailing suits and white-lace pinafores. The husband passed over their information with a protective hand on his wife's back, their bumbling baby upon her shoulder between them.

"Where you headed?" the dock master asked.

"My wife and I plan to open a restaurant. We heard there are lots of hungry men and no one to feed them. She's the best cook there is."

"Yer right about that. We got a number o' places, but plum few decent ones. You can be sure I'll be by for a meal. Welcome to San Francisco."

With a smile, the dock master waved them down the gangplank and Cade stepped forward. He had barely spoken to her since Julep disappeared. She knew he blamed her and what argument could she make against it? His daughter had been in her charge. When she and **Tleyuk** ran back to town for help, she couldn't forget the haunted glaze upon Cade's face or how his hand grappled his chest like his heart was giving way. Without a word, he had returned to the woods, followed closely by his brothers. For over nine hours, they searched with no success. Cade increased in desperation until Jamison forced him to drink a tincture that made him sleep until morning.

Jamison assured Martha that really, it wasn't her his brother blamed, but himself and Alice Ann. Alice Ann for leaving when a child needed her mother and Cade for his inability to fill both roles sufficiently. It was Alice Ann who should have been tasked with watching her daughter on the shore, not Martha. Sarah suggested

9

perhaps Julep's mother had stolen her in secret, although the others agreed it to be unlikely. Alice Ann was not known for a quiet demeanor. If she returned, she would have made herself known and probably in an immense way.

"Papers, girl?" the dock master demanded. She had missed his exchange with Cade who now waited at the foot of the gangplank.

He adjusted his grubby hat and glared at her. "I said, you got your papers?"

"Yes, sir. Course." Eyes on her boot toes, she handed over her freedman's papers, which acknowledged her status as a free person, rather than a slave. California was not a slave state; nevertheless, the fugitive slave laws were still in force. Even with proper papers, there was no retribution for unlawful capture. With a silent prayer, she hoped the dock master was not actually a bounty hunter.

"Freedman, huh? Where you headed, girl?"

"Just hopin' for a job," she mumbled, knowing stupidity would be expected. Her learned speech and proper stature, courtesy of Sarah, wouldn't be.

Thankfully, the man sniffed and handed her papers back, then stepped aside to let her pass. He didn't welcome her to San Francisco as he had the others. She didn't mind. The less notice, the better.

With her papers again secured, she set off down the gangplank to join Cade, uncertain where to go, wondering who they could trust to provide directions. The city stretched out before them, a vast unknown that threatened to gobble her whole. At least there were many other colored folks, as well as Asians and natives, to blend in with.

"Outta the way, girl!" Someone jostled her shoulder—a man with a wooden hand cart—and she tripped sideways. Her boot landed in a putrid puddle of discarded fish guts and she yanked her skirt hem away seconds before it swept through the mess. Her nose crinkled from the odor and she barely managed to keep her breakfast down, what little of it she had on board. The cart owner's profanity rang as he hustled away, but she gave no notice or reply. She had forgotten how cruel the world could be outside of Larksong.

"Do you know which direction the hotel is?" she asked Cade.

"The dock master said to follow this road and turn at Randall's Saloon. It's about a mile down the road, close to the water."

Cade started off and Martha followed, again a step behind with eyes downturned. According to Garrett, last year had been formative for the city. A recession blew in, gold became scarcer, and prices dropped on everything from dry goods to housing. Families started to move in. A police force was established and reformed sinners filled the churches weekly. Still, there lay a sinister undercurrent that made her nervous. She wanted to find Garrett, complete their task, and return to Larksong as quickly as possible.

Thankfully, the hotel wasn't difficult to locate, a large wood-planked sailing ship wedged between two fully wrought buildings. *How strange*, she thought, *to have a boat sitting along the road as though it belongs there all the time.* Although the body of the ship remained, it would not be seaworthy again any time soon. Her masts and sails had been removed and replaced with two additional stories, each with full glass-paned windows. Those upper floors, she assumed, must contain the guest rooms.

A tavern sign replaced the usual masthead, a large wooden board which swung in the breeze on polished hinges. Black painted lettering read, "The Screeching Peach Hotel." How had Garrett come by such an odd name? No wonder he hadn't shared it with her in his letters.

As they stepped into the foyer, her breath quickened along with her heart rate. Six years apart and now she had to face him under desperate circumstances and ill-prepared for her response to his declaration. She knew what she wanted, but his letters could have painted the ideal rather than the reality. What if he was nothing like the words she had fallen in love with?

"A hotel in a boat," Cade murmured. "Alice Ann would love this place." His eyes moistened as they roved across the foyer's charming maritime décor, and Martha wouldn't dare to imagine the thoughts rushing through his mind. Of his estranged wife and where she might be, if she regretted abandoning her family for the sea, if she thought of them at all. Alice Ann had always been headstrong, abrasive, and might Martha say, profoundly selfish. Her leaving only confirmed everything their families most feared when she and Cade first found

11

companionship. As much as Martha disliked Cade's pain, she prayed that Alice Ann would never return. Better for him to find someone else who loved him as she ought.

Martha nodded toward the desk attendant who was dressed in starched livery. "He should be able to help us find Garrett."

"Oh, yes. Right." Cade led the way. The attendant glanced up at their approach and his tidy cinnamon beard surrounded a warm smile.

"Good afternoon, sir. Warren Gypsem at your service. Are you seeking accommodations?"

"Perhaps momentarily," Cade replied, "Might you inquire of the hotel's owner, Mr. Lark, if he has a moment to meet with us? The matter is of great importance."

Mr. Gypsem's brows raised slightly. "Whom shall I say is calling?"

"I'm his brother, Cade."

"Are you then?" In an instant, the attendant visibly relaxed, all suspicion melting away as he extended his palm outward. His smile broadened even into his eyes. "It's a pleasure, sir. Mr. Lark has indeed mentioned his brothers often. He's all up and anxious to be getting back to you in a few months, although—" He leaned in. "I'll admit the staff isn't too eager. Whoever purchases this place is bound to not be as courteous as he is." He released Cade's hand and stepped back. "Mr. Lark didn't mention a visit. Do you plan to be long in town?"

"Not long I hope."

If Garrett's Gift worked, they would either find Julep here or know her whereabouts. It was only eleven in the morning. Depending on the distance, they could find her even before nightfall.

"Mr. Lark is seeing to business at present, but you are welcome to wait in the parlor. It was recently outfitted with new carpeting and furniture imported from Atlanta. Mr. Lark told us how you brothers were plantation men. I think you'll find the parlor contains some of that same Southern charm."

Cade's dour expression mirrored Martha's thoughts. There was a reason they left all that "Southern charm" and neither of them wished to run back to it. How strange that Garrett, who hated his father's life most of all, would wish to be surrounded by it.

"Perhaps you could show us to our rooms after all," Cade said. "I'll require one for myself and one for Miss Louis. Please fetch us when Mr. Lark is unengaged." His words sounded breathless and somewhat stilted as though forced through his teeth. He probably wanted to beg the man to find his daughter then break down into a puddle of tears on the floor. He had done so twice back in Larksong, both in front of Jamison, with Coraline recounting what she heard to Martha in confidence.

Around anyone else, Cade was more stone than human. He wanted to keep the peace. That had always been his way and nothing would drive him from it.

Mr. Gypsem wrote their names in his ledger and slid two brass keys across the counter. "Rooms four and eleven. Unmarried ladies lodge on the starboard side of the upper deck and gentlemen on second upper. Married couples and families stay on the port side from the ladies. All guests may walk the promenade for a touch of sunlight. Meals are served at six and six in the galley opposite the parlor."

"Where will I take *my* meals?" Martha asked, bracing herself.

His brows raised, higher this time. His chin hitched sideways in confusion. "In the galley, ma'am. As I said."

"You mix folks together?"

"Of course. All are welcome at The Screeching Peach. If that is a discomfiture, I could inquire to Mr. Lark if a meal might be sent to your room."

She looked to Cade, but he had already retrieved his traveling bag and was heading for the stairs. Without a backward glance, his soft tread disappeared upward. Perhaps he hoped she would be told it was all a mistake and to leave. She was only here, after all, upon her own insistence.

Martha turned back to the attendant. "No, thank you. The galley will be fine." She reached for the key, but as her fingers wrapped the metal, Mr. Gypsem's wrapped hers. There was unexpected kindness in his smile, almost as though he understood what she had gone through. But how could he?

"Mr. Lark is lucky to have a progressive financier who cares nothing for one's background. He would as soon invest in a colored man as he would a white one, so long as it is to his benefit. You, miss, have a connection to one of his most proliferous clients. I assure you, with Mr. Sterling around, no one will ever turn you out." With a light squeeze to her fingertips, he released her.

With a nod, she snatched the key from the counter, lifted her carpet bag, and hurried up the stairs.

3

At thirty-four years of age, after six years living in San Francisco, Garrett Lark prepared to close up shop and head home to Larksong. Of course, it wasn't his home *yet*. The last home he knew was in Charleston before his parents died. That home he never wanted to return to. The memory of his mother's death made him sick and his father's memory made him want to burn everything to the ground. Instead, he focused on all he had accomplished to finally greet his brothers with a clean slate and a happy spirit.

It had been his navigational Gift which sent him to The Golden City on a mad impulse he still couldn't quite explain. For even more mysterious reasons, his friend and father-figure, Josiah, agreed to follow him. For years, they lived without figuring out who—or what—he had been sent to find. The gold mines resulted in disaster, he'd spent most of what they made anyway, and he ended up falling from odd job to odd job. While his Gift's physical ill effects had diminished over time, they never fully vanished and, eventually, he learned to live with the nauseous discomfort and sometimes outright headaches. His Gift led him without direction, like a compass whose needle went spinning.

A fresh ocean breeze blew through one of the two windows in Garrett's office, rustling the ledger pages on the desktop. He moved the miniature bronze anchor paperweight to keep them in place. When he decided to build his hotel into the abandoned *Fly Felicity*, he had kept the original captain's quarters for his own. The front room served as a combined parlor and study, while the rear provided a sleeping space and much needed privacy. Although, with the constant bustle of business, opportunities for both were rare and fleeting. Especially with a financier as invested as Ashley Sterling.

Mr. Sterling currently sat in one of the two wingback chairs facing Garrett's desk, his black top hat upon his knee and wiry beard oiled to a gleam. A firm believer in, "The appearance makes the man," he never squandered on first impressions. As part of his investments, he kept Garrett, and all those under his employ, clothed in the height of fashion and expected them to pass along that luxurious service to all their guests.

Garrett truly marveled at all he had achieved in these two short years under Sterling's guidance. His hotel wasn't the first to be built into an abandoned ship, but it was the most prosperous. Other establishments had suffered from last year's recession, but The Screeching Peach only continued to grow. As much as he disliked frivolity, there were many aspects of Sterling's generosity he would miss once he returned to Larksong. Then he remembered the stack of letters in his dresser drawer, read and reread, creased until several of them had torn straight down the middle, and knew that home was exactly where he wanted to be.

"It'll be a shame to lose you, Lark," Sterling said. "You've been my finest partner. Helped me out of some real pickles with the profits from this place and helped our city's police force catch their share of men." He chuckled. "You've made me very wealthy off those bounties."

"Likewise, sir. I was dead broke and a sorry sack when I met you and now—" He swung his arm around the captain's quarters. "—I have all of this. I'm eternally grateful."

"As you should be." Mr. Sterling rubbed his beard thoughtfully. "I know you say you want to return to Larksong, but what is there for you to accomplish in such a miniscule place? If the hotel game isn't your preference, perhaps I can convince you with another venture? You are, of course, welcome to join me in management of Sterling's Theatrical. I could use a right-hand man."

"You have a right-hand man," Garrett chuckled. He shifted back in his chair, kicking his heels up on the desk. "Kayus wouldn't appreciate me trying to usurp him."

"Usurp? Who said usurp? I'm asking you to join him at my right hand."

"You only have one right hand and therefore, can only have one right-hand man."

"Then be at my left. Holly day, Lark, I'm offering you the world and you're making jest."

"I don't need the world anymore. I only need a piece of it. And I'm sorry, Sterling, but that piece is in Washington. I've been away long enough. I've never even seen the town my brothers built and it's far past its infancy."

"What about Josiah?" Mr. Sterling asked. "What if I offered the job to him?"

"Josiah's twice my age. He has the freedom to make his own mind."

To be honest, Garrett hadn't considered that Josiah might choose to stay. His father's former butler had been like a father to him and his brothers since the day they were born. They had their own father, of course, but Alonzo Lark was akin to the devil's confidant. He had been nothing like a father should be and Garrett decided long ago to stop claiming him as such. Whenever anyone asked, he told them his father was dead. All other details were inconsequential.

As a former slave, Josiah had never received Alonzo's permission to marry, never had children or a home of his own. His ancestors had served the Larks without even so much as a last name bestowed upon them and once emancipated, Josiah chose not to take one. For as often as Alonzo belittled the man, his wife and sons had loved him. The Larks were the only family Josiah had and Garrett could not see him abandoning that for things like wealth or a prestigious placement.

"And if he should stay?" Sterling pressed. "You would allow that lifelong bond to break?

Garrett sighed. The man was relentless, always had been. "Yes, it would be an unfortunate change; however, there is another reason why I cannot remain in San Francisco."

Sterling smiled. "Ah, now we come to the truth after these many months. Tell me, what truly keeps you from, as you say—" He swung his arm about the cabin. "—all of this, so I can convince you to forget it."

Disappearing through his bedroom door, Garrett retrieved the wooden box which contained two simple gold bands and a third with a peach pearl at its center. The pearl he bought off one of the oyster men down at the docks for an exorbitant sum and set it in the band when first he could afford it. That had been two years ago and mere weeks after his decision to change his life. He had figured if he saw the ring every day, he wouldn't fall back into bad habits. It would remind him of a future worth fighting for. So far, it had worked.

He set the box on the desktop and opened it. "I've got a lady waiting for me."

Sterling's lip twitched. "A woman? That's what this is about? You give me some nonsense about guilt over leaving your brothers, when really, it was just a woman? Lark, you've been with lots of women. What's this one going to think when she finds out about the others?"

Garrett stared at the rings. "I don't know. I haven't figured how to tell her." Would Martha even want him once she knew? It wasn't as though his number of conquests was low. Despite the assurances of San Francisco's increased morality written to Martha, this whole town was full of scoundrels, perverse men, and those just looking to make a buck any way they could. He himself had spent far too much on immoral amusements. If Jamison knew even half of what he had done, he wouldn't merely quote the Bible at him; he would throw it.

It was the entire reason he hadn't attended Sterling's establishment in two years, since the night he pledged to create a life Martha would be worthy of.

MAY 1856

Sterling's Theatrical was the premiere entertainment in town, a three-story plantation-style behemoth constructed in the city's popular octagonal design. Its eight conjoined annexes surrounded an enclosed central show floor with a dirt equine track and seating for an audience of over 400. A family-friendly attraction with a hidden side stage of carnal depravity. Parents and children watched exciting circus acts—equine acrobats, trapeze artists, clowns, and strongmen—from the stands while male patrons satiated their most intimate desires behind closed doors. The circus performers were not sold inside the brothel, however. One of Sterling's firm and fast rules: always keep clear division between your assets.

But that night, Garrett's mind couldn't seem to keep clear division between anything. He kept thinking of Jamison's recent letter, the one warning him how their supposed friend, Clinton Reed, was actually hired to pass information on their Gifts to his boss in California. This was ironically discovered after Clinton's wife, Gabriella, went missing on the westward trail, becoming the sole person Garrett had ever been unable to locate.

Amid the circus fanfare and chandelier light glinting off the trapeze swings, with the fire dancer so close he could smell the sulfur and feel the heat of her batons, he had worried for his brothers and their families, for their new townspeople, and most especially for Martha.

It was unbelievable how much he missed her.

A young woman in a pale green mask leapt from the trapeze platform and swung over his head. Masking was the only hard and fast rule of visiting Sterling's Theatricals. Even when in the back-room brothel, both patron and performer remained anonymous. Garrett adjusted his own black mask unnecessarily as the acrobat released the swing and her counterpart grasped onto her hands before she fell.

Within the applause, another thought came unbidden: He should marry Martha.

Marry Martha? What a ludicrous idea. How could he marry her and not the others he had shared a bed with? At Sterling's alone, he had lost his good reason no less than nine times, not to mention every other senseless place he'd been. Confronted with the reality of his perceived failures, it was too difficult not to embrace temptation. But according to his mother, such behavior was meant for a wedding and a promise of forever. He couldn't promise forever to all those other women. He didn't even know where most of them were. Why would he promise it to the one he hadn't even touched?

Because you love her, and love never fails.

Wonderful. Now he was starting to sound like Jamison.

He cinched his mask again as the trapeze artist flipped above him, her skirts swirling high above her knees. Back in Charleston, the ladies would have fainted at the sight. Here, the audience cheered and mothers encouraged their children to stand and clap. All while being ignorant of—or unwilling to acknowledge—everything they couldn't readily see.

Here he could wear a mask and be himself and no one cared. He could watch the show with families around him and act like he was one of the decent ones, someone who could go home, marry the belle, and have a history she would want him for.

Martha wouldn't want him as he was. She said she did, or at least her letters relayed some hint that she might, but he couldn't imagine that she would. Not with all he had done. He honestly couldn't even believe she was still writing to him. Some of the things she said...they gave him hope he didn't deserve. But what could he possibly do to make himself the man she needed?

Hadn't he always said the only person you could believe in was yourself? Had one woman really made him forget what years of life lessons smacked into him, most of those thwacks coming from his own father's hand?

He turned to Josiah seated on the bench beside him, his friend's too-small mask standing out against his midnight skin. "I'll be back before the end of the show." Without waiting for a response, Garrett edged out of his seat and down the aisle. Applause muffled his steps as the trapeze artists' act came to a close, followed by the audience's laughter as child clowns took the stage. He sidestepped a man exiting the brothel's familiar green door and ducked inside. Paying the doorman, he waited for his room assignment and practically sprinted to Number 24.

Garrett was going to go in; take what he needed; and leave. Like every other time. A transaction, nothing more. Once the exchange was made, the relationship would be terminated. No thoughts of the future or the girl he left behind. Just tonight and what he wanted.

Marry Martha. Give her the life only you can understand.

The door swung open, seemingly without his prompting, with his grip still tight around the handle. Candlelight cast a warm glow over the room's lavish décor, its Louis XVI style and pressed fleur-de-lis wallpaper indicative of Sterling's usual extravagance. Rainbows swayed from the crystal chandelier, flickering across a slim copper-skinned figure standing near the window. She turned and her charcoaled lashes blinked slowly behind a crow-feather-bedecked mask. Assaulted by a bounty of black lace and garters, his imagination didn't require much stimulation to know what else awaited. He wanted to back her onto her silk-covered mattress and give into every sinful desire until the fire inside burned him alive.

And it would *burn you, Garrett.*

Seriously, enough. Where were these thoughts coming from? His conscience? His soul? God?

He had bid goodbye to God after his father persuaded his mother to hang herself and Father Corbin refused her the decency of a Christian funeral. Garrett had toppled the church's sacred statues and the candles before being banished from the sanctuary. He never stepped foot in one again.

He was the only one of his brothers who hadn't.

What would they say about him being here with this soiled dove?

Tobias would likely try to fix him: "It's a terrible idea, Garrett, and you know it. You shouldn't have gone to San Francisco in the first place. You should be home, keeping your promises."

Jamison would try to save him: "Our mother raised us to be upstanding citizens and devout Catholics. You know what you're doing is a sin."

Cade would want nothing to do with it: "I won't verbalize an opinion because any opinion would cause strife. All I want is to keep the peace."

Whereas their eldest brother, Daniel...well, Daniel had done what he wanted as much as Garrett had. He had taken his inheritance, tossed them their share, and waved them out west without so much as a how-de-do. Garrett supposed he should expect the same indifference now.

He stood frozen in the doorway until a thick hand came to rest on his shoulder, a hand he could trace up an arm as wide as his thigh to the seven-foot height of Josiah's mountainous form. The man who practically raised Garrett now gazed on him with disappointment, his soulful eyes peering out from behind his mask.

He didn't speak, simply turned Garrett around and down the brothel stairs to the circus floor. Back into the roar of the show and the equine acrobats now galloping around the show floor.

"What kinda man ya become?" Josiah hissed as he stopped Garrett in the empty shadows at the back of the stands. "Ya have a lady waitin' for ya.—Yah, I know about Martha. The way ya talk, it ain't hard to figure out.—She'd marry ya in a heartblink and here ya are, dallyin' around with Sterling's women."

"Sterling's women can't be disappointed. I can't legally marry Martha."

Josiah's grip tightened. "You could marry her in Larksong. Get ya back to Wash'ton. Yer time here is done."

Garrett ran a hand through his dark and tangled curls as he watched the equestrian performers streak by and the crowd cheered. The horse acrobats were always the first and the last act of the evening, easily the crowd favorite, and a final reminder of the show's excitement to persuade them to return.

Maybe he was ready to give up this fiasco and hide in the wilderness, away from all of San Francisco's filth and double-crossing son of a guns. In a shocking turn of events, he wondered if he'd actually had enough of loose women, late night drinks, and early morning brawls. He had given his brothers nothing to be proud of, helped Josiah accomplish nothing, and was in no fit shape to marry Martha, should he somehow find a way to do so...or even want to.

"I can't go back with nothing to my name. We have barely more money than we came here with. I promised my brothers I would bring them gold and answers. I have neither. Is it fair to face Martha as a failure and ask her to share that life?"

"Ya speak as if she has never failed at anything. Are we not all sinnas?" His voice grew soft. "Some of us more than others."

"I need a job, Josiah. A proper job that pays regular, something to call my own. I need to know why my Gift sent us here before I can entertain any thought of returning to Larksong. Especially before I can consider anything with Martha."

Josiah's hand remained on Garrett's shoulder a moment longer before he said, "Wait here. I think I's might know a way."

At the end of the show, Garrett was still sitting in the stands, even after the last stragglers departed and he could hear their hootin' and hollerin' from between the foyer doors. That was when Ashley Sterling appeared with Josiah from backstage. At that point, Garrett had only known him as the show's ringleader. Anyone who attended the show knew who Ashley Sterling was.

He claimed the seat beside Garrett, Josiah standing at a distance. "So, Mr. Lark, I hear finding people is your specialty."

Garrett balked. His eyes flicked to Josiah who stared at his boots. "Who says that?"

"Your big friend over there. He told me how you saved a girl in a storm."

Years ago, on the westward trail, Garrett had used his Gift to find a missing girl in a sea of prairie grass and an impending tornado. Why would Josiah tell this man about that day? He thought of Jamison's warning letter currently folded in his dresser drawer.

"A search party went out. I was but one of many."

"Now, don't be shy. Take credit where it's due. A man isn't much if he can't recognize his assets and expand upon them." Sterling smiled. "Your friend tells me you're in need of financial capital. Well, it just so happens I'm in need of a business partner."

"I'm not a businessman."

"Ah, many say that in the beginning, but you're a plantation man, are you not? Used to overseeing slaves and all that?"

"I *used* to," Garrett gritted out. "It's not something I like to tell tales about."

Sterling raised his hands with a chuckle. "Now, hold on, hold on. I'm not asking you to go back to all that. I'm merely emphasizing that plantation work is no small task. This'll be much simpler. All you need to do is find people. You tell me where they are and in return, I'll invest in any business venture you choose."

"Find people? That's all?"

"That's all."

One year later, Garrett had money in the bank and a hotel to call his own. He was known about town, well respected, and well liked. He didn't understand his Gift's calling, but Josiah's suggestion to Mr. Sterling had changed his life. Sterling brought him names of wanted men and women and Garrett provided their locations. He didn't need to collect the criminals himself, yet still reaped the rewards.

God forgive him, he knew he'd made mistakes, but he loved Martha. He *did* want to marry her. He wanted to sell the hotel, pack up all his money, and run back to Larksong. He'd build her a house. He'd give her a family. Maybe he'd harvest some crops like he was supposed to before he bailed on his brothers and ran away.

Please, Lord, he wondered. *Would she make an exception for someone like me? If you tell her to, I bet she would, and I promise to never be that man again.*

SEPTEMBER 1858

"I still do not understand." Sterling's voice returned Garrett to The Screeching Peach and the present conversation. "Why must you return to Larksong? Why not bring your bride here? We already make splendid partners, so take a position with my circus. You and your wife shall live at the theater and manage the hotel's finances from there. In your absence, Josiah will be here to captain the ship, so to speak."

Bring Martha to California? Hardly. "It isn't that I don't appreciate your generosity, Mr. Sterling. It's that...you see, she's a colored lady and you know the laws. Larksong will welcome us, whereas here, well..." He raised his palms and shrugged. "Bringing her to San Francisco isn't an option. Not a wise one at any rate."

"What is wisdom, Mr. Lark, if not opportunity? The circus doesn't care what color you both are. We have performers of every race and creed. You can raise a family there and never will you hear a complaint or a criticism. You would have money and lots of it. A city like San Francisco offers you more than a town in the woods without even a port of call or a stagecoach to her name. You must seize that opportunity."

It's a bad idea, a voice nagged. *You would take her right into the place where you bed nine other women? You would be walking right among them and never even know who they are.*

No, he and Martha needed a fresh start. That's all there was to it.

"My family has become Martha's family. I'm sorry, Mr. Sterling, but she couldn't leave them any more than I could."

Sterling's lips pressed into a thin line then parted slightly, a sharp inhale across his tongue. Before he could speak, however, a knock sounded at the door.

Garrett snapped the ring box shut and hid it in his top desk drawer. He slid the drawer shut and locked it, pocketing the key. "Enter," he called.

Warren Gypsem stepped into the room. "Sorry to disturb, Mr. Lark, but your brother, Cade, has come to call."

Of all the names he expected to hear, it certainly wasn't that one. After six years with no visits from his brothers, for what possible purpose would one be here? His brothers despised this place. Or at least, their letters certainly indicated as such. Did it have something to do with the spy in Larksong?

"Did he say why he was here?" Garrett asked.

"No, sir. I told him you were otherwise occupied and showed him to his room."

"Ask Josiah to fetch him and meet me here." Garrett glanced at his financier. "I believe we're finished?"

Sterling cast him a cool glance but nodded. Resituating his top hat, he reached for his ornamental cane and tapped it against the floor as he stood. "I believe we've discussed all we need to. See to your brother. Oh, and Lark..." He stepped around the desk so his shoulder brushed Garrett's. He leaned close. "You would be remiss not to reconsider my offer. Josiah would tell you likewise. Good day."

Garrett listened to the tap of his cane all the way down the corridor.

4

arrett folded his hands upon the desktop as the seconds
ticked by on the sideboard clock. Agitation tingled his
fingertips while he waited for Cade to arrive, which wasn't
like him at all. He didn't get nervous about much. Or at least, he
didn't use to. Now, he couldn't help but wonder about all that hadn't
been said in his youngest brother's letters. Was he still angry that
Garrett left? Would he be glad to see him? Should Garrett have been
able to read between the lines the way he could with Tobias and
Jamison?

Perhaps he should decipher why his brother had come in the first
place.

A breeze blew through the windows, cooling his face and
tempering his anxieties. He remembered when he commissioned the
ship's lower deck portholes to be replaced with glass-pane windows,
allowing more natural light into the guests' common areas. Then he
white washed all the walls and commissioned a visiting photographer,
Henry Frye, to provide several landscapes for even brighter ambiance
and gaiety. The sailing ship theme had gone over spectacularly and
few seemed to mind that he permitted colored patronage. Yet one
block away sat another hotel where Josiah wasn't allowed to step foot
inside the door. Life was so mixed up sometimes.

With a knock on the office door, Garrett rose, striding around the
desk to lean against its face. He crossed one ankle over the other and
hooked his thumbs around his suspender straps. There, that was
better. Cade had never known him as a businessman, but he had

known him as an immature upstart without a care. A nonchalant pose would be a more comfortable transition to their new relationship.

"Enter," he called.

Josiah appeared first, then held the door aside for Cade to enter behind him. Garrett could hardly believe that the man before him was his youngest brother; his appearance had altered so. The once smooth-faced boy now possessed a full beard, close-cropped against his jaw. Although his familiar charcoal curls remained, they now brushed the edge of his collar. A lost and lonely stare revealed how life must ache inside him. He had certainly grown in ways his letters never let on. Garrett, however, barely had time to consider any of them when another figure stepped into the room.

He swore the world ceased spinning.

Martha Louis stood ten feet away, exactly as he remembered and yet not at all. She, too, had aged. Slight wrinkles lined her eyes and mouth, evidence that she was on the closer side to forty. Her dark hair twisted into a mass of tight curls against her neck, as abundant and beautiful as he remembered. He recalled sitting near the campfire and imagining how it would feel to run his fingers through those curls, draw her close, and kiss her as soundly as he had kissed every Southern belle back in Charleston. No, more soundly. With as much sound as he could muster.

Good grease 'n gravy, Garrett. Why don't you focus on why she's here before you focus on what you'd like to do with her? San Francisco isn't a city that an unmarried woman would willingly enter unless she had a very good reason.

Somehow, he managed a sincere smile as he greeted his brother first and shook his hand. When Cade half-smiled in return and accepted the gesture, Garrett was able to breathe a little easier. Maybe he hadn't ruined their brotherhood after all. The real test would be Tobias and of course, Jamison's high holy expectations, but this seemed a positive beginning.

Now, time for the real test. Martha's brown eyes rolled up to meet his from under thick lashes. He took her gloved hand, held it between both of his, and then grinned like an idiot. "Why, Miss Louis, what a pleasant surprise. How did my brother finagle you into coming all this way?"

"I wanted to come alone," Cade interrupted, casting both their attentions his way. "But no one believed I could handle it myself. Martha thought she'd have the best chance of convincing you, even though I told her your Gift won't work. She told us you two are involved, but I still don't know why she would think she'd stand a chance. You do what you want; everyone knows that."

Oh, golly, Garrett thought. Maybe their brotherhood wasn't in as solid a place as he thought. But was that because of what he'd done in the past or because of his recent romantic omissions? At any rate, he was grateful to have it all out in the open.

"Don't pay his words any mind," Martha said softly. "He's been through so much. He's desperate."

"Desperate how?"

Cade blinked and folded his arms. He focused out the window while the cool air blew his dark hair askew. "Julep...is...gone."

"What do you mean, she's gone?" Josiah asked.

"Martha can tell you."

Garrett raised both eyebrows. "Why can't you tell me?"

When Cade didn't answer, Martha took Garrett's arm and turned him into her. They stood less than a foot apart and, despite her charming dress and delicately pinned curls—beyond gorgeous—he also caught a whiff of fish and ship's lacquer. The stench should have put his mind to rights quickly enough, but he figured she could have smelled like garbage and horse manure. It wouldn't have mattered. Her hand was on his arm and all he could think about was the ring in his desk.

Good grief, man. Pull yourself together.

"Garrett." Martha squeezed his arm and he refocused. Her soft irises searched his, their color like copper mixed with the evening sky, a perfect match to her skin's soft hue. "We need your help. Julep was kidnapped. Cade blames me, and I'm not sure he's wrong."

He opened his mouth to tell her that she was, in fact, wrong. Either wrong about Julep being kidnapped or wrong about it being her fault; he was having a hard time comprehending either. But before he could, Josiah released the bellow of hellhounds.

"Julep was taken?" he shouted. Martha jumped as Josiah pounded a fist upon the desk. "What'd they look like?"

"I don't know," she told him. "I didn't see them. Tleyuk did—that's Julep's friend who was with her—but he's a mere child himself. Said they were tall, broad of build, one pale and the other dark. It isn't much."

"It isna anything!" yelled Josiah. "I canna believe they took her."

"Josiah, take it easy. She's only the messenger." Garrett didn't understand why his friend was in such straits. Julep's disappearance was a terrible shock, yes, but Josiah's reaction appeared more profound than Cade's, and Cade was Julep's father. A fact that rather annoyed Garrett right about now.

All the emotions from their younger years percolated inside him, feelings he thought long since buried beneath his work. Annoyance with Cade for always being such a coward and a wet blanket. All through their youth, Garrett had ridiculed him for his baby ways. He had thrown insults even their father never used. He shouldn't have, but he never could understand why Cade couldn't step up and be a man. For pity's sakes, his brother was now twenty-six years old. He was married. He had a child. He should be able to take the reins and fight for something—or someone—without sniveling. How would anyone ever take him seriously? Sometimes Garrett felt poorly for his brother, but other times, it was no wonder why his wife had left him.

That was no excuse for Alice Ann to have left Julep though. She had only been a baby.

"Anyone else gone?" Josiah asked Martha. His muscles visibly tensed beneath his shirt sleeves, but at least he didn't shout this time.

"No. We can't explain why they would take Julep but leave Tleyuk. Maybe because he's Chinook. They may have only wanted white children."

"Seems unusual though, don' it?"

It did to Garrett, too. Taking both children would have provided additional time before anyone noticed the children missing. Whoever stole Julep left Tleyuk behind on purpose, almost as though they wanted him to tell the others.

But why?

The words of Jamison's letter galloped across his vision: *It appears Clinton Reed may have sold our secrets, to whom I do not know. He did not say what his employer planned, but I am assured it was nothing decent.*

What could Reed's employer possibly gain from a four-year-old girl? She had nothing of value, except for her Gifted family, and they had been left alone.

He snapped his fingers. "I've got it! Where's the ransom note? I can track the person who wrote it. We'll find her easy."

"There is no ransom note." Cade's hands were in his hair, fingers gripped tight around the strands as he sagged against the wall and sank to the floor. "For a month, our townsmen went up and down the Washington coast, to Olympia and Seattle and Astoria, and found nothing. Heard nothing." He stifled a sob. "You're all we've got."

A month missing meant slim chances of ever finding her. What if she was sent back east or onto a ship? She could have been enslaved by one of the native tribes. What if she wasn't even alive?

"You ain't gonna find nothin'," Josiah groaned. "They don't want ya to." He stumbled over to the sofa against the far wall and sank into its navy blue upholstery. The sofa was made for two, but his mass easily claimed the space. He lowered his head into his hands, mirroring Cade's preferred position of distress.

Garrett focused on Martha, his tone lowered to a mere whisper. "I can't find her. Even if we don't know her Gift yet, she's still one of us. In thirty-four years, I've never been able to find another one of our kind."

Martha's hand was back on his arm, distracting him with its warmth. "Jamison used his Gift to save Tobias and Coraline. Coraline used hers to translate for all of us. I believe you can, too. You just need to try." She swallowed. "Please, Garrett. Please try."

What he wouldn't give to kiss her right then and there, even in front of his brother and Josiah. Those four simple words, "I believe you can," threatened to undo him.

Taking both her hands in his, he closed his eyes and reached out into the darkness. He allowed his Gift to search as it desired, feeling for any remnant of his niece. The familiar ache prodded his temple and only grew the deeper he searched. As much as he wanted to find Julep, this was a hopeless endeavor.

Resigned to the emptiness, he opened his eyes. Martha's pooled with tears. "I'm sorry. We can create a search party—"

"It won't be enough. You have to try again. Julep's all Cade has left in the world."

His annoyance flared. "That's a kick in the pants to the rest of us, don't you think?"

She glanced at Cade now huddled within the corner, knees to his chest, arms wrapped tight around them. His eyes glazed over, focused on unknown thoughts within. "You weren't there when Alice Ann left," she whispered. "It completely broke him. After that, Julep became like my daughter. I helped raise her. Please, isn't there anything you can do?"

How could he witness her turmoil and tell her no? There wasn't anything he wouldn't do for her and finally being together solidified his confidence in that decision.

"We could go to the circus."

She blinked. "The circus? How will that help us find Julep?"

"My financier is the owner. He has almost as many connections as my father did. He's always receiving leads on people requiring location and I help him. In exchange, he lent me the money for the hotel."

"What do you mean you locate people for him? Like a bounty hunter?"

"I wouldn't put it that way. I don't capture the people; I just tell him where they are. They're all outlaws anyway."

Her brows rose. "Are you sure? Clinton Reed was a bounty hunter for someone in California. Isn't it curious that he dies and you suddenly earn a similar role?"

"Coincidence. Bounty hunters are high and low in the west. They're always roaming through town searching for their next big reward. Sterling invested in me when I didn't deserve it, and I've returned that trust five-fold in sums. Why would he do all that if he was only interested in sabotaging us?"

"Mr. Sterling's the best option," Josiah said. His forearms braced his thighs, hands clasped between his knees. Slowly, his eyes lifted. "The police won'a help. There's no time for a missing child. Peopa are always missing. Sterling has the resources."

"You mean he's wealthy," Cade said. From where he huddled, his head lolled sideways with a red-rimmed gaze. "Garrett, you used to hate the rich. You said they reminded you of Father."

He had used to say that. He used to think it, too. Anything that brought reminders of their good-for-nothing father, he'd wanted to destroy. Alonzo Lark made his fortune through manipulation and Garrett would rather be poor than make money that way. But he also couldn't drag himself back to his brothers with nothing. If it took wealthy men to buy him decency, he would need to turn a blind eye.

"That wealthy man is going to find Julep," he replied. "You can harp on my personal sins after she's home."

Cade nodded without comment. Julep was *his* daughter; he should be leading the charge. Instead, he sat immobilized, staring at his clasped hands. Unwilling to fight, even for this. Garrett had had it with his brother's pacifism.

"You and Martha can stay here," he spat. "Josiah and I will visit Sterling's and ask him about Julep. It obviously isn't a place you'd be comfortable in."

"It isn'ta place you should be comfortable in either," Josiah muttered.

"There's nothing the matter with the show. Families attend the circus with their children."

Josiah might be a hulk of a man and an overprotective surrogate father, but Garrett wasn't the Lark brother people pushed around. Never had been. Never would be. He hadn't changed *that* much.

"Then why can I not attend?" Martha asked. "I won't be left behind due to what I look like."

"It isn't a matter of race."

"Then why, if it is as harmless as you say?"

The heat from Josiah's glare could have seared him. Every shadowed line in his friend's face felt like a summons to reveal all his faults right here, right now. Martha's white-gloved fingers still gripped his, waiting for an answer. She had spent most of her life as a

32

slave, resigned to the shadows, but had evolved from timidity to graceful strength. He was at her mercy, and he hated it. But he also didn't want to hide anymore. Not from her.

If she rejected him, well, maybe he would stay in San Francisco. He still had the hotel, after all, and Sterling's promise.

"The circus is only part of the show," he admitted. "I was usually there for the uh, feminine entertainment. The kind you hide from children."

Martha didn't respond. Her expression remained unreadable, although her chest rose in a deep inhale. How upset was she? Had his honesty ruined everything? If he proposed now, would she tell him to go drown himself?

"That's what you came here for?" Cade choked out. "You could have been home. You could have stopped me from—stopped them from—Julep—" His face blushed bright as a bowl of their mama's favorite sweetened strawberries. He held his hands out in front of his face. The digits were shaking.

Rising from the sofa, Josiah squatted beside him. He pressed a hand to Cade's shoulder and searched his eyes. "Now, son, calm ya down. Yer brother made mistakes, but we gonna get 'er back."

Cade shook his head. He grappled for Josiah's sleeve, gripping it between both hands "You have to take me with you. Julep's my responsibility. Don't leave me behind."

"We won't, son. We won't. Now, let's get ya rested before the show."

Gripping Cade by the arms, Josiah raised him up and set him on his feet. His arm looped the smaller man's shoulders, mostly to keep him upright. Cade's chin raised an inch, revealing eyes bloodshot and waterlogged. Salty streaks traced his cheeks.

Quickly, Garrett looked toward a framed oceanscape of San Francisco Bay, before the gold miners arrived and crowded the port with abandoned ships. That was how Garrett felt right now. Elated to rush after gold while also lost and abandoned.

"I's meet ya back in the galley fer dinner," Josiah said. He opened the exterior door to the squawk of a disturbed seagull, then led Cade past its roost on the deck rail. When Martha turned to follow, Garrett tightened his grip upon her hands. "Would you please grant me a moment?"

Her eyes narrowed as they searched his for clarity. No doubt she wondered how he could use manners like "would you" and "please" seconds after admitting to a list of lady lovers and none of them were her. He didn't want to consider that her incredulity was also a precursor to his rejection.

It was then he realized his head didn't ache. He didn't have a trace of nausea or stomach pains. His heart pounded, but for once, not because of his Gift's effects. In fact, he felt better than he had since the day he jutted off the westward trail and chased a worthless golden nugget. The last day he saw Martha.

All these years, he had thought his Gift needed to show him a reason for being here before he could head home.

But he hadn't needed to find anything.

The reason had been staring him in the face all along. Writing him letter after letter after letter. All the way from Washington.

Cade was right. He should have never left Larksong.

Maybe this was all his fault.

5

Martha had tried to prepare herself for this moment, when she finally stood face-to-face with Garrett again. What she would say, what she would do, how she would feel. No preparation was enough.

If I were a wiser man, I'd ask you to forget me, he had written in one of his more recent letters, *but we both know I'm not wise. You know me better than anyone, and you know I will always be a fool.*

He ran a hand through his hair, shorter than it used to be, but still as dark as night. Martha wondered if he had been this tall on the westward trail? He must have been. He was far past his growing years. Now, she had to look up a few inches to hold his gaze and she didn't remember that before.

Even at thirty-four years old, he was still so handsome. She had always found him so, even in the trail dust. She remembered the swagger in his step, the curl of his smirk, the rough persona she believed only she truly saw through. He behaved differently with her than anyone else. Told her things without his usual touch of arrogance. Back then, she never expected them to end up here. Back then, she wanted her babies to look like her, and Garrett's creamy skin was a laughable departure from her own.

God's plans hardly ever went the way one expected. But was it truly God's plan for her to be with him after what he told her? After all those women…

"Cup of tea?" he asked. He gestured toward the corner where a tea service sat, probably prepared from his previous guest. In all the commotion, she hadn't noticed it.

"No, thank you. I don't think I could manage—"

"Yes, of course." He nodded, then cleared his throat. He looked around the room, finally settling on the sofa. "Please have a seat. Unless you wish to stand. Whatever you prefer."

"A seat would be lovely." Sitting would offer a minute to compose herself and formulate a coherent thought. How incredible that, to this point, their friendship had been nothing but words and now, sensible sentences escaped them.

They crossed to the sofa, taking seats on either end. Her straight-backed posture juxtaposed to Garrett's as he crossed one leg over the other and leaned an elbow upon the armrest. Taking a moment to observe the study, she noticed tidy spaces and businesslike décor, more reminiscent of Southern homes than the maritime theme of her upstairs guest room. This must be what his plantation was like as he helped to manage the rice fields and calculate sums. She could read and write, of course, but she had never learned proper arithmetic. Even what few lessons she possessed had been granted by her mistress outside of the law's provisions. Whereas Garrett was a learned man with a university education and no restrictions to the lengths such instruction could take him.

No, she scolded herself. She must put these types of debasements from her mind. They had both left those lives behind. They were equals now. He had never treated her any different.

But it still wasn't a life she could easily forget.

"How was the voyage from Larksong?" he asked. "I've heard those sailing vessels can be rough."

"It was fine, I suppose. Fair weather. I stayed below decks for most of it. Cade didn't say much."

"Because he blames you for Julep?"

How kind of him to air her laundry like a urine-stained sheet on a clothesline. She flattened one of the arrow seams of her skirt and watched it pop back up again.

"Martha." When she glanced at him again, there was no smirk upon his lips, nothing of the arrogance she remembered. "I don't think you could ever be responsible for such a crime."

"I gave her permission to go into the woods."

"We all ran off sometimes as children. That isn't a recipe for being captured."

"It was for me."

"Oh." A shadow crossed his expression, a humility and realization of all the ways they stood apart. Of course, running off would mean capture for her. Slaves didn't simply run off and not expect someone to follow them. Even as a young child, she understood that.

A painted landscape hung above the sofa, its view of a peach orchard, each tree swollen with ripe fruit, their branches hanging low for picking. Beneath, a smattering had fallen to the ground, a reminder of happier childhood days.

She pointed to the painting. "We had peach trees on the plantation where I grew up. We picked them for the mistress's pies, but she thought them worthless otherwise. And we had such an abundance. So, we stole them as snacks and took them home to our families." She could almost taste the sweet tang as she bit into the first moist fruit of summer, and a sad smile brushed her lips. "Papa loved them."

"He called you his sweet peach."

She glanced at Garrett. His expression had turned thoughtful. "You wrote about it in one of your letters. You said there wasn't much you missed about the South, but you did miss the peaches."

"I can't believe you remember that. I only wrote it for something to say."

"No, you wrote it because it was important to you. Jamison would tell you that very few things we say are ever arbitrary." He reached for her hand and cradled it between his. "Why do you think I named my hotel The Screeching Peach? That was for you."

"You think I screech?"

He winced. "Sorry about that. Josiah said The Sweet Peach sounded too feminine. He didn't care for the Screeching Peach much better, but it rhymed and was more unique than half the businesses in this town."

She focused again on the painting. It was there because of her. He had named his hotel after her. How many colored women had *anything* named after them? Not many, she'd wager. Perhaps none.

Certainly none designated by a white man. Definitely not one who also declared his love for her.

He scooted closer, closing the breach between them. His thigh pressed hers, sending a jolt into her stomach. No one had ever made her feel this way, not during her slavery, not on the trail, not in Larksong. Not even Garrett had brought such an intensity when they sat around the trail fire or walked beside the wagon.

"Have you thought about what I said?" he asked. "In my letters?"

Thought about it? It was embroidered on her heart: *I love you, Martha. After chasing too much and finding too little, there's only one thing I want and that's you.*

She opened her mouth to tell him...whatever could she tell him. There was so much to say... All the words of all his letters crowded her heart for attention. Words were what they needed now, but it was not words that came. Rather it was her lips which stole the possibility of his words, her hands which drew him close as she explored the greatest "what if" of her life.

Without hesitation, he embraced her with a response her "what if" never took into account. His lips found their way to her neck then drifted back to her lips. With every breathless advance, she longed to be ever closer while knowing they shouldn't. Her fingers tightened around his jacket's loose fabric while her heart beat a steady, "You. Are. A. Fool. You. Are. A. Fool," and willed her to end this folly.

He was white. She was black. They weren't married, nor could they be, not until they were in Larksong, and legally, not even then. Their babies would be illegitimate. Never to claim land or move away from Larksong. They would resent her and Garrett for stealing their freedoms. Why, why, why didn't it seem to matter?

It was his lips which stole her reason. His hands upon her sides, pushing her backward into the sofa. She shouldn't let this go any farther. But stars in the heavens, she wanted it to.

She thought of Alice Ann and Cade somewhere in the woods or on the seashore where everything went much farther than it should have. She always thought Alice Ann seduced Cade—that girl was the wild one, after all—but maybe it wasn't that simple. Cade didn't walk away either. Now, Julep was without a mother and with a father who mourned her loss.

Garrett hadn't initiated this, but by his own admissions, he was unlikely to stop it. He hadn't stopped with those other women. He had pursued it.

Without marriage, she would be no different than the others.

"Garrett," she whispered against his lips. "We shouldn't."

He responded with another slow kiss before muttering, "You started it."

"It wasn't wise."

"Well, I'm known to make a lot of stupid decisions. If you make a few, we'll be a matched set."

His forehead pressed against hers, both of their labored breaths coming in time together. His fingers kneaded her waist in frustration, but not in pain. "I know there are things I don't know about you," he breathed, "and much I'll never understand. But I know that I love you and I think that's enough. Martha, won't you be my wife?"

"Your *wife*?" How wonderful that sounded. "But we've only just reunited."

"I told you I loved you in my letter. What did you think that meant?"

"I don't know. I mean, I suppose I did know, but...it's illegal, Garrett."

"If you truly cared, you wouldn't have kissed me."

"Colored women regularly find themselves in situations of compromise with no expectations of more."

He leaned back and held her at arm's length. His brow crinkled into three symmetrical lines. "You are not that type of colored woman. Am I wrong?"

"You're not." She stood, her skirt brushing out of his open reach. There was no safe place to wander, and she couldn't be in such proximity with a clouded mind. The open window beckoned her forward. She closed her eyes as its cool breeze fluttered against her face. What did she want? If she could have anyone in the world, no complications, would she choose Garrett?

His broad palms slid around her waist to clasp over her stomach, then eased her back against him. Her cheek found the curve of his chest, right above the steady rhythm beneath shirt and skin.

"Martha," his voice rumbled above her. "I know a priest here who marries mixed couples in private ceremonies. Or, if you prefer Larksong, Jamison wrote of a Father Lionett. Perhaps he would be willing."

"We could be married in a church?" A marriage before God meant more than any government approval.

"Yes." Garrett's lips brushed her crown. "If you can forgive me my sins, we can be married this afternoon."

His sins...for a moment, she had forgotten. Until today, he had never spoken of them in detail, only in youthful arrogance on the westward trail and in passing innuendo through his letters. Delicate hints of his past, and never in such vulgarity as they probably deserved. She had always considered what it would be like to bare their souls without paper and ink between them, but she never thought it would happen, not completely. If it did, not until he stepped foot on Larksong soil.

She loved Garrett. Could she overlook all the other women in his bed? Plantation women, trail women, soiled doves... How many had there been? She couldn't ask for fear of the answer.

Not that she had ever expected her future husband to be pure as hawthorn blossoms. Whether enslaved or free, she hadn't the luxury of such naivete. On the plantation where she was born, slaves were sometimes matched without marriage to create children with ideal characteristics. It may have been her had she not been sold into Sarah's care. The Walcotts never forced her against her will, but she wasn't foolish enough to believe all slaves were so fortunate.

Turning in Garrett's arms, she opened her eyes to find him studying her with remorse. "Martha, I'll ask you to forgive me, but I won't beg you. That isn't me. You'll have to believe me when I say I can be faithful. I can't change the law. I can't make our children legitimate in Uncle Sam's eyes. But I won't leave you or them. I'll be there. In Larksong, we can make it work."

Her eyes flitted to the floor then back to him. "You created so much here, Garrett. When you wrote to me of a hotel, I never imagined it would be all of this. Are you certain you want to give it up for a lifetime in Larksong? We don't even have a general store."

He chuckled. "Your point is fair. My brothers do think I'm a selfish good-for-nothing."

"I didn't mean—"

"Of course, you didn't. You wouldn't. But it is true. My brothers don't think much of me. Cade's reaction is proof in point. Don't you think it's high time I returned home and set things right?"

She nodded. "I do. Once we find Julep."

He frowned. "You heard what I told Cade. My Gift won't locate her and you've searched up and down the northwest coast. If tonight doesn't—"

"Garrett, please." The words hardly sounded in her throat. She didn't want to hear there was no hope. For two years, since Alice Ann left, Martha had helped raise Julep. That child was as close to her own flesh and blood as one could be. She could not—would not—so much as think that the daughter of her heart was gone forever. "Please, Garrett," she said. "Think about if she were ours. What would you do then?"

His fingers rose to brush her cheek gently then lingered there. "I would stop at nothing." Bending, he kissed her softly. "I've missed you, Martha. This isn't how I expected our reunion to be."

Me neither. She never thought she would ache for someone who wasn't related to her. For years, ever since she was ten years old and sold at market, there had been a pain inside her from want of family. Mama and Papa. Roma and Lemuel. For a cabin and a home she would never see again. For a while, she even longed for her tiny room in the Walcotts' attic in Hawthorn Ridge. It too had been home for longer than it hadn't been. The other kitchen maids held an understanding, a friendship unique to the enslaved, something impossible to describe to those outside of it.

But her desire for Garrett these last six years had been outside of reason. Something forbidden she tried to pray away, but God never answered the way she thought he ought. He had only inspired more letters and permanently sealed the ache inside her heart.

"Let me show you something." Taking her hand, Garrett led her behind his desk and through the door to his bedroom.

"Garrett...I don't think we should—"

He squeezed her hand and smiled. "It's not what you think."

He directed her to two large traveling trunks—one brown, one yellow—positioned against the far wall. Reaching under the dresser's center drawer, he popped out a hidden compartment and removed a key from within. When he slipped it into the brown trunk lock, the latches released and the lid popped, allowing him to raise it the rest of the way.

Inside contained a host of household items—pretty china dishes and lace linens. Click went the second lock to reveal neatly packed dresses and shoes and underthings. It made her blush thinking about how he selected it all and held it in his hands.

"Your trousseau," he explained.

"My...pardon?"

"For two years, I've wanted nothing more than to build a life you would want to share. The life you had isn't the life you deserve. As a slave, nothing belonged to you. I know Tobias provided you clothes and supplies out of obligation, but I want to be the one who does those things. I want to give you the life you never had."

She lifted a pale blue day dress from the trunk. It was stunning. She remembered the first time she wore anything with color. That dress had been blue too, one Tobias made for her to wear on the trail. It was long gone now in a rag heap, but she remembered how beautiful it made her feel.

She had never expected Garrett to buy a hotel, amass wealth, or give her everything she wanted. Her happiness had never been based on things. The generosity of his gifts, however, was not lost on her. Before Larksong, she had never hoped for much. She never dreamed too far ahead or considered whom she might marry or when. She knew the chances were that if she did, there was a risk that one day, her children could be sold. Hadn't she been stolen right out from under her parents while they worked in the fields? She and Roma and Lemuel, one day all gone.

No one knew how long their journey might be on this earth or what the circumstances might include. In Larksong, she could have a marriage without any of the usual derision granted to colored couples. It would never be legal on paper, but it would be to them and to God. That was all that mattered, really. What reason was there to wait when tomorrow was never guaranteed?

A pause, then finally a small smile. "Do I get a ring?" she laughed then waved a hand to erase the notion. "I'm kidding. Someone would probably think I stole it."

"Just you wait." Grabbing her hand, he rushed them back to the office where he unlocked the top desk drawer. From within, he lifted a box, and from inside that, a ring of gold with a peach pearl. He slid the band onto her fourth finger.

She gasped. "How long have you had this?"

"Two years."

"Two *years*?"

He smirked, that lovely arrogant smirk she remembered.

"My lands," she breathed. "You were serious when you said you'd changed."

He stepped closer, desire reigniting in his eyes. "Darlin', I'm as serious as a hurricane in Charleston Harbor."

She looked from him to the ring and back again. "You say we can be married today?"

"If you but say the word."

She smiled. "Consider it said."

6

Martha rested her forehead on her closed hotel room door and listened to Garrett's steps descend the corridor. He had carried her trousseau chest upstairs and insisted that she select a gown from its depths for the wedding and entertainment to follow. He would fashion her a mask for the circus from his current ones and meet her in the hotel foyer at five o'clock sharp.

Was she truly set to be married in a matter of an hour?

She butted against the door and gripped the handle beside her. The room spread out before her in silence, but for the waves breaking outside the window. The late summer sun blanketed the room from its wooden wall panels to its prominent four-poster, and the golden light hinted at the intimacy to come. Would Garrett join her here for their first night as man and wife? More likely, she supposed she would join him in his quarters.

She swallowed. Soon, Garrett would be hers, and she his.

Crossing to the trunk, she flipped the latches and lifted the lid. She removed the delicate tissue from atop two stacks of prettily crafted gowns. The first stack was sewn from sensible cotton with matching sun bonnets and a singular petticoat, in a similar nature to her usual style. The others were far fancier with dainty bows and cream lace trim, unrealistic for work in the Washington wilderness but perfect for a wedding. Immediately, her eyes sought the blue dress. It was the first color Garrett ever saw her in, and she had looked lovely in it. Coraline, however, had married Jamison while wearing blue.

Garrett wouldn't know that, of course. He hadn't been there. But she would know. Therefore, no blue. Alice Ann wed Cade in green and Sarah wed Tobias in yellow, which left ivory, pink, brown, or red.

Sarah should be here. She had been like a sister for over twenty years, always closer than housemaid and mistress. They spent their formative years running through the fields, staring at the stars, making wishes, and naming their babies. They read stories by the firelight, despite it being against the law for slaves to receive an education. Martha had comforted Sarah when her first great love, Linden, died followed by six others. She was there for Sarah's wedding, when she birthed her son, Philip, and lost her stillborn daughter, Mary Grace. That loss had also torn Martha's heart in two. To think they might lose Julep, too...

No, she wouldn't think of it. They would find her and they would bring her home. If Garrett trusted this Mr. Sterling enough to ask him, she needed to trust him, too.

She laid the pink and ivory dresses across the bed and determined them both perfect options. She should count herself lucky to even have an option. Her mama was married in the same plain wool she sheared and carded herself. No fancy outfit or a wagon to take her to church. She'd been married by the plantation master, as all marriages must be approved by him. She had loved Papa, but theirs had been a fortunate arrangement.

What would Mama say about Martha marrying a white man? Garrett had always been kind to his family's slaves. As overseer, he protected them from his father's hand. He never had a say if they would be kept or if they would be sold. The law was the law, and he and his brothers did what they could with an impossible situation.

These were things she understood because she had grown to know the Larks. Her years living and working side-by-side them taught that every fellow from the South couldn't be measured by the same scale. Unfortunately, not everyone had such an opportunity.

"Don' you forget what they done," Roma had spat the day they parted at the St. Louis slave market. "Don' you forget who it was that split us apart." At twelve-years-old, Roma had been the oldest and sold first. Martha cradled seven-year-old Lemuel in her lap, holding him close, one hand smoothing his tight curls as she sang Mama's spirituals, all the way until they came for her.

"Don' go!" Lemuel cried. He ran after her, but his left leg was shackled to the next boy in line. He stumbled, and the other boy caught him before he fell. He stood crying, his bare toes clenched against the hard stone floor of the storehouse. "Sissy, come back!"

Martha tried to reach for him, but the chain upon her wrists pulled taut. It yanked her in the opposite direction. "You be good," she called. "You 'member what Mama taught us!"

Be as Christ to you. It had been Mama's daily prayer.

Papa had a different view: *Stay calm. Stay quiet. Stay alive.*

"'Member what Papa said!" she shouted, but she was already out the door. Warm sunshine sang of a beautiful day, but not one meant for her. The guard gripped her shackled wrists and dragged her tripping through a throng of unfamiliar faces. To a set of white marble stairs topped by pillars taller than any on the plantation porch.

"Up," he ordered and she did as she was told. One step at a time, then turned to face the sea of strangers. Mothers and children and plenty of men. A white woman in a feathered hat who held a colored baby in her arms. Was the child hers? Had she purchased it or was she selling it? Martha wondered what would be its fate.

"Oh, Mama, her!" a little voice cried. "She's the one I want!" Peering into the crowd, Martha saw a middle-aged man raise his hand and call out a number. Beside him stood a beautiful woman who must be his wife and between them a little blonde girl, her soft curls bouncing as much as her heels. Probably no more than eight years old, she ogled Martha with a smile as wide as a crescent moon. She waved her tiny hand, but Martha didn't move an inch.

Stay calm. Stay quiet. Stay alive.

"SOLD!" Papers were signed and bank notes exchanged. She was shoved back down the stairs toward the couple and their daughter.

The woman extended her a small smile before turning to her husband. "Oh, do unchain her, Redmond. I don't think she'll run, will you?" Her sights swiveled back to Martha who shook her head without a word. Where would she run? She had no way to return home.

The man motioned to her guard who removed the shackles, then left without another glance.

The blonde girl immediately grabbed Martha's hand and squeezed, her entire face alight. "I'm Miss Sarah Walcott. This is my papa and my momma. We're going to be the best of friends. I know we will."

Mr. Walcott cleared his throat. "Mind your manners, Sarah."

"Oh, I'm sorry!" She gave a little curtsy, oblivious to the dismay her parents exchanged at their daughter's unorthodox behavior. Surely, it had been Sarah clasping a slave's hand—and later the curtsy—that Mr. Walcott took issue with, not her lack of a formal introduction.

Sarah took no notice. "What's your name?" she asked.

Martha stared at her bare feet beneath a too-high dress hem and a bodice too snug for her growing figure. "Bakhita," she whispered.

"That's a funny name," Sarah giggled. "I like it."

Mr. Walcott, however, was not amused. "She won't be able to serve our friends with a name like that. Elda, surely you can devise something better?"

That was when Bakhita became Martha Louis. For the name meant "pleasantness" and Martha in the Bible was a hard worker.

Elda Walcott had been a kind mistress, although often melancholy over the loss of her babies. Martha had tried to fill the void, but a colored child could never be an acceptable substitute. Nor could Elda be the mother Martha longed for. A colored child could not be dressed in lace and crinoline and shown off to the ladies at tea. A colored child could not worship in the Walcotts' pew at church, join family meals, or sit for the painted family portrait. Above all, a colored child would not bear any blonde-haired, porcelain-doll children. Martha had been loved, although not always wanted. Soon, Sarah forgot that her dearest friend had ever been called another name at all.

If only her family could be with her today—Mama and Papa, Roma and Lemuel. Then they would see what she saw. Service to one's husband and family, although that family may be white, could not be compared to forced servitude. Once they met Garrett, they would have surely shared her joy.

A knock startled her from her thoughts. Leaving the dresses where they lay, she opened the door to find Cade waiting.

He appeared less flushed than before, although his folded arms revealed tension wound within his muscular shoulders. His dark curls flipped out at angles which he quickly patted down. It made no improvement.

His eyes drifted past her to the open trunk, spilling over with garments. "Trying to choose a wedding gown?" He attempted a smile which only half-landed. "Garrett found me in the hall. I suppose I should offer best wishes."

"Thank you." She was simply relieved she didn't have to reveal the news herself. "Look at all the fine things he bought me. I hardly deserve them." She stepped back so Cade could enter the room. Rather than approach the trunks, he moved to the double window which overlooked what had once been the rear of the ship. He studied the ripple of the waves, the sea calm and skies clear.

"You're good for Garrett, you know. He needs someone like you. Someone to keep him steady."

She observed him for a moment. "But you're not happy."

"I rarely am." He quieted. "I'm sorry I became a mess earlier, and I'm sorry I blamed you for Julep's disappearance. It wasn't your fault."

"It wasn't yours either." She thought she heard him sniff, but the sound was so quiet she couldn't be certain. "Cade, it wasn't your fault."

He stood stock still another moment, staring out over the water, and she wondered if he even heard her. What thoughts must be in his mind. No doubt, he thought of Alice Ann out on that ocean instead of here, with him, trying to find their daughter together.

Abruptly, he turned. "You'll give my apologies to Garrett, won't you? At the wedding, I mean."

"You're not coming? But you must. You're brothers." Even as she said it, she knew how foolish it sounded. Garrett hadn't been there for Cade's wedding. Even if word could have been sent in enough time, everyone knew Garrett wouldn't have bothered to attend. That had been over four years ago, before his supposed conversion, when he held a plank in his eye no one hoped to ever dislodge.

Except for her. She had always held hope.

"Please, Cade. You must come. For me at least."

"I can't."

"Will you be there when we meet with Mr. Sterling?"

"Yeah, I'll be there." His eyes sought the door, followed by his steps. "I am glad for you, Martha. You'll make him a better man."

"Cade..."

He turned, his hand on the knob. He nodded to the trunk, its contents overflowing. "Keep above suspicion. Wear the brown." Then, he was gone.

7

"What do you mean, Cade's not coming to my wedding?" Garrett followed Josiah through the dining room as his friend smoothed the creases from each tablecloth. Two hotel maids flitted around them, dusting curtains and angling chairs beneath each table. Meanwhile, Martha remained upstairs, choosing a wedding dress from her trousseau, and making it increasingly difficult for him to focus on anything else.

Josiah smoothed another table crease. "Exactly as I's said, Garrett. He won't be there."

"He's my brother. He has to be there."

"There ain't no law demanding it."

"The law of hospitable etiquette demands it." Garrett paused when he noticed the maids dusting far slower and in the same place. He cleared his throat which caused them to jump and look his way. "Those curtains seem clean enough, ladies. Perhaps the parlor needs tending to."

"Yes, sir, Mr. Lark." They both nodded and scurried off through the main doors.

Once they latched again, Garrett turned back to Josiah. "Since when did Cade become so argumentative? Normally, he goes along with whatever everyone else wants."

Josiah shifted to the next table, eyes on his work. "You don'ta really know him like ya think ya do. Time's passed."

"It has, but we still wrote. He never sent me anything that might be the least bit upsetting."

"He did ta me." Josiah paused. He studied Garrett, the wrinkles around each eye puckered in consideration. "Ya got to understand. The last wedding yer brother was at were his own. Then she left 'im. He ain't got the kinda mind to handle that easy."

"I know he misses her—why I don't know—but I'm his brother. Can't he put all that aside for an hour?"

"Why do ya have sucha need to marry Martha today? Ya had yer heart set on marryin' her back in Larksong, why not stick to it?"

"Because she's here now and there's a priest willing to marry us. I've been faithful as a fiddle for two years, Josiah. For the sake of holiness, don't make me wait any longer."

"So's it all 'bout meetin' yer physical urges? Get away from me. I's got work to do." He strode off to the kitchen and Garrett ran after him, dodging one of the waiters as he ducked into the dining room with a stack of plates.

They passed Cook Marcos directing the kitchen assistants and scullery maids in preparation for that evening's meal. The sweet scent of garlic and cilantro filled the air. "It isn't *all* about that," Garrett insisted.

"It ain't?" Josiah opened the linen cupboard, a room with barely enough space for two. Garrett thought it would make an ideal spot for a rendezvous with his new wife. He could picture it now: him and her, them together... Garrett scratched his temple. Maybe his "urges" were more prominent than he thought.

"Fine, you know my dark past. I can't stifle that completely, but Martha isn't like those other women. I believe it was you who told me to stop chasing the doves and settle on one." Garrett reached for the basket of freshly-trimmed candles and began to search for the matchbox. The maids had an ongoing issue with replacing it properly. He opened the cabinet above him. "I love Martha," he told Josiah as he searched. "She loves me. That type of marriage doesn't waltz its way in every day. It didn't for my parents. It didn't for most of the folks back in Charleston." He shut the cabinet and opened the drawer below. Nothing but silverware. "Cade might've chosen a wench, but that's his problem, not mine."

Josiah opened the corner drawer, withdrew the matchbox, and

dropped it on the hutch's tabletop with a clank. "That's yer sista-in-law. Show respect."

"Like the respect she showed Cade and Julep? I doubt Julep would be missing if she had two parents to tend her instead of Martha trying to be everything to everyone. She also has Coraline to care for. It's too much for one person to handle alone."

"It is. Mighta been kind to have an extra pair of hands around town to help."

Garrett opened his mouth then shut it. Dash it all, he'd walked himself right into that. "You weren't there either." It was petty to toss the blame back, but annoyance was winning over courtesy.

Josiah's eyes darkened. "Love ain't somethin' ya do in a blast of stupidity. You're rushing this, Garrett, like ya've rushed everything all yer life." He opened a drawer and lifted a stack of folded napkins, speaking over his shoulder. "You've been engaged for half an hour. I wouldn't be saying this if I wasn't trying to protect you."

"I don't need protection."

"Ya do. Why do ya think I's wanted to come here with ya?"

Garrett couldn't answer that. Whenever he asked Josiah why he refused to leave and live in Larksong, he said, "Bein' here is somethin' I's needs to do." Was it really just to protect him?

Garrett leaned back against the hutch, flicked the edge of the matchbox with his fingernail, and said nothing. Josiah stared him down a minute too long, then shrugged and turned toward the door. "Don't matter none, but I's don't want ya to make the same mistake I made."

"What mistake?"

Josiah left Garrett to march back through the kitchen. No way was his friend about to leave without finishing this. Garrett grabbed the basket of candles and the matchbox and easily sprinted to block Josiah's exit into the dining room. "What mistake?" he repeated. The words echoed in the now silent kitchen.

Josiah glanced at the cooks paused in their meal preparations, the two scullery maids stirring soup while their ears perked in the men's direction. It wasn't every day that the owners of The Screeching Peach confronted each other in the middle of the work day, and certain to be more excitement than they usually saw. Garrett paid them well, but not enough to attend the theatre or run with any other classy crowd. Even the circus was pushing the envelope.

"Everyone is free to take a fifteen-minute break," he announced.

Incredulity gaped back at him. "But, sir," one of the scullery maids exclaimed. "If we leave, the soup will burn and so will the bread. We won't have supper ready to serve at six."

Of course. Garrett knew that. Now he looked like an idiot in his own hotel.

"Right, yes, of course. Carry on. You may all knock off fifteen minutes at evening's end."

"Thank you, sir," the kitchen staff responded in unison. They promptly turned back to their work.

The next ten minutes were followed by silent arrangement of dining tables, folded napkins, and the flash of sparks against candle wicks. China clattered with each of Josiah's subsequent trips to the cupboard and wary glances exchanged with each arrangement of silver. At last, supper service was ready and the staff vacated the room.

Garrett glanced at his pocket watch. Quarter 'til. Martha should be nearly ready. They would take their supper after the wedding, once the other guests had their fill of Marcos's scrumptious cuisine.

And we've had our fill of each other, he thought, and immediately regretted it. *Focus, you fool. Josiah first.*

He pulled out a dining chair, spun it around, and sat down, arms folded over the chair back. He rolled a hand toward where Josiah stood near the window. "Might as well tell me what's on your mind or I'll hound you and you know I will.

Josiah folded his own arms, his biceps bulging. "You shouldn't get involved with a colored woman."

"*Excuse me?*" Despite their father's prejudicial upbringings, he would have never suspected Josiah to hold such tendencies. Maybe marriage was where he drew the line. "So, that's what this is all about? You don't like that she's black? You are too and about as dark as they get."

"Watch your tone, son. The problem isn't that she's black and yer white. The problem is ya haven't thought about what that means."

"I don't care if it's against the law—"

"It ain't the law I worried about. It's yer children."

"Now who's rushing things? I suggest marriage and you've already made me a father." Garrett laughed. "You think Martha and I didn't discuss these sorts of things? Of course, we did. In Larksong, none of that makes a difference."

"Today it don't, but what if the town expands? What if more folks come who aren't as understandin'? Mixed babes turn out black. Rarely white. Yous can try to keep it secret, but everyone gonna know. Are ya willin' to watch yer family suffer the insults and shame?"

"Tobias and Jamison won't let them. Those aren't the rules of Larksong."

"Yer brothers ain't the ones who have to answer fer what they done. What if someone turns ya in to the police? They'd take Martha back to the South. Yer children, too."

"Martha has papers. I can create some for our children."

Crossing the room, Josiah rested his hand on Garrett's shoulder in an uncharacteristic gesture of familiarity. "Ya know it ain't that simple. Nothin' ever is."

An hour ago, Garrett and Martha had hashed out all these same arguments. She said the same words and it all seemed so logical to dispute her. After they kissed, nothing sounded like a valid consideration for why they shouldn't be together. Larksong was Larksong—different, perfect, and without flaw, or not many anyway. Where a man could be a man and a woman a woman and nothing else stood a chance. Then why did it sound different from Josiah's lips? Why did the same arguments seem to grow legs and dance around, mocking him?

"You told me to wait for her," he argued. "That night at the circus. You told me to stop wasting my nights on other women when there was one waiting for me at home. You told me she was worth giving all that up for." He pushed his chair forward, standing up and catching Josiah unaware. His friend's hand fell from his shoulder. "You told me I was allowed to love her. You, Josiah. You said it was permissible."

"I did." He reached for Garrett again, but let his hand drop back at his side, emotion flickering in his eyes. "Yer like my son, Garrett. I love you with every breath. But I seen the pain of lovin' someone ya can never truly call yer own. That is a pain ya never pass."

"How do you know?"

"Yer mother," he whispered. "Her pain was great."

"Because my father never loved her."

Josiah looked away. "He did not."

"I'm not Alonzo. Martha means everything to me. I would do anything for her and endure the pain."

A knock sounded from the entryway. Garrett swung his chair around and back in perfect angle beneath the table. He tugged on the hem of his jacket and exhaled before calling, "Enter."

Warren Gypsem stepped in with a grin. "Mr. Lark, Miss Louis is waiting in the parlor. I must say she's pretty as one of them Southern paintings you admire. Where are you taking her?"

"To the circus, Gypsem. But first, to church."

"On a Friday, sir? I believe the daily Mass was in the morn."

"I've petitioned Father Bolin for a special service. For Miss Louis, as she missed the morning Mass."

"Ah, how kind of you. Shall I fetch the wagon from the livery or will Mr. Josiah be accompanying you this evening?" It had been Josiah's request that he handle the reins whenever they rode together. Garrett had never demanded Josiah to be his chauffeur; that was something Alonzo would have done. Nevertheless, given Josiah's coloring, folks assumed it anyway. The two men carried on as they had done since Garrett's childhood, when he still needed Josiah's strong arms to swing him up into the saddle.

He turned to his friend, a silent question in his eyes. Would Josiah really abandon him, too? He had said Garrett was like a son to him.

"Yer set in goin' today?" the older man asked.

Garrett nodded. "I can drive the team on my own, but I'd rather you joined us."

"Then I best get my hat. We shouldn'ta keep a lady waitin'."

55

8

As Cade suggested, Martha wore the brown day dress from her trousseau. Rather than her usual prairie bonnet, however, she allowed herself the luxury of a straw bonnet with a single rose ribbon, which added a touch of sophistication, like a real city lady. It may have been the gloves, dress sleeves, and hat brim shielding her skin, but no one stopped the wagon to ask why she, a colored woman, rode so proper beside a white gentleman, acting above her station. Even so, she scooted a little farther away from Garrett on the bench seat. Best to not encourage talk of any sort, especially not on their wedding day.

It had been Josiah's idea for Martha to join Garrett up front with the team. "It ain't right fer a lady to ride in back," he insisted, "and it'll call 'tention ifa two black folks share the seat." Therefore, Garrett now rode beside Martha in better than his Sunday best: an ebony frock coat, gold-threaded waistcoat, and black trousers purchased for exactly this occasion, although he originally planned to wear them in Larksong. His silk tie fastened in an asymmetrical knot which he claimed to be the latest style, while a top hat accentuated his brunette waves yet tamed them into submission. Every few minutes, he caught her stare and would smile with such affection that she couldn't help but remember back on the trail when his smiles were rare. Those that did emerge were often attached to a curl of the lip or a snide remark. Who would have believed that six years and a stack of letters would change him from a man who believed in nothing and no one, sharp around every edge and crevice, to a man who pledged his entire devotion to her?

They trotted down Clay Street and past Portsmouth Square, Martha taking in everything around her. Well-manicured paths crossed through the park to a central circle, like wheel spokes on a wagon, each path lined with small trees and shrubs. No doubt, once they were fully grown, this area would be a place of shade and relaxation from the summer sun. Even now, there were several men and women out for a stroll within its iron-fenced perimeter.

"This area of San Francisco is different than what I expected," she told Garrett. "It's far nicer than near the pier."

"Not everything here is garbage," he laughed. "Although if you had visited five years ago, it wasn't at all fit for company."

"Now look at ya, Martha," Josiah cut in from behind them. He held on to either side board, legs dangling off the back of the wagon bed. "Ya as fit a lady as any of 'em."

Heat flushed her cheeks and she wondered if they could tell. She peered in the opposite direction, following a fine covered carriage as it ambled past.

"Josiah's right," Garrett said. "Except a lady would have chosen a more becoming gown on her wedding day. I only added that one out of necessity. It's the cheapest in the bunch."

She managed to face him again and pasted on a smile. "Which was quite astute as it is necessary. We shouldn't draw attention when what we're doing is illegal."

"I know," Garrett sighed. His fingers released the reins and seemed to move toward hers, then raised at the last second to sweep hair behind his ear. "I wish I could give you a perfect day like Sarah and Coraline had."

Although she longed to reach for his hand, too, she only smiled. "Their days weren't perfect either, but they were full of love, and I already have that. I don't mind what I'm wearing."

"Listen to her," Josiah grunted. "Ya don't wanta land in jail again." Back on the trail, Garrett had spent a few hours in the Fort Hall garrison after spouting vulgarities at one of the guards. His actions had been in defense of his friends, but it still wasn't an event to repeat on their wedding day.

"Yes, yes, I'll follow the clock's reminder," Garrett told him. As the wagon slowed before St. Mary's Cathedral, he waved a hand at the brick-inset clock of the central spire. Beneath an inscription read, "Son, observe the time and fly from evil!"

While he secured the horses to the hitching post, Martha hopped from the wagon, overcome by the majesty of the cathedral. Never had she seen a building so expansive. It was nothing like their small chapel back in Larksong with Father Lionnet's once-monthly Masses. St. Mary's brick façade contained three arched entryways with wooden doors at least twice as tall as she. Above each rose rounded windows created from thousands of pieces of colorful glass in intricate patterns. She didn't know what to call such artwork, but she could appreciate the effort it must have taken to produce.

Before moving to Larksong, the Walcotts' plantation slaves had always worshiped together whenever they could find the time. Sarah's family had been Catholic, so the slaves were also instructed in the Catholic prayers, although without the fullness of a priest to say Mass. While in Larksong, Coraline's husband, Jamison taught Martha more about the faith and her Baptism last year brought everything together. While she still didn't understand all the Latin prayers, she understood enough to know that there was something deeply reverent and substantial within the Eucharistic celebration—Christ's presence come to life. Blessed was she to be wed in such a place. It had been a journey and she cherished every step, the blessed and the broken. She prayed it was a faith which would only continue to grow.

Removing his hat, Garrett opened the church door. Her heart skipped as they passed under the threshold and into the cool hush of the sanctuary. Two columns of pews—likely enough to seat a thousand or more—drew her eye down the central aisle to the communion rail and on up to the altar. An intricate stone and gold tabernacle and crucifix created a backdrop for worship. Marble pillars along the central aisle ascended into a lofted ceiling where a second white rail indicated the presence of a balcony which, no doubt, contained more seating for parishioners. Upon it all, sunlight cast through those whimsical colored windows, and she could see they included detailed images of people, probably saints or Bible stories.

How had such beauty been created out of nothing but broken glass? In awe, she raised her hands, allowing rainbows to dance over her white gloves.

"Inspiring, isn't it?"

She snapped her hands to her sides as the priest approached through a side door, already dressed in vestments of white and gold. Hazel eyes smiled out from a face much younger than she expected; he couldn't be more than her thirty-six years. Having only Father Lionnet to compare with, she had assumed most priests to be older, but that seemed silly to think now. Of course, priests could be any age. Hadn't Jamison once wanted to join the clergy?

The priest glanced at the vaulted ceiling of the sanctuary. "The cathedral was dedicated only four years past. Built by the Chinese immigrants with brick brought straight from the East. Such hardworking men and so hungry for the Word of God." He extended his hand to her followed by Josiah. "Father Bolin. I'm the assistant rector here at St. Mary's."

Somehow, she found her voice beneath her nervousness. "Martha Louis. It's a pleasure, Father."

"Likewise. I have heard much about you over the years." He grasped Garrett's hand. "I was surprised to receive your request, Mr. Lark. Delighted, to be sure, but never did I expect it."

Garrett withdrew his hand and ran his fingers through his hair. "I know it isn't the plan I told you."

"The Lord always has a better one. Come, let us begin." He continued to speak as they moved up the center aisle. "Out of discretion, I did not request an altar server nor inform the bishop. I trust your understanding if we cannot perform the full nuptial Mass?"

Garrett looked to Martha and she nodded. "As long as we're good and married, Father," he said. "That's all we want."

Father Bolin instructed them to stand at the center of the communion rail, with himself behind it, and all directly beneath the watchful eye of Christ's presence in the tabernacle. Garrett held her arm tight as the priest retrieved a pitcher of holy water and instructed Josiah on how to hold the missal and turn the pages. The cathedral's expanse covered them in all its splendor, dizzying as she peered up into its breadth.

"Are you certain?" Garrett asked, a question for her alone. His brow furrowed, a series of tight lines she longed to smooth away. After today, she could do so every night for the rest of their lives. She pictured them back in Larksong, sitting together before the fire, Garrett resting his head in her lap after a hard day's work with his brothers. Her fingers would glide across his scalp, her voice soothing in song as she erased every care of that day...and the next...and the next.

She nodded with a smile. Even if the law said she was wrong, she knew in her heart to be right.

"Garrett Lark," Father Bolin began, "will you take Martha Louis here present for your wife, according to the rite of our Holy Mother, the Church?"

"I will," Garrett promised, his face alight with joy. How different than the day they met when all he did was brood and complain. Today, there was genuine happiness in his expression and it delighted her to be the cause.

"And Martha Louis, will you take Garrett Lark here present for your husband, according to the rite of our Holy Mother, the Church?"

"I will."

"Please face one another and join your right hands. Mr. Lark, repeat after me..."

This was it. The moment all the indecision and confusion of her life found purpose. Everything had meaning. All those lost years, the heartache that stole her from her family and brought her to Hawthorn Ridge, also brought her in line with Garrett. *God makes all things new and for his good.* Hadn't she been promised that a million times, first by her mother, then by Sarah and Jamison and Father Lionnet? Now it was Garrett's turn to truly show her how Christ kept His promises. In that, a curse had turned to blessing.

Martha allowed Garrett to hold her gloved hand in his. "I, Garrett Lark, take you, Martha Louis, for my wife, to have and to hold, from this day forward, for better, for worse, for richer, for poorer, in sickness and in health, until death do us part."

"Now, Miss Louis, I will ask the same. Repeat after me..."

"I, Martha Louis, take you, Garrett Lark, for my husband, to have and to hold, from this day forward, for better, for worse, for richer, for poorer, in sickness and in health, until death do us part."

"Garrett and Martha, I join you in Matrimony." Father Bolin raised his right hand, tracing a cross before them. "In the name of the Father, and of the Son, and of the Holy Ghost. Amen."

"Amen," they responded as one.

When Garrett handed over the rings, the priest sprinkled them with holy water followed by several blessings in Latin which Martha couldn't translate. Even after years of Father Lionnet's monthly visits to Larksong, she still wasn't able to understand more than a few Latin prayers here and there. She had always been wistful of Coraline and her natural Gift of translation for any language, without need for even a single lesson. Today, she remained simply thankful that at least their vows were recited in her native tongue.

"O Lord," Father Bolin continued, "these rings which we bless in Thy name, so that they who wear them, keeping faith with each other in unbroken loyalty, may ever remain at peace with Thee according to Thy will, and may live together always in mutual love. Through Christ our Lord. Amen."

"Amen."

Unbroken loyalty...ever at peace...always in mutual love. For the first time in her life, she truly believed that she could have those things. That she was worthy of them. Love and loyalty would bring them peace always.

Gently, Garrett removed the glove on her left hand and returned her engagement ring to her finger along with a thin band of plain gold. His eyes ever set on hers, he promised, "Martha, take and wear this ring as a sign of our marriage vows in the name of the Father, and the Son, and the Holy Ghost. Amen."

With the simple gold band handed to her by the priest, Martha placed it on Garrett's finger. "Garrett, take and wear this ring as a sign of our marriage vows in the name of the Father, and the Son, and the Holy Ghost. Amen."

"We're married," Garrett whispered. His smile glowed with the sunlight through the broken glass windows, a colorful array within his eyes. There in the center of either iris, she saw herself reflected as he must see her, with the radiance of a new bride. Her breath stilled at its beauty.

She couldn't speak, only smile, her eyes spilling over as the sprinkle of holy water rained upon them. She felt as though she were being baptized all over again.

"May God fulfill you in His blessing; so that you may see your children's children to the third and fourth generation and afterwards possess everlasting and boundless life. Through our Lord who reigns forever and ever. Amen."

"Amen."

Garrett kissed her then, right in front of Josiah and Father Bolin, even though she was fairly certain he wasn't supposed to. His lips brushed hers with such tenderness, unlike their hurried kiss before he proposed. This was soft and sweet and spoke of much more than physical longings.

All her life, the world had told her she was ugly and insignificant because of the color of her skin. Not once had Garrett ever made her feel that way. Not even back then. Not even at his worst.

And he certainly, most definitely, wasn't looking at her like that now.

9

Well, how-dee-do, they'd done it. They'd actually gotten married. Garrett Lark, womanizing addlepate according to his brothers, had settled down with one woman. He had never—*ever*—thought he would come to this point, where he loved and trusted someone enough to commit himself for his entire life. For Martha, he had reformed his life. For her, he had done everything. Her letters had made him feel like they stood in a room of eligible bachelors, but for some reason, she only focused on him in all his imperfections. Now that wonderful woman was his for the rest of his life.

Other married men in San Francisco told him he would get bored. That he would go back to the brothels soon enough. That's what they did, but he couldn't imagine it. Not this time. How could he ever get bored with Martha at his side?

The drive back to the hotel was agonizing. The familiar twenty-minute distance suddenly felt as long as the totality of miles on the western trail. Having Martha beside him, her knee occasionally brushing his, the ribbon of her hat fluttering out of the corner of his eye, had his nerves on fire and fingertips tingling. Once they reached the hotel, he handed the reins off to Josiah and allowed Martha to return to his room before him, lest anyone gain suspicion of their criminal escapades. However, when he entered the room fifteen minutes later, the shy flutter of her lashes caused him to slam the door in his haste.

Slow down, he reminded himself. *This is your wife, not another conquest. She deserves more than ten minutes of your time.*

But oh, how he bit hard on his lip as he approached in agonizing slowness. His eyes forced to hers, his hands trailing to her waist, then around her back. Her curves were rounder than he remembered, but that had been years ago. He, too, had gained a few pounds since giving up his time in the mines.

"I can't believe this is our life," he said.

Martha suddenly averted her eyes, seeking out the floor. She stepped back out of his touch. It seemed so unlike the woman who strode into his office—leading his brother more than Cade leading her—and demanding that he help them find Julep.

Was she questioning her decision to marry him?

He tipped her chin up until she met his gaze again. "What is it? Are you sorry you married me?"

She gripped his upper arms, and brought them back around her waist. "No, not at all. I love you. I just—"

"Don't. Whatever it is, forget it." He pulled her into him and kissed her, soft and slow, before—with inhumane restraint—he eased away again. "Don't you ever avert your gaze from me. Don't you ever look at the floor like we aren't proper partners." He jerked his chin toward the door. "Maybe out there we can't go around like we'd prefer, but here you're the same as me. Better than. Don't let those uneducated idiots dictate how we're going to live."

Softly, she inhaled then exhaled. The sunlight flickered within her brown irises as she lingered within his examination. She was searching for something within him as much as he searched within her. Some sort of confirmation, although he didn't know what that was.

"Where is your confidence, Martha? Where is the woman who kept alive what little spirit I had all these years, who insisted I could do things I never thought myself capable of?"

What he intended then to be another gentle kiss, once prompted, quickly turned to fire. Martha's insistence tossed another several logs on the flames and all too soon, they blazed and fell to embers. All sound evaporated within their one focus, an unbearable two years of celibacy finally drawn to its terminus.

Afterward, arms wrapped around one another, Garrett lay listening to Martha's soft breaths from where her head rested within the crook of his arm. Her fingers splayed upon his stomach while his eyes traced the lines of the deck boards in the ceiling above. They grew more difficult to discern as the sun dipped beneath the horizon and cast the room into violet shadow.

"Bakhita," Martha whispered.

He tilted his chin down to look at her. "What does that mean? Is it the African language?"

"African isn't a language, and no, it isn't. I don't think." The tips of her fingers traced over the scar on his far side, the one from the day his father slashed him with a fire poker. The same poker he had turned on Tobias and Jamison at least once in their younger years.

"What does it mean then?" he asked. He didn't want to talk about his scars if he didn't have to. Martha already knew about his father's abuse from their late-night trailside talks and his letters. *Let's leave it in the grave where it belongs.*

"Bakhita means 'fortunate,' but I don't know in what language. It's the name my parents gave me. I haven't said, and barely thought, that name in over twenty-five *years*." The final word drew upon a whisper, a slight sound like the voices in the wind at night, when one imagines ghosts along the halls and slipping through the window sashes.

Martha's real name is Bakhita. He traced the ceiling shadows, unable to reconcile this truth with the woman he loved. He knew her name had been changed when she was purchased by the Walcotts; she told him so on the trail. Once he asked her what her real name was and she simply said, "Martha is my real name now."

Both legend and religion claimed that knowing the real name of someone gave you power over them. For a former slave—used to being overpowered by her master—a decision like that became monumental.

He swallowed hard. "Why did you tell me?"

"You asked where my confidence went. It's with the girl I used to be before she was sold. Ever since being in Larksong, I've found her a little more. All your letters made me believe in the wonderful words you said. I'm glad to have married you, Garrett, so glad. But once you brought me home, truly as your *wife*, all the fear came flooding in. Being where everyone looks at me how they do...that they'll jail my husband for loving me...that they could kill me for loving him... The truth is we're not in Larksong and might not be for a while, and I feel like that girl on the auction block being told I'm only worth a 'fair price.'"

Grieved, Garrett drew his wife in tighter. A drop of water touched his chest, one of her tears threatening to break him in two. A life together was much more difficult than a life of letters. This time, he couldn't even piece words together to offer her comfort. He wasn't used to comforting a woman when she cried. He was used to leaving her bed, walking out the door, and rarely wondering what she did once he was gone. Did those other women cry, too? Did they wish they had someone to pour their wounds out to? They must for, although he loathed to admit it, he always wished he had that, too.

He supposed now he did.

"Martha...Bakhita..." he began, uncertain what to call her. "I love you. We'll make it through this. We'll find Julep and we'll return to Larksong. There's nothing to fear." Sterling would have the answers, he reminded himself again. Sterling would help them and they'd be home in no time.

Her face turned up to him, sweet tears against her cheeks. She smiled. Even in the darkness, he could feel its warmth.

"I still want you to call me Martha." This time, she nodded to the door. "Because out there, Bakhita is nothing but a shattered child, but in here?" She wrapped her arms around him and pressed her cheek back to his chest with a sigh. "Here, Garrett, Martha is your wife. Everything I am is yours."

10

Torches lit the night as Martha, Garrett, Cade, and Josiah passed through swirled wrought iron gates into the world of Sterling's Theatrical—a rush of music, laughter, and mystery that dizzied the mind and dazzled the senses. Excitement engulfed her like the rush of ocean waves against a shore. Patrons in tantalizing attire, each with a unique sparkle, the flutter of feathers, or near transparent muslin, were certain to cause a scandal. Yet, in the same glance, she caught sight of families in outfits no different from her own everyday fashions. Their masks had probably been crafted out of scraps from the rag bin.

She had never been to the circus, nor the theater, so she'd no idea what to expect. Garrett had insisted she change into one of the fancier ensembles from her trousseau. Not wishing to be too bold, she paired the red dress's double silk skirt with the brown's more sensible blouse, its ruffled sleeves fluttering with every step. Unlike the typical Southern fashions, she was able to secure herself easily within their folds. Back in Missouri, it had taken her over an hour to lace and button, curl and pin Sarah into her party attire.

Back then, Martha always stood out of sight. She watched from doorways or tucked behind window curtains as the carriage whisked her friend away and left her behind. Now, however, it was her turn to have the adventure.

And find Julep, of course. That was their reason for being here. But today was also her wedding day and her new life begun. A marriage was meant to be a joyful occasion. Even if she could not share it with the world, for a tiny time, she could allow herself to celebrate being Mrs. Garrett Lark.

Her husband led her into the thickening crowd, Josiah and Cade not far behind. To match her attire, he had chosen to wear tails with a red asymmetrical cravat, while Cade and Josiah preferred less formal frock coats and trousers. All three wore simple black masks which concealed from forehead to cheek bones, and Martha's covered her features in delicate black lace.

As they neared the theater doors, white marble plantation-style pillars rose three stories on each of the building's eight sides, with the western portion overlooking the Pacific cliff. There were no exterior windows; instead, banners hung at regular intervals, each portraying a different circus act: a young white woman rode upside down on horseback, her bare legs pointed to the heavens; a black man with biceps twice the size of Josiah's held a horse aloft; and a slim black girl walked on fiery coals and tossed a flaming baton into the air.

White marble floors and white wood-paneled walls welcomed them into a high foyer almost too bright after the exterior twilight. Two curved staircases wrapped either side with black iron banisters in the same swirled design as the boundary fences. At the top of each stood two closed doors with white half pillars at either side.

"Ready?" Garrett asked.

"My heart is racing. How am I allowed to be here?"

"Everyone's allowed to be here." He ducked his head, pressing a kiss to her lips before she could stop him. Her lips parted to scold but softened when she caught his boyish grin. He was happy, and so was she.

After he paid for all four tickets and handed out programs, they were ushered through a second set of doors into the main theater. An enormous central room, lit by stunning chandeliers, was the foyer's visual opposite with dark walls and crimson velvet curtains in each of its eight corners. Wooden audience stands—also cushioned in red velvet—rose five rows deep around the circular show floor, a dirt track hugging its perimeter. Between the wall curtains, glass-paned and iron-barred windows lined the top two stories while the main level contained only doors. Save for one side, nearly every window lay dark.

"The performers' quarters and the company offices," Garrett explained. "Mr. Sterling has a fully contained town; everything they need is imported or made right here. The performers each have their own living space, a kitchen, and gardens; there's even a school and a hospital. Sterling doesn't allow non-performers upstairs, but his description was rather impressive."

"There are children here?" Martha asked.

"They're the performers' children. They act as clowns at the end of the show. I think you'll enjoy it."

She smiled. "I'm sure I will." *I would like it better if Julep were with us*, she thought. *But she isn't and this may be my only chance to attend. I should appreciate what I've been given.*

As they moved to take their seats, she noticed a green door positioned directly behind their area. A copper plaque read, "Gentlemen Only," but she didn't see another for the ladies.

"Garrett, where's the ladies' parlor?"

He paused with one foot on the bottom step of the stands. His brow furrowed, one wrinkle visible above his mask line. "There is no ladies' parlor. Do you need the necessary? I can escort you to the outhouse in the courtyard."

It was her turn to quirk a brow. "Are the ladies truly expected to relieve themselves in the elements while the gentlemen have a chamber pot in here?"

"No. There's no gentlemen's lounge either. I—" He finally caught the direction of her gaze and the visible portion of his face paled. He coughed. "We should find our seats."

Gripping her hand, he tried to direct her up the stairs, but she stopped him on the second step.

"Garrett, where does that door go?"

"Uh, nowhere. I mean, it goes somewhere, of course. All doors do. I just haven't been in there since..." He glanced away at the show floor and the red velvet valances that swept the ceiling. "Since the last time I was here."

"Oh. I see."

"Yeah." He gripped her fingers as though he expected her to turn tail and run. "I'm sorry."

"Stop yer apologizin'," Josiah grunted behind them. "It isn'ta worth worrin' over. We'll get Julep and you'll never haveta see this place again."

She thought she heard Cade mutter, "I hope not." She squeezed Garrett's hand and smiled, inviting the memory of their marriage bed rather than her imaginings of his bare limbs tangled in some other woman's sheets. One last glance at the green door, then she forced herself to settle in her seat and focus on the show.

"Greetings, my friends!" A man in black tails and scarlet waistcoat appeared at center stage, his head bowed against the foot lamps that encircled the ring. With a flourish, he removed his top hat and sent it sailing into the audience. Unlike the performers, he bore no mask. His smile matched his jaw's trim slant, his beard and hair cut short and oiled to a shine. Whistles and cheers deafened his next words, and he pressed his palms toward the floor, ushering silence once again.

"That's Ashley Sterling," Garrett whispered.

"Your financier?"

"Mmm."

"Why isn't he wearing a mask?"

"It's his theater. He likes to make himself known."

Mr. Sterling did have charm, although his roguish glances made no mistake why he tended a brothel. After so many years serving others in silence, Martha had developed a way of noticing things. Some folks had a look that declared no one else could top them. No higher calling to answer to, no one to place a foot against a door that shouldn't open. It was how so many horrible men came to power. To them, integrity became a stumbling block to success.

Garrett, however, believed Mr. Sterling was the key to his conversion. Without his investment, he wouldn't have his hotel or his confidence. Mr. Sterling helped him to find his place and as a result, became the type of man who could be a faithful husband. She needed to give him the benefit of the doubt. Perhaps his egotism was more show than reality.

The audience roared as a set of wide stable doors opened and two lines of dazzling cream-colored mares paraded out, each set carrying a matched female and male rider. Every rider was draped in azure costume, the men with bare chests and the ladies' skirts cut scandalously up their thighs, white feathers secured around their eyes. Their bare skin indicated a mixed range of cultures: midnight brown, copper, bronze, beige, pale, and peach.

One by one, each female rider raised her arms toward her partner. Gripping their waists, the men rotated the women to stand inverted, palms upon their shoulders and toes pointed high. Then the men rose themselves. Each one's feet perfectly balanced upon his horse's bare back while the animal maintained perfect stride. Truly, an incredible feat.

Martha applauded as the final horse entered, this one an ebony mare whose mane rippled like water. Its rider rode astride, the same woman featured on the banner outside the building. Her chestnut curls hung loose, her miniscule turquoise costume glittering all the way up to her bejeweled mask. Full peacock feathers sprouted down her arms from either shoulder, their eye swirls like an aviary window to another world. Even masked, she outshone every other performer.

With a wave of his hand, Mr. Sterling directed the audience's attention. "Ladies and Gentlemen, I give you my life, my love, the ever gifted and glorious Rella!"

Without warning, the peacock woman—Rella—lurched sideways. Martha's fingers hit her lips, certain the woman would plummet to the ground and be trampled by the riders coming full circle. Instead, she gripped her horse's mane and twisted in midair, her toes barely touching the floor before bouncing back again. She flipped backwards onto the horse, riding mere seconds before somersaulting halfway off the horse's withers. Somehow, she managed to keep her grip while her legs performed an impossible dance in midair. Rolling feet over head, she pushed up on both hands, one leg pointed to the sky and the other bent to her knee. With a final twist, she vaulted from the horse, completed a double flip, and landed perfectly before Mr. Sterling as the audience erupted in cheers.

Mr. Sterling held her hand and raised it high. "My beautiful Rella!" The other riders continued their parade, each performing tricks that had Martha leaning forward in her seat. How were they able to do such things? It was truly amazing.

The horses exited through the stable doors and Kayus the Strong Man was announced. The banner hadn't lied about him either. He hefted cannon balls with ease and finished his act by lifting a horse over his head, pretty rider included.

The show progressed from contortionist to fire tender to trapeze artists with equine acts scattered in between. Except for the skimpy costumes, the acts were appropriate entertainment, even for the children. They laughed extra loud as the jugglers hopped back and forth. Seeing the wide grin on Garrett's face, she could almost forget about the illicit acts performed so discreetly or the real reason why they'd come.

Her eyes shifted to the green door. Another man slipped inside and it closed behind him. Garrett had gone in that door, too. Many times, he had visited without remorse. He claimed the performers weren't sold in the brothel, but with everyone masked, how could he be certain? The blonde acrobat dangling from the trapeze, her legs wrapped around the wooden bar, could have been one of them. Or the peacock woman with the ability to ride a horse and hold her raised foot in her hand. Perhaps he had been with her.

She pressed a hand to her chest, the heat of the crowd igniting like the fire tender's batons. Had he been with *her*? Her striking dark skin and hair and eyes would be difficult to dismiss. When Garrett had held Martha, in the height of their passion, it felt like he wanted her. It seemed like he was pleased. What if he wasn't? What if he was thinking of one who performed better? Her chest tightened. How much did she truly wish to know?

From the corner of her eye, she caught Garrett watching her rather than the show. His eyebrows tented in concern. A glance behind her showed the same expression on Josiah's face while Cade—poor Cade—appeared to be more weathered than ever before. She faced forward and ignored the green door. The show was almost over and then they needed to find Julep.

The acrobats descended the heights and ran backstage through mighty applause. She forced her palms to mimic their enthusiasm.

Once...twice... On the third clap, Garrett caught her hand and held it.

She glanced at their clasped fingers then up at him. "We can't do this here."

"We can do whatever we want here."

The applause continued as the second to last act moved onto the stage: tightrope acrobats, The Couple McKay.

"What's the matter?" Garrett whispered. "Aren't you enjoying the performance?"

"I am."

"Then what is it?"

Don't look. Martha pleaded with herself not to glance at the green door again, but her eyes flicked in its direction of their own accord. His expression crumpled.

"You're never going to forgive me, are you?" His thumb traced a circle on her palm, while the McKays performed an intricate dance on a one-inch wire.

A set of cymbals crashed and they both startled, their hands jumping apart. Another stage door opened and a line of little clowns waddled out, garnering laughter from the audience. In oversized clothes and wigs knit of everything from corn husks to knotted fabric scraps, it was hard to tell if they were midgets or merely children.

Rather than the show, Garrett watched her, waiting for an answer.

Voice frozen, she turned the opposite way, straight into Cade's horrified stare. His jaw slacked as the clowns tumbled to and fro and high-pitched squeals pierced the air. "Julep," he breathed, then louder, "Julep!" He leapt from his seat and shoved his way into the aisle, knocking people out of the way as he went.

"Cade?" Halfway down the stairs, Garrett caught his brother's arm, yanking him out of his mad dash for the show floor. "Cade, get back in your seat." People in their area stared, although the rest of the theater seemed focused on the show. Clowns crowded center stage, piling into a tipsy pyramid while laughter filled the room.

"Let me go!" Cade managed to free his arm from his brother's grip. Shoving Garrett away, he stumbled back and fell down the remaining stairs. Two men dressed in black tails and full masks appeared to restrain him, but it didn't stop his hysteria. With mumbled apologies,

Martha and Josiah hurried to join them.

"That clown is my daughter," Cade told the men, expression desperate. "The one with the black hair and the big shoes. Garrett, tell them."

Martha followed Garrett's stare toward the show. The clowns' face paint and wigs made it impossible to tell girls from boys, let alone if one of them could be Julep. None appeared to have black hair and all wore big shoes.

Garrett grabbed Cade by the shoulder. "Stop making a fool of yourself."

"I'm not. That clown is Julep. Your financier kidnapped my daughter."

"You've lost your mind." Garrett leaned into the man holding Cade's left arm. "Could you manage a meeting with Mr. Sterling for us? Tell him Garrett Lark needs to speak with him. It's urgent." He lowered his voice, which seemed unnecessary in the show's uproar. The trick riders had returned for the finale. "Perhaps we could meet at Harvest Hill."

The man's lips parted, and he didn't speak for a second. Then he nodded. "Come with us."

As they followed the two men, still restraining Cade, through the foyer and up the marble staircase, Martha leaned into Garrett. "Where's Harvest Hill?" she whispered.

"It's what Mr. Sterling calls his private office. Only someone in his circle would know that name."

11

Garrett paced Sterling's office as the minutes passed in a silence so dense, he could hear the clock gears whir. He pressed his palms atop the mahogany hutch and studied the device, wondering how long Sterling would keep them waiting. He worried that if it took much longer, his brother was going to throw himself through the glass window, including the iron cross bars, and go on a mad search for Julep himself.

Cade stood with arms folded, scowling at the circus floor one story below. The show had ended over twenty minutes ago and the audience efficiently ushered out through the foyer and into their waiting carriages. The low rumble of stragglers' conversation filtered through the office door, juxtaposed with the clatter of cleanup from within the theater.

His boot heels echoing off the marble tile, Garrett joined Martha on one of two sable horsehair sofas, Josiah having claimed the other. Along with a pair of corresponding Dutch highback armchairs, they surrounded an octagonal coffee table and faced a blazing black marble fireplace. Its elaborate façade belonged with the rest of Sterling's extravagances, such as the gilt pheasant wallpaper, lifelike enough to fly right off the walls. Inset bookcases covered the remaining wall space, although they contained few books. Most held framed newspaper clippings and circus advertisements; one contained a worn set of fire batons and an antique compass. Nearer the windows, a massive desk and inset wall cupboard completed the aesthetic with two stallions carved into the side panels and a sailing ship on its front. Except for an ornamental globe paperweight and whale oil lamp, the desktop lay clear, all items relegated to its drawers.

"Is he going to keep us waiting forever?" Garrett grunted. He tugged his mask off and tossed it on the coffee table in frustration. This was his wedding night, an evening he did not want to spend with his employer, his brother, and his surrogate father. His wife sat an inch away, more attractive than any Southern belle, and more enticing than before they married.

Assuming she forgave him for his indiscretions, which he oscillated between certainty of and eternal doubt.

With no outlet to vent his passions, he chose to focus his annoyance on Cade instead. He was still irritated at his brother's outburst during the show which, as far as he was concerned, was unfounded and would only hurt their chances of Sterling's cooperation. If anything, the circus master would insist Cade be committed rather than be capable of caring for a child.

Martha's fingers brushed his knee, which only flared his fevered mood. "He'll be here," she said. "He wouldn't keep you waiting."

He would though. Everything Sterling did was in his time and never anyone else's. What was that saying about how important people are always on time, even when they aren't? That was Ashley Sterling to a T.

Garrett offered Martha a smile that, based on the worried tilt of her chin, probably came across as more of a grimace. When he brushed a stray hair behind her ear, she turned her head to press a kiss to his palm. Maybe he still had a chance.

"Martha, I want to talk about the green door."

Her voice was soft, her eyes on Cade rather than him. "Now? Can't it wait?"

"It can, but we were married today. I don't want to go home tonight and have you refuse to sleep in my bed."

Her lips rose in a shy smile. "Nothing could make me that angry."

"You say that now—"

Like a winter gust, the office door opened, ruining the moment.

Cursing bad timing's name, Garrett eased away from his wife.

Ashley Sterling strode toward them, followed by his wife, Rella, and his daughter, the fire tender Clary, both still masked and in costume. He had never met either woman personally, but heard much about them both. He noted that, away from the show's flickering chandeliers, Clary's skin carried much darker than originally perceived. He had believed her warm copper tint came from the fire's glow, when in reality, she must be of mixed parentage. No wonder Sterling had conflicting feelings on Garrett's own mixed marriage; it probably reminded him of an old flame once gained and too quickly extinguished. As far as he knew, his business partner had never once mentioned a late wife, or even a lover.

"Mask on, Mr. Lark," Sterling snapped. "You know the rules."

You don't wear one, Garrett wanted to retort. With a huff, he secured his mask ties once again.

Gripping Martha's hand, he helped her rise as Sterling joined them. His frown flipped easily into a warm smile. "Who have you brought to me, Mr. Lark?"

"My wife, Martha. And over there is my brother, Cade." Cade half-turned from the window but had the good sense not to speak out of turn. He butted his shoulder against the frame and tried to appear relaxed while only looking ill at ease.

But Sterling wasn't paying attention to the quiet boy in the corner. "Married?" he exclaimed. "You were quite the singleton when last we spoke. When was the blessed event?"

"This evening, mere hours after my bride and brother's arrival to our city."

Sterling reached for Martha's free hand and raised it to his lips, his eyes never leaving hers for an instant. He gave a low whistle. "My, my, your husband did not exaggerate your beauty, Mrs. Lark. You are indeed stunning. It is rare to see such a radiant shade of bronze from one of the African faction."

Garrett felt Martha's body tense against him. Her eyes immediately dropped to her shoes. "Thank you, sir."

She shouldn't be thanking him! If Garrett had been annoyed by the delay before, now he was irate. Why would his financier say such a thing to his wife? How would such an insult help their partnership?

He barely heard Sterling provide introductions for his wife and daughter, the former of whom was eying him rather strangely. Her peacock blue mask covered most of her face, hiding any distinguishing features, but her demure brown eyes did possess a striking familiarity. If only he could place it. Perhaps he was thinking of Coraline. He thought he recalled her having brown eyes.

"Drinks, Rella," Sterling ordered. His wife skittered off to the hutch where she withdrew three crystal-cut old-fashioned glasses and a bottle of Hackmeade Glenn scotch whiskey. At one time, it had been Garrett's favorite, but he seldom partook anymore. One drink usually led to half a dozen, and this was a conversation he needed full sobriety to pursue.

"None for me, thanks," he said when Rella attempted to hand him a glass. Her lips peaked and she glanced to Sterling. He had already downed half his glass.

"It's a prime year, Mr. Lark. You won't get much better. Please, as my guest, I insist."

Rella shoved the glass at him, and Garrett was forced to accept it or let it slosh over his waistcoat and trousers. He nodded his thanks and raised the glass, letting the most miniscule of rivulets pass through his lips. His eyes widened. "This isn't Hackmeade Glenn. What'd you put in this?"

"Oh, I assure you, it is. It's distilled especially for my associates." Sterling removed his ringmaster's tailcoat and handed it to Rella who draped it over the nearest highback. He lowered himself onto the seat and patted a palm along either arm, inviting his wife and daughter in beside him. "Now, let's get to the heart of this visit, shall we? My men informed me that you, young man—" He nodded at Cade who swallowed a sip and choked, coughing through the end of Sterling's sentence. "—caused a commotion during the show."

Breathless, Cade abandoned his glass on the desktop and slapped his chest. Another coughing fit followed and he stumbled to the opposite highback, still heaving. Rella rushed to fetch him a glass of water.

"You," he finally gasped. "You...have...my...daughter."

Sterling propped an ankle upon his knee and sipped his whiskey.

"Do I? I have so many young girls in my circus. Which one is yours? Lissie?"

"Julep."

"Ah, yes," he smiled. "I do know Julep. She is a lovely child."

Cade's water glass slipped from his fingers and exploded upon the floor. Shards skidded across the tile in every direction and Rella immediately leapt up to clean it. "You...you admit that you...took...you took my daughter?" All color left him, his dark hair the sole element not that of a specter. "But, she's mine."

Sterling's eyes flashed, in contrast to his relaxed demeanor. "No, boy, she isn't, and if that's what you got in your head, you had best be puddling right back where you came from."

Cade leapt from his seat at the same time Garrett did. He grabbed his younger brother's shoulders before he threw himself at Sterling like a fool. Cade's fingers clenched and unclenched at his sides, but it wasn't fury in his eyes but despair. "Don't do something stupid," Garrett hissed. He shoved his brother back into the armchair and rounded on Sterling himself.

"What in the blue-heeled devil? You kidnapped my niece? Explain. Now."

"Or what? Please tell me, Mr. Lark, what will you do?"

Garrett paused, staring down at his financier with fists clenched and chest heaving. With Martha three feet away, horror in her eyes, she probably wondered what her new husband would do. Would she watch him beat this man bloody? Had she made a mistake in thinking him reformed? Even he wasn't sure, but he knew it wouldn't do him any good to test those questions.

Backing away, he dropped onto the sofa and reached for Martha's hand. With measured breaths, he said, "My apologies. You must have a reason and I would be grateful to hear it." The syrup in his tone made him want to punch a wall.

After Sterling sent Rella for another glass of whiskey, then ingested an abnormally slow sip of that whiskey, he rested the glass on his knee and sighed. "You think me a villain, but I am no such thing. I am an opportunist, same as so many in this city. When I see a good deal, I snatch it up, exactly as I did with you. I think it's time I let you in on a few secrets, Mr. Lark. I didn't only hire you for your reputation for finding people. Any investigator could do that. Your Gift goes beyond that. Your brothers', too. Cade can predict the weather. Tobias is the builder, Jamison the doctor. All with extraordinary precision. Am I correct?"

Garrett clenched his jaw to keep it from falling open. How could Sterling know that? He glanced at his brother whose lips gaped, astonishment slapped across his expression. Josiah's oversized hands curled around his knees.

Sterling chuckled. "If you find that puzzling, imagine your surprise when I say that I've known your father since infancy. Our great-great-grandfathers sailed together on the ill-fated *Oblique*. We both valued Giftedness; we merely understood it in different ways."

Wait a minute. Sterling had an ancestor on the *Oblique*? He knew their father? If they were so close, why had the brothers never met him? Why had their father never even *mentioned* him?

Garrett felt like he'd been kicked in the head. "Why didn't you mention your association when we met?"

"You hate your father. If you knew we were friends, you would never have trusted me."

That much was true. Garrett would have cut off his hand before he would have shaken it in partnership with any of his father's friends.

"Why take Julep?" Cade rubbed both palms down his face and stared at the ceiling. "Haven't I been through enough?"

"My decision had nothing to do with you, Mr. Lark. I couldn't care less if you have a good day or a bad one. But the situation is this: your father and I made a deal long before you were born. We divided the country and divided our children. He thought heading west was a waste; I saw it as a gold mine. He thought sons were all that mattered, but I knew the value of daughters. So, we agreed to a trade."

"A trade?" Cade moaned. His fingers gripped in his hair as he doubled over. "We're all your sons, aren't we?"

Garrett's stomach flipped. Were they related? Was that better or worse than being Alonzo Lark's son? Ashley Sterling had given him his life back, lent him money for the hotel, helped him become a man of valor worthy of Martha's love. For two years, they had shared a trust. Could it truly be for reasons he never suspected?

He glanced at Clary. She focused on the fire as though this story came as no surprise. Perhaps it didn't. Having lived with Sterling her entire life, she might well know all her father's secrets.

The Lark brothers always suspected their father of murdering their infant sisters. What better reason than to keep them out of Sterling's hands?

Everything made sense now. The whole messy line of events throughout his life and everything Tobias and Jamison had written to him.

"Clinton Reed was your informant," he told Sterling. "You hired him to abduct Coraline, but then he drowned, so you had to hire someone else to kidnap Julep. You knew they were Gifted women. According to the rules of your agreement, they belonged to you."

Sterling's fingers snapped. "Ah ha, now the boy's thinking like someone truly Gifted. Your father could persuade anyone to do his will, but I utilize potential. And to ease your concerns, your blood is from Alonzo. I'm sorry to say, he received far more profit in children than I did."

An odd mixture of relief and sadness settled over him. He snatched up his whiskey, liquid sloshing as he tossed his head back and swallowed it down. His throat burned as he held out his glass to Rella. "Another, please? Fill it all the way." Martha's stare seared into him, but he didn't turn to meet it. He'd fallen into the hole, might as well dig himself a well.

Sterling laughed, loud and long. "There's more where that came from. I told you this afternoon what I could offer. I want you in my business, Garrett. You have never failed me and I know you never will. I want you, your wife, and your brothers—your entire family!—to be part of the Theatrical. All the Gifted come together under one roof to share a common goal. The circus is, after all, known for its oddities. As I'm sure you've found, the outside world is not ideal for our kind. It's the same reason Tobias created Larksong, is it not?"

"Tobias never kidnapped anyone."

"He purchased them though. Even now, he holds the papers to numerous slaves."

"Freedmen. He holds those papers for legal reasons, to keep them safe from the slave catchers."

Rella deposited a fresh whiskey in his hand, the fill line only an inch below the rim. Martha placed her hand over his, and his fingers spasmed. He raised the glass to his lips anyway.

Finally, Cade spoke. "If you know all that, sir, and you're a father yourself, you must understand how much I want my daughter back."

Sterling tented his fingers, his lips pressed tight in consideration. "Mr. Lark, I do appreciate the predicament I've placed you in. It can't be easy. But do consider what I'm offering. While here, Julep can grow into her Gift with confidence. To be who she was meant to be without prejudice or fear. Without a single reason to hide. I welcome you to stay and be a part of it. All I ask is a few simple rules."

That caught Cade's attention. "What are the rules?"

"Cade, shut up," Garrett hissed. His brother wasn't asserting his authority as Julep's father. He was, as usual, expressing his faithful ability to concede. That cowardice caused his wife to leave him. If they weren't careful, he would bend to Sterling's will and agree to kidnap children, too.

"Surely, you can see the flaw in your design," Garrett said. "You can't kidnap people and not expect them to be riled. Eventually, you'll cross paths with a target who sets you on the darkened end of their rifle. Everything you've worked for will be gone."

Sterling's lip curled. "This is your trouble, Mr. Lark. You've forgotten your own role in all of this. Only a few years past you were as depraved as I. Selfish. Lustful. When you changed, you wanted so desperately to become a new man for your bride." He nodded at Martha. "That desperation made you blind. It was easy to manipulate you into breaking your new rules without you even realizing you were doing it." He smirked and Garrett realized he was currently swallowing another dredge of whiskey, one of those vices he vowed to keep under control. His face warmed clear down the back of his neck. With the intent to set the glass on the table, he misjudged his own force and slammed it down instead.

Martha didn't even try to reach for him this time. He hated himself.

"You're right, I messed up, but all my problems were mine. I never hurt anyone else."

Sterling laughed again and to Garrett's unease, so did Rella. They exchanged a secret smile. "Have you forgotten all those people I paid you for? I asked for their whereabouts and you provided their locations so readily. Did you never think to ask why I sought them out or why there were so many?"

"You said there was a reward. I assumed the law was after them and you wanted to claim the glory."

"You didn't want the glory for yourself?"

"No, I..." He glanced at Martha. "I wanted the money to pay for the hotel. I needed enough to repay you and go home." How reckless he had been. How utterly senseless. His one-track mind allowed him to be manipulated without even missing a step. Clinton Reed had been duplicitous, but at least he knew what he was. Garrett had destroyed families and never even realized his corruption.

But if he was able to find all those people, and they were Gifted, then that meant he should be able to—

He dove into his Gift, following the halls of the circus, through each of the eight buildings surrounding the stage floor. There he found Julep on the southernmost side of the complex, one floor above them, down the corridor, second door. He could see her location as clear as anything. Reaching out again, he found Tobias at home with Philip and Jamison and Coraline in their sitting area with little James. Six Gifted and he could find them all.

That shouldn't be possible.

His hand reached for Martha's, practically of its own accord. He gripped her fingers until he was sure it must be too far, although she didn't flinch, didn't say a word. She shifted toward him, but he turned away, unable to meet her judgment. The disappointment. The shame. He stifled the urge to scream and smash things. His father had been wrong. The Larks weren't the last of the Gifted. No, Garrett had helped Sterling steal the last Gifted away from their homes and their families to become circus slaves or worse, and he did so without question.

For once, he didn't have the heart to mock Cade for the tears on his cheeks. His brothers were right to loathe him. This was unforgivable.

"You told him where to find Julep?" Cade asked softly.

"No, Cade, no. You have to believe me, I didn't tell him anything about Julep."

His brother's gaze bore into him. "That's the problem, Garrett. I don't believe you."

"Boys, boys, steady now." Sterling's lips held a grin, but all previous amusement and gentility had been replaced by impatience. "It's true that Mr. Lark more than tripled my hotel investment and doubled my performers. Some would call that contemptible; I say it's simply good business. He brought us both what we wanted, so where is the fault? To be fair, your brother did not betray your daughter to me. For that, you can thank your father's butler."

Josiah?

As one, they focused on the man hunched against the sofa seat. A seven-foot tall, over three-hundred-pound goliath whose expression held the shame of a runaway child. Sterling pointed him down. "This man's strength, his ingenuity, are assets I wish were part of my Gift. When he is for you, you can accomplish great things. However, when he is not..." He raised Josiah's untouched whiskey in salute then turned the glass upside down, releasing its contents. Copper splashed onto the coffee table and spread outward. Martha drew her skirts back as the liquid spilled off the edge onto the floor.

"Josiah," Sterling scolded, "you knew what happens to those who cross me. Garrett was living in San Francisco since the golden glory days, yet it took you years to bring him to me. And, despite our agreement, it was Clinton, not you, who first sent news of Julep's birth. Shame he's dead. Now, *that* man was loyal."

Tears ran down Cade's face unchecked. "Josiah, why?"

Josiah's fingers wrapped his scalp as a groan escaped from deep inside. "He stole my dau-ter, too. I did what I hadta do ta get her back."

"You have a daughter?"

"I did. Yer father sold her ta him."

Sterling shrugged. His arm snaked around Clary's waist

possessively. "Traded would be the more appropriate word. I paid nothing for her, nothing but the agreement Alonzo and I made."

"Alonzo wasn't her father, though," Garrett spat. "Our sisters died. I saw them buried. What right would he have had to give her to you?"

"Slaves are property, Mr. Lark. Property can be sold or given away. Whether they work a rice paddy or perform in my circus, they belong to someone. How they arrive there makes no difference. Your father wanted to get rid of Clary and I didn't. Simple."

"Mr. Josiah is my father?" Clary's voice rose. It was the first time she had spoken since they arrived, and her expression shifted between disbelief and despair. Her life was a lie, nothing but a business deal.

"You are mine." Sterling's other hand lashed out, his fingers curling over her wrist. She winced as he squeezed. "You would do best to remember that."

She gave a silent nod, signaling Sterling's release. He returned his sights to Josiah, but the other man only had eyes for his daughter.

"I's lost my soul fer ya, Clary. Forgive me fer what I done." His expression crumpled in such agony that Garrett hated Alonzo Lark all over again. The brothers had grown up in their father's shadow, with his persuasion filling every aspect of their family, destroying their mother's mind, and keeping them all from ever truly living. All this time they believed Josiah had no family, that without the Larks, he was alone in this world. But it was the Larks who had made him that way. Clary seemed only a few years younger than Cade. How painful for Josiah to lose her and then watch his master lose three more daughters one by one.

Not once in Garrett's thirty-four years had Josiah ever once mentioned being in love.

Unable to contain the mess inside him, he jolted from his seat and paced to the window. The show floor lay completely dark, but ethereal shadows shifted from behind the lit interior windows.

He paced back to the sofa. "Why didn't you tell us, Josiah? I would have found her if you'd only asked!"

"No, ya couldna have. Same as ya couldna find Julep or any other of them Gifted. My great-great-grandpap served yers on the *Oblique*.

Why'd ya think yer father insisted I always stay close?"

"You're Gifted, too?" Cade rose from his seat, his breaths heavy and eyes swinging erratically across the room. He grabbed Martha's untouched whiskey and upended it straight into his mouth.

"Cade!" Garrett grabbed the glass, dark liquid splashing on both their shirts and the floor. His brother's breathing didn't slow. He gripped his shoulder. "Cade!"

Somewhere behind him, his brain recognized vague snips of conversation. "I couldna come," Josiah said. "Not until...Clary, had ta...said he'd kill her if I didn't."

Garrett whipped around and caught Sterling's sly smile. "Mr. Lark, I do believe our business is at an end. Rella, kindly summon Kayus and Julio."

Rella opened the door and waved two men inside, the strongman Kayus and another—no doubt Julio—who sported a whimsical black and grey feathered cloak and mask. Garrett remembered him in attendance at the show, and now he knew why. Not as a patron, but as a guard. He displayed enough muscles to show he could subdue someone with no need of a weapon.

Martha grabbed Garrett's arm, close against his side. "Do something."

He shoved her behind him, between himself and his brother. What in the devil's name was he supposed to do? Without knowledge of how they had been alerted, more guards swarmed through the door and surrounded them, all in Julio's same black coat attire and feathered masks.

Garrett ripped his own mask off. Behind him, Rella gasped, a sound for which he couldn't be bothered. He turned to his wife and pressed a hurried kiss upon her lips. "When I move, you run out that door and keep running."

She clenched his arm. "No, Garrett, please."

He ignored her plea. "Cade, get Julep. She's in the south building, second floor, second door. Don't wait for me." He yanked his hand out of Martha's.

"Garrett, no—"

With a gruff cry, he lunged at Sterling. His shoulder collided with the man's chest and together they toppled over the highback and into the hutch. Dishes clattered as a porcelain vase slid to the ground. Its side cracked against the floorboards and spun while their shoes slipped across its spilt contents. Garrett drew his fist back first, but was met with Julio's blow to his stomach, sending him to his knees. He wheezed as the guard roughed both his arms behind him and shoved his face to the cold marble. Across the room he caught sight of Martha. Kayus had her pinned against his chest. Cade, likewise, was restrained by a third man who seemed no less eager to end him when commanded. Pressed against the far wall, Josiah submitted to three more.

Martha's chest heaved against Kayus's grip, her expression full of terror. *My wife,* Garrett lamented. *I was supposed to protect you.*

Sterling's emotional mask had fallen away, revealing disheveled hair above the emerald-laden eyes of a demon. If his Gift was opportunity, he knew how to play his cards well. But no one was playing anymore.

He swiped both palms down his jacket and flicked them toward the floor. "My, my, Mr. Lark. Where are your manners? I've been more than fair to you. I gave you an opportunity to join me. I offered you fair compensation. I even agreed to include your woman. We could have made for lucky partners. But I do not grant second chances. In fact, allow me to show you firsthand what happens to those who betray me. Stedmann, do what you do best."

In a single movement, the burly man on Josiah's left reached beneath his coat, drew a Bowie, and plunged it into Josiah's side. Martha's cry was barely audible within the wail that flew from Clary's mouth. Her eyes locked with her birth father's as he stretched to cover the wound, impossible with his arms restrained. Instead, the gash leaked more every second until finally his knees buckled. His gaze shot to Garrett, then Cade, before rolling upward, his weight forcing the men to release him. With a crash as expansive as his seven-foot form, he landed in a heap.

"Sterling, you—" Garrett released a torrent of vulgarity that should have made him ashamed with Martha there, but all he saw was red. Clinton had spied on Larksong, but so had Josiah. He had been closer than a father, then betrayed them. It was no coincidence that Sterling approached Garrett, no grand gesture that he offered him the money for the hotel, and no simple business agreement. All this had been planned to lure him, and eventually his family, into Sterling's clutches, and Josiah had been a part of it. Some would say he got what he deserved. Garrett felt like the blood on the floor was his own.

Cade's sobs rent the air; his eyes scrunched closed like he was eight again. That was the year their mother had died, leaving them with an abusive father, and Josiah had taken Cade under his wing more than any of them. Now his mentor was gone and likely, he was next. His daughter was doomed for a life of servitude, as was Josiah's. As was Martha.

My wife, I should have protected you.

Garrett had brought them here. Their presence in this place was because of him.

Sterling flicked his wrist. "For the sea, men."

A sack dropped over his head and after that, all was darkness.

12

Stay calm. Stay quiet. Stay alive.

Martha's father's words came alive as Julio's fists battered Garrett and yanked a potato sack over his head. Another of the guards looped a stretch of twine around his neck to secure the bag; she prayed not tight enough for him to suffocate. He groaned as they wrapped his wrists with more twine behind his back. They shoved him toward the door with Cade close behind.

"Sterling, you lousy pig," he shouted. "Kill me if you want but let her go!" He turned his shoulder into Julio in a mad attempt to knock him off balance, the result of which landed the guard's fist to Garrett's gut. He doubled over, and Julio knocked him in the back, Garrett's forehead slamming into the door frame.

"No," she breathed, a soundless plea, yet he still turned his head toward the sound.

"Martha," he gasped. "I love you. I'm sor—"

Julio's backhand cut off his apology.

Stay calm. Stay quiet. Stay alive. That was what she had told Lemuel before they were separated for the auction block. Slaves were dispensable. If she fought, they would probably kill her. Helpless, she watched as her husband was shoved through the door, Cade directly behind. Josiah lay on the floor, his shirt soaked crimson with blood oozing from his wound. It took four tough men to lift his immense form and haul him away, while Clary watched dumbstruck beside her stepmother. Blood spots trailed a path across the floorboards, through the doorway, and vanished from sight.

"What do you want me to do with her?" Kayus asked Mr. Sterling, his brawn squeezing Martha tighter. "She'd be easy enough to crack right here."

"I grow weary of aggression, however necessary." Mr. Sterling's eyes swept the room as though he had entered a kitchen after supper preparations were completed but the mess not yet cleared away. He strode toward Martha and stopped a foot apart, arms folded as he studied her. "Rella?" His wife appeared immediately, her expression impassive. "Do you think you can train her within a fortnight? I wouldn't want to give up more talent if there's a way to save her. The show could use a new attraction."

"Not to worry, darling. I'll make sure she's ready."

"Very good, my sweet." He gestured to Martha's guard. "Allow Kayus to escort you to your new quarters. I think you'll be rather satisfied with the accommodations."

Kayus loosened his grip and instead, offered her his arm. When she didn't immediately take it, he grabbed her wrist and threaded her arm through his, close against his side. In the commotion, her mask had come loose and now hung by its ribbon around her neck. He perused her features, making her feel more exposed than ever. Even as a slave, neither of her masters had leered at her with such derision. He was colored folk like her; how could he do this to his own kind?

Her eyes sought out her dress hem then his shoes. A blackened scar in the floorboards. Anywhere to not meet that stare. "Where are they taking Garrett and Cade?" she whispered. *Stay quiet*, her inner voice scolded, but she had to know.

"That you needn't worry about," answered Mr. Sterling. "Be assured they will not return for you."

Kayus led her forward, stepping over the blood trail as they moved to the door, Rella close on their heels.

They traveled down a long marbled corridor, ablaze with sconces along either wall. Interestingly, there were doors on one side of the hallway and a blank wall on the opposite. A door at the end of the hall angled into the adjoining building followed by another corridor exactly the same as the first. Up one flight of stairs to the third floor, then down a third identical hallway to the fourth door, which Rella opened and led the way inside. A quaint sitting room of warm pastel upholstery and spruce flooring lay beyond.

Three young women glanced over at their entrance, silenced mid-conversation. Two black women lounged on opposite sofas and the third—a petite white girl and too pale to be healthy—sat cross-legged on the floor, her back against the sofa's upholstery. None of them could be more than twenty and the littlest one appeared as young as fifteen. All had removed their masks and costumes and now wore silky black dressing gowns with tight braids over their shoulders.

Kayus released her and departed. She heard the distinct turn of a key in the door's lock.

Rella breezed across the room. "Listen close, ladies. This is Martha, our new recruit. Martha, this is June and Nora, two of our equine acrobats, and Lissie, who performs trapeze. Ladies, be kind; Martha lost her husband today."

Because your *husband took him from me!* Martha wanted to shout but remained silent. Her wedding rings suddenly felt like a great millstone upon her neck. She had been reunited, married, and lost Garrett all in one day. In less than eight hours.

Exhaustion overwhelmed her and she reached for the sofa, somehow managing to lower herself beside June with only a slight stumble. Its cushion was more comfortable than anything she had ever known possible, and she hated it.

"Oh, you poor dear!" Lissie leapt from the floor. "You can have my bed. It's the best one because it's near the window. There're bars on the outside, but if you raise the sash, it lets in a little air and almost feels like being outside." She waved a hand toward an open doorway with four plush beds beyond. "We sleep in there."

"I don't want the best bed," Martha muttered. "I don't want to be here."

The girls laughed in unison. "We know it's shocking now," said Nora, "but you'll adjust."

She had to stay strong for Julep. Was her niece truly an orphan? She couldn't imagine that Mr. Sterling's men let Cade live when they murdered Josiah so cruelly. Which also meant Garrett was probably—no, she wouldn't even consider it.

She must find a way to recover Julep and escape this place, whatever it took. Her niece may not have her parents, but she still had family who loved her. Martha would get them back to Larksong or die trying. If she could, she would steal away Clary, too.

Lissie's hand lighted on hers. "You should listen to Nora. This place really does become better with time."

"Unless you've got Rella's bad luck and have to marry Sterling," said June. She picked at her thumbnail, already dangerously short. "Sharing a bed with him, can you imagine?"

Lissie giggled. "He's not bad to look at."

"He's not good to look at neither. That man's got the eyes of a devil, and he's so *old*. I don't know how you stand it, Rel."

With a roll of her eyes, Rella moved to the wardrobe and began shuffling through its contents. She retrieved a nightgown, silk dressing robe, and a pair of plush velvet slippers, the same sort the other girls wore and which she now handed to Martha. Then she opened the other wardrobe door and sighed. "We've no rags or towels. You girls are supposed to tell me when you run low. I'll return in a moment." With a no-nonsense stare around the room, she unlocked the door and slipped out, locking it again behind her.

Without pretense, the girls swarmed Martha. Nora slid across the coffee table and leaned in close. "Now that she's gone, we can give some advice."

June sniffed. "Rella's a two-bit Jezebel." She flipped her braid back over her shoulder. "We'd never call her that to her face, of course, but everyone thinks it. She's dear Ashley's darling puppy."

"Don't bother trying to leave the theater," Nora added. "It's basically pointless. The guards are everywhere."

Martha shook her head. "I met them. There were about ten, but not enough to man this entire complex all the time. There weren't more than a few even at the show."

Nora and June shared a glance and a secret smile. It reminded Martha of her and Sarah and her heart constricted.

Nora leaned forward, her elbows on her knees. "You met his most trusted men, like Kayus, but there are others. Mr. Sterling employs more guards than we are even aware of. They rotate days and arrive at random hours. Blend into the audience in ever changing costumes so we can't keep track. He's very thorough when it comes to protecting his assets."

Assets? These women were slaves and they didn't even realize it. "I used to be enslaved, but I escaped from that, and I can help you escape from this. If we work together, we can find a way out."

"Listen, sweetie." June leaned back and kicked her heels up on the coffee table, one silk-slippered ankle crossed over the other. "Being here ain't like being down south—I know 'cause I was there, too. Just think like Sterling's your master now, and the best way to be taken care of is to be docile and peaceful. It isn't so bad on this side of the theater. He gives us nice things if we listen and do as he asks. Beautiful clothes, comfortable quarters, and all we want for food. I even learned my sums and how to read. Not like the girls he sends to tend the Garden."

"The Garden?"

"You know, behind the green door?"

"Oh."

When Nora spoke next, her smile seemed genuine. "We were all scared when we arrived, but June's been here longer than almost everyone except Clary. She helps us see the good. The west fell into a depression last year, the gold is drying up, and fires and floods and earthquakes are plaguing the city every few months. Some of the girls think it's the end of the world and the Lord Jesus is going to carry us all away. That's hogwash and the rest of us knows it. But see, even in all that, there's customers still willing to be frivolous. Spend their money on entertainment and attractive women. Unlike the gold, our shows have never dried up."

"As I said," June sniffed. "It's not so bad on this side of the theater."

A key turned in the lock and Rella strode back through the door, arms bearing a stack of towels, rags, fresh sheets, and a toothbrush and charcoal round. She laid everything at the foot of Martha's— formerly Lissie's—bed and returned to the sitting room. "Were you ladies having a pleasant chat?"

"Yes, ma'am," all three responded in unison.

"Delightful. Now, Martha, I need you to come with me. We have one more visit to make."

Martha untied her mask from around her neck and laid it on top of the bundle of borrowed night things. Silently, she followed Rella from the room, down the corridor and across the threshold into a third adjoining building. At the second door down, Rella unlocked a set of double doors and directed her into an elaborate sitting room, twice the size of the one the girls shared. Four windows overlooked the stage floor framed by full-length gold brocade draperies. All the furnishings portrayed a distinct Southern style, reminiscent of—yet more embellished than—those in the parlor of the Screeching Peach. A lavish pink and gold rug with gold fringe trim spanned the floor and another massive black marble fireplace emitted warmth throughout. A second set of double doors revealed the largest four-poster bed Martha had ever laid eyes on, raised on a central dais and covered in green embroidered satin. Flowering potted cacti covered every table and corner floor.

"Is this Mr. Sterling's room?" Were they supposed to be in here? If he caught them—

"No, this is my suite. I wished to speak with you alone." Rella untied her elaborate mask and shook out her long dark locks. As her brown eyes raised, Martha gasped. It couldn't be... "Gabriella Reed?"

Excitement flashed behind Rella's gaze. "You recognize me? When did we meet?"

"1852, on the westward trail. You rarely left your wagon and then one day, you disappeared. We searched everywhere. It troubled Garrett that you were the only person his Gift couldn't find." Obviously, due to Rella being Gifted. Over the years, as Garrett had fine-tuned his own Gift, he had been able to help Sterling without realizing who he was searching for.

"What a relief. I knew Garrett looked familiar when his mask came off, but I couldn't place him. I'm sorry I don't remember you." Rella gripped Martha's hand and pulled her to the sofa. "Sit. I'll pour us some lemonade."

A pitcher sat on a small sideboard against the far wall, a tea tin and various glasses and wine goblets settled beside it. A kettle hung on a hook near the fire, but not over it. Rella poured two glasses and handed one to Martha. "Tell me about the wagon train. Where were you headed? Why was I going there with you?"

Something about the way she asked, her tone and the tilt of her chin as she settled beside Martha set off warning bells. What did she truly know about this woman? Her first husband, Clinton, had gained their confidence only to prove their downfall. Her second husband held hundreds captive, had murdered Josiah, and possibly done the same to Garrett and Cade. June's words echoed inside her: *She's dear Ashley's darling puppy.*

The peacock woman couldn't be trusted. Martha deserved answers, not the other way around.

"Don't you remember any of it?" she asked.

Rella sipped her lemonade. "Bits and pieces. It's more like a dream, impossible to make sense of what was real and what wasn't. I know Clinton Reed was real. I know I married him, and I know he's dead now. Ashley told me that much. He was quite the comfort to me in those days..." Her tone of admiration made Martha want to retch.

"But how did you end up *here*? Were you running from Mr. Reed?"

"No. I loved Clint. My father specialized in cattle—Clint was his ranch hand—and when I shared my dreams of equine acrobatics, Clint supported me. He even married me to prove his commitment. When my family was murdered, he was right there to pick up the pieces. The night we packed for Larksong is the last night I fully remember."

She rubbed her temple as though it might help restore the lost memories. "He drugged me, or that's what I was told. One of Sterling's recipes, the same kind the other hunters use when collecting their finds. It keeps us lucid enough to care for ourselves, but unaware enough so we won't run. I was handed off to another of Sterling's men at Independence Rock. It's a popular spot for exchanges. So many people and merriment that no one notices."

If only the Larks had known of Clinton's duplicity from the start, and that Josiah was to follow. Everything could have been solved in that moment. They could have saved Rella from becoming Sterling's wife, saved all those Garrett had found for him, and most importantly, saved Julep and their family from being torn apart.

Rella gripped Martha's hand, jolting her back to reality. "Oh, Martha, I'm so relieved to find someone who remembers me. You can fill in the missing pieces. It will be like having family here."

Family. Martha's family wasn't here. They were scattered.

"Where are Garrett and Cade? You tell me that first."

"Didn't you hear what Sterling said? You don't need to worry about them."

"But I am worried. Help me find them, Rella, like we tried to find you. We can take Julep and return to Larksong. You can come with us."

Rella dropped her hand. Her smile faded to stone. "You're not listening. Once Mr. Sterling sets his sights on you, you are his. There is no escape and no negotiation. You acquiesce or you wish you had. Mr. Sterling's loyalty only extends so far as your usefulness. If you remember nothing else, remember that."

Darkness pressed on Martha's periphery. Her drink's sweet and sour scent threatened to undo her. She set the glass on the oval end table and gripped the sofa arm, blinking back panic.

Rella could have been their saving grace, but she was as entrenched as the rest of the girls. When a sharp rap sounded at the door, the younger woman abandoned her lemonade and went to answer it.

"Ah, there you are!"

Martha spun at Mr. Sterling's voice. When he caught her eye, he smiled, but there was nothing companionable about it. His lip rose farther in a sneer, and Martha's memory slipped back to another time and another place. A childhood as Bakhita she would as soon rather forget.

Now, Sterling wasn't Sterling, but the man who had chained her siblings and shoved them in a train car, away from their parents without a chance for goodbye. He was the switch that struck her as she was corralled into the slave market warehouse and waited for her number to be called. He was the voice that announced a price while her bare feet froze against the courthouse steps. He whispered in Mrs. Walcott's voice, "My husband's sold you, Martha. You have to run!"

Then Garrett's: "If I were a wiser man, I'd ask you to forget me, but you know that I will always be a fool."

"Martha?" Sterling stepped forward. The floorboards creaked with every step.

She stood to face him. The sofa between them became her shield, as useless as it was for protection. She clutched her skirt and felt the blood pulse up her arms, every bruise from Kayus's stronghold made apparent.

"All is well, Ashley, dear," Rella soothed. "I wanted to instruct her in the ways of our little family, away from the other girls. I think she understands well enough."

"Good." His grin widened. "I look forward to seeing her Gift in action."

What did he mean, her Gift? She wasn't Gifted.

When Martha remained silent, Mr. Sterling's grin faltered. "Now, now, I know your husband wouldn't marry someone without talent. Do tell me what you can do."

"Where is my husband?"

She shouldn't have said it. The circus master's eyes flashed. He lunged forward. She raised her arms to shield herself, but then Rella was there pushing her husband away with a flirty laugh as her fingers whispered over his trimmed beard. She glanced at Martha with a hint of warning. "Oh, Ashley, you're making the poor girl uneasy. This is all an awful lot to adjust to unexpectedly. Remember my first day? Give her time."

His brows raised. "Time to determine what her Gift is? She is well past the age when most discover these things."

"Time to grow used to our way of life. Let me ply her gently. Help her work her Gift to its utmost potential." She leaned in close, her lips fluttering across his cheek. "Imagine the crowd we shall draw with two fire tenders. It will be delicious."

Those words were all it took. His grin turned up in slowest fashion, his eyelids slightly hooded. "You can tame fire like my Clary?"

"Of course, she can." Rella's tone warned that Martha had better agree or suffer the consequences.

Martha couldn't trust her but she also knew she needed alliances if she had any hope of escape. Clary had recently suffered a blow to all she knew. Perhaps Martha could use that vulnerability to her advantage.

"Yes, sir," she told Sterling. "Although, it is not so much a Gift to manage fire as the stories one can tell with it. Story and song, that is my Gift." Thank goodness for a childhood of her mother's spirituals and Sarah who insisted she learn to read. Thank goodness for her years living with Coraline and Alice Ann, the two most bookish women she knew. As a result, her mind overflowed with beautiful stories and songs. She would weave them with Clary's fire dancing and captivate the circus's trust.

That was how she would rescue Julep. That was how they would survive.

13

Garrett hurt everywhere. His head throbbed from where it had slammed into the doorframe and his jaw felt like it was going to fall off. A searing pain shot up his spine from when Julio had shoved him to the ground.

Under this blasted sack, all he saw was darkness. The place where he sat smelled of sea salt punctuated by the lap of water somewhere close. Twisting, he managed to touch his bound hands to the ground beneath him—rock. To the wall behind him—also rock. A slight breeze whistled past...a tunnel, maybe? Or a cave? He had never used his Gift to search for someone underground. He was about a mile from the circus building, but otherwise couldn't grasp on any specifics.

He remembered walking down several flights of stairs then through a dank stretch that smelled of overturned earth; it reminded him of death and decay. Was this a catacomb? Did they even have those here? Jamison always talked about how he would like to visit the catacombs of Rome or Paris one day. He had explained how way back in medieval times, they would create intricate artwork using human skeletons. Something about that never sat right with Garrett and imagining dead bodies mere feet away where he couldn't see them...well, it nauseated him. And he wasn't one to be sickened by anything.

"Where are we?" he asked. The echo returned within seconds, possibly indicating a tunnel rather than a cave.

"What does it matter?" Julio's voice returned. "You're never coming back here."

"Then where am I going?"

"Into the ocean if you don't shut up."

So, at least he knew they *weren't* intending to throw him into the sea.

A low moan followed by a sob turned his attention. An ounce of relief poured into him as he located Cade twenty feet away and then a torrent of relief when he found Josiah about fifty feet farther. Based on what he took to be Josiah's groan, he wasn't in good shape, but also based on his groan, he was still alive. Perhaps due to his size, the knife merely slit muscle and didn't rupture any vital organs. He wished Jamison were here; he would have known.

Garrett immediately withdrew the thought. He didn't want any of his brothers in this predicament. It horrified him enough that Cade was.

This was all his fault. Because of him, they were here. Because of him, Martha was trapped in that crazy circus to be used for Sterling's twisted amusement. What would he do to her and Julep? It horrified him to think. Cade should never forgive him for this. Ever. Nor should any of the families of those people he helped Sterling capture. Why had he never asked questions? Because he was a selfish jackabout and had gotten what he deserved.

He couldn't focus on that now. He had to find a way to escape. Then he could save them. Eventually, this bag would have to come off and he could gauge his surroundings. There was a way out of every situation; he simply needed to find it.

Rough voices woke him hours later, still trapped in burlap blindness. The commotion rattled down the tunnel, bringing foul language along with it. There was a metallic clang, then what sounded like a board being tossed to the ground. He searched for Cade and Josiah and found them in the same positions as before.

"Cade," he whispered loudly. "You all right?"

"Thought I told you to shut up." Something smacked Garrett in the face, right across his injured jaw. He clenched his jaw to keep from crying out which only sent pain into his temples and threatened tears.

"Stand up," Julio ordered. "Walk." Garrett heard the snap of ropes around his feet, then was shoved forward, stumbling as he hit some kind of ramp. Julio held his arm to keep him upright, and a few steps later, they moved from the ramp onto solid ground...which shifted and caused Garrett to fall onto hard wooden planking.

The ground shifted again, and not from an earthquake. He had grown used to what those felt like with San Francisco having tremors multiple times each year. This was a gentle rocking rather than a shock. A ship? He had never been on an ocean vessel, but it made sense. Sterling's Theatrical overlooked the Pacific. The lapping water he heard must be ocean waves against a stone pier.

Suddenly, all the pieces clicked. They were being shanghaied. He had heard miners talk about it when he lived over the saloon. Men captured and sold as ship slaves, then sentenced to hard labor across the seas in China.

They stripped off his tails, waistcoat, cravat, socks, and boots, leaving him barefoot upon the splintered deck. His money disappeared along with his pocket watch. He supposed he should be grateful he retained the rest of his clothing, although he wished they would remove the sack.

Cade shivered beside him, the sound of his tears filling Garrett with an unexpected need to defend his brother. He used to hate how Cade cried at everything; now, he wanted to smash someone's face in for causing that grief.

Impossibly, Josiah also stood nearby, his grunts as they searched him the sole indication of his ongoing physical anguish. As far as Garrett knew, no one had doctored him. He was likely in excruciating pain and possibly suffering internal damage. Why hadn't Sterling finished him off? Josiah was not a small man to lug around. None of this made any sense.

"Ring," demanded Julio.

"What?"

"Take off your ring."

His wedding ring? Only when pigs flew and waddled. "No."

"You take it off yourself or I'll break it off. Your choice."

Garrett had no doubt that he would. Agonized, he removed his wedding band and Julio snatched it up.

"Gentlemen, they're all yours."

A new pair of hands led him down a steep wooden staircase, more akin to a ladder than an actual stairwell. He could barely hold himself steady to keep from tumbling down. At the bottom, they were ushered through what sounded like a corridor, then down another staircase. Another door opened to a blast of heat like noon on a July day in Charleston. The difference was that back in Carolina, summers were sticky and humid, while this new location sucked moisture like a blazing bonfire. Struggling to gain his bearings, his ears detected metallic bangs and the hiss of steam. Behind them, the door clanged closed.

Unfamiliar hands untied the twine from around his neck and lifted the sack, sending him blinking, although the room was not in itself overly bright. Cade stood beside him, his face flushed.

Enormous circular reservoirs lined the space they stood in, each metal tank around twelve feet in diameter. Two round openings emitted steam from each tank, their open doors backlit by fire's orange flickering glow. Those same flames provided the room's only light, save four weak lanterns. In front of each reservoir worked men in soot-stained clothing, their faces so black with grime that Garrett couldn't tell which race most of them were. They clasped shovel handles like weapons as they studied the newcomers, not a friendly face in the room. Between them towered piles of coal ready to be cast into the fire.

A medium sized man with a brown beard and frayed suspenders stood apart from the others, his face significantly less filthy. He also had the luxury of wearing shoes. "You got names?" he grunted. Garrett opened his mouth, but the man immediately overrode him. "Ya know what, don't care none." He sniffed at what was left of Garrett's black tail attire. "I'll call you The Aristocrat and—" He nodded at Cade. "—that sniveler is Baby Cakes. Your negro gets a number; how 'bout twenty-seven. I'm the engineer and you don't need my name."

He pointed to the tank on the end, both of its round doors closed. "Captain's looking to light the final furnaces for this trip. We use 'em to power this girl's paddlewheel. Should one break or blow—and we don't all perish in a fiery death—we continue by sail alone. Crew on deck handles that. You two will be shoveling coal with these stokers for as long as I tell you to. Ya behave and you might get a break every now and then."

Garrett glanced at Josiah who leaned against the wall. His wound had stopped bleeding, but every breath sounded like torture. "What about him? He needs a doctor."

"We'll get 'im fixed up. I gotta keep 'im looking nice to get the best price."

Best price... Garrett's stomach roiled. "You're transporting slaves."

The engineer stretched his suspenders and grinned. He appeared downright proud. "Got a number of 'em in the hold. Don't want to work 'em and ruin our chances at a good sale." He waved his arm across the stokers. "Unlike these white boys. Can't sell you all for peanuts."

Good to know where they all fit into things. Garrett controlled himself from lunging out and belting him one, which wouldn't gain him freedom and might find him dead. He needed to be smart about this.

"Due to the nature of the cargo, Congress says we can't ship 'em over land at Panama." The engineer snorted. "Makes 'em a foreign import or some fool thing. Gotta go around the Horn and back again."

Garrett tried not to sigh in relief. This ship wasn't headed for Asia after all. It was going around the tip of South America, which was still incredibly dangerous, but then it was headed to dock in the States. Probably even somewhere near his home state.

"Which market are you headed for?" he asked. "I used to be a plantation man myself. The Charleston Slave Mart usually has good stock, but I've always found the prices to be better in Atlanta."

Cade stared. He knew his brother's disdain for the South's black hospitality. Garrett had repeatedly attempted to free his father's slaves and helped a few to escape with Tobias's help. He had tried to convince his brother to purchase and free all the Walcott slaves in Missouri, despite full well knowing the insensibility of that idea. No wonder Cade was confused by his supposed change of conviction.

The engineer quirked an eyebrow, his expression on the edge of suspicion. "You sure ask a lot of questions, Aristocrat, and none of 'em concern you. Now, get over and light that fire while I take this one to the hold." He snatched up the rope around Josiah's wrists and pointed to a door on the opposite end of the room. "Through there, Twenty-Seven."

Nope, Garrett wasn't going to be able to contain himself. He didn't care if he did have a splitting headache and wanted to vomit from the pain in his ribcage. He was going to belt this guy into next Wednesday.

Only the spark of gratitude in his brother's expression stopped him.

"You promise?" Cade said. "You'll make him better?"

"I don't need to promise nothin' to a slave."

As the engineer stalked away and shoved Josiah through the door, Garrett wished he'd decked him.

14

G arrett learned several things in his first week aboard ship. The *SS Arletta* was one of the fastest sail and steam ships on either American coast. She carried three sails, but her main power source stemmed from two side paddlewheels, each thirty-three feet in diameter. Those wheels were, in turn, powered by two oscillating engines, each with seven single-sided boilers that contained two furnaces a piece. He and Cade were two of twenty-eight stokers shoveling coal in shifts twenty-four hours per day.

Thick black coal dust spat upon every surface—in the air, in their lungs—and the work of hauling it was more strenuous than his time in the gold mines. After a week, no one would guess his shirt had once been white. The bruising on his face had improved, but the rest of him remained sorer than ever. He craved a bath and missed his bed more than on the westward trail, which was a whole heck of a lot. A home cooked meal would have been like heaven, even a decent meal like singing with the angels. More than any of that, though, he missed Martha.

Throughout the monotony of his daily work, as sweat ran from his hairline and dripped from his chin, he dwelled over his last conversation with Sterling and every conversation before that. His former financier knew too much about the Larks, and there was other information Garrett couldn't recall now if he had let slip or not. With every shovelful into the fire, his anger blazed over his own stupidity, over Josiah's betrayal, and most of all, over what he'd done to Martha. They hadn't even had a chance to start their life together. Why had he made himself a better man if only to be punished in such an awful way?

Because you made bad choices, Garrett.

Shut up. He took his inner consternation and locked it in a mental closet.

The second the engineer stepped out—probably for the mid-day meal which the stokers and slaves didn't receive—Garrett slammed his shovel's flat side against the coal pile in frustration. Bits of black skittered from the metal edge and full pieces rolled to the floor. He kicked one down the line of boilers where it clanked off a furnace and hit one of the workers in the behind—a slender fellow with a face that looked like it had met the end of a fist one too many times.

Wonderful, Garrett groaned. Flat Face already hated him. All the stokers hated him. Waltzing in here in fine attire, then being dubbed The Aristocrat, led them all to believe he was some priss rich top hat. So, of course, they all wanted him to get what they felt he deserved.

Flat Face jammed his shovel into the coal pile with a scowl. "Hey, Crat," he snarled. "Ya got somethin' yaw wanna say, just get over here and say it."

Garrett turned his back and scooped another shovelful. "No, sorry. Just a mistake. Kind of like your face," he muttered quietly.

Not quietly enough.

Flat Face's footsteps pounded across the floor. Garrett was whipped around by the shoulder, his shovel landing on the floor with a bang. Flat Face glared at him, one eye listing downward. "What'd ya say?"

"I think you heard me."

"Garrett," Cade hissed from the furnace beside him. He held his shovel in a white-knuckled grip. "Don't make trouble."

Garrett glanced from his brother's frightened expression to the tightness in Flat Face's jaw. "Fine," he relented. He picked his shovel back up. "Sorry I hit you. It won't happen again."

But Flat Face apparently wasn't finished with whatever nonsense he wanted to play. He had ribbed on a few of the stokers over the past week; it seemed to be a favorite pastime of his. Usually, the engineer looked the other way, unless it interfered too long with their work.

Right now, however, the engineer was gone. Moreso, none of the stokers were asleep or on a break, so the three of them were the only ones loafing off. The ship would press forward even without their shovels.

Flat Face elbowed Garrett out of the way and peered down at Cade instead, his nose mere inches from the younger man's. The corner of his lip drew up as Cade's turned down. "Aww, look at the little boy baby, so worried about his brother. Are you sad because you don't have a high style vest or fancy shoes?"

Like Garrett's clothes were anywhere near high style anymore.

"Leave him alone," he said. "Your problem is with me."

Flat Face ignored him. He stepped closer, his nose bumping Cade's who took a step back, slipped on a loose piece of coal, and fell bottom-first into the coal pile. When he attempted to rise, Flat Face kicked him in the chest, one foot pressed against his sternum. "What're ya gonna give me to let ya go?" he sneered.

Cade said nothing, like he hoped it would all simply go away.

Garrett grasped Flat Face's shoulder. "Leave him alone. He doesn't have anything. None of us do." Apparently seeing an opportunity for some entertainment, the rest of the workers began to one-by-one abandon their shovels and circle around them. He glanced at the engineer's corner, but the man hadn't returned. *Absolutely fantastic. He never leaves for more than a few minutes and now, when it might matter, he goes on holiday?*

"I told you he doesn't have anything valuable," he tried again. But Cade's fingertips slipped to his waistband and hovered there suspiciously. Did he have something Julio hadn't managed to confiscate when they came on board?

When Cade failed to produce anything of value, however, Flat Face took it as an opportunity. He shoved Garrett backward, knocking him to the floor, and lunged on top of Cade. Cade screamed and tried to scramble away while Flat Face groped at his trousers, calling, "Let's see what Baby Cakes has in his secret spots." One soot-covered hand slipped beneath Cade's waist band. "What's this, ya barbs?" he laughed.

From the floor, Garrett tackled Flat Face around the waist. They slid across the scattered coal in a heap of flailing limbs, but neither one managed to throw a punch before two other stokers dragged them apart. "Don't you dare lay a hand on my brother!" he shouted.

Someone's boot landed square on his behind and the men at his arms released their restraints. Caught off balance, he toppled face-first onto the deck amid raucous laughter.

"Aw, don't get yerself so sore," Flat Face griped. "I just wanted to see what he was keepin' warm in there. All's I found was this." He brandished a folded bit of parchment in front of Cade's nose, but when Cade reached for it, he held it aloft.

"Give-give it ba-back, please," Cade stammered.

Please? Garrett wanted to kick him upside the head.

"I will once we see what it says. Don't let yer brother get all uppity again, ya hear, or I'm gonna tell the engineer how he started the whole thing." He pointed at Garrett, who picked himself up and clenched his fists but remained silent. Flat Face lounged against the coal pile and flourished his hand like he addressed the local congregation. "Let's see what it says. 'Dear Cade'—ah, so it's a letter. A love letter perhaps?" His brow hitched. "Man or woman?"

"Probably a man," one of the others—Crow Caw—snickered. "Gotta be."

Cade sank behind the wall of coal, aghast as he searched for an exit that wasn't available to find.

"'Dear Cade, I planned to leave without a word, but decided it better to tell you. I can't be married to you anymore.'—Aww rats, guess it is a woman—'I can't be a mother either. I'm not good at it and I never will be. I'm meant for the sea...'"

Dung weed to a bank shot, Garrett thought. This was Alice Ann's farewell letter. He didn't even know she'd written one. His brother just carried it around, torturing himself?

As the reading continued, the sentiments grew worse. She never apologized, she didn't even sound remorseful. The way she spoke of the sea—she yearned for it as most young women yearned to be mothers. Cade shouldn't have kept it. If Flat Face ripped it to pieces, it would only improve his brother's fragile state. Garrett should let him, except he knew Cade wouldn't survive the loss. Not today, at any rate.

Odds were that, sooner or later, life aboard *Arletta* would kill them both. He would never make amends with Daniel or Tobias or Jamison and never have a chance to tell Martha that six years was too long to realize love was worth more than hotels and notoriety. Out of all of his brothers, Cade had written to him the most, almost every week. Even though out of all of Cade's brothers, Garrett had flung more insults at him than anyone.

Looking back on his life, he had consistently ignored every opportunity to set things right between them. It never felt like the right time to do this thing or that thing, to be a better man or a more supportive brother. He always assumed he had tomorrow or next week or next year for valor.

"'I never understood you,'" Flat Face continued reading, "'and I know you never understood me. I want adventure. I want to fight pirates and sea monsters, not run away and hide. I want a husband who isn't such a gully-washer.'" With each continued insult, Cade shrank further. If he could burrow into the coal pile, he no doubt would.

"Stop," Garrett growled. "You've read enough."

"I'm not done yet. I wanna see how Baby Cakes got his name."

Garrett snapped. The past week's betrayals, the lack of sleep and food, and the feeling of helplessness combined with his injuries broke something in him. In order to have any hope of escape, he knew he needed to remain in control, except he no longer held hope of that. They were completely doomed and he was furious. He wanted to destroy something. Anything. Everything. Maybe *he* actually wanted to be destroyed. He didn't care. At least, he would go down defending his brother rather than being like Alice Ann, flinging insults and running away. He had already done that.

In a satisfying crunch, his fist connected with Flat Face's nose, spinning the ugly fellow sideways. Garrett kicked him in the side, a horrific scream echoing from his lips and all around the metal boilers. His shouts punctuated each blow and even when someone slammed a shovel into his shoulder, he didn't stop. In his heyday, he had walloped five so-called gents on the Lark Plantation's back walk, dressed in full top hat and tails, and barely took a bruise. After being humiliated by Sterling—a man he thought he could trust—he needed to win this one, even if in the end he lost.

Other stokers leapt forward to restrain him, but he twisted away, kneeing one in the groin quickly followed by a jab to the other's jaw. He snatched the letter from Flat Face, simultaneously sending Crow Caw to his knees. He stumbled to Cade's side, feeling rather victorious, until the engineer strode across the room on the captain's heels.

I'm an idiot, he thought, and this time, his ego wasn't arrogant enough to disagree.

The stokers parted at their leaders' entrance, creating a blockade from which Garrett could not escape. He remained where he was, drawing deep breaths as four other stokers groaned on the ground around him. Cade backed still farther with nowhere to go.

The captain stopped a pace away, arms folded across his broad chest, his boots twice as wide as Garrett's and broad knuckles that reminded him of Josiah's. He wasn't as tall, probably two past six, but with a glint to his blue irises that threatened with everything Garrett deserved.

"I'm Captain McCullen." His voice was rough, like he choked on sand and it settled in his lungs. "What happened here?" he asked Flat Face. The man had risen to his knees and cradled his bruised ribs. His cheek had already begun to turn a sickly shade of purple. He wheezed without sound.

Crow Caw spoke instead. "Flat Face stole some scrap of parchment from the little guy there." The man thumbed at Cade over his other shoulder then to Garrett. "This here's his brother, was trying to steal it back. Started beating the dirt outta everyone, but the rest of us didn't even do nothin' to earn it."

The Captain's eyes narrowed. "I don't tolerate brawling on my ship. Especially not from slaves."

Garrett snorted. He shouldn't have, but he couldn't help it. It was an involuntary reaction. "I'm not a slave, sir."

"Were you hired on this ship? Did you willingly sign your name to a line? Am I paying you a wage? Do you even know how you came about this post?"

"No, sir, but my brother and I really don't belong—"

"Then as none of those apply to you, you are, therefore, a slave. My slave. And rebellious slaves are either lashed or thrown overboard. Would you prefer the latter or the former?"

Well, he certainly didn't *want* to die. It might be inevitable, but he wouldn't ask for it. To be lashed, however...he still remembered every slave his father had beaten. Worse, when he whipped eight-year-old Cade for simply giving food to a starving slave. After that day, his brother lost all his courage. Their father had ruined him forever.

Garrett was already ruined anyway.

"I choose lashes, sir."

A slow smile curled the captain's lips. "Good lad. To make certain you won't try anything so daft again, you've chosen your brother's punishment instead."

"*What*? He didn't do anything."

"Precisely. If I punish him every time you fall out of line, eventually, you'll be as docile as any other member of my crew." He snapped his fingers and the engineer snatched Cade's arms behind his back. He dragged him toward one of the thick black masts that held up the ceiling. Cade's terrified expression locked with Garrett's.

In a blink, they were children again while their father dragged his son kicking and screaming to the whipping post. The engineer became Alonzo Lark, tying Cade's hands and securing his waist to the beam.

"No!" Four stokers grabbed Garrett as he lunged forward. "You can't do this! Please, I beg you! Punish me. Throw me overboard."

The engineer strode from the room and returned with a four-foot bull whip. Cade turned away and vomited on the floor.

Garrett strained against his restraints, to no avail. "Please! This isn't fair! He didn't do anything!"

Slipping a knife from his boot, the engineer slashed the back of Cade's shirt from collar to tail. It fell open, revealing the abundant reminders of their father's abuse. Not a space of skin had been spared. Everyone silenced, the sound of Cade and Garrett's labored breaths breaking through frozen time.

The engineer stepped back aghast. "What in the land-lubbin' hollyhocks happened to you, kid?"

The captain studied Cade's scars, then narrowed his sights on Garrett. He plucked Alice Ann's note from his hand and tossed it into the nearest furnace. "Seems your brother ain't all straight and narrow either, is he? If he's lived through it once, he can survive it again." He nodded at the engineer. "Give him double the lashings."

15

A week after Cade's lashing, his screams still echoed in Garrett's nightmares...and his wakefulness, too. His brother had been offered minimal care after the ordeal and once he recovered enough to be coherent, he was thrust right back onto the furnaces. His ripped shirt hung from him in tatters, having been turned backward to provide his wounds some protection against infection. With the strain of his duties, however, scabs were slow to form. The first several days, Garrett's frequent glances revealed bright red stripes seeping through his brother's shirt. He imagined the pain it must cause and regretted that he wasn't the one forced to experience it instead.

As expected, the engineer separated them immediately following Cade's punishment, each one paired with another stoker at opposite ends of the boiler room. Cade had been paired with a man the engineer called Limey, a brisk British fellow who performed two shovels for Cade's one, but never complained. Garrett, rather, had been partnered with Mumble, dubbed so due to his distinct lack of a tongue. That was fine by Garrett; he had no desire to make friends.

Lest he get his brother into more trouble, he remained silent and completed whatever the engineer asked. How Alice Ann could actually want to be on a ship day in and day out was beyond his reasoning. To him, out here in the middle of the sea, surrounded by water, guards, and locked doors, it felt so hopeless.

He used his Gift to keep watch on Josiah, making sure they hadn't thrown him overboard. Had they fixed him up like they promised?

The engineer hadn't been fooling when he said Josiah would be easier to sell in one piece. Having a slave as tall and strong as that, especially one not often prone to aggression, would be an expensive commodity on the market.

Garrett, however, *was* prone to aggression. Or at least, he used to be before he decided to make himself a better man for Martha. He had even gone to Mass again for a time, then more sporadically as the hotel got its feet underneath it. The more successful he was, the more often he found himself with other obligations on Sunday morning. He supposed he should be grateful Father Bolin agreed to marry him after only a quick confession.

Would it be sacrilege for him to pray now after all his mistakes and how messed up everything became? He wasn't any kind of saint, never would be. Didn't really want to be. What kind of God would give him what he wanted after he placed his trust in Sterling without asking enough questions and knowing all the facts?

What kind of man blindly accepted the word of someone who ran a brothel as a legitimate business? The kind of man who purchased the first man's pleasures, that's who. Deep inside, he wanted to justify his actions. He wanted to prove that what he did wasn't so terrible. But all it led to was more terrible. Helping Sterling kidnap innocent women and men, giving him the directions to kill their families. He led Martha to the same fate and his brother to the whipping post. Yes, Josiah had also betrayed them, but somehow it felt more honest than what Garrett had done. Maybe it wasn't, but it felt that way.

Sterling guaranteed to change Garrett's life. At least that part had been true.

He wiped a palm across his forehead, flicking sweat to the floor. Then he shoveled another mound of coal into the furnace and watched it blaze. It was a perfect penance; he loathed every minute of it.

"Aristocrat," the engineer barked. "Ya got fifteen minutes."

Garrett speared his shovel into the coal. He wondered how quickly he'd be killed if he rammed it into the engineer's face instead. He left that thought where he found it.

"I'd like to see Josiah—I mean Number Twenty-Seven—and Baby

Cakes, please." How it grated to add the please onto the end when he wasn't pleased any of the sort to ask it.

The engineer frowned at him. "Did ya forget why you and Flat Face are shackled to the furnace while them other boys work free?"

"I remember." Garrett shook his leg where the metal ring had chafed his ankle and the top of his foot raw. Last night, the blisters broke open, and he made a paste of soot and spit, hoping to stave off infection. Jamison would think him addlepated—he was probably helping the infection worsen—but as the engineer said on the first day: he couldn't be sold and was easily replaced. There was no reason to offer him medical care. He had to work with what he had.

"It's been a week and I hoped maybe you would trust me now," he told the engineer. "I promise I won't cause any trouble. If I do, you can throw me overboard." His gaze dropped to his bare toes, black and calloused from weeks of labor. As filthy as the rest of him, his fine wedding trousers torn and shredded, stained with sweat and soot and blood—some Cade's, some his own, some the louse he had beaten.

He kept his eyes to the floor, even as the silence lengthened. His precious minutes away from the coal pile dwindled within the wait.

Finally, the engineer sniffed. "Fine. Ya get ten minutes, but you're gonna have to trade your supper for 'em."

Garrett barely suppressed his surprise. If he showed any kind of pleasure, it'd probably be squashed immediately. He paused a beat before replying. "Deal."

"And your brother stays here."

Not as good of a bargain. Still, he would take it. He nodded.

Free of the shackle, he offered Mumble a nod of acknowledgment before limping with the engineer to the door Josiah had vanished through two weeks prior. They followed a dark corridor then through a double-barred door, leading to an enormous room that rose the height of all three decks. The left side was stacked high with wooden crates, nailed closed and covered in netting to keep secure during sea swells. On the right side, at regular intervals around the wall, sat colored man after colored man, their hands shackled together and feet chained to the bulkhead. Each had enough length to stand and stretch, but not enough to reach the door or any of his fellow prisoners. Sunken expressions stared from empty eyes and not a one's lips rose or fell in greeting. They simply existed.

Not too many years ago, Garrett would have tried everything to help them—probably thrown some of his father's money at the captain to buy their freedom. Since then, he had learned that money could buy plenty, but it couldn't solve everything. At least half of these men were probably free before they landed here. Maybe they accidentally left their manumission papers at home when they went into town. Maybe they were plucked from the fields or the mines and their papers torn to bits. They could be married. They could be fathers. Where had their families been taken? Did someone out there play the role Garrett had, giving information of these men to the Sterlings of the world? Destroying families without consideration?

He wanted to help, but what good was he now, when he had become a slave among them? They weren't even allowed to use the chamber pot without someone keeping track. There was nowhere to escape except to the fish.

He blew out a burst of air and limped forward, his eyes scanning the wall for his friend.

Toward the far end of the room, Josiah rose in a rattle of chains liken to Marley's ghost. A rock the size of all Garrett's thirty-four years wedged into his heart. For all of Alonzo Lark's horridness, he had never chained Josiah. Not once.

"You have eight minutes," the engineer said.

"You gave me ten."

"It took two minutes to walk down here. It'll be seven soon." A key turned in the locks with his departure.

Seven minutes wasn't much time to say what was needed.

He stumbled over to Josiah, his ankle flaring the entire way. His friend's features twisted in the lantern light.

"Can you forgive me?" Garrett blurted. "I put you here. I almost got you killed."

Josiah extended his open palms. "I should be beggin' yous forgiveness. No betrayal goes so deep as mine."

"Except for mine."

"You been lost a long time, Garrett, but cha didn't even know most ya sins was sinnin'. Ya thought you were doin' somethin' good and it turned out wrong."

Oh, he had known enough to recognize a sin for what it was. Most of the time, he just hadn't cared. The times that hadn't been intentional, when he partnered with Sterling under the guise of redemption and building a life for Martha, could he truly say he hadn't had suspicions? No. The warnings were there. He was the one who chose to ignore them.

To not waste his final few minutes on pointless arguments, he lowered himself to the floor, his ankle thanking him for temporary relief. He visibly searched the slash in Josiah's shirt from where the knife had pierced his skin. A crusted copper stain circled the fabric, joined by grime and sweat from their proximity to the boiler room. "They're taking care of you, then?" he asked.

Josiah tugged up the edge of his worn shirt. His dark skin was smooth, not a scab or scar in sight. Almost as though he had Jamison to assist him.

"That's incredible work. Is the ship's doctor Gifted?"

Josiah crouched beside him. He didn't speak at first, his lips making subtle movements but not sounds. Then finally, he stared at his hands and turned them over. "No, that's *my* Gift."

"It is not," Garrett laughed, but Josiah didn't. "Oh, you're serious." He had assumed his Gift was strength; anyone who looked at him would probably assume the same. "How?"

"Yous knew my family served the Larks since the *Oblique*. We were on the ship. We were there when it happened."

"I understand that. I meant, how does your Gift work? Do you have a healing touch?" He stuck his injured ankle out. "Want to fix this up?"

"Ya know Gifts don't work like that. Some, like mine, only help the bearer. I heal quicker than most, but wounds cause more pain than most, too. I guess every Gift has its dark side."

His eyes followed the line of men all chained to the wall. "Yeah, I guess it does."

There was one more question he needed an answer to, something he couldn't believe none of the brothers had ever known. "Josiah, who was Clary's mother?"

"Aristocrat!" The engineer had returned. He leered at them from the doorway. "Your time's done. Back to work."

"Five more minutes?"

"What do I look like, your momma? Ya get your round little bottom over here or I'm tossin' ya to the sharks."

Garrett didn't want to leave. There was still too much left unanswered. Even so, he stood and masked the pain of his swollen ankle. He grinned at Josiah as though life-changing conversations weren't happening five seconds ago. "I'm glad you're feeling better."

"Take care of yerself and yer brother."

Of course, Josiah didn't know about the whipping post or the brothers being separated since.

"I will," Garrett promised. He followed the engineer back to the furnaces while his questions multiplied like weeds that threatened to strangle the sun.

16

Fire tender training hadn't gone as planned, but it had gone exactly as Martha expected. Clary was fabulous. She made it appear as easy as tying one's apron strings. Martha, on the other hand, was as worthless at tending fire as she would have been at any other circus act. Her batons landed on the floor more often than in her hands and she repeatedly leapt out of the way to keep from catching fire. Even so, she singed her skirt more than once. Dread filled her in anticipation of the day Mr. Sterling insisted she perform a more impressive challenge, like walking on embers or swallowing flames. Both of which Clary could accomplish without batting an eye.

"What is the matter with you?" Clary admonished. "You said this was part of your Gift, didn't you? It's like putting on your shoes or rubbing the sleep from your eyes. It'll come back with a little practice. Watch again." She twirled her baton singlehandedly, then flipped it in the air, nearly twenty feet. As it descended end over end, she completed a pirouette, and caught its center before it touched the ground. Her feet snapped together with perfect poise. "See?"

Martha didn't see. Her two-week training was almost at an end. She was never going to make this act believable, Mr. Sterling would know she was a liar, and Julep would become a permanent part of the show. She hadn't even talked to her yet. Every day, she was escorted to meals, escorted to the show floor for rehearsal, and escorted back to her room. Kayus even escorted her to the outhouse. She had hoped that might be a way to escape, but a second glance at his sturdy muscles made her reconsider.

At least, she knew her niece was alive and assumedly well cared for. Every night from her window, she watched Julep dance with the other children during the second to last act. Although the steam calliope's music blocked the little girl's laughter, it couldn't block the memory of her giggles. That lovely laugh was all too familiar.

Martha tossed the burning baton into the air, said a prayer, and watched it spiral back toward her. She was supposed to complete a pirouette and catch the baton in one hand as she let it trail inches above the show floor. Clary had demonstrated the trick nearly thirty times and Martha had practiced it as many, but when it came to the actual moment, all she saw was fire. She spun, reached out her arm, and fumbled. Pain seared her nerves as the red-hot end slapped the back of her hand and bounced across the dirt, still sputtering.

"You are hopeless!" Clary snapped. She retrieved the flaming spoke and held it out to Martha. "Try again."

"But my hand—" The red and tender skin had already started to blister.

"Will heal." Clary shoved the baton at her, forcing her to either take it or have her face burned off. Martha grasped it with both hands and when her fingers curled, the pain in her left hand forced a hiss from between her lips.

But she didn't have time to complain. She knew she needed to learn this or suffer the consequences. She glanced at the windows set in the building on the octagon's left side, the ones she knew led to the "garden." Nora and June told her that the girls there—"wilted flowers" they called them—weren't allowed to leave their rooms. Meals came at set times and were cleared, along with chamber pots, before arrival of the evening's clientele. Except for customers, the wilted flowers received no guests, their doors always locked from the outside. From their sealed and barred windows, they watched a life they could never again join.

"Do you want to end up there?" Clary said. "Because you will if you can't do this."

"Couldn't I focus on my Gift for story instead? I'll sing and you throw the fire?"

"You were the one who told Mr. Sterling you had two Gifts. Now

120

he's enamored. Ya get what ya get for lying."

Except Rella had chosen Martha's Gift. Mr. Sterling had backed them into a corner and she did what she could to save them in that moment. Martha was grateful but feared Rella's temporary relief would only result in her demise later on.

Between rehearsals and housework—cleaning, laundry, and the like—Sterling hadn't given her an hour to truly contemplate the gravity of her situation. Garrett and Cade were both missing and could be dead; Josiah had betrayed them and definitely was dead; and she had no one here to trust. She wanted to curl into a ball and cry her heart out, but she also knew from her time enslaved that tears never changed your trajectory. Action did. She wasn't Bakhita anymore. She was Martha Lark and she would find a way.

"I'm sorry about your father," she said softly. She meant Josiah, but best to let Clary interpret however she wished.

Up above, Lissie and Rodrigo swung from rung to rung on the trapeze and Kayus eyed them from the corner of the stands. Within the hour, Rella and her equine performers would enter for their turn on the show floor. Clary twirled her baton, her eyes on the flames. "Nothing to be sorry for," she replied impassively. "He was obviously a threat. Mr. Sterling did what he had to do."

Martha observed the fire tender's drawn lips and her fadeaway glance toward Kayus. Was her impassivity to protect herself or was she truly so cold?

Finally, Clary sighed. Taking the baton from Martha's hand, she stuck it in the water bucket, immediately dousing the flames. She pointed to the building which housed the school and hospital spaces. "Go see Miss Serena in the hospital. Third floor, center of the hall, across from the children's dining room. There's a sign on the door, so you can't miss it." She held up a single finger, pointed skyward like a scolding. "You get ten minutes to tend that burn. Ten, you hear? Straight there, straight back. Understood?"

"What about Kayus? He escorts me everywhere." The guard hadn't moved from his cross-armed, wide-legged stance, eyes narrowed on the situation.

Clary rolled her eyes. "You let me explain things to Kayus. You've

121

been here almost two weeks; he can loosen his hold."

Martha didn't hesitate. She strode toward the hospital building as calmly as she could, fighting the urge to run the entire way. Clary trusted her enough to go "straight there, straight back." Therefore, she should honor that trust and do as she was told. She shouldn't risk herself or Julep or anyone else's safety.

The instant the stage door closed, she sprinted down the hallway. She took the stairs up to the second floor two at a time and paused at the top, peeking around the corner before proceeding into the empty corridor. She passed several empty dormitories and a large playroom filled with toys, books, and comfortable furniture.

Right now, however, the children would be in their classes with Miss Charlotte, known for the best memory, but not the brightest mind. Creeping farther along, she ducked into an empty workroom as a guard appeared at the opposite end. He paused on the staircase landing between the buildings.

How could she steal Julep away from a crowded classroom and find a way past the guards?

She glanced at the back of her hand, red and raw and throbbing. Of course. What was the one thing you never yelled unless you meant it? Sarah had told her about some ox of a boy screaming it in a theater once and "causing such a commotion as you never did see."

With an inhale, she shouted, "Fire! Fire! The building's on fire!"

Sure enough, within seconds, a child's confused voice echoed, "Miss Charlotte! Someone said there's a fire!" A young woman's voice followed, presumably Miss Charlotte: "Quick! Everyone down to the courtyard!"

Dozens of diminutive footsteps scattered through the halls, stomps and pitter-patters echoing off wooden paneling. Squeals blended with their rhythm, rising in volume as they passed by Martha's hiding space.

As Julep neared, Martha lunged, drawing the girl into the dark room with her. "Jewel, it's me," she whispered before the child could cry out and reveal them. Julep threw her arms around Martha's waist. "Auntie Marta!" Her wide eyes searched her aunt's. "Are you here ta stop the fire?"

Martha hoisted the child into her arms, one tiny leg on either side of her hip, and ignored the protest from her injured hand. "There's no fire, little jewel. I'm here to take you home."

Julep's arms immediately circled her neck. "Papa too?"

Of course, she would expect her papa to come for her. Every father should be his little girl's hero.

Martha couldn't tell her. Not like this.

"Your papa, too. He's readying the ship."

"Yippie!"

After checking the hallway and finding the guard gone, Martha rushed toward the stairs. She would have to take her chances with the main entrance door. She already knew the other stairway offered no exterior escape.

Her feet had barely touched the bottom landing when she was tossed forward, losing her grip on Julep and sending her flying. The child screamed as she hit the tile, sliding across the marble entryway, and into the theater's main exterior door. Dazed, she blinked at the ceiling and whimpered as Clary burst through the theater doors. Quickly, she scooped Julep off the floor and against her shoulder, rubbing her back in soothing tones. "There now, Julep. You're all right."

"*She's not all right!*" Martha wanted to scream, except her mouth was covered by a hand twice the size of her own. She flinched as Kayus's grip tightened on her upper arm.

Escape had been so close, right in front of them. Ten more paces and they would have been outside.

"Tsk, tsk, Mrs. Lark. Causing such a scene."

Ashley Sterling descended the marbled staircase. One hand languidly brushed the railing, while the other adjusted the gold button on his jacket. He shook his head and tsked again. "I was taken with you when you arrived, offered you substantial accommodations, and you now attempt to steal one of my performers?" He bent to study her. "I had such high hopes for you."

"I don't think she meant any harm," Clary spoke up. She cuddled Julep who inhaled great sobs, her face buried in the woman's chest. "She's afraid as they all are when they arrive. They don't understand that being here is for the Gifted good. But she'll learn. They always do."

Whatever was in this woman's head, she couldn't honestly believe this place was for the so-called "Gifted good," not after what had happened to Josiah right in front of her. Perhaps she felt she had no other choice. She was born of a black man, raised by a white man, and unlikely to be accepted in either world. With Josiah dead, she had no other family to turn to. Still, Martha must believe that if Clary thought she had any other option, she would take it.

"Might I suggest something, Father?" Clary asked. Mr. Sterling nodded. "Allow Martha's niece to share her quarters. Let them room together and even perform together. I don't mind adding Julep to our act. Such a gesture would help them acclimate."

Surprisingly, he appeared as though he might consider it. He tilted his chin as his attention shifted from Clary to Martha then back again. He gave an almost imperceptible nod.

"Perform admirably tonight and I'll consider that request."

"Tonight?" Clary scoffed. "You promised two more days. She's not ready. She'll ruin my act."

"Then, my daughter, I suggest you make her ready, because she performs tonight. I've advertised for two fire tenders and our guests expect to see them."

The young woman straightened. "And if I, your *daughter*, refuse?" She spit the word "daughter" like it was bitter herbs.

He strode toward her, his grin wicked as he cupped the back of Julep's ebony curls with a gentle palm. The child peeked out, her eyes wide while his thumb stroked her cheek. "If your new protégé does not go on tonight, then this child's little pinky will be on your breakfast platter come morning. Ask yourself if that's a decision you can carry."

"Now," he smiled. "How about we return to work?"

17

Who knew six hours could pass in the blink of an eye? Despite additional rehearsal, Martha's fire tending showed no improvement. Her final rehearsal was so awful that Clary flung her baton across the show floor, leaving Martha to wonder which one of them would set fire to the theater first.

Her legs swayed and hands trembled as Kayus escorted her, Nora, June, and Lissie down to the backstage area after supper. Clary greeted her with the warmth of a Missouri winter and instructed her where to locate her costume and face paint. Yes, makeup was necessary even if her mask covered half her face. The visible half must be smooth as a sculpture. Yet another aspect Martha was certain to fumble over.

But if she didn't perform, and perform to every standard, she had no doubt Mr. Sterling would carry out his threats. That might be a decision *he* could live with, but she couldn't.

Now, she sat on a tall ottoman, one of many in front of a wall of speckled mirrors, several other female performers seated in line beside her, while the men readied in a similar room next door. Ladies skittered about in various states of undress. Some layered on their full costumes first, while many chose to paint themselves in their underthings. June lifted her leg onto her stool and rolled her stockings all the way up to her thigh, showing more leg than would ever be considered decent in society circles. Not even decent in the slave quarters. When she caught Martha staring, she grinned and slowly pinned her garters one by one.

Two fingers snapped in Martha's face.

"Are you listening?" Clary asked. Her brows had folded in on themselves. She held a shiny red and black dress Martha feared could not belong to her, yet also feared it was. The skirt was only slightly longer than her partner's mid-thigh-length ensemble.

"Is that mine?"

Clary flung it at her. "Yes. Chemise first, followed by the overdress, and then the petticoat goes on top to show off the ruffles. Laces face back like a corset. Don't ask for help; no one has time." She handed Martha a mask, far more elaborate than the one Garrett had fashioned for her. Long black feather plumes draped down her back and smaller feathers peeked up in front from beneath black lace around the eyes. She hadn't yet rehearsed in a mask and now wondered at the wisdom of that decision. Her sightlines didn't feel too hindered; would it be enough to ward off disaster?

Clary lowered herself onto the ottoman beside her. She crossed one delicate leg over the other and opened a wooden cigar box on the table top. Inside were all number of cosmetic pots and brushes. Unscrewing the top of one, she tapped a thin brush into the cream. "I'll show you how I do my paint. Watch carefully because you'll need to mirror it on yourself."

Martha tried to pay attention, adding a bit of rouge here and charcoal liner there. But the activity of the room wouldn't let her focus. June and Nora chatted away in her periphery with three other equestrian acrobats, their laughter decidedly out of place given their imprisonment. Most of the women, in fact, acted as though this were any other working position. They reminded her of the Walcotts' old kitchen slave, Tildy, who carried Martha under her wing those first months in Missouri. Tildy had been the one to insist she dry her tears and get to work, that there was nothing for feeling sorry for herself or expecting another way. The life she had was the life she had and the sooner she accepted it, the happier she would be.

Martha eventually did find happiness at Sarah's plantation home. Little by little, her new friend added a layer of kindness around the hole in her heart. Nevertheless, she always missed her parents and siblings. She never forgot those nights in the Carolina slave quarters, singing songs and telling stories together by the communal fire.

In the end, her makeup replication was far from perfect, but was decent enough to earn Clary's distressed nod of acceptance. That complete, she proceeded to dress. Despite the costume's hemline falling only to her knees, she must admit to its overall support and surprising comfort. Its layers of scarlet and black lace fluttered when she moved and felt like clouds against her skin. Rather inappropriate for public display, but would have made for intimate newlywed attire.

Her fingers fumbled on the costume ties as thoughts of Garrett trampled through her like a stampede of Sterling's horses. His gentle embrace was all she wanted on this night, not the ogle of every other man in San Francisco.

Clary studied her in the mirror. "What are you crying about? You aren't the one who loses a finger if you ruin the act."

Of course. Julep. She couldn't help Garrett, and her niece's fate also hung in the balance. It was selfish to think of anything else.

She palmed her cheeks, careful not to smear her rouge. "You don't understand. Julep is like my daughter. I held her when she cried, cared for her when she was sick. I would give my life for her. That's what parents do, Clary. They protect their children."

Clary didn't reply. Replacing the cosmetic pots, she closed the lid on the cigar box and reached for her batons tipped against the dressing table.

Martha clasped her wrist as she turned to leave. "Does it ever grieve you, knowing what he did? He kidnapped you and forced you into this life. He murdered—"

"No, Martha, it doesn't bother me. Mr. Sterling had reasons for what he did. He made an agreement with Alonzo Lark and that agreement needed to be carried out. If Josiah wanted me, he should have fought for me. Instead, he left me here. God built that man like an eclipse; he should have blocked the sun to find me."

"He was a slave. It didn't matter how strong he was, he never could have—"

"He could, Martha. We lived in the same city for six years. Why didn't he come before? It's not difficult to figure out where Mr. Sterling bides his time; his posters are plastered on every block and building. As you said, parents protect their children. In the end, Josiah may have given his life, but he didn't give it for me."

She twisted her wrist from Martha's grasp. "Excuse me, I have tasks to tend to before tonight's show. You know how my father hates to be set off schedule."

The crowd roared, an unending rush through Martha's ears as she awaited her turn on the show floor. The prior act finished, the contortionists dashed back through the velvet hangings. She pressed flat against the wall to let them pass and said another *Our Father* to calm her nerves. *Thy will be done*, she prayed, but what if His will was for her to flop her performance? Good things came from bad situations all the time; would He choose this moment for such a purpose?

Mr. Sterling's announcement filtered through the closed curtain. "Now, it's time for a real treat, ladies and gentlemen—a triple act! For your pleasure, I present our Royal Flyers, the Two-Time Jugglers, and for the first time, the dual fire tending talents of Miss Clary and The Smoldering Lark!"

Clary poked Martha's shoulder. "We're on."

Her stomach roiled as Clary painted a wide smile on her face, drew back the curtain, and strode into the chandelier lights and applause.

"You're going to be wonderful," Lissie assured Martha. She gave her shoulder a quick squeeze as she and Rodrigo hurried to ascend the rope ladders to their trapeze platforms. The jugglers, Benson and Hubert, followed them to their place on the show floor.

Gripping her batons, Martha entered and attempted to let the commotion float right off her. Every audience bench was occupied, hands clapping to the calliope's entrance tune and children kneeling on the seats to see over heads in the front rows.

Mr. Sterling had moved into the wings where he always waited during acts, watching them so intently. Was it desire or fury which drove his thoughts? She couldn't tell, but even her mask couldn't conceal her bare shoulders and legs, leaving her more vulnerable than before. He had never seen her so exposed and she couldn't tell if it delighted or infuriated him.

Somewhere to her left, a man whistled from the audience. Her hands instinctively went to her skirt hem, trying to tug it lower, but her occupied hands and rigid hemline prevented it. This wasn't her, but somehow it had to be. For Julep.

The calliope quieted, signaling the start of the act. Lissie leapt off her platform immediately, taking one, two, then three swings on the trapeze before releasing. With a double flip—and a number of gasps from the audience—she caught Rodrigo's hands from where he hung from his knees on the opposite trapeze.

Right on cue, Benson and Hubert began their performance. First, two balls circled round then two more were added, then they began swapping back and forth. Every ball was retrieved from the air with ease; not a one fell to the ground.

"Ready?" Clary hissed from the corner of her smile. Without waiting for an answer, she lit her batons from the brazier and Martha did the same. Clary spun hers with the same awe-inspiring beauty she always had. She twirled in one direction, then the next. She tossed her baton up and completed a one-legged windmill maneuver while it spun back to meet her open hand. The audience loved every minute, exactly as they did every night she performed.

Sterling's daughter gave a slight curtsy and flourished her batons toward Martha, her cue to begin the next part of the act.

Despite the burn still fresh on her left hand, Martha flung the baton into the air. Rather than performing a graceful spiral, however, it shot to the right, clunked off the theater wall, and hit the floor. She snatched it up before it caught the wooden paneling on fire.

Unlike the others', her performance elicited silence from the audience. Even cloaked in shadows, she could see them exchange confused glances. She could almost hear their thoughts: *Aren't the performers supposed to be good?* Across the ring, the jugglers sniggered.

She strode back to the center of the floor and raised her baton again. She smiled, but no one was cheering. Up went the baton, she performed a wobbly pirouette, and misjudged the timing. She dove out of the way a second before the flames would have set her mask and hair ablaze.

"What's this bunkum?" A man stood in the third row and pointed at Martha. "Get her out of here!" A few others called in agreement. "I didn't pay for this garbage!"

Hubert and Benson cackled like clowns, throwing exaggerated gestures as they switched to tossing bottles and jumping sidelong. That garnered some laughs and the irate patrons returned to their seats.

Clary caught Mr. Sterling's eye from the wing. His lids had folded to slits. Quickly, she turned and extended her arms to the audience with a wide grin. "Would you like to see me eat fire?" she shouted. Cheers met her announcement. "I thought that might please you!"

Exchanging her batons for a metal spoon, she proceeded to swallow three burning coals from the lit brazier, all with the cheeriest of smiles. Thunderous applause resounded, drowning the circus as Martha stood petrified, her lit batons smoking at her sides.

Lord, help me.

Her faith had always been strong, even on the plantations, even in the railway car, even on the auction block. She had been miserable and hopeless and terribly confused, yes, but she had never doubted that God was with her in the pain. Why did she have trouble trusting He could be with her here?

Lord, do not let me fail Julep. Show me what to do.

Overhead, Lissie flipped from the trapeze, her nimble flight catching Martha's eye. She twisted and turned with grace, like a bird in flight. *No*, she thought. *Like a Lark*. She had once told Sarah how larks sang as they flew, how they were simply happy to be alive. Martha was a Lark now and she needed to sing.

After their opening tricks, they had planned for her to sing a song popular with the miners about golden fire being plucked from the earth. "Sure to be a crowd pleaser," Clary had told her. "When the men are happy, they're more likely to spend money on treats and souvenirs."

"And more likely to purchase tickets to the Garden?" Martha had asked.

Clary shrugged. "They visit the Garden whether they're happy or not, makes no difference."

Wearing this dress, as exposed as she was, that song seemed all wrong now.

Lord, bring me the words.

A tune came to her from childhood. Every night, her mama's soft voice would sing lullabies, spirituals, or other melodies straight from her heart. When Papa returned bruised from the overseers, she would soothe him with one song in particular.

Martha extended her arms, flaming batons warm against her face. A hush fell across the crowd as they waited to see what would happen next. Even Lissie paused atop her platform, Rodrigo's trapeze creaking from where he sat upon it. The jugglers jibed each other and Mr. Sterling watched them, one finger to his lips, his thumb beneath his chin in contemplation.

He needed to watch *her*. How could she help Julep if he wasn't even paying attention?

She must make him pay attention. Her mama's tune with brand new lyrics.

"Little one, come to the tale I will tell,
the one of the plagues of Egypt
Sickness and blood and darkness and hail,
these are the plagues of Egypt
T'was a tale we all know, a tale we all lived,
don't forget, don't forget of Egypt."

While she sang, she twirled her lit baton and walked the perimeter of the show floor as Clary dumped coals on the dirt and proceeded to walk barefoot across them. After a moment, Lissie and Rodrigo continued their act, but the audience appeared mesmerized by the tune. Encouraged, she sang all the louder.

"First came the blood in the waters,

the wells, the rivers, and streams
No one was spared, not a single cup poured,
they were red, always red, always bleeding.

Then there were frogs, the gnats, and the flies,
every room, every dirt, every floor.
Pestilence came and the food died away,
and they called to the Lord, nevermore, nevermore!
Yes, Egypt called to the Lord, nevermore."

From the shadows, Sterling stepped forward. His expression remained impassive, but she sensed a slight twitch to his lips. It may have been her imagination—an optimism for which she prayed—but one lip tilted upward, more smirk than smile. Some part of him must be pleased.

Lord, please let him be pleased.

She slashed her baton like she wielded a sword, fire blazing a dark path through her vision.

"But the Lord wasn't done and the hail blazed down,
swept through the fields, burned the sky.
When the locusts arrived, they completed the task,
we shall starve, we shall starve, they all cried.

Then darkness, darkness, darkness,
three days Egypt lost its sight.
Still Pharoah refused, his heart was hard,
and the Lord took the first in one night.
Yes, the Lord took them all in one night."

As she approached the final verse, her voice descended to softness. She held the baton in both hands, arms extended straight. The light from the flames danced across her and from the corner of her vision, she saw the acrobats complete their final tricks and pose on the platforms. The jugglers captured their balls and bottles. Sterling hadn't moved. She chose her final words for him. And for Julep.

"Egypt wept and they mourned, but me, I was spared,
every one of us safe, Israel.
We were cursed, we were blessed, but we still praise the Lord,
praise the Lord, our good God, Israel.
Praise the Lord, our good God, Israel."

She tossed one baton skyward, performed a single turn...and Clary snatched it out of the air before she could. The two women's eyes met over the flickering fire as the audience exploded in applause, every person on his or her feet.

With quick curtsies, the women doused their batons and hurried backstage where Rella waited to meet them. "What was that?" she exclaimed. "Clary, did you know what she was going to sing?"

Clary shook her head.

"I let the Lord guide me," Martha admitted. "Do you think it's enough to save Julep?"

Rella folded back the stage curtain. The audience still cheered, men on their feet, two fingers to their lips as they whistled in appreciation. "Lord have mercy, would you look at that crowd?" Rella watched the audience, eyes glistening. "I think we may have found Sterling's newest Gifted star."

Later that evening, as the women readied for bed, a key turned in the lock of the sitting room door. To Martha's surprise, Rella entered, leading Julep by the hand. Dressed in a nightgown and two dark braids, the child raced into her aunt's arms, tears in both their eyes. Martha squeezed her precious jewel, never wanting to let go, while June, Nora, and Lissie watched from the bedroom doorway.

"Just for tonight," Rella told them. "I'll collect her at eight for morning lessons."

"Thank you." Martha met the woman's gaze. It contained sincerity along with a sorrow she couldn't quite place. "I am so grateful."

"It's Clary you should thank. She insisted that the star of the show be granted some concessions. Let me provide a friendly warning, however. Mr. Sterling is never this forgiving. From this day forward, he will expect your act to be nothing less."

"I understand."

Rella locked the door behind her and after quick introductions, Martha and Julep snuggled under the blankets together. After bedtime stories and lullabies, the child fell fast asleep, cocooned within the warmth of her aunt's embrace.

Martha laid her cheek on Julep's soft cottontop. As she drifted off, she raised a silent prayer. *Thank you, Lord, for protecting all ten of my niece's precious little fingers.*

18

"You lied to us, Martha," Nora said at breakfast the next morning. The three roommates and Julep sat at their suite's round dining table discussing yesterday's show over plates of hard-boiled eggs, citrus fruits, and salted salmon. "Fire tending isn't your real Gift. Your real Gift is that voice of yours."

Martha paused mid-peel of Julep's orange. The little girl blinked up at her. "It's a sin to lie, Auntie Marta."

Called out by a child, but if she didn't keep to her story, she would be calling Rella a liar instead. If word made its way to Sterling, they would all be in trouble. *Forgive me, Father, for I'm about to sin again. It will be much longer until I can confess it.*

"I didn't lie. Yes, song is my primary Gift, but so is fire."

"Oh, please," said June. "We're not stupid. You can barely twirl the baton much less catch it. Who taught you to sing like that?"

Martha finished with Julep's orange and laid the pieces on her plate. When the child reached for a wedge, she was met with her aunt's firm headshake. "Prayers first, my jewel." She caught Nora and June's shared incredulity as she took Julep's hand and they bowed their heads. Today's was the first meal she had prayed over aloud. "Lord, bless this meal, the hands that made it, and the women who enjoy it. Amen." She smiled when Lissie joined with a whispered "Amen."

Martha pierced her fork into a bit of salmon and chewed slowly. "In answer to your question, June, no one taught me how to sing. I didn't even know what would come out when I started."

"See?" June laughed. She picked up the conversation as though nothing had interrupted it. "No lessons and you're that good? Only one explanation." She nodded at the other women knowingly. "I wish I had a better Gift. There are twenty-two equine acrobats here and I'm plain as day. No one's interested in me, honey, but you've got talent. Honestly, last night, half the guards were gushing over how they want you to bear their babies."

The words drove like a knife to her heart. "I already have a husband."

"*Had* a husband. He's gone now, same as all our families. Luckily for me, I left mine behind at the plantation. Better than most of the girls here whose families died."

"All your families are dead?" Martha asked, redirecting her focus to lessen the ache in her chest. It didn't work, not even a little.

June plucked an orange wedge from her plate and tossed it in her mouth. "At least all those who weren't enslaved before. Nora was free when she came here, but her family got butchered by the natives. Parents, two brothers, three sisters, all gone. She walked the Sacramento streets for three years before Sterling found her and brought her here."

More like Garrett found her and told Sterling, Martha thought.

Rather than grief, however, Nora's eyes flashed with anger. "Which is why I have no intention of tending the Garden—ever. I will gladly take this over that any day."

"Where's the Garden?" Julep asked. "Can I see it?"

Martha's fork clattered to her plate and bounced onto the floor. She ducked beneath the chair to retrieve it. Lands, she had forgotten the child was listening.

"You have seen it, precious," Nora quickly deflected. "You've been in the courtyard for the daily walks, haven't you?"

Every afternoon, the performers were granted an hour outside in the rear courtyard to stretch their legs, converse, and play games, if they felt so inclined. It was also where they planted, cared for, and harvested the circus's vegetables and herbs. Now that Martha had passed the test of a successful initial performance, today would be her first day to join them.

She mouthed Nora a "thank you" and received a nod of mutual understanding.

Julep's nose wrinkled. "There aren't any flowers there."

"See," Nora said, "that's because we're not good at tending them. No one here wants to do it, therefore, nothing grows."

The child inspected her plate thoughtfully. Then her chin lifted and she smiled. "We need ta hire a gard-ner. My papa said his papa had one in Char-ston. He said we don' need one in Larksong 'cause we got all the mamas and Auntie Marie's been gard-nin' since she was small. She's real good at gard-nin'."

"Which sorts of flowers do you plant?" Lissie asked.

"We don't. Ours grow wild." She pouted her little lips and counted on her fingers. "Roses...and dandylions—my uncle Jame-son brought those back from Sattle—and...Oh! The thislies. Those are pretty, but they got pricklies on 'em."

"That sounds nice," Lissie said, her voice wistful. "I used to live in Savannah—you ever been there?"

"'Vannah?" Julep looked to Martha who shook her head. "Nope, I neva been there."

"Well, in Savannah, we grew flowers everywhere. My family had a big ole house with three floors and balconies on every side. But what I liked best were the gardens. Momma simply adored flowers and insisted we have no less than three acres of 'em. You probably don't know what an acre is, but it's a big space. There were these pebbled paths and statuaries throughout, a few fountains, and simple seating tucked away between the azaleas. Sometimes, I'd sit there and pretend the garden could listen. Maybe that someone was listening. Someone good."

"God?" Julep's mouth made a little "o" as she whispered the word.

Lissie shrugged. "Maybe."

Over the girl's story, the pain in Martha's middle finally began to ease. The gardens she spoke of so fondly reminded her of the ones Garrett had written of their Charleston plantation: *There were magnolia trees out back and Live Oaks lined the drive. Spanish moss draped down, sometimes to the groundline, and Tobias always spoke of how he wanted to walk his wife beneath it. I hated that house so much, I never imagined I'd take anyone there, but I guess maybe with the right woman, I might have found a way to enjoy it.*

To find a kindred spirit here, in this place of depravity, became a most welcome thought.

"Are you Catholic, Lissie?" she asked.

The girl flushed. Clearly, she hadn't expected to be called out on her story. "Lutheran. Is that similar?"

"I'm not sure. I've never met another Lutheran, but I am glad to know you. I heard you join in our breakfast prayer. Maybe we can say some other prayers together?"

She had expected Lissie's quaint smile and perhaps a sparkle to her eyes. What she did not expect was for the light to leave them. "Thank you, Martha, but I don't think so."

Gathering her dishes, she pushed back from the table and deposited the remains of her breakfast on the serving tray. "Please excuse me. I need to rest before rehearsal." The click of the bedroom door finalized her exit.

"Don't fret about her," June sniffed. "She's touchy about church. Sterling took her on her way home from service one Sunday. She still don't know if her parents were spared. Given the stories most of us have, we suspect they weren't."

"That's terrible!" Julep exclaimed at the same time a key turned in the exterior door. It opened to Rella's smile, the woman already dressed in her rehearsal attire, which thankfully included a knee-length skirt, rather than her usual barely-there acrobatic flounce.

"Did you enjoy your evening, Miss Julep?" she asked.

The child leapt from the table, her napkin fluttering away. She skipped to Rella and grabbed her hand. "Oh, yes, Mrs. Sterling! Auntie Marta and I had such fun. We got ta share a bed and tell stories and she sang me *two* lullabies, instead of one."

"It sounds like a lovely time. Perhaps, if you are a very good girl, you may have more visits with your aunt. Would you like that?" Her words were kind, sugary even, but they were aimed at Martha and laced with warning. Julep's fate entirely depended on Martha's cooperation.

She felt numb as she gave her niece a quick hug and wished her a good day at school. She assured her that they would see one another for break in the courtyard without knowing if that were true. How many ways could she manage to lose that as well?

The instant the door closed, she rounded on June and Nora. "I need answers. Are all the children stolen? Or only Julep?" *And Clary*, but she needn't reveal that secret.

Nora bit her lip like she didn't want to say but then sighed. "Only Julep. The others are ours."

"Yours? You and Mr. Sterling have children?"

Her eyes narrowed. "Of course not. Mr. Sterling may be perverse, but he is faithful to Rella. I meant that the children belong to all of us. Every woman is matched with one of Mr. Sterling's men, especially chosen Gifts paired to create the best of our kind. After you're here long enough, he'll find someone for you, too."

"She'll be with someone tomorrow," June snorted through a mouthful of eggs. She pointed her spoon at Martha. "As I said, they all asked for you."

Collecting her now-empty dishes, Martha returned them to the tray and exhaled slowly. "And as I said, I'm married to Garrett."

"That hardly matters. None of us are legally married. Besides, there are laws against interracial weddings, so your wedding to Garrett doesn't make any difference."

"We were married before God. That's the *only* difference that matters."

"Not to the law. Even if Garrett did return, you would have to hide forever. At least here, you'll be matched with a man of your own race, who is bearable to be with. You're Sterling's new star; he might even take your preference into consideration."

Her words aimed another knife even larger than the first. This was a full-length sword, perhaps one of those fancy ones soldiers wore. Martha's heart fluttered like a moth edging closer and closer to a flame. Worse, this was the life now planned for Julep.

She addressed Nora, knowing she might have rational answers. "You've all been matched, then?"

"I have, yes. June and Lissie, no. Mr. Sterling matched me to Moses a few months after I came here; he cares for the horses. Has the gentlest touch with them, almost like he can speak their language. We had our first son about six months ago."

Yet, there was no child in this room. "What happened to him?" she whispered.

Nora's brow crinkled. "Nothing happened to him. He's in the nursery with the other children safe and sound."

"You never see him? You don't get to raise him? That's terrible."

"It isn't though. Sterling's Theatrical is a community. It isn't supposed to be about one woman raising one child. We're mothers to all the children, raising the next generation of Gifted."

"You can't honestly believe that?" But the ease of everything—Nora's words, her relaxed posture, how she sipped her coffee without a care—indicated that this life didn't bother her at all.

Nora reached across the table to grasp Martha's fingers. "Isn't it better to accept what is than to hope for what will never be? There's no point in fighting it. I meet with Moses once per week and he's always kind. The entire time I carried our son, he insisted I be well cared for. Back in Sacramento, I rarely had the same customer twice, and they were anything but gentle. Our madame took most of what we had. We were practically starving. Would you rather I returned to that?"

Martha could understand her feelings. She remembered living on Walcott Plantation and being so thankful to be purchased by a family who treated her well. She and Sarah were close as sisters. But in the end, she hadn't been Mr. Walcott's daughter. All the kindness in the world hadn't made them family nor given her freedom. Like her, all these women were enslaved. They just didn't see it since they weren't harvesting hemp or pinning their mistress's hair.

"I understand, Nora, I do. I used to be a slave, and it wasn't as bad as it could have been. But then I found something better. Now, I live in a town where we still have our troubles, but we marry whom we wish and decide the kind of life we want."

"No such place," June interrupted between bites. "You won't convince us to start an uprising. We'll lose and even if we won, what're ya gonna do? Lead us into the desert to die?"

Like the Israelites, she thought. Saved from the plagues and led out of Egypt, only to wander the desert and quickly forget about all God's promises.

Nora squeezed Martha's hand, genuine concern within her gaze. "I suggest you forget about Garrett. Even if he isn't dead, Mr. Sterling will never let you be with him now. He isn't the type of stock Mr. Sterling wants. Listen to what we're saying—if the wrong folks make a baby with the wrong blood, we doom that child, too."

Martha grew colder by the second. Everything she heard horrified her more than being at the slave market huddled on a cold floor, surrounded by desperation and uncertainty. Mr. Sterling had found the perfect façade to capture beautiful and talented women—and men—and breed them like prize mares. It was no different than what some Southern plantations did, except that he wrapped it in pretty accommodations, three square meals a day, and a whole heaping mess of lies.

Oh, Lord, where are you? she prayed. *Please don't let us spend forty years in this desert.*

19

EARLY DECEMBER 1858
ABOARD *ARLETTA*

For two months, Garrett lived as the epitome of a contrite sailor, yet he had been afforded no allowances. No rewards for all the shenanigans he endured. He'd been slapped by the engineer, lost his dinner for reasons he couldn't glean, and been called slurs he hadn't even known existed. As someone who used to work the gold mines and frequent San Francisco's saloons and brothels, that was saying something.

At least his ankle had healed. The engineer never did remove the shackle; instead, Garrett had torn a strip off his already ruined trousers to wrap around the metal. It was enough to protect his skin from further damage, although he knew it wouldn't last forever.

His ten minutes with Josiah had been the last time he was allowed out of the boiler room, save for short bouts of sleep. Apparently, the engineer figured, now that Garrett had seen his friend alive and mended, he had no need to ever see him again. Unfortunately, that also meant he thought Garrett had no need for any familial interaction. With Mumble as his digging mate, the clink of metal on coal and the furnace's sizzle became his only worthwhile conversation.

Over the months, he kept an eye on Cade as much as he could from fourteen furnaces apart. They were never allowed to sleep, eat meals, or take their singular break at the same time, and he worried about his brother. First, his wife left, then his daughter kidnapped, and Josiah stabbed right before his eyes. He had been whipped until he passed out, then woken up and whipped some more. What was it all doing to his fragile nature?

He had desired for Cade to mature, but not like this.

Sometime in the early morning hours of December twenty-fifth, the engineer banged open the boiler room door with a "Merry Christmas, ya louses!" and the instruction to prepare to enter port in a few hours. Buenos Aires would be their first stop since rounding the Horn—surprisingly accomplished with fairly calm seas—and they'd make berth for a few days of merrymaking. Well, merrymaking for the crew up top, not for those chained below.

As a Christmas present, once the fires were doused and their ankles shackled, all twenty-eight stokers were corralled into a cabin with four bunks, no bedding, no porthole, and a single lantern with a candle half as tall as it should have been. It wasn't unexpected; that's how they were placed every night while they slept. The engineer set a crate of bread, jerky, and two clay jugs on the floor. "Here's yer holiday feast!" he announced and locked the door.

Garrett dashed forward. He barreled through the men to grab a handful of jerky and leapt backward as Crow Caw's shoulder grazed his back. The other men shoved each other to and fro, fighting to seize one of the bottles. Whether they contained water or mead mattered not. Garrett knew he would need something to drink by tomorrow, but he wasn't willing to receive more blows over it or inflict additional punishment on Cade.

Speaking of, he found his brother hunched in the corner behind one of the bunks, his elbows on his knees and palms cradling his head. As he approached, he observed him up close for the first time since his lashing.

And. He. Looked. Awful.

Downright dreadful.

But then again, Garrett probably appeared much the same.

Both of them were so filthy, it was hard to tell where their clothes ended and their skin began. Unlike Garrett, however, who held firm to the torn and charred remains of his shirt, Cade had discarded his altogether. His beard and chest hair matted with coal dust, minus thin trails where sweat had marked a path through the grime. Similar to Garrett's, his trousers were no longer than a boy's knickers and his dark curls, once neatly tended, hung in tangles slicked with sweat.

Flat Face decked Crow Caw at that moment, sending the other man to the floor, which resulted in Jack Jaw jumping into the bunk and being clobbered by Flat Face. Garrett slid down the wall, squeezing up against his brother shoulder-to-shoulder while the other men fought over the bunks in a tumble of ankle chains and fisticuffs.

"What's wrong?" he asked Cade.

"What isn't wrong?"

"I mean with you, specifically. Are you ill?"

"There's a storm coming. I can feel it, and it's about to turn my stomach."

Garrett jabbed his brother's arm with the jerky. "Here. This might help."

Cade released the grip on his temples to accept the proffered meat. He ripped off a bite and chewed. "Thanks."

Garrett stuck his portion into the back waistband of his trousers. If he had been anywhere else, it would have been a disgusting move, but in their current situation, it made sense. They only had so much food to last until the engineer returned—sometime within the next forty-eight hours—and they needed to ration it. He could wait.

"Is the storm going to be bad?" he asked.

The stokers were finally settling down on the bunks and the floor, having created an unspoken hierarchy amongst them. With the exception of Crow Caw, who lay dazed in the middle of the floor, their conversation and sloppy saliva chews created a background the brothers' conversation could blend into.

Cade ripped off another bite of his jerky, already appearing better. "Storm'll throw the ship around some, toss a few waves on the deck. If they're not apt sailors, somebody might go overboard. But it isn't as bad as some we've seen. Like that tornado on the trail or the squall when Alice Ann...you know what, never mind."

Garrett hadn't been there for the squall and none of his brothers wrote to him about it. He wondered what had happened, except it involved Alice Ann, so fewer words on the matter were better.

"I think this is the first you've mentioned your Gift since you showed up at the hotel."

Deep creases lined Cade's forehead, straight down the bridge of his nose. He scowled at the remains of his jerky, then stuck it in his waistband as Garrett had done. "It's a trivial Gift. I figured you wouldn't want to hear about it."

Garrett thought for a minute. "Do you talk about it in Larksong?"

"Yeah, all the time. Tobias and Jamison always want to know when the rain will arrive, when the best time is to plant crops and when to harvest. The natives ask when the seas are calm enough to fish."

"They value your opinion."

"They do." And clearly, he believed Garrett didn't.

Because until now he hadn't. He *had* felt Cade's Gift was fairly trivial compared to the rest of theirs. It had been helpful on the plantation when tending the rice paddies, and it probably helped to tend the fields in Washington, but most of the time, his Gift didn't seem to serve much purpose. The Carolina seasons were fairly predictable. Summer was hot, winter temperate. Rain was rain, unless it was a hurricane, and they had the local fishermen to inform them of those weather changes as they arrived.

The difference was that Cade's Gift had never gotten them into trouble, not like Garrett's had. Cade hadn't used it to imprison people, destroy his marriage, or lose the woman he loved. He may have done other things to drive Alice Ann away, but his Gift hadn't been one of them.

Garrett leaned back against the bulkhead, closed his eyes, and reached out into the void. He found Martha in one of the rooms of Sterling's theater, Julep in another on the opposite side of the octagonal compound. Probably bedrooms, given the holiday and the time of day. He focused on that whisp of Martha's spirit and considered how she spent her time. Performing most likely. What had Sterling decided her Gift was? The question plagued him every day. She was a beautiful and intelligent woman, but she possessed no theatrical talents that he was aware of. Although, they hadn't spoken of such things in their letters. Perhaps she would amaze them all.

He missed her. Fervently. More than he ever had when they were states apart and only sharing letters. Their marriage had lasted but hours, and it shocked him how deeply he fell during that time. It couldn't only be their mind-altering intimacies. Those had been top shelf, front page; her taking charge had been like a thousand champagne bottles uncorked all at once. But he had experienced that with other women, too. Several of whom he'd even courted, as fleeting as it may have been, yet not one did he think on longingly when they parted. That had never been his way.

Until Martha.

Absently, he traced the path of his missing wedding ring around his finger. Any indentation had vanished by the morning after Julio took it from his hand. He hadn't worn it long enough to leave a lasting impression. Now, he wished he had.

"You have to stop doing this to yourself."

Garrett's eyes popped open. Cade studied him with obvious pity.

Pity? What was that about?

"Stop doing what?" he asked.

"Using your Gift to find Martha."

"What's the matter with that? I need to know where she is for when we make it back."

His brother glanced to the side. "We're not making it back."

"You might not be, but I certainly am." His forced laugh wasn't fooling anyone. He leaned back again and focused on the ceiling. "I could tell you where Alice Ann is."

"I know you could."

The resulting silence stretched for a full five minutes before he couldn't take it anymore. "Then why don't you ask?"

Cade drew his legs further into himself until his knees hit his lowered chin. His fingers visibly shook as he clasped them around his shins, his ankle chains rattling. The indentation on his ring finger was nearly gone, but still visible if you knew to look for it. Back in Charleston, people thought Catholic men were a curious bunch for wearing rings—Garrett had too for the longest time—but it was a centuries old tradition. Sometimes it was nice to have one thing you knew would never change.

"I've wanted to," Cade finally admitted. "I thought about writing you at least a dozen times. But what if you told me she was close to Larksong? Then again, what if she isn't? Either way, she has no intention of coming back, and I'm not either now. So, what good will it do to know?"

"We're going home."

"The lines on my back say differently."

The comment landed like a punch to the gut, although not one unwarranted. If Cade died on this ship, it was Garrett's fault. A few months ago, he would have lashed out at his brother's quick remark. He probably would have been snide about how Cade needed to crawl back into his hole of passivity, despite constantly ragging on his brother to crawl out of it. Now, he just felt weary.

A thought invaded of finding Alice Ann right now and forcing his brother to know the truth. Garrett had followed her around in his head for years, growing more furious each time. It was time for Cade to be done with it. If he made it back—no, *when* he made it back—he could choose another wife. No one would blame him. Divorce was legal, and he didn't even need Alice Ann to agree to it. He could divorce her for any number of reasons, whether they were true or not. Given the circumstances, he could probably even convince the Church to grant an annulment.

But he couldn't do any of that if he was dead.

An idea lit in Garrett's brain. "You need to tell the engineer about the storms. When they're coming, how strong they'll be, all that blather you always tell Tobias."

"I already told him. He laughed at me. Told me I was trying to get in good with the captain."

"Exactly."

Cade's brows rose. "What do you mean, 'exactly'?"

"You *are* going to get in good with the captain. After the rain today arrives exactly as you said, the engineer will remember what you told him. The next time there's a storm, even if it's a little one, you're going to tell him again, in detail, what to expect. He won't believe you, but you keep telling him. Every time, you hear me? Eventually, he'll tell the captain and they'll invite you up top to work the deck. You'll listen to everything you're told and obey every direction. You won't mention me or Josiah. You won't even whisper about life anywhere else. Then when you get a chance, the next port we're in, even if you have to jump off the ship and swim for it, you go. You get to Larksong and our brothers'll help rescue Julep and Martha."

"I'm not leaving you here. Or Josiah."

"Yes, you are. If we stay on this ship, no one will know what happened to any of us. One of us needs to make it back and it needs to be you. For Julep, if no one else."

A tear slipped from his brother's eye. He wiped it away. "I'm not brave enough. I could never convince them."

"You are. You had the courage to come to San Francisco. You would never have done that before. You took lashings for me. You deserve to go home, not the other way around." He squeezed his brother's shoulder. Any minute, one of the other men was bound to notice, peg him a johnny-jump-up, and probably beat his face in. He didn't care. "I believe in you, Cade."

His brother's expression lifted slightly. "Do you?"

Did he? Or was he talking out of the horse's rear? He honestly wasn't sure. Cade had never proven himself a man of strong will before. He annoyed Garrett with every fiber because of his weakling behavior. If he told his brother that, though, Cade would curl back into his turtle shell and all hope would be lost. He needed to take the chance to get his brother off this ship, even if it meant he never saw Martha or the rest of his family again.

"I do, Cade. It's time for your Gift to do something good. All I ask is that you help our family remember that, just one time, I did something good, too."

20

From its marble staircases to its chandeliers, Sterling's Theatrical had transformed into a true holiday sensation. For most of December, every minute not spent in costume was dedicated to crafting decorations. Once Christmas morn arrived, branches and baubles were distributed throughout the foyer and theater space, ensuring everything glistened for that evening's special holiday performance. Almost every performer received at least one new accessory, if not entirely new costumes. Martha and Clary's were stitched of black lace with delicate silver embroidery that glittered underneath the gas chandeliers and turned crimson from the firelight. Martha had prepared a never-before-heard song, Rella readied a new acrobatic stunt, and Lissie and Rodrigo claimed their double-twist-flight was sure to "set the crowd acrow." If one didn't know any better—which most of their patrons didn't—they would believe the circus was an upstanding place of business, full to bursting with Christmas spirit.

In reality, the performers all understood the gravity of this performance. Christmas Day was historically one of Sterling's most highly attended with dual performances at four and eight o'clock and a special patron supper provided in between. Only his wealthiest customers were invited with lavish courses and special wine reserves offered in his private dining room. With the exception of Rella and

Clary who served the meal, and Kayus and Julio as personal bodyguards, none of the performers were in attendance. Instead, they were granted a Christmas meal all together, seated on blankets in the courtyard and careful, of course, not to muss their costumes.

"Will those in the Garden be invited?" Martha asked Nora as she untied her mask and laid it carefully upon the dressing table. Clary's chair remained empty between them, as she had been summoned to the patron dinner immediately following the final bow. Thankfully, their first performance had sold out and proceeded without complication. Now, the second would need to go as smoothly.

Nora removed her mask, shaking her head. "The wilted flowers have to remain in their rooms. You know that."

"They deserve a holiday, too."

"Christmas is one of the busiest days in the Garden. All those men spending lonely holidays come a calling. Some of them more than once. You can't expect Mr. Sterling to give up all that coin."

Martha could and she did. It was horrible how those women were treated. She would never wish that on any of the performers, especially not this lovely woman she had gotten to know so well. She watched Nora repin her hair and dab an extra bit of rouge on her lips. Her friend popped them a couple times in the foggy mirror and smiled.

"Why the extra care?" Martha asked. "You're almost acting like you have a real beau."

Nora replaced the rouge pot in her cigar box. She turned and butted against the dressing table, fingers lighting upon its edge. "I do. Moses, you know that. I don't see him often outside the bedroom and I want to look my best."

"But why? I thought you were forced to be together."

"We were, at first, but you know how things can change. Moses cares for me as much as he is able. Maybe I am even... Could it be?" Her lips parted in surprise. "Why lands, Martha, I think I love him. You are so good to make me realize it."

Had she done that? She hadn't meant to. She couldn't imagine how anyone could love a man she had been forced upon. Perhaps Nora simply mistook proximity for love, rather than survival. After three months, Martha still hadn't been partnered with anyone. Every night that passed, she breathed a sigh, but then a guard would cast her a flirtatious glance, and the fears came rushing back.

To her surprise, the only one without interest had been her own guard. Kayus led her to and from rehearsals, to and from performances, to and from the outhouse, and never said a word. It was that silence which unnerved her more than the others' outward flirtation. After all, he'd had a direct hand in her husband's capture, a fact not easily forgotten.

Lord, please return Garrett to me, she prayed for the thousandth time. As much as she still hoped for him to be alive and well, as time stretched on, her hopes faded with it.

The call came for Christmas supper and Nora looped Martha's arm, ushering June and Lissie along with them. As they cut across the show floor to the courtyard doors, Martha observed the line of men outside the green door and the lit windows of the Garden above. She raised a prayer for those inside and the loneliness they must feel.

Had Garrett been a holiday visitor, she wondered. This would have been their first Christmas together, both since they'd met and since becoming man and wife. They should have celebrated in Larksong surrounded by family, singing carols, and eating delicious food—rich salmon smoked by the Chinook and venison by the Lark brothers. The little ones would act out the Christmas story as they did in years past. Martha had sewn Julep a fleece lamb for her darling shepherd's costume, and she had carried it everywhere, bleating as she went. Would aunt and niece get to see one another tonight?

Despite the evening's chill, the four women savored the feel of fresh breezes and the sweet salty scent of the sea. They couldn't see the waves past the courtyard's brick walls, but they could hear the rush as each swell crashed against the cliff face below. Lanterns illuminated blankets spread about the courtyard, each with a stack of bowls, spoons, and glasses at its center. Above them, the sky glittered with stars, tiny sparks that seemed to fly upward through the night. She missed seeing them from Larksong, but took comfort in knowing that the ones she gazed upon tonight were the same as those her family saw.

As the performers situated themselves, the kitchen staff bustled about, bringing pots of buffalo stew, boiled salt pork, and preserved fruit, jarred from their own small courtyard orchard. The children scurried about with pitchers of tea, filling glasses before joining their parents on the grass. Usually, they ate separate from the adults, but for this one day, an exception had been made.

Martha resented Mr. Sterling for so many things, but as Julep cried, "Auntie Marta!" and snuggled into her side, she was grateful. It may have been Rella's doing more so than Ashley's, but *why* didn't matter so much as that they were together again.

"Merry Christmas!" Julep laughed.

Martha kissed her crown. "Merry Christmas, my jewel. Let's thank Jesus for bringing us this nice meal and good food."

"Should I cross myself?"

Martha glanced at the guards near the doors. "Best not to." She took the child's hand in her lap and silently prayed. After another few seconds, she gave it a squeeze and proceeded to hand Julep her bowl and spoon. "Careful. It's still warm."

After blowing on the steaming stew, Julep took a tentative bite with the edge of her teeth. Immediately, she spit it back in the bowl. "Hot."

Martha chuckled. "I told you it would be."

The girl cradled her bowl in her skirt and turned wondering eyes up at her aunt. "Auntie Marta, why isn't Papa here? Did he not get our note?"

After their unsuccessful escape attempt, Martha had told Julep that she sent a note to Cade's ship, informing him of their delay. "He'll head back to Larksong and return with the others," she told her. "Your uncles will know what to do." Julep accepted the falsehood, but months had passed since and reasonably, she wanted to know why.

Martha could feel the other women watching, wondering how she would explain their circumstances. "Julep, your papa loves you very much. If he hasn't come, there is a good reason." *Such as his death,* she thought. She swallowed hard and continued. "Your uncles and aunts love you, too. I am certain they pray for us each day and do all they can to bring us home."

"But I want to go home now." Her tiny lips quivered. Martha blinked and looked away, across the courtyard, around to all the performers happily enjoying their holiday meals. Why weren't they as distraught as she? Had she been away from slavery for so long that she had forgotten the many ways she used to protect her broken heart? She had. Larksong had changed her, unable now to handle such conversations with the ease her mother had.

"Martha." Lissie's hand nudged her arm. Her outstretched palm held a piece of green ribbon. "I almost forgot. This arrived this morning from Julep's pa." She turned her bright blue eyes on the child. "So, good of you to remind me, young miss."

From Cade? Impossible. It was but a bit of Lissie's costume, ripped from the hem. But Julep latched onto the fabric and clutched it to her chest like flakes of digger gold. "From Papa?" she asked her aunt.

Martha forced herself to laugh, amazed at how genuine it sounded. "Of course! He said he might send something, but I didn't want to lift your hopes. He's sad he can't be with us this year, but has faith you'll be together again soon." She gave Julep a quick squeeze and mouthed "*thank you*" to Lissie over the child's ebony curls. Lissie smiled and spooned another bite of stew.

As Martha released Julep, June's shoulder pressed against hers. "You're such a liar," she breathed.

"I am." Martha shifted away and reached for her bowl. *Forgive me, Father, for I have sinned. Forgive me again for I am not sorry to have done it.*

In less than a month, her niece would turn five, and she already wondered if Julep would be too old to play with ragdolls and stuffed lambs. She already didn't remember her mother and soon would forget her father. Martha's heart broke at the thought. Children grew up quickly. It was unconscionable that Sterling forced them to grow up faster still. When all they could cling to was hope, God might forgive her the lies it cost to keep it.

Throughout the next hour, she tried to enjoy the holiday as best she could. They told stories of Christmases past and wishes for the new year, albeit none that could be construed as a betrayal of Mr.

Sterling's perceived magnanimity. The stew, although a simple meal, was delicious and sugar for the tea, a rare treat. Their bowls were nearly empty when a girl of perhaps thirteen arrived, her plain blue dress and white apron identifying her as one of the governesses. A sleepy infant snuggled against her shoulder, one dark-skinned hand fisted around her apron strap and his sweet curls pressed up against her chin. At their approach, Nora's expression lit with glee and the child was transferred to her arms. "Ladies, this is my son, Hiram. Little one, these are your new aunties, June, Lissie, Martha, and your cousin, Julep."

"Neither of you have met him?" Martha asked June and Lissie. They shook their heads.

"We have no reason to visit the nursery," June told her. "We haven't given birth, yet."

Minutes later, a young man arrived, the blackish-blue of his skin a match to the sky and with hair and irises just as dark. His smile, however, was bright as sunlight when he sat beside Nora and kissed her cheek. She giggled and plucked away a bit of straw stuck in his wooly beard. *Her husband, Moses*, Martha surmised. Seeing them together made Garrett's absence all the more apparent.

"Who do we have here?" Moses asked the babe. The young boy had fallen back to sleep in his mother's arms. "This can't be Hiram. He was but a mite last April."

Martha silently counted backward. "You haven't seen your son since he was two months old?"

It was the wrong thing to say. Moses's eyes narrowed on her. His palm splayed protectively across his son's back. "Aye. And who are you?"

Nora spoke up. "Moses, this is Martha, my roommate. Remember, I told you about her, the fire tender?"

"Aye. The one who sings. I've heard you through the stable doors."

"Yes," Martha said. "You must be Moses, the stable hand. Nora's told me how she cares for you."

"Is that so?" His scowl lessened a bit. He turned back to his wife and placed a hand on her knee. "You care for me, do you?"

Nora's lids lowered to focus on the baby. "We have our next

meeting on Thursday. Let's speak of it then."

"Oh, I intend to," he whispered. "But for now, let's enjoy the feast." He kissed her cheek again before finally turning back to the group. June's lips quirked, parted, and then chose to remain silent, but Martha knew they would hear her opinions later. Lissie said nothing while she watched Julep fold and unfold her new ribbon.

Once dishes were cleared and the kitchen staff off to their next tasks—principally setting dough to rise for the morning—the stable and stage hands left to ready the show floor, Moses among them. For the next half hour, the performers circled the courtyard while the children ran tag and tossed pig bladder balls in their made-up games. Nora offered Hiram to her friends to hold, giving her sore muscles a rest. Unlike Martha who was used to carrying Larksong babies every day, Nora only cradled Hiram on special occasions.

"Nora, he is such a darlin'," Martha told her as she handed him off for Lissie's turn. The child's smooth skin turned even darker against Lissie's pale complexion. He gurgled as she tickled his belly, tiny bubbles popping from between black cherry lips. The women all laughed then, even June.

"I wonder if I'll have one soon," she sighed.

"Why, June," Nora grinned. "Does that mean you've found a partner?"

June pursed her lips, her secret smile evident. "There is someone. He is around us all the time."

Nora let out a girlish squeal. She clutched her friend's hands and ushered them all into the corner of the courtyard, right where the brick walls met. Quickly, she glanced around at the guards then back to June. "Tell us who it is! No, let me guess. It's Kayus, isn't it? You're set on him. I can see it in your eyes!"

"It is! Do you think he'll choose me?"

Across the courtyard, a horrendous screech overrode Nora's affirmation, sending the guards running toward the well. Two of the kitchen girls backed away from the stone basin, continuing to scream and pull their braids. They pointed at the well's wooden bucket spilt over on the ground, its rope still attached to the roof of the well house. In the lantern light, Martha couldn't see what could have them so alarmed.

"It's blood!" one of them screamed at the nearest guard. "The water's turned to blood."

His chin cocked sideways. Martha didn't need to see his face to imagine his raised brows. "You've gone mad."

The other kitchen maid pointed at the well. "Raise a bucket. You'll see."

Lifting the bucket, the guard tossed it down the well where it landed with a splash. Hand over hand, he drew it back up and raised his lantern close to observe the water. When he dipped his fingers in, his usually pale skin drew out dark red, the same as if he had skinned it raw.

His eyes shot up. "Lord in heaven, it is blood. Raymond, check the barrels!" Another guard sprinted from one courtyard corner to the next, checking each rain barrel, before disappearing inside. Minutes later, he returned, eyes wide in the moonlight.

"They're all the same. Even the one in the kitchen. Every last drop."

Murmurs spread through the crowd, a lull drone like cicada wings in summer, starting softly then rising in pitch. They gawked and pointed, rumors about *her* and her song. The song that brought the plagues upon them.

Hiram was spirited from Lissie's arms, without so much as an allowed goodbye from his mother. Julep, too, was dislodged from Martha's grip. She called her name, but could not locate her in the crowd. The children were rounded up and moved inside, the guards coming to encircle the performers at the center of the courtyard. Martha pressed between Nora and Lissie, clasping their hands as her heart raced with fear.

One of the guards gripped her wrist, yanking her away from her friends. "Go fetch Sterling," he called to the nearest guard. "He'll want to speak with her."

21

"Y ou're very clever, Mrs. Lark. I will grant you that."

Martha sat opposite Mr. Sterling, hands folded in her lap to keep them from visibly shaking. After the blood discovery in the well, he had been summoned from his private supper, none too pleased to be called away from potential revenue. He had sent Kayus to bring Martha to Harvest Hill, instructing that she speak to no one else. Except for his presence at attention behind her chair, the remaining performers had been ushered backstage to ready for the next show in thirty minutes' time. Clary would need to prepare for a possible solo act.

Mr. Sterling placed a glass jar on his office desktop filled with small crystals, their hue's variance from deep red to light pink. "Salt," he explained. He nudged the jar farther under her nose. "We purchase it from the salt ponds outside the city. It's the bay's algae which turns it red. Safe enough to ingest, although its color causes rather the commotion." He smiled. "But you know all this already."

She didn't know any such thing. She hadn't known salt ponds existed or that they provided seasoning for the circus food. Larksong didn't store much salt, being able to purchase only meager amounts during Cade's visits to Astoria to sell oysters and salmon. What they did obtain was rarely used for daily meals, so highly needed was it for winter preservation.

Kayus's broad hands folded over the high back of her chair, his fingertips brushing her neck and setting goosebumps along her spine. Did he anticipate the order to snap it? He was the circus's strongman;

he could do so with ease.

She glanced to the door but would find no help there. "Anyone could have put salt in the water, Mr. Sterling. The kitchen staff have access to the stores. The rest of the performers could have pocketed some at meals and tossed it in when no one was looking."

"A performer such as yourself?"

She faltered. Yes, she could have taken salt from the table bowl in their room. Every day, she could have pocketed the entire bowl, then dumped them into the well and courtyard rain barrels. But how could she have also turned the kitchen barrel red?

"It wasn't me."

"Yet, you are the one who regularly sings of water turning to blood, of slavery uprisings and turning against one's master."

"I didn't sing that tonight. Tonight's song was a compilation of Christmas carols, exactly as you asked."

"Yes, and you performed spectacularly. However, you have sung of plagues for months. Perhaps you simply waited long enough that you believed it would hold you above suspicion."

"The plagues are not the only songs I sing." The shows rotated regularly, allowing patrons to attend three times per week and never see the same show twice. "On Tuesday and Friday, I sing of the trumpets of Jericho; yet, no one has broken down the walls."

Behind her, Kayus sniggered, immediately silenced by Sterling's glare. "Apologies, sir," he said.

"Mrs. Lark, your Jericho song is another of oppression. As is your tale of Esther and Mordecai. I ignored their deeper meanings due to the attraction among the audience. Since you joined the show, our attendance has increased twenty percent. No business man could ignore that." He rubbed his temples as though this were simply another issue of revenue, a complication of how to fill seats. The furrow of his brow indicated exasperation rather than genuine anger. "Perhaps I shouldn't have given my people so much freedom. The Christmas courtyard supper is a gift I bestow every year, but this is the first anyone has made me regret it."

"Please, Mr. Sterling," she tried again. "The salt may have been a practical joke. After all, you said it yourself, salt in the water isn't enough to kill anyone. Might make them sick, but any sensible person should notice its taste after but one sip. Or they may have thought the color to be holiday cheer." She considered Nora and Moses cuddling Hiram, who they hardly had a chance to see. Despite Nora's supposed support for Sterling's mission, Martha knew she would be devastated if she lost yet another day with her son. "Please, sir, don't punish everyone."

Kayus's hands jostled the chair. Almost as though to warn her of the dangerous ground she trod.

"Then who, Mrs. Lark, should I punish?" Mr. Sterling's palms slapped the desktop and he leaned forward, dark irises boring into her. "Need I remind you that this is *my* circus. These are my people, not yours. Like the Larks, I aim to build the ideal society, except, unlike them, I only accept the best. Nothing comes in that I don't want here. My Gifted know they are not safe outside these walls. They know I am saving them from a worser fate. If one of them breaks, the entire show will break. It would mean the end of everything."

Martha *wanted* everything to end. She wished she had the influence to incite a rebellion among the performers. Except she did not. She had no power here. None of them did. Maybe the guards did in their own way, but even Kayus, situated at Sterling's right hand, had been silenced with a mere stare.

Stay calm. Stay quiet. Stay alive.

Had those words kept her father alive? Unlikely.

"I know you despise me," Mr. Sterling sneered. "You have reason. I killed that faithless Josiah. I sent your husband and his brother off to sea, probably dead by now anyway—"

Probably? Did he say Garrett and Cade were *probably* dead? That meant they might not be. But how could they not be, if he had thrown them into the ocean? Unless sending them to sea meant something altogether different. Alice Ann had wanted to "go to sea" on a ship. Is that where they were?

Quickly, she schooled her expression, forced it to erase as she had every day as a house slave. She could use those years to her advantage now. If there was even a sliver of chance that Garrett might be alive, she must cling to it and never let Mr. Sterling realize that she did.

He continued speaking, apparently, thankfully, unaware. "I suppose I should have expected this of you, so that oversight lies with me; however, I suspect you did not accomplish it alone. Have you sent word outside these grounds? Perhaps to your friends back in Larksong?"

"How could I, sir? I am watched every moment of the day."

"Except when you are not. You nearly escaped once already." He tilted his chin and examined her like he might consider a purchase. As though he wondered if the investment would meet his expectations or be a waste of funds. Shoving back his chair, he stepped around the desk, folded his arms, and propped thumb and forefinger to his chin.

"Was it one of my girls? Are they helping you?"

"I don't know. I did not do this."

"One of my men, then?"

She shook her head. "No."

"Kayus? Have any of the guards turned her head?"

"No, sir," he replied evenly. "Although nearly all of them have admitted desire for her."

"Good." Mr. Sterling's attention swung back to Martha. "It is unseemly for you to choose for yourself, and I would rather not part you from someone you want, yet is found unsuitable."

You already have! she wanted to scream. *Garrett was both unsuitable and the one I want.*

He considered her a moment. "Was it Rella?"

"No. She would never."

"Hmmm."

In horror, she realized that her defense of his wife made her appear guilty. How could she know Rella wasn't involved unless she also knew who was? "I...I meant Rella would never betray you. She has too much respect for her position."

In a lurch, his hand claimed the back of her neck, his fingers clenched tight against her scalp. She winced as the roots tugged taut. "Tell the truth."

"I...I am." She wished she hadn't stammered; it only increased his suspicion. His irises swirled with a mix of fury and desire. God help her, she was terrified and barely holding herself together. "Please, I...I

160

don't know anything."

He gave her another cold stare before he finally let go and stepped away. Rounding the desk, he returned to his seat and began rifling papers, dividing them into neat stacks. "I must say, you are a terrible liar. I know my wife loathes her position. She hates me and she hates the circus. She would leave today if she thought she had anywhere to go. I have earned her loyalty because I have made myself the only option. You will learn from her example—" His hands stilled and lids lifted, venomous sights set on every inch of her. "—one way or another."

She felt Kayus's fingers light against the back of her neck again, making her aware of his continued presence. Ensuring she knew she was always watched, never alone.

With a broad sweep, Mr. Sterling drew the four careful stacks of papers together into one and fisted his knuckles upon it. "Never again will you disrupt my show or my performers' loyalties. I will not allow their heads to be turned by the likes of you. Not unless you wish to find yourself in the Garden with the same women your husband so enjoyed."

The blow landed exactly where she knew he intended it, squarely to her already shattered heart. Tears slid down her cheeks and she could not stop them. It was such weakness for a slave to allow her master to see her emotions. It lost her what little dignity she had left.

"There, there," he crooned. "You now see what comes of singing these rebellious songs. It's a complicated business, slavery, and no one wants to think about dour things here. Our audience wants to be entertained, to forget. As do the performers. Let's help them do that, yes?

Stay calm. Stay quiet. Stay alive.

She nodded and wiped tears from her eyes. "Yes."

"Good girl. Kayus, let's take her to the show. Oh, and Martha?" His lips rose in a satisfied smile. "Do have a merry Christmas."

That night, Martha lay curled in bed, wishing Julep could sleep beside her instead of in the children's quarters. Despite her "good and docile" performance at the evening show, it had not been enough to convince Mr. Sterling that she would not act out of turn again. Separation from Julep ensured she wouldn't misbehave.

Her three roommates lay asleep in their beds, their forms but grey silhouettes against the darkness. Even they had maintained their distance from Martha until they returned to their bedroom for the night.

"Did you do it?" Lissie asked once they were safely locked inside.

"Of course, she didn't," Nora snapped. "She knows better."

"But does she?" June kicked off her slippers and wiggled her toes. "Mr. Sterling did kill her husband after all. She probably wants revenge."

"That would be a foolish thing to do. Sterling would kill her."

"No, he wouldn't." Martha clutched her nightgown to her chest, the memory of Sterling's harsh words flooding her again. "He said he would send me to the Garden."

"Oh, sweetie!" Lissie rushed forward, her arms around Martha while their tears fell in tandem.

Nora tied her nightgown laces as she peered out the darkened window, her jaw clenched with unspoken emotions. She had spent three years in a similar situation once, until Mr. Sterling saved her from it. She likely didn't want to say anything that might send her back there.

"So, did you do it?" June pressed. She stood in her underthings, a hand on either hip, her dark hair cascading over her shoulders tempestuously, as though she belonged in the Garden instead.

Martha looked away. "No. I didn't, and I have no idea who did."

Now, alone in her bed, fresh sobs stifled into the comfort of her pillow, she prayed for guidance. *What am I to do, Lord? I cannot stay here, but how can I move when there is no path forward? When everyone suspects me so? How can I hope to escape?*

She felt for her wedding rings, still safe on the long chain beneath her nightgown, and folded her hands around their smooth bands. *Please, Lord, be with Garrett. If he is alive, help him to withstand his trials. Bring him back to me. For Julep's sake, please return Cade as well. Be with our family as they wonder where we are. Find us a way home to them.*

A sharp click sounded from the exterior lock and she rolled over, listening as soft footsteps padded through the sitting room and stopped outside the bedroom door. She hid her wedding rings back beneath her nightgown a second before the door eased open. A female figure stood in silhouette, outlined by the dim flicker of a light within the adjoining room, probably a lantern brought to light the way. Martha could make out nothing of the woman's expression, however.

The figure halted at the end of her bed, whispering. "Shh, it's Rella. I'd like to speak privately."

"It's the dead of night," she whispered back. "Your husband will think we're conspiring."

"He won't. I take night walks often. He thinks I'm checking on the babies."

"Your babies?"

"Shh, let us speak elsewhere, not to wake the girls." Rella paced out of the room, leaving Martha no choice but to follow. She couldn't afford to have her captor's wife upset with her as well. Lands, who knew what he might do then. Grabbing her dressing gown, she shrugged it on and quietly closed the bedroom door behind her.

On the coffee table, the flame of a handheld oil lamp flickered behind its glass chimney. Rella sat on the sofa, still and straight as a fire baton, the skirt of her burgundy dressing gown tucked against her ankles, her hands folded upon her lap. She gestured to the opposite seat. Tugging the knitted throw from the sofa back, Martha draped it over her lap and drew her dressing gown a little tighter. "How can I help y...you, Rella?" A yawn escaped with the question.

"I am sorry to wake you, but something's weighed on me since this evening's first performance."

"About the babies?"

Her brow crinkled. "What? Absolutely not. I wanted to ask you about your lovely story of caroling on the seashore and the children with the candles. Did you sing that of Larksong?"

Whether she realized it or not, her question still focused on babies. Martha wondered if she and Mr. Sterling had any children together.

Or if she had children with anyone else. Had she been partnered with someone later found unsuitable? Was that why she went to check on the babies at night? To ensure breath still filled her child's lungs? June and Nora said everyone mothered the children, but would Sterling hold to such a rule for his own offspring? To hand it over with no say, to play the same role as every other?

"Yes," Martha replied. "The story was about last Christmas in Larksong."

"And the children you spoke of? Who were they?"

Why did she wish to know? So that she might take the information to Sterling and capture still more of Martha's precious family?

For the sake of whatever alliance might be forming, she wouldn't ask, but she would be cautious. Since Mr. Sterling valued Gifted daughters, Rella could assure him none other existed.

"Julep, of course. Then Tobias and Sarah have a *son* and Jamison and Coraline have a *son*. There are many other children, mostly Chinook, none Gifted."

"Are they happy? There's enough food and their parents treat them well?"

"Of course. We've had to make our sacrifices, same as any family, but we manage. The Larks are the kindest men I've ever met. They were my family long before I married Garrett."

Rella gave a soft, sad smile. "How lovely to have so much family for so many years. I do hope that in time, you'll come to think of the Theatrical as family, too."

To Martha's ears, it sounded like a forced line, something Rella had to say rather than something she truly believed. Her tone implied a deeper hurt she refused to admit to, but that could be an act as well. If they knew each other better, if they had built a friendship along the westward trail, Martha would have reached for the younger woman's hand. Being as they were, however, rather than as they should have been, the gesture would have been unwelcomed on both sides. Trust may not exist, but there was still a sympathetic draw, a desire to show Rella the life that could have been.

Just as every day she drew closer to Nora and Lissie and June. Even she and Clary had formed a temperate bond, despite her early indifference. She would gladly allow them to join her and Julep in their escape plans. But how could she possibly plan an escape which included all of them? Their only chance was to leave with as few people as possible. How could she, in good conscience, leave so many innocents behind?

In the end, she knew she would have no choice. She couldn't save them all, but she must save Julep.

"I already love the people here," she said slowly. "I assured Mr. Sterling I would never do anything to harm them."

"I hope that is true. I told him as much."

Rella had defended her? Was that before or after he threatened Martha and claimed his wife hated him?

"Thank you," she whispered. "You did not have to do that."

"I believe punishments should be fair. While I believe you capable of such an act, I do not think you would jeopardize Julep in that way."

"No, I would not."

A heavy silence descended then, while the desire for words prickled across every inch of Martha's skin. Each person at the circus, from performer to prostitute, had a million stories about their time with this place, perhaps none more than the woman who sat before her.

"I wish I had known you on the Westward trail," Martha said finally. "I think we could have been good friends."

"Yes, well, no wisdom living in the past," Rella replied, her tone rigid once more. She smoothed her dressing gown and stood, lifting the oil lamp from the table. "I believe I've heard all I need. Best to get some sleep. It's another busy day tomorrow." She turned for the door.

"Rella, wait. Please."

The woman's slim silhouette paused, the lamplight flickering eerily across her features. "Yes?"

"You said you often go at night to see the babies. Have you noticed anyone else? Anyone who might have been able to enter the courtyard and taint the well unnoticed?"

"The night guards. They certainly had opportunity but lack motive. They have no reason to sabotage us, and everyone else is locked in their rooms."

"Then someone has a key."

"No. Only three have keys to the bedrooms: Ashley, Kayus, and myself. Be satisfied with that. Good night, Martha." The key clicked in the lock as the door closed, taking the light with it.

22

"I wonder what my father is waiting for?" Clary muttered during rehearsal a week later. "It's obscene how they drool over you. Like a dog with a bone." She rolled her eyes with perfect timing as Benson strode across the show floor toward them, juggling pig's bladder balls as he went. He walked a circle around Martha with a slow smile, then tipped his chin as though he wore an invisible top hat, before walking off. Three other men had offered similar flirtatious glances during this week's courtyard socials. And how they stared as she walked the halls! Openly gawking, whistling, propositioning...she may as well have been in only her underthings for how they behaved. Where the women kept their distance since the well incident, the men took her supposed rebellious act as a challenge.

For just last evening, she had discovered Rodrigo leering as she and Kayus entered the backstage dressing room. He filled the threshold between the women's and men's areas, thumbs hooked in his waistband and raised brows beckoning. Kayus directed Martha toward her dressing table with a brush of his arm. "Get walking, Rodrigo," he grunted.

"She's gotta end up with someone."

"Ain't gonna be you." Kayus gripped his shoulder and spun him around. "Sorry for the insult," he told her as he directed Rodrigo back to his proper place.

Now, standing in the center of the rehearsal floor with Clary's question dancing in her mind, Martha wondered the same. What was

Mr. Sterling waiting for? He assumed Garrett was dead, even if there could be a chance he wasn't. How long until he declared her a widow and insisted she break her vows?

Lifting her batons, she spun them aptly, having finally mastered the art of twirling, if still poor at everything else. Clary stepped into place for her planned routine, and Martha began to rehearse her latest song. Heeding Sterling's warning, she had chosen a tame story, one far from political. It told of a time when a cloud of grasshoppers invaded the Walcotts' hemp fields and devoured nearly all the crop. Mr. Walcott had joined his slaves to tirelessly replant the field. Although the harvest arrived much later and did not produce the desired yield, it saved the plantation from falling behind in the accounts. It wove a tale of master-slave camaraderie and she didn't see how it could be used against her.

On the final notes, she tossed her baton into the air, determined to catch it for once, even after dropping it twelve times in their previous rehearsal. However, as the baton circled above her, horse hooves pranced into her peripheral vision, causing her to glance sideways. One of the equine acrobats watched her performance, a white fellow about six inches taller than her and with a face peppered with pock marks. His bare chest, however, rippled with broad muscles that belied his facial disfigurements. Distracted, she fumbled the baton to the dirt. One end sizzled out upon impact.

"Olo!" Clary huffed at the rider. "You spoiled the act."

"I think you both did wonderfully." The rider smiled at Martha. "I'm Olo."

Clary picked up the fallen baton and handed it back. "She knows who you are. The bells haven't rung, so the show floor isn't yet yours. Why don't you wait in the stable with the rest?"

His grin didn't waver. It was like he had pasted it on. Ignoring Clary, he extended one hand to Martha, holding the horse's reins in his opposite. "Moses tells me you share quarters with Nora. He says you're in need of a partner."

She ignored his hand. Two men offering requests within an hour? This was escalating at a pace she couldn't contain. "I'm sorry, Olo, but I've already been partnered."

"Oh? That's not what the men are saying."

"The men are mistaken. Perhaps we'll see one another in the courtyard?"

Finally, his smile turned downward. "Oh. Yes, perhaps we will. Forgive my assumption."

"Of course."

He rode away and Clary twirled her baton, flames drawing an orange circle around her outstretched arm. She tossed it up and let it land back in her outstretched palm. "If you don't pick one, they're liable to do something drastic."

"Choosing one would be drastic, and why should I? Sterling hasn't matched *you* up yet."

"I'm his daughter. He'll let me choose in my own time."

"Yet, you're halfway through twenty-four and haven't chosen."

"No man here entices me. They're all disgusting. They visit the Garden every other night."

Martha glanced at the barred windows above. A shadow moved within one, quickly ducking back from the curtains. "Sterling allows his performers to visit prostitutes? I thought he only wanted babies of certain breeding."

"He does. Gifted or not, he considers those babes half-breeds. Rella takes them to the steps of St. Mary's."

"Rella's permitted to leave? Isn't Sterling worried she won't return?" After everything he had said, it seemed strange for him to allow such a freedom.

Clary stared like she was daft. "She's his wife. She has no other family. Where would she go?"

Perhaps Rella had nowhere else to go and no skills to get her there, but what if her opinion could be swayed? Over the past four months, for as cold as she could be, there had been glimmers beneath her softly cracked surface. Times when she seemed almost human, questions asked that seemed to warrant more than the words she spoke. Martha still didn't trust her, but there were few people that a slave truly trusted. Survival depended on those you could offer something to, with those who saw worth where others didn't.

Rella wasn't happy here. Sterling had said so and Clary had

admitted it, although not in so many words. If Rella hadn't been kidnapped, drugged, and transferred to Sterling's men, she would have continued on to Larksong. Surely, by her questions the other night, she understood what she had lost.

Martha had thought Clary could be the key to her and Julep's escape but time was running short. She needed another way.

Once the bell rang, she hurried to the dressing room and straight to Rella. "Do you think you could find time for Julep and I to spend together? It's been a week and I really miss her."

The younger woman's lips lifted into a smile. It seemed she might agree when a scream sounded from the adjoining corridor. Frantic whispers of "What was that?" and "Is it another plague?" shuffled around them as performers and stagehands rushed into the hallway. Glass shattered from within the kitchen, followed by feminine cries.

Not again, Martha thought. *I cannot afford more suspicion.*

As one, they raced to the pristine kitchen, their performance slippers barely heard on the polished floorboards. The head cook, Louisa, and her three younger chefs stood inside the fully-stocked pantry, their attention focused at something on the floor.

"Stay away, stay away!" she called as the performers crowded in, filling the kitchen. Her arm circled as a pinwheel. "There are vermin everywhere!"

Several of the younger girls shrieked and fled the room, forcing two guards to give chase, while the rest of the performers moved closer, shoulders bumping together. Martha squinted between the multitude. A shattered rice crock lay near Louisa's boot heels, many small white worms wiggling proudly between the grains.

"Good jiminy, it's only maggots, Lou," Nora said. She shoved her way forward and bent over the mess, squinting at the worms. "It's no tragedy. The pantry is fully stocked. We won't even miss a meal."

"You stupid girl. 'Tis not just the one jar. There are worms and flies in half the food. Look."

One by one, she held up several baskets, their once fresh fruit buzzing with gnats. After that, she revealed the ceramic crocks—ten in all—which, when opened, showed either dead black specks or fat white worms within their ingredients. "I noticed it when I came down to prepare supper. St. Peter help me when I check the ice house. I'd bet anything all the meat's lost, too."

"Who woulda done such a thing?" one of the shortest cooks asked. She appeared barely old enough to see over the stovetop.

"Bet it was the storyteller," came the return whisper. Once the speculation began, it was impossible to silence. In, out, and around it wove until everyone confronted Martha in accusation.

"It wasn't me. I promise it wasn't."

"Why should we believe you?" Rodrigo asked. "We all know you hate Sterling for murdering your husband."

"Don't *you* hate him for murdering *your* family?" She slapped a hand over her mouth as the words fled her lips. Her escape plan could not include antagonizing those who, like June and Nora, truly believed Sterling made them "better off." She was just so angry about everything. Even while on the plantation, she had been helpless, but she hadn't been angry. Perhaps it was remembering her and Garrett's fleeting serenity which made her so. He had become a better man, they had finally found love, and then...all gone.

"What is this ruckus?" Mr. Sterling bellowed as he marched through the kitchen. He wore no jacket and had missed a button on his waistcoat, his hair slightly mussed on the right side. Clearly, he had been summoned in a hurry which displeased him greatly, for the fury in his eyes did not match the nature of the crime.

He halted before Martha, who now stood alone before the broken crock, a four-foot semi-circle between her and the other performers. As their master surveyed them, their eyes swept to the floor until he finally returned to her. Then they popped back up like baby vultures eager for food.

His eyes bored into her, so close she could smell the sticky scent of sweat and count the beads of moisture upon his brow. "What did you do, Mrs. Lark?"

"Nothing, sir. It wasn't me."

"I believe I've heard that song before."

"It's as true today as it was then."

He bent to observe the spoiled rice, then glanced over the fruit basket still in Louise's arms. With a growl, he brought his boot down on the rice maggots with a sickening squish.

"It's exactly like her song about the grasshoppers," Rodrigo offered. "The red water in the well, too. We all heard her at rehearsal. She's out to ruin the circus."

"That's not true!"

"Oh, so you didn't sing those songs? You're hoping for the show to thrive?" Rodrigo smirked from behind Mr. Sterling's back. He was seeking revenge for her rejection earlier and twisting facts to obtain it.

She had no counter argument. It was as he said—she had told those stories, and she did want the circus to be ruined. She despised Mr. Sterling and was homesick for Larksong. She wanted his entire show to go up in flames.

"I warned you, Mrs. Lark—" he began, only to be cut off by Nora.

"They're maggots and flies, sir. They're liable to grow on any rotting food. It's coincidence, that's all."

Without rebuttal, Mr. Sterling stepped forward, drew back his hand, and as Nora recoiled, he turned instead to whip the back of his knuckles across Martha's cheek. Without Nora's quick grip to steady her, she would have tumbled to her knees. Refusing to rub her cheek or allow tears to fall, she focused on her dainty black performance slippers, their shadows reflected in the floor polish.

"Do we allow our food to rot here?" Mr. Sterling asked the group.

"No, sir," they replied.

"Then how could this happen? How could there be maggots when we have no rotten food? Fruit flies without rotten fruit? And so many to top it all!" He extended his arms, opened them wide, and turned a circle. "Tell me, my friends, for I would sorely like to know."

For a moment, there was silence. Then the steady hum of syncopated breaths, growing more fevered with each passing second. No one dared offer a suggestion lest they be accused of the crime. Even Rodrigo remained unusually silent.

"No one? Hmm, that is most disappointing." He clapped his hands together, causing several performers to flinch. "Louisa, collect all the stores from the pantry, the cellar, and the ice house. We will take them to the courtyard and see them burned."

"But, sir!" Louisa cried. "Our stores hold a week's worth of provisions and the pestilence has affected only half. The garden is also dry from winter. Would you have us starve until the next shipment?"

"The next shipment is in two days' time. You'll survive. I cannot allow my performers to suffer from food poisoning."

"But you would allow us to suffer from empty bellies?" Nora asked. "We cannot perform without food to sustain us."

Even when his enraged expression turned her way, even when he grasped her arm, she didn't cower. Something transformed inside her with those words: *You'll survive.* Yes, Martha reasoned, they would survive, but they would also do little else. They would certainly not live as God designed. Each performer held such promise and so many wonderful Gifts, yet none could use them to their potential, only to Mr. Sterling's profit.

She was afraid, too—yes, so afraid. Her insides screamed to remain silent, but her brain lost all control. It was as though it left all good sense behind, running to catch up. Then it tripped and stumbled and fell and she simply continued on without conscience.

"Mr. Sterling, leave them all be. I know you blame me for this."

His heated stare met hers, but he didn't release Nora's arm. "Are you admitting to it?"

"No. I do not have access to the kitchen, and my meals are brought to my room. You want to punish everyone because I refuse to take blame for what was not mine? Food rots in *every* kitchen. Even yours."

He brought his face close to hers. "The evidence is against you, Martha."

"Because I sing songs and they come true? You wanted us all to be Gifted. Perhaps, that is simply more of my Gift."

Martha drew back as he raised his hand again, and prepared herself for the blow. Except it never came. Nora seized his arm and forced his palm back into his own face, slapping himself in the nose. Then she lifted her own and struck it across his cheek.

"It was me, you ratbag!" she shouted. "I did it, and I'm glad for it."

The guards overtook her in seconds, Martha jostled to the side as they seized her friend's arms and slammed her up against the pantry cabinets. Sterling rubbed his cheek, evil in his eyes.

"Nora, no," Martha gasped. "Mr. Sterling, please. It wasn't her."

Nora shook her head, her eyes wet but determined. "Don't defend me, Martha. I know what I'm doing."

"But Hiram...Moses." And the unspoken question, *How can you leave them?*

Nora held her chin higher. "They'll understand. Now, Mr. Sterling, let me tell you how I did it..."

That was the last time she saw her. Nora's bed lay empty and Martha wept, knowing her true friend went to the Garden for something she hadn't done.

Worst of all, Mr. Sterling knew it, too.

23

T
he *Arletta* listed heavily starboard as another wave struck, nearly knocking Garrett into the furnace's open door. His short leash of an ankle chain caused him to stumble, his shovel clanking against the heated metal instead of his bare hands.

Over a month had passed since he told Cade to cozy up to the engineer and thereby make his way above deck. To their luck and his surprise, several well-timed rain showers and rough seas occurred soon after, allowing his brother to predict each perfectly. Then, one day in mid-January, the hoped-for call came—Captain McCullen requested Cade's presence in the pilothouse.

He prayed his brother had managed to keep pace with those undoubtedly surly sailors and also managed to hide his emotional afflictions. He only needed to blend in until they reached their next port of call—St. Augustine, Florida—then he could make his escape. At least he would be on United States soil and familiar with the Southern territory. Hopefully, his Carolina accent would encourage someone to take pity on him.

Garrett dug his shovel into the coal pile, bracing himself as the wave descended.

"Ahhhh!" Three furnaces down, one of the stokers, a stub of a man, held his wrist against his chest, his lips pressed tight in pain as the ship finally leveled out.

"What's the matter, Stinky Two Toes?" the engineer barked. No one was quite certain how he had earned the nickname when all ten of his bare and filthy toes were visibly attached. Flat Face speculated he must have been part of a railroad gang that removed toes as souvenirs. Stinky Two Toes refused to say.

"That wave made my blad shovel come back and slap me," he seethed. "Darn metal's hot, too."

"That all? Sounds like ya's need to work harder. That storm ain't gonna blow itself out. We gotta get through 'er."

"Be a lot easier without this blad chain on my ankle. Can't keep my balance worth a penny."

Tonight, for once, Garrett and Flat Face weren't the only stokers chained to the furnaces. Everyone had been shackled, as the engineer claimed, "to keep ya in place during the storm." It meant constantly bumping into one another and dropping more coal than fed the fire.

"Somebody gonna set the ship on fire," Jack Jaw said. "One mishaul, a few of those hot coals flung wrong, and the planks around us'll go up like tinder. Neptune takes us to the bottom."

"Are you refusing to work?" asked the engineer.

"No," he muttered. "I just don't wanna die."

With the waves' next roll, Crow Caw gagged and lost his meager breakfast all over his feet and the floor. "What a bunch of landlubbers," muttered the engineer. He strode over with a bucket of sawdust and dumped it across the muck. "Else y'll go sliding into the furnaces and I'm down a man." Crow Caw grunted and continued shoveling. The faster they made it through the storm, the fewer chances for trouble.

Everyone's sights jolted to the ceiling as a great crash sounded above, a monstrous roar of wood and metal such as if a train engine barreled straight through the upper deck. *Arletta* pitched starboard, angling sideways like rice slides at a plantation threshing mill. Garrett fell into Mumble, the two of them landing on the coal pile. One rock dug into his shoulder while another ground against his leg shackle and subsequently into his ankle joint. Fury jolted through him, and he couldn't contain the foul language that passed his lips. He had grown up on a plantation for goodness sakes, the largest in South Carolina, perhaps in the entire South. He was the owner of a luxury hotel. He used to wear silk waistcoats and engraved pocket watches and received invitations to dinner parties. Men had respected him and women had admired him. His wife had loved him. *Him*, of all people. Now he was nothing. Nothing.

God should send him to the bottom of the sea and be done with it.

Another boom came from above and the ship shifted to its port side. Arms flailing, he snatched up his shovel and braced it across the furnace opening before he tumbled into the flames beyond. Heat singed the hair from his forearms, leaving the scent of char in its wake.

Mumble pulled him back and both men fell to the floor, panting.

"What kind of devil storm is this?" Crow Caw gasped. He too had nearly fallen into the furnace.

"One that wants to kill us," Garrett replied. They all scrambled to their feet as the engineer continued his rounds, barking orders. Mumble dug his shovel back into the pile, unable to say a word, while Stinky Two Toes cursed around the pain of his burnt arm.

The storm raged for hours. Three more stokers received burns, one so bad two sailors were called to remove him from his duties. They carried him away still screaming.

One of the sailors returned shortly after. "Someone's gone overboard," he told the engineer. "They need you up top." They ran out and slammed the door before Garrett could ask who had fallen. *Not Cade*, he prayed. *Please not Cade.*

"Wait!" Flat Face yelled after them. "Let us help too!" The other stokers shouted their agreement, but their cries fell on deaf ears. The engineer wouldn't return until the storm had passed, not if one of the sailors had been lost. Perhaps he wouldn't even return until they reached St. Augustine and could hire a new crewmate.

Garrett didn't hesitate. He yanked the remnants of his shirt over his head and dunked it in the cooling bucket, thankfully still latched to the floor. Over half its portion had been lost, but enough remained for a mild soak. He wadded the wet shirt through his shackle and down over his ankle and foot. Then, lifting his shovel, he thrust it into the furnace's hot coals.

Once one scoop landed on his ankle chain, he went back for another. It wasn't long before he could feel heat rise around him and prayed it didn't burn through the floor. The deck boards sat on a layer of iron, but beneath that this ship was no more than a wooden toy.

"What are you doing?" Crow Caw asked.

"Getting out of here. The hot coals should weaken the chain enough to break. The wet fabric will hopefully protect my skin from any links still attached."

"Where ya think ya gonna go?" Flat Face asked. "We're on a ship. They'll toss you overboard if the storm don't."

"Not if we all escape. We have fists, we have shovels, and we have hot coals. The chains on your ankles will do damage as well. Between us and the slaves in the hold, we can use the storm to our advantage and win our freedom."

"Or be dead," Jack Jaw grunted.

Garrett swiped at the sweat running into his eyes. "This place will eventually kill us anyway. How long do you think we'll survive down here breathing soot and never seeing the light of day?"

When his ankle chain glowed red hot and he couldn't bear the fire anymore, he counted another two minutes, swept the coals aside, and raised his shovel overhead.

As he brought the blade down on the weakened chain, all the men gaped like he had lost his mind. He cringed as the rough shackle drew against his leg with every blow. He wouldn't allow himself to consider how much damage he might cause, if he would be able to walk afterward, or how he could escape a ship in a storm. He had this singular opportunity and he wouldn't miss it. With one final clang, the metal cracked, freeing him from the furnace wall.

"Whooee!" Flat Face shouted. He raised his shovel overhead. "Ho, men! Crat here's free!"

"Whatcha say?" Stinky Two Toes called.

"I say the crat's got himself free. Dump hot coals on the chains and they'll break!"

One by one the stokers began retrieving coals by the shovelful and dumped them on their restraints with various levels of efficiency. Garrett heard at least two agonized shouts as someone missed their mark and struck an ankle instead.

"Once everyone is free, lead them on deck," he told Flat Face and Crow Caw. "Take your shovels and buckets of hot coals. Whatever else you can find that could be a weapon. I'll meet you there with reinforcements."

With Flat Face's nod, Garrett sprinted toward the hold, all the while ordering himself not to scream from the pain in his ankle and the hot chain slowly toasting through the wet shirt wrapped there. He could wallow later. Or he would be dead, in which case, he wouldn't need to.

As he had hoped, there was no guard posted outside the hold door. Every sailor must be on deck helping to keep *Arletta* afloat. Like last time, a ring of keys hung on the wall outside the door. Could it really be that simple?

He braced himself through the next swell, then raising a prayer to heaven he didn't deserve to have answered, he tried each key until one turned the lock and opened the door. Another released his battered ankle.

Shaking the chain aside, he hobbled into the hold, drawing his damp and burnt shirt back over his head as he went. Josiah and the other slaves braced themselves against the bulkhead as best they could, but from their exhausted expressions, he guessed it had not been easy. He grabbed for the nearest rope net as the ship lurched again. Once the vessel righted herself—or nearly so—he scrambled to unlock each prisoner before the next wave met them.

"Fellas, we're taking over the ship. Grab whatever you can use as a weapon and head up on deck. Now is the only time you'll have."

Most of the men stared as though nothing mattered, but a few expressed a rising hope behind their brokenness. One by one they dragged themselves up and followed Garrett to the door.

"Yas might lead 'em to their end," Josiah breathed as they moved through the corridor.

"Perhaps, but would they not prefer it to what else will be? I would give them a chance."

Josiah grabbed his shoulder, holding him back as slaves and stokers rushed upstairs into a midday dark as night. Thunder boomed above the sailors' shouts as they caught sight of their mutinous crew.

Garrett didn't want to see anyone die, not even the men who had captured him. It might give him pleasure now, but later on, when he escaped this place, it likely would bring him little joy. He would still be guilty, lonely, and hollow. Some storms could be sailed through, others must be fought.

He tried to step past Josiah, but his friend held him fast. Difficult emotions crossed his expression before he said quietly, "I'm proud of ya, son. What else happens, I's want ya to know."

Those words...he had always desired them from his father and never received them. Never been good enough, although he rarely tried to be. Now, Josiah was offering them in his father's place at a time when Garrett had tried, yet fallen so short. "I don't deserve it, Josiah."

"No. It's good neither of us got what we's deserved." With a squeeze, he released Garrett's shoulder. "Let's see what is to come."

Up the stairs they trudged, only to be struck full force by driving wind and rain like buckshot. Garrett squinted, trying to adjust to the near darkness after the lantern light of the corridor. The extinguished deck lanterns swung wildly from their posts, only one element of the chaos that swirled around them. *Arletta*'s foremast had broken, its top section fallen through the pilothouse where rain flooded inside. Broken crates littered the deck, their contents slipping from rail to rail in ruin. Lightning drove into the sea, jagged white beams against charcoal thunderheads. In the next burst, he caught sight of Flat Face and Crow Caw, knuckles tight around their shovels as they headed for a group of sailors struggling to stretch and nail the torn foresail over the pilothouse roof.

Someone gripped Garrett's arm and he swung around, fists at the ready. A man's dark-skinned fingers wrapped his bicep, the whites of his eyes ablaze in stark contrast to the storm. They darted from side to side with almost animalistic movements. Although clearly a colored man, his drenched sailor's attire indicated him to be neither an enslaved stoker nor from the hold. How had he been awarded such a role? Was his plan to turn them in?

"Garrett?" he shouted over the wind.

"Yes?"

"Your brother sent me. Is this Josiah?" Garrett nodded. "Good. We have to go."

"Where? How? Who are you?"

But the sailor was rushing across the deck, past his crewmates working to save the ship while being set upon by their captives. Garrett slid, tripping, falling, and being upheld by Josiah's grasp as the formerly oiled deck became like mossy rocks under his bare feet. Like a strange dream, he glided, barely aware rather than with full participation. Rivulets of coal soot washed from his skin.

A bolt of lightning ignited the sky, and he locked eyes with the engineer, the massive paddlewheel whirling behind him. Without the stokers, how long would it be until the furnaces dimmed and the wheel slowed? A crack of thunder exploded as the engineer started toward him, fists raised.

This was it. Garrett was prepared to go down swinging. He raised his own fists until their new friend jerked him away by his tattered sleeve.

"You're not dying yet," he said. "Cade made me promise to get you off this ship."

"We're taking it over. All these men need to return to their families, not only us."

The sailor's stare hardened. "You stay and you die. These men have no hope of survival."

"We won't harm you if you help us."

"If I help you, I'll die, too. Captain McCullen's men are ruthless. Trust me when I tell you this."

"Why should I?"

"Because I was one of the slaves who mutinied the last time. The only one who survived. I won't tell you what I had to do to get the captain to spare me."

Time seemed to right itself again. Garrett became painfully aware of the agony in his burned and battered ankle, the sting of the wind against a face chapped from months before the furnaces. His now shoulder-length hair slapped his cheeks and he pushed the strands aside in an effort to see. The engineer slipped in the deck puddles, yet drew ever closer as the battle raged on. In a flash of crimson, Stinky Two Toes slammed face first upon the deck boards, a sailor's sword withdrawn from his belly. His killer stepped over his body and made for his next victim. Had Garrett sent all these men to their deaths like he sent so many to Sterling?

"I recognize that look," the sailor said. "Guilt over it later. Now we run."

Run they did—for as much as the slanted deck allowed them to run—toward the stern where a young man struggled to uncover the only lifeboat aboard. His sailor's clothes marked him as belonging to the crew, but his dark curls matched Garrett's.

"Cade!" The wind tossed his words away, but Cade still turned. His eyes widened at the sight of his brother and then the engineer in close pursuit. He rolled his hand to hurry them along. "Quick!" Turning back to the lifeboat, he yanked off the cover's final corner and shoved the entire mass into the boat. The stranger leapt up onto the rail and called for them to jump in. Josiah hefted himself into the boat, but Garrett hesitated.

"But what about—" he began. The deck crew had abandoned defense of the ship in favor of aggression toward the stokers. Somewhere aft, he detected a gunshot.

"Forget them!" the man shouted. "Get in!"

Another lightning strike brought the engineer's face into focus, bearing down on them in fury. Garrett braced himself as the engineer charged, no doubt determined to barrel him into the deck rail and over it.

As *Artletta* shifted downward on the crest of a wave, however, Cade dove from the lifeboat, tackling the engineer. They crashed to the deck, sliding into the wooden rail. The engineer pressed a palm upon the deck to raise himself, but Cade recovered first. His fist launched into the other man's cheek, the full impact silenced within nature's terror. Cade cursed—legitimately and with a word their mother would have fainted over—as he cradled his injured hand. The engineer sat stunned, slumped over against the rail.

Garrett was shocked...and proud. His brother had punched someone. He supposed he should have placed more faith in him after all.

"We have to go!" He grabbed Cade by the sleeve, shoving him over the rail into the lifeboat. The stranger tossed Garrett a knife, holding another in his opposite hand. "Cut the rope!" he shouted. "On the count of three."

"*What?*" Ocean waves slammed against the ship's hull, threatening to engulf the lifeboat the moment it entered the sea. If they cut the ropes, they would fall three decks into the water. They would all drown.

If they stayed here, they would die anyway.

"On the count of three." He motioned with each number. "One...two...three!" Together, the two men cut the lines and the lifeboat fell from its moorings.

24

Throughout the afternoon, the sea threatened to upend the four men in the middling lifeboat. By each thunderclap, it struck with the darkness in its many fathoms. With fevered strokes, the escapees rowed from *Arletta*, while every gunshot, shout, and lightning flash cast the fate of those aboard into clear impressions. Many would die that night and not from nature's mighty hand.

Garrett refused to consider the part he had played in what was certain to be the demise of many. For the sake of his family and his wife, he had done what he needed to do. Or that was what he told himself. Between bailing their feeble boat and rowing against the sometimes near-vertical waves, his concentration focused on survival, rather than the stokers' and sailors' fates. *They whipped your brother, stole his letter, and chained you to the furnace,* he reminded himself.

But what of the slaves you released? They did nothing to you.

He stood by what he had told Josiah—his decision gave them a chance rather than to walk to the auction block without hope. Despite what their sailor friend told him, it was still possible that the slaves could overtake the sailors and claim control of the ship. Flat Face's brawn alone might be enough to finish the job.

A wave crashed over them and Cade grasped Garrett's arm, yanking him back into the boat before he washed overboard. "Pay attention!" He pointed northeast, the opposite direction of *Arletta*'s current due west trajectory. "That way! Twenty minutes to calmer waters."

Those twenty minutes were both their savior and a kick to Garrett's poor opinion of Cade's Gift. Rather than taking them through the storm, Cade led them around the errant waters, until they cleared the thunderheads into the light of day. To every side, water lapped for miles with *Arletta* nowhere in sight.

Drenched and dog-tired, the four men huddled under the lifeboat's canvas cover, too near to maintain a gentleman's propriety, yet none caring. Garrett sat tight between Josiah and Cade with the unknown sailor on Cade's opposite side. To afford scant more room, he shifted sideways and eased his brother's shoulder into him. Obediently, Cade curled his knees into his chest and leaned against him, his eyes sinking shut almost immediately. Garrett held him close, remembering their time together as boys. He had been sixteen when their mother died, Cade only eight and missing his mother, but left with only brothers to fill her place. At first, he allowed Cade all the hugs and snuggles he asked for. As the months wore on, however, Garrett's affection turned to ridicule, ashamed that on the cusp of being a man, he might still need his mother, too.

He eyed their sailor companion who lay bent over one of the boat benches, head asleep upon his folded arms. Was he truly a friend or a foe? Garrett's head lolled with fatigue, but he forced it upright. He couldn't sleep when so much was at stake.

As though hearing his thoughts, Josiah's warm voice rumbled above him. "Get some rest, son. I's keep my eyes on ya."

"You need sleep, too." Garrett murmured, but his head tipped against his friend's shoulder and before he could say more, sleep claimed him.

Based on the sun's position, Garrett surmised that two hours passed while they slumbered. For now, they remained huddled under the lifeboat's canvas cover, one corner lifted to allow light and fresh air, yet still ward off some of the ocean's chill. The brothers now sat side-by-side, Cade no longer against him. "Where to now?" he asked. "Do we know which direction *Arletta* went?"

"I do," said their sailor friend. "I have a compass and a map. I can keep us far from them." He reached into his coat and extracted both, the map rolled within an oiled sealskin. Unrolling it, he draped it across his knees, examining first the map and then squinting through the canvas gap toward the horizon. He considered the compass and nodded north of the setting sun. "That way."

"Why should we follow you?" Garrett asked. "I could just steal your map and dump you into the sea instead." He didn't really need the map. He could simply lock onto someone and paddle in that direction to find land. But this stranger hadn't yet earned the privilege of such secrets.

The young man's eyes twinkled in amusement. "You could, except I got you off that ship, which means you now owe me a great debt." He extended his hand with a white-toothed, surprisingly intact, grin. "Melvin Whittle and *Arletta*'s boatswain. Or was. I've been trying to get off that hellhole since I was twenty. It's been thirteen years if you're good with numbers."

Garrett wondered when, during that time, Melvin had gained his title. If he couldn't say what he'd done to spare his life, how much more had he done to elevate from ship's slave to minor officer?

The man's hand hung in the air between them. "Honest, I ain't gonna cast you in the sea. Would have done it during the storm and made it look like an accident."

"You can trust him, Garrett," Cade said. He had reverted to his old self, voice low and shoulders rolled inward. He shivered as a sea breeze blew through the canvas gap and across his damp clothes. "From my first day on deck, Melvin's been an ally. He collected supplies and stored them under cover, a little at a time, ready for whenever the next storm came. He thought to tie them to the oarlocks, otherwise, none would have survived. He thought of things I never would have."

During the storm, at least one sack had still gone overboard, along with Garrett's knife, as the force of the boat's descent met the strength of the sea. Still, two supply sacks had survived, including one containing grog and water jugs, something Garrett wouldn't have considered, leading to dehydration long before starvation.

"He saved all our lives, Garrett. If you won't take his hand based on his own merits, at least take it based on mine. I did what you asked, didn't I?"

Yes, he certainly had, unexpectedly so. When Garrett sent Cade above decks, he doubted if his brother would rise to the challenge. Yet, he had. In that moment, he didn't look so much like a pitiful child; he showed the heart of a man Garrett hoped would never fade.

Tentatively, he accepted the proffered hand. "I don't give my trust easily, Mr. Whittle. You'll have to earn it."

Melvin released his grip with an amused smile. "Ah, and yet you call me, a colored fellow, by my title, which tempts me to believe I haven't far to go."

"I'm married to a colored woman," he said by way of explanation.

"So, your brother's told me, and I look mighty forward to meeting her." He snapped the map and repositioned it across his lap. "Now, back to business. Assuming Captain McCullen squashes the mutiny, *Arletta*'s next port of call is at market in St. Augustine. They'll unload as many slaves as they can before heading to the Carolinas to sell the rest and purchase goods. Which means we need to head somewhere in between. Jacksonville..." He paused, considering. "Hmm, no, Savannah would be better."

"Charleston," Cade said.

Melvin frowned. "Charleston is exactly where I said we shouldn't go. 'Sides, I lived there once and I got no desire to go back."

"That's where our brother is, and he has money. He'll help us."

Would he? Garrett very much doubted it, but what choice did they have? They'd already traversed the pits of hell, hadn't any coin, and no way to return to California. Begging their brother's mercy was the only sensible option, short of robbing a bank or holding up a stagecoach. Garrett could get a job, but that would take time, and who would hire him appearing as he did? Whether they purchased passage on another ship or joined a wagon party, it would already take months he didn't wish to sacrifice.

"Cade's right," he said. "Daniel is our best option."

Melvin's frown soured into an outright scowl. "No. Savannah is our best option. We don't have enough food to last us to Carolina. At least a third of what I stowed away fell overboard in the storm. We's lucky to have saved anything, and will have to ration as it is. If you don't care for your survival, hop out and swim to Charleston, because this boat is going to Savannah."

Did he speak to everyone with such nerve? Or was his impudence reserved solely for their lifeboat's unusual circumstances? It seemed Melvin wouldn't have made it very long if he responded to everyone this way.

"What about Savannah's slave market?" Garrett asked. "Don't you worry about the fugitive laws?"

"Mr. Lark, if you knew the price I paid for my survival, you would consider my freedom earned. Let the slave catchers try. I will kill them before they can claim me. Should I die in the process, there's a better life after this one, and I will welcome it."

"We'll defend you," Cade said. "On my life, I promise it."

"I believe you would try."

Garrett wondered what had occurred over the past weeks while he toiled in the boiler room. How had his usually timid brother managed to gain such confidences, find the wherewithal to belt the engineer, and now promise defense of a black man? From his fiery determination—an emotion Garrett had never once seen on him—he believed Cade truly planned to follow through on his promises.

As Melvin had implied, however, Garrett also doubted his brother's ability for success in such an altercation. Despite his defense of Garrett with the engineer, without help, his defense of Melvin would truly be "on his life."

"I will stand by you as well," he said. "With my gratitude. As you said, we are no doubt in your debt. All I ask is that, once we resupply in Savannah—once we know *Arletta*'s passed us by—we continue on to my brother's place in Charleston. Once there, you are free to do as you please."

Melvin didn't appear convinced. "If I take this risk, you must allow me a place in your homestead. Cade's word says you have a town and thousands of acres between you. I want a piece of it to call my own— at least fifty acres, plows for planting, and help at the harvest. No added conditions."

Garrett's brows rose. "*Fifty* acres? That's almost half what the government was offering when we arrived in '52."

"Seems fitting then, considering the government only thinks of me as half a man."

Without warning, a jolt shot through him, a pain that hit Garrett's head like lightning in his brain. He wanted to vomit in the bottom of the boat.

It had been so long since he had felt a definitive pull toward someone without explicitly knowing why. Was this his Gift's way of telling him they needed Melvin in their town? As far as he knew, the sailor hadn't been on Sterling's list of bounties. From what he could tell, the man wasn't Gifted either. Then what was the reason for his distress?

"None of that land carries my name," he bit out. "I can't share it with you."

"He can have my share," Cade offered, seemingly oblivious to his brother's discomfort. "What good is it to me? I make most of my living on the shore." Fishing and oyster mongering because that's what Alice Ann preferred. Yet another aspect of his life reconfigured by that horrid woman.

Garrett, however, couldn't even properly focus his anger. Not with this wretched headache.

"Garrett?" his brother asked. "Do you agree?"

He dragged his eyes open, not realizing when they had closed. "Fine."

Cade eyed him, finally seeming to understand. "Are you all right?"

"I have a headache."

His brother's grey irises asked a hundred questions without words, none of which could be answered with Melvin in the boat. Cade had experienced plenty of Garrett's headaches before, his worst being the day he assaulted a soldier at Fort Hall, landed himself in the garrison, and then abandoned his brothers for San Francisco hours later. When he noticed Melvin staring, he held the man's gaze, despite the rip of pain that sliced through him at the gesture.

"I'm fine. Josiah, you've been awfully quiet. What say you?" The effort of keeping those few words steady nearly did him in. Sweat beaded upon his brow and he quickly wiped it away.

Josiah gave a low grunt, his arms folded in sour silence. He leaned into Melvin, his enormous shoulder square against the other man's normally-sized bicep. "I'm witcha, Melvin, but don'tcha hurt my boys. I already lost my dau-ter. Ya hurt my sons and I'll take ya to the bottom of the sea."

With that, the canvas cover was set aside, oars were taken up, and stroke by stroke, they set out for Savannah. All the while, Garrett wondered if his head would shatter before they arrived.

25

By their sixth day on the water, only half a water jug remained between four parched tongues. Their food had run dry that morning. Between damp clothes, the chilled ocean air, and meager rations, Cade developed a cold which quickly escalated into rumbling coughs. He rowed on without complaint, however, wearing himself down, and forcing Garrett to offer him extra rations from his own share. Using Melvin's knife, Josiah had fashioned strips of the canvas cover into capes, but even so, Cade began to shiver.

The four men now huddled under the remains of the lifeboat cover while a steady drizzle pattered down upon it. Tight within Josiah's arms, Cade slept soundly, his fevered skin radiating warmth. Concern puckered the older man's lips and brow as he dabbed Cade's forehead with a wet cloth torn from his shirt, no doubt wishing he could bestow some of his healing Gift upon his youngest "son."

By then, Garrett's own headache had reduced to a low throb, still noticeable but manageable. Despite the hunger pangs within his belly, he no longer felt the constant want to vomit, weep, or pass out, so he considered that a point to the positive. Unless it actually meant the opposite, and his stomach had shrunk to the size of a walnut, each labored breath bringing him closer to death.

"We won't make it to Savannah," he whispered to Melvin as Cade released a particularly ugly cough. His brother moaned and settled back in against Josiah.

The sailor wrapped his arms around his knees, his chin propped against them. "Then we die out here."

"We're only fifteen miles southwest of Georgia and the wind's in our favor. We could be to Brunswick by nightfall. The river there will have fresh water and the town, everything else we need."

"We have nothing to trade. How do you expect to pay?"

"I don't."

"Don't steal it," Cade mumbled. His eyelids fluttered, but didn't rise, and Garrett wondered how much he had truly heard.

He reached for an oar. "Josiah, wrap him in the canvas for warmth. The rest of us get to rowing."

By the time they washed up in the coastal town of Brunswick, his arms screamed for relief. They had arrived in less time than anticipated, but the extra effort now threatened to undo him. As the boat slid to a stop upon the sand, he threw a leg over the side and darkness filled his vision. He stumbled forward, falling on his face in the water. Salt rushed into his mouth and he retched. His malnourished time at sea had done him no favors.

"We almos' there." Josiah's steadying grip lifted him by the elbow and set him on his feet again. He focused on his friend's broad chest and blinked. If he looked up and saw compassion there, he would finally relent to the emotion he'd stifled all those months on *Arletta*. Once he was home, then he could bawl his heart out. *If* he got home. And when he did, what if Martha wasn't there? What if he was too late?

For now, he could see that she and Julep were still at Sterling's, and for now, that was enough to keep him moving.

While Cade slept on the shore, they stripped the boat, prying away the bench boards for a makeshift stretcher. From their supplies, they kept only two empty jugs, but retained both sacks, and filled one with sticks from the nearby scrub. Josiah helped Garrett strap Cade to the stretcher and together with Melvin, hauled him toward town.

What a pathetic sight they must appear to the residents of Brunswick. Looking and smelling like a heap of gutter garbage, their clothing in rags and hanging loose from their emaciated forms. Char marks crossed Garrett's shirt from being wrapped around the heated shackle, while salt, sand, and sunburns left their exposed skin dry and in places, blistered. When his bare foot landed in a mound of horse manure, he just kept walking.

As they passed a restaurant, his mouth watered, the scent of sausage and calf's liver taunting him through windows left ajar. Without money, however, it was a wasted dream. An elderly woman crossed the threshold, saw them, and pressed a handkerchief to her wrinkled nose, her *tut-tut*ing none too quiet. Likewise, a mother quickly ushered her two young children into the rail depot while they peeped with curiosity around her wide skirt. Through the window, he saw her speak to the station agent and point in their direction. Hopeful the man might offer some assistance, he stepped closer. A minute later, however, the agent appeared on the stoop, fingers wrapped around his rifle and warning them to "get along."

Garrett would steal food and medicine if he had to, but hoped it wouldn't come to that. His eyes scanned the sky for steeples, his ears perked for the sound of distant bells. Surely, the Church would help. He would beg them on his hands and knees if he had to.

"Stop!" Cade croaked. The singular word set off another coughing fit which left him panting. He jerked for the canvas strap around his waist, clawing to release himself from the stretcher. "Josiah, let me out of here!" His eyes snapped to something down the street, then to Melvin. "Cut these ties away! Now!"

Garrett tried to ease him back, but Cade's fist flew out, cuffing his brother around the ear. Garrett dropped to a knee, ear ringing as the stretcher fell from his grasp. He barely comprehended his brother somersaulting into the street, finally freed from his bonds, as his stomach threatened to upset again.

"Garrett, are you's all ri—Cade!" Josiah hauled Garrett up, both hands steady on his shoulders. "Ya hafta go afta him. I's can't be. Not here."

Garrett blinked, his vision swimming as two versions of his brother chased down a shiny covered landau. What the blue devil was he doing?

"Alice!" Cade screamed, his voice like gravel. He coughed and stumbled, but managed to continue forward. "Alice Ann!"

He thought he saw his wife? Here? Garrett reached out to find her, which took more energy than he had left. He retched again, right in the street beside a pile of manure, his head screaming back at him.

Josiah's hand was on his back. "Are ya ill?"

He nodded, but Melvin stepped in and elbowed Josiah out of the way. "Go get your brother," he ordered. "Josiah and I go and this town'll think we're out to murder him."

A black behemoth like Josiah charging down the street in Southern Georgia? He'd have a bullet in his back before Garrett could blink twice. And blinking was rather difficult at the moment.

Once he had an appropriate amount of food and a good night's rest, he was going to slap Cade into next Tuesday. He stumbled forward, forcing himself to maintain focus on his brother, rather than the darkness at the edges of his vision. Had that punch concussed him? Jamison would've known.

Up ahead, a supply wagon crossed the street, tied high with wooden barrels and blocking the landau's path. Its driver pulled up on the reins, finally bringing the carriage to a stop. Cade yanked open the narrow black door to a feminine shriek and a man's shout of "What filth is this?"

Cade shook his head, his complexion as pale as his white-knuckled grip upon the door. "No, I...you're not...I thought you were her." He released an alarming mix of weeping and coughs, illness clearly driving deeper into his chest. If they were in San Francisco, they would have had the money to hire a doctor, but Cade would have never fallen this ill to begin with. Another black mark on Garrett's name. If his brother died because of him...

Practically falling against the carriage, he gripped what remained of Cade's sleeve to keep him grounded. "My apologies," he gasped at the landau. "My brother...he's ill. The fever's ad...addled his mind."

A wispy feminine voice replied. "Mercy me! What's happened to y'all?"

"Pernella Mae," an older man hissed. "These vagabonds are not our concern."

"We're not vagabonds," Garrett said. "We're just slightly mad with hunger."

"Beggars then and no better."

Garrett finally straightened, taking in the landau's occupants. A middle-aged man glared at him from the upholstered bench seat. Fevered breaths puffed his mustache whiskers in a flutter while the exterior breeze barely shifted the hem of his black frock coat. Clearly affluent, although not sensational about it.

Across from him, an adolescent girl, barely older than a debutante, extended him a wide-eyed stare, her irises the color of lake lily pads. The way her rose-tinted lips curved into a smile despite his unkempt state suggested a naivete that would one day lead her to ruin. Back in his youth, she would have probably landed in his bed. Exactly as Alice Ann had done with his brother.

For Pernella did look incredibly like Cade's wife. Her bright crimson hair was piled at the base of her neck, streamers trailing down from beneath her pink-ribboned bonnet. The way the waves framed her face, combined with those smoldering eyes and a curve of hips too womanly for her age, all suggested Alice Ann Owens Lark. It was no wonder why Cade, in his delirious state, would give chase, expecting to find his wife at last.

"As I said, my brother is not well," Garrett told them while Cade stood stricken and shaking. "If you could provide directions to the Catholic Church, we'll seek assistance there."

"Oh, Daddy, no." Pernella slid to the edge of her seat, her gloved fingers on her father's arm, her eyes focused on the brothers. "Don't you think we could take them in? For a few days, at least? We have so much more than the Church can give."

Garrett cut in before the man could outright refuse her. "Please, sir, miss, there is no harder case, I assure you. A shipwreck caught us off the Floridian coast. We've been adrift with our servants for nearly a week." May God—and his friends—forgive him for the lie, but desperation demanded it. None of them could stand straight as it was; instance on Josiah and Melvin as freedmen might lose them this chance.

The man's brows rose an inch. "Servants, you say? That them there?"

Garrett startled to find Josiah and Melvin quite near, each attempting to remain out of the flow of street traffic while keeping their eyes planted on the ground. Like a proper servant, Josiah's thick fingers folded across his middle while Melvin's slender ones curled into fists at his sides. Garrett turned back to the man and nodded.

"Daddy, please," Pernella tried again. "Fancy clothes, fancy negros. They're just like us, except fallen on hard times. We have to help them."

Garrett bristled at how easily the word "negros" fell from her lips. He was not like these people, not at all. But for today, he would have to be. "Our father's Alonzo Lark of Charleston. We're trying to get home."

"You're Lark's sons? Every rice farmer knows of Alonzo. Shame you lost him too soon." The man's expression relaxed, exactly as Garrett expected it would. His father's persuasion had reached far and wide in the South, and it was no surprise that his influence spoke all the way down here.

"Does that mean you'll help him, Daddy?" This time Pernella was finally rewarded with her father's smile.

"God must be watching over you this day, gentlemen. I cannot allow you in the carriage in your current state—you understand—but my negros are collecting an order with the wagon. Stay near the depot and I'll send them on down." He handed a calling card out to Garrett by its edge. "We've got a few dozen rice paddies up north of town at Spalderton Plantation. You're welcome to stay on awhile. We'll get you fixed up all right."

"Thank you, sir." He offered a slight bow which had him warring between gratitude and unconsciousness, his temples pounding as the landau drove away.

Melvin was about to spit nails. "I'm your slave now, am I?" he seethed.

"We can' talk here. Let'sa wait at the depot." Josiah gestured to a narrow space under the raised wooden platform of the rail depot, hidden beneath the crossed support beams. Leaning on each other, they shuffled inside, glad to be out of the mud and mist. From here, they would have visibility to Spalderton's servants' arrival but remain far enough away from prying eyes.

"So, this is what I get for helpin'?" Melvin sat inside the triangle of two cross-beams, one foot upon the opposite post. He glared at the ceiling where railway passengers hustled by unaware. "Sold back into slavery."

"Stop being dramatic," Garrett shot back. "Do you want to eat or not? I had to tell them that."

"You didn't have to tell them nothin'. I would have been better off taking that boat and leaving you all behind."

"You wouldn't have made it off the ship without me to cut the rope."

"With the knife you *lost*."

Garrett snorted. "At least I didn't lose a third of our rations."

"Who do you think stole those rations to begin with? Oh, that's right, it was Melvin, the *slave!*"

"Stop fighting! Please!" Cade collapsed to his knees. Deep gasps gripped his chest, and his fingers grasped the skin there, as though he could rip the pain straight through his rib cage. He coughed, then coughed again, until he fell to his side, curled in the dirt.

"Why does this keep happening?" he wailed. "How weak am I that I keep looking for her? That I can't hold myself together? How weak am I?"

Garrett didn't know what to do, and from Melvin's expression, neither did he. He had seen his younger brother act pitiable. He had seen him retreat from fights and cry over things his brothers found meaningless. He was the family peacemaker; always had been. But this was something else.

As Cade's breaths grew shallower and his coughs deeper, the terror in his face became so clear Garrett wondered if someone could indeed die from fear. All thoughts of his own hunger and exhaustion fled in that feeling of helplessness, watching what he was certain was his brother's last moment before his eyes.

Josiah crouched beside Cade, drawing him in close. His large palm covered half of his hunched and scarred back as it rubbed back and forth, back and forth, the movement nearly hypnotic. Ever so slowly, one frozen second at a time, Cade's breaths grew longer, his body calmer. He leaned into Josiah and closed his eyes. "What's wrong with me? Why am I like this?"

"'Cause God gave ya much love. They who love much, feel much.

I's loved once, too. Ya never stop lookin' for it even after ya know it's gone."

How long had Josiah looked for Clary without hope? Knowing she wasn't in Charleston, but praying that Sterling might return her someday. Then living in San Francisco, knowing she wasn't far away, but with no means to bring her home again. Of course, every girl he passed would take on Clary's form. You never stopped searching for the ones you lost.

"I don't want to love her," Cade coughed. "Every time Tobias and I went to trade in Astoria or Jamison took me to the mission or even in San—" He gave a deep cough while his hand clutched the torn remnants of his shirt. "—Francisco. Every red-haired woman gives me hope."

"You gotta stop that." Melvin stood, hands on his hips in disgust. "I lost both my parents and two sisters within days of each other. I know they're gone. I know there's no hope. There's only me and my freedom. Do you wanna be free or you wanna keep that shackle on your leg forever?"

Cade glanced up at him, his eyes red and cheeks blotchy. "I don't know how to escape."

"You leave behind everything you can't change and you hold onto everything you can. We get you well, get to Charleston, and get your brother's money. Then we go get your daughter and go back to Larksong."

"And back to your fifty acres," Garrett muttered.

"We all gotta live for something." Melvin shot him a glare. "Guess we better start headin' toward it."

Spalderton Plantation accepted Garrett and Cade like long lost brothers. They were offered the best of everything, including the best for their servants, although Josiah and Melvin stayed in the slave quarters while the brothers slept in spacious rooms with downy beds. Even so, all four were provided with ample bathing accommodations and fresh outfits. Garrett ate dinner like the world depended on his intake, then slept for nearly an entire day. When he woke, he found Cade much improved, still coughing, but with renewed color and his fever gone.

Walking the plantation house conjured unpleasant memories; to be back in a home so like his father's made him think of his childhood and a life he despised. He had accepted the opulence of Sterling's Theatrical because, to him, it had been a place of business, not his home. He recalled his bedroom at Larksong Plantation, the high ceilings and broad windows, the mosquito netting surrounding his bed in the summer to protect from the risk of malaria and yellow fever. Not that it protected him anywhere else, especially after their mother died. Without her gentility, the rooms had filled with his father's hardhanded aggression.

The second evening at the Spaldertons', once dinner was through and Cade retired, Mr. Spalderton took his newspaper to the parlor while Garrett escorted Pernella through the garden, the gnarled branches of the live oaks still full and green even in February's chill. The girl's creamy fingers lay long and thin, perfect for playing the pianoforte or the harpsichord or for draping across his forearm with a flirtatious laugh as she did now. He could imagine her within his arms at one of his father's parties, her giggle light as she leaned in to tempt a kiss. Ultimately, however, she would have offered her dowry to Daniel. His brother had been the eldest and the heir. All the women would kiss Garrett and pour out their pitiful hearts to him, but in the end, never choose him. So, he never chose them either. He would rather chip off his own hand than be saddled to someone so selfish and petty, even if he had acted the same way.

Not so with Martha. Never with Martha. She was neither selfish nor petty.

He would never be able to give his wife a luxurious home or walk her arm-in-arm through a crowd. Part of him grieved all he could not offer her. Marriage should be a place they traveled together, *every* road together. It wasn't fair they couldn't. Life never had been, though.

"You're rather quiet, Mr. Lark," Pernella said as they rounded the roses, their thorny branches pointed to the sky. "What's got you thinking so?"

"To be honest, Miss Spalderton, I was thinking of my wife."

"Oh. I didn't realize you were married."

He had figured as much. "Yes. We were newlyweds when we were forced apart."

"What forced your separation?"

"It is difficult to discuss. Many mistakes on my part."

"And now she waits for you in Charleston."

"She waits for me, yes. Or I hope she still does." Tentatively, he reached for Martha in his mind and found her in the theater, likely in preparation for a performance due to the hour. Julep was in a room nearby. At least he knew where to find them, even if he knew nothing else.

Pernella's fingers tightened on his arm. Her sweet smile tipped to cast her light his way. "Oh, bless your heart, Mr. Lark. You must miss her just terribly."

"Thank you. I do."

"Be assured, Daddy has promised me he'll get you home. The railway don't go direct to Carolina, but it can get you there round about. We'll send you with everythin' you need. All the finest, so when you get home, everyone'll know that we sent you off just right."

He realized then that he didn't actually have a home anymore. The Screeching Peach was surely lost to him by now; Sterling no doubt led the staff to believe him dead. He had never visited his brothers' town, so when he arrived in Larksong, he wouldn't have a waiting home there either. Until recently, Martha had shared a cabin with Jamison and Coraline. Moving in with his brother and his wife, especially as a newlywed, felt too uncomfortable to consider. Charleston, while it had been home once, hadn't beckoned to him since he left almost eight years ago. He only traveled there now out of necessity.

Then again, if he didn't rescue Martha, these questions wouldn't mean anything.

"What of your brother's wife?" Pernella asked, oblivious to his ongoing internal monologue. "The one he thought I was? Where is she?"

"She, I'm afraid, is long gone." He started to search with his Gift then decided against it. As Cade had said, "What good will it do?" It was time they let Alice Ann fade into obscurity. Perhaps with time, the less they spoke of her, the more his brother could begin to heal.

"May I ask how she died?" Pernella's voice was quiet, her eyes wet and dewy. He felt her lift on her toes, slowly, as though even she was unaware of her decision. He could ask much from her in this moment. A kiss, her virtue, anything he wanted. The Garrett of two years past would have, and he knew she likely would oblige.

Lights flickered from the slave quarters down the lane, where Josiah and Melvin also made their beds this night. He should be with them. There was no reason for them to be separated. But as much as the Spaldertons didn't want their slaves to share their quarters, the slaves equally didn't want white folks to stay in theirs. Two different cultures, two different worlds. The Americans had purchased them but the Africans had sold them and somewhere along the way, up became down and down up and no one knew which way was the way to go. He could see their silhouettes shuffling about like ghosts, their eerie songs and mumbled stories floating toward him on the wind.

"Mr. Lark?" Pernella whispered, her lips inches from his.

He blinked and stepped away, letting her feet slip back to the pebbled walk. "I think it's time we said goodnight, Miss Spalderton. Allow me to escort you back."

"Oh. Yes, yes, of course. Forgive me for keeping you out so late. I suppose you must be tired."

"I am." He was indeed tired of a good many things.

Back in his borrowed room, he lay awake, listening to the strains of a servant's fiddle through the open window, reminding him of the tunes his friend Levi had played along the trail. The wagon train had indulged in dancing, a rare occurrence of genuine joy for him. It was the first, and the last, time he ever danced with Martha. Spun her 'round and 'round and 'round. He couldn't get enough of those sweetwater eyes.

Looking at him like he meant something.

Like he meant everything.

As he drifted off to sleep, he recalled her voice, her words on their wedding day. *My name is Bakhita.*

"Why did you tell me?" he murmured to the darkness.

Because everything I am is yours.

"Everything I am is yours, Martha," he replied. "Everything I am is yours."

For as long as he lived, everything would never be enough.

26

Martha lived in a state of constant fear. Mr. Sterling hadn't summoned her back to Harvest Hill, but every time he addressed the performers, his eyes held hers without affection. Kayus continued to escort her to rehearsals and performances in their usual silence. That was fine by her. The less time she had to speak to any of the men the better.

The end was coming. She could feel it as surely as a baton flame to her skin. A pink scar remained on her hand from the burn she received the day of her unsuccessful escape. It reminded her of the slow death of all her dreams and the sacrifice Nora made so she could keep them. Only that realization and love for Julep kept her upright day after day. Her darling jewel was the glimmer of hope which threaded its way in and tortured her with possibilities.

All she could do was pray.

Pray for courage. Pray for strength. Pray for hope.

Place a hand over the spot on her chest where her wedding rings hung and pray for a solution. *Please, Lord, help me find it.*

Pray, pray, pray.

All the female performers gave her long pitiful looks as she followed Clary to the show floor curtains. Each one kept her distance. Unlike Nora, they would not take the fall for Martha's misdeeds.

They likely wondered what she would sing tonight. Would it

devastate the circus and bring them to a swift and certain end?

Rella met her at the stage curtain with a reassuring smile. "You'll do exceptional. I know you've learned your lesson, and Mr. Sterling knows it, too."

"If you believe it was me, you must let Nora out of the Garden. She didn't do anything wrong."

"You're admitting to the deed?"

"No, but Nora didn't do it either."

"Martha, someone is responsible. Nora admitted to her culpability. What's done is done. I suggest you be grateful you are not the one currently tending flowers." With that, she held the curtain wide and pushed Martha to the show floor beyond.

After her act, Martha retreated behind the corner curtains, peeping through their edges at each act, hoping for a glimpse of Julep. To her relief, in the second to last act, the girl skipped out with the other child clowns. She tumbled in her too-big shoes, performed a somersault, and laughed like the show was her favorite thing. A few weeks back, she had turned five with no knowledge of the occasion. No celebration, no favorite meal, no happy family to present her with a patchwork doll or whittled horse.

As the clowns began their dance, Rella paraded out atop her mare, hands in the air and feet clenched upon its back. Her peacock costume glittered, its feathers fluttering. The audience cheered as they did every night. One more lap and the next set of equine acrobats would ride out to join her.

However, as the lap completed, no one else arrived. Rella glanced at the door as she passed a second time, although her smile remained intact. She repeated her previous round of tricks and as she neared the stable doors for a third time, called out, "We welcome back Sterling's acrobats! They may be nervous, but they are always appreciated. Let's encourage them with some applause!" She whirled her arms, striking a round of cheers and whistles from the stands. The final act was always one of the most memorable. The audience expected it to steal the show and a failure at the end would land heavily on them all.

Ashley Sterling directed from the center ring, arms raised, nothing amiss in his chiseled expression. But even he could not ignore the horrific clatter which sounded then from behind the stable doors. A shriek raised such as had never been heard, then another and another. Inhuman cries that reminded Martha of squirrels being devoured by hawks back in Washington. Even when you knew the cause, you wanted to clasp your hands to your ears, for the sound suggested tortures one shouldn't even imagine. Of whipping posts and auction blocks, men who lost a foot when they tried to flee, and the plaintive wails of mothers as they watched their children starve.

The audience rose to their feet, children clinging to their mothers and wives to their husbands. Half-dressed men stumbled out the Garden door, sights frantic as they tucked in shirts and peered in every direction.

Rella's mount bolted, causing her to slip and fall hard onto its back. She grasped its mane, hanging on with one hand, but in two attempts caught the other side, swinging herself back into position.

The stable doors burst open then, and Mr. Sterling exclaimed, "Ah, at last! Here are the Sterling Riders!" except there were no riders, only horses. The mares streamed out and around the dirt track, their brilliant white coats splattered crimson. Every one bore a horrific slash across their sides and now raced pell-mell, blood dripping down their legs and trailing the show floor. The audience screamed and rushed from the stands, fleeing the theater and the macabre sight which followed them.

Mr. Sterling sprinted toward the stable doors, shouting unintelligible commands. As he neared the threshold, Moses stepped from the shadows into the chandelier light. He caught the ringleader's eye.

Did you do this? Mr. Sterling asked with only a glance.

Moses simply smiled, an expression that, for Martha, required no words. He knew what had happened to Nora, and he wasn't going to stand by in silence. If he had wanted to kill those horses, he could have slit their throats and left them in their stalls. That would have sent a message, but Mr. Sterling had the means to purchase others. Such a gruesome public display said, "I'm going to destroy you and I want everyone to know." Something like this couldn't be brushed away. It would make the newspapers. Moses's defiance could mean an end to everything Mr. Sterling had built.

Time was up. Martha and Julep needed to leave—now.

She rushed across the show floor, her heart past her throat and screaming through her lips. "Julep!"

Little legs pedaling, the girl crashed into her, her arms trembling as they circled her aunt. "Auntie Marta, they're going to kill us!"

"No, they're not." Hurrying to the stands, Martha snatched two discarded frock coats and draped one around Julep. It swallowed her, dragging the ground. Martha shoved her arms into the second coat, and lifted the child, securing her legs around her waist.

"Don't be afraid, my jewel. We're going home."

"Home to Daddy?"

"Yes, home to Daddy. We're going to run now. Hold tight and close your eyes." The girl did as she was told, five-year-old fingers clasped around her aunt's neck.

Martha raced them toward the entrance where the audience had congested in their effort to escape. She elbowed her way into their center, then evened her pace to match the crowd, becoming one with them as they shuffled across the blinding white entryway to the main doors. Guards stood on either side, their eyes focused on attire rather than faces, likely searching for costumed figures. She tightened her grip on Julep and averted her gaze, ducking out the doors a moment before Julio's attention swung in her direction.

Cool wind hit her face as they descended the front steps and temporarily blinded by the darkness, she squinted for the wrought-iron gates. Pandemonium reigned as wagons and carriages circled the drive and men untied their horses from the hitching posts. With a holler and a slur, they mounted and rode away. At the end of the drive, the open gates welcomed their departure, not more than fifty paces away. Martha could see them waiting.

Blazing braziers flickered in her periphery as she hurried toward freedom. So close. So close. "Julep, we're almost there," she breathed, although a moment too soon.

A brawny woman blocked her path, a scowl on her face and her equally solid husband at her heels. Without a word, she snatched at

Julep, trying to rip her from Martha's arms. Julep screamed as Martha clung tightly to her and tried to knock the woman off.

"Leave us be! Leave us be! She is mine! You cannot have her!"

The woman pulled at Julep all the more, and the child flailed, the oversized coat falling from her shoulders. She threw herself back around Martha and clung tight. "I wanna go home!" she wailed as tears dripped against her aunt's neck. Martha tried to push past, but the woman's husband snatched both her arms from behind, holding her firm.

"You stole this child!" the woman screamed at her.

"I didn't! She's my niece."

"Ha," said the man with a mirthless laugh. "We'll get to the bottom of this."

Of what? There was nothing to get to the bottom of, except for the hill that lay beyond the open gates. That was where she needed to be now. Else Kayus or Julio or Mr. Sterling himself was liable to exit the theater and drag them both back inside.

The woman ran between theater patrons, even ducking in a few carriage windows. "Please, are you missing a child?" she asked. They shook their heads and many continued on, but several lingered, apparently having decided the exterior commotion was a preferable show to the interior danger. "Do you think we should summon the police?" the man asked his wife.

Too late, Martha realized their assumption. A black woman carrying a white child. Of course, they assumed Julep to be kidnapped.

Heart racing, she struggled against the man's grip, but it was no use. Everywhere she turned, someone else closed in, ensuring that even if she wrestled him away, she wouldn't make it to the gates. But they were so close, so very close. How could she fail mere steps from freedom?

Lord, help me!

Through the theater's front doors strode Kayus, set in her direction. This was the end. If he took them back, Mr. Sterling would blame her for this plague as surely as the others. Even though he knew of Moses's guilt, he would cast the shame upon her. Heaven only knew what he would do to Julep. She wasn't old enough to be matched or sent to the Garden, but was there truly a limit to his depravity?

"Give her to me."

Martha turned at Rella's voice. She sat atop her mare, a brown woolen cloak about her shoulders, her mask removed. She opened her arms, her long creamy limbs extended, her costume exchanged for a simple day dress. "Give her to me. I'll keep her safe. I'll get her out." Martha saw Kayus approach, running toward them now. The woman's husband still held her arms.

"Are you this child's mother?" he asked Rella.

Martha wanted to scream, "No! Her mother left her, but I raised her! She's mine!" Except no one would believe her. Even if they did...they would only think her a white man's strumpet.

"Yes." Rella flexed her outstretched fingers. "Please, let me take her home."

Stay calm. Stay quiet. Stay alive.

Then, for the first time since entering Sterling's Theatrical, she heard her momma. *Be as Christ to you.*

She had no choice. She laid a hurried kiss on Julep's crown and lifted her into Rella's waiting arms. Julep's frightened eyes sought hers.

"Go, my jewel. She'll take you home. I'll be right behind."

Rella settled Julep in front of her and raced for the gates, her cloak rippling as the mare passed through.

Please, Lord, Martha prayed. *Keep my baby safe. It's all I ask of You.*

Rella had planned to escape alone. When the commotion began, she recognized her opportunity and took no heed to second thoughts. As Sterling's beautiful horses bloodied the show floor, she steered her mare toward the dressing room, changed her dress, snatched her cloak, and rode back out through the front doors. She wanted to get away, as far away from Sterling as she could ride. It mattered little where she ended up, so long as she never returned.

Then she saw Martha and Julep. As she came upon the scene, she remembered Martha's lovely stories of Larksong and how she said the children were always cared for and loved. She knew, then, that she couldn't ride by without conscience. Martha was beyond help, but she could save Julep, and she suspected that was what mattered most to the woman anyway.

Martha carried a mother's love, and a mother's love sacrificed her own good for the good of her child. Rella had never felt that sort of connection. Her only child died in infancy and Sterling expressed no sympathy. He never did. The other performers' children she cared for, of course, but never loved. She shared them with the rest of the community, exactly as Sterling trained her to do.

Except Julep hadn't been born into Sterling's circus. She had a family in Larksong who loved her and wanted her. Her father might be dead, but there were others who would do right by her. Martha's loss would not be in vain.

As they galloped away, she held Julep close, soothing her tears and praying for her Auntie Marta's soul.

27

Martha woke not knowing where she was or how she had arrived there. She was in a bedroom, but it wasn't hers. Except for flickering light through the edges of the window draperies, the room lay dark. The space wasn't large, but contained a double bed with a plush mattress and soft sheets of finest quality. Atop that, a lavish coverlet kept the bed cozy and warm.

Whose room was this? The last she remembered was Rella riding away with Julep. Kayus had dragged her back into the theater. After that, nothing.

She pushed herself upright only to fall back against the pillows as the room spun and every part of her ached. Had Kayus beaten her amidst her escape attempt? Had she suffered a blow that stole her memory? Significant bruises circled her wrists and stung when she rotated them. She felt along her arms where rough knots lay beneath the skin. On her shins and calves, too.

A horrid realization swept through her.

She gripped the sheets so hard, her forearms throbbed. Ever so slowly, she shifted her thighs together and bit her lip to keep from crying out. She couldn't remember a thing, but knew with certainty what had happened. Only one type of abuse carried bruises like that.

Oh, Lord of my life, how could you leave me here?

Tears leaked down her cheeks and blinded her. It wasn't enough, however, to stop the images flooding her mind. Her body trembled at the thought of Kayus charging at her, holding her down, and silencing her screams with a rough hand upon her lips. She couldn't remember, but she could imagine.

All those years hearing horrible tales about masters taking slave women for themselves, and not once had she experienced the same. Thirty-six years and somehow, God had saved her purity for her husband. Now that, too, had been spoiled.

She reached for her neckline and the chain that held her wedding rings, but both were missing. Her last precious remnant of Garrett stolen. At least her costume had been exchanged for a more modest nightdress.

On further inspection, she realized that her entire body, while sore, had been bathed. The usual post-performance grime was gone and when she lifted her wrist to her nose, she could make out the faint aroma of jasmine. Even her hair had been brushed and braided. Someone had cared for her after her ordeal. She very much doubted her assailant would go to such lengths.

Had Kayus been the one? He had found her, but maybe he brought her to whomever had done it. Rodrigo, perhaps, or Julio? Maybe even Ashley Sterling himself? He would find great delight in ruining her. Likely, he drugged her so she wouldn't know. The question would haunt her more than the answer.

What did it matter? What was done was done. They couldn't take it back.

Overcome, she allowed herself to weep until exhaustion turned to sleep. She awoke to the sound of a key in the lock and peeled her eyes open as a masculine figure stepped into the room, oil lamp in hand. She blinked, willing her eyes to adjust. Not until he closed the door and sat beside her did she distinguish who it was.

Kayus set the lamp on the bedside table where the flames stretched shadows across his somber expression. Deep furrows lined his brow and if she didn't know better, the creases about his eyes could be construed for concern. Those eyes held hers, their white outline bold against the darkness.

"How are you feeling?" he asked.

She focused on the square ceiling bevels and said nothing.

"I know this isn't what you want, but the Garden would have been worse."

She tugged the blankets higher, right under her chin. "So, it *was* you."

His eyes widened. "Don't you remember?"

"I don't remember a thing." Of course, it had been the strongman. No wonder she had bruised so badly. She supposed she should be grateful he hadn't killed her.

Tears sprang anew and she couldn't flee the bed fast enough. The sheet fluttered to the ground as she stumbled to the window, her legs so sore she could barely stand. She grasped the window frame with both hands to steady herself. She wanted to throw herself through the glass to the show floor below. Only the few ghost lights flickered at this hour, with no way to tell the time except that the Garden was quiet. No customers and no rehearsals meant the hour must be sometime between 5 and 7 a.m.

"*If you open the glass, it lets in a little air and almost feels like being outside,*" she recalled Lissie saying on her first day here. It wasn't. The circus air tasted stale and empty and hollow. She longed for the fresh air of the courtyard, the sweet breeze she felt when she thought freedom was upon them.

"You had a choice," Kayus said. "You chose me."

She stared at the window's iron bars. "Why would I ever do that?"

"After you tried to leave, Sterling was furious. He wanted to send you to the Garden. I offered to be partnered with you instead. He didn't care for the idea, but I convinced him that it would be a shame to lose you from the show. I promised to keep an eye on you, so he gave you the choice. Once we got the commotion sorted, he married us in his office."

Her palm pressed to her racing heart. It pounded so hard, her entire chest shook with the pressure. *Married? To Kayus?* And she had *chosen* it? "I...I don't remember."

"Musta been the stuff we gave you. You were throwing a fit in the yard, hadta have somethin' to calm you down. I wish you remembered our wedding night, but I'll try to make the next time just as memorable."

"You stay away from me!" She swung around, but Kayus remained seated. He watched her, but not without compassion.

212

"Martha, every man wanted you. Do you know how many times Sterling hadta set them straight? You could do much worse than me."

"I already have a husband. You are not him."

"According to Sterling, I am."

"Not according to God."

"God doesn't exist here. Here there's just me and you and Sterling's watchful eye." His voice quieted. "We're Gifted, Martha, and we're negro. There's no other place for us but here. This is what we haveta do."

"Or what will happen? What consequences remain? You've already taken everything from me."

His eyes lowered to his hands, as large as soup bowls and as powerful as a bear. "If you think everything's already been taken, you haven't begun to understand how much more Sterling is willing to steal. You used to be a slave. So did I. You were taken from your family. So was I. You ended up here against your will. Again, we are the same. You lost your husband, but you didn't see him die. I saw my wife killed right in front of me by one of Sterling's men. Of course, I wouldn't learn that until I ended up here and saw the criminal guarding the door. By then it was too late. I have heard the stories that walk these halls. Going to tend the Garden is not the worst one can suffer here. Sterling will find everything you love and he will destroy it. That town you come from, those people you left behind? He can order them dead with a wave of his hand. My arms are strong, but I am not. There are not many left I care about, but I have no doubt he would be able to find them."

As he spoke, he rounded the bed to stand before her. His hands lighted near her upper arms, but did not rest upon them. "Trust me when I say that Garrett is not coming back for you. At least here we have the other Gifted. Here we can raise a family. Here we have a chance at what passes for happiness for people like us." Slowly, gently, he lowered his palms against her shoulders, so soft she barely felt them, even with her bruises.

His eyes and his touch and the steady rise of his chest all spoke more than his words. Like Rella, he had been conned into coming here and had lost his world violently in the process. When he spoke these things to her, they weren't idle threats, they were promises he knew could be fulfilled. If he said Garrett wasn't coming back, it was because he knew he couldn't. Like his own wife never could.

Garrett had to be dead. Cade too. Her one condolence was that Julep had escaped...assuming Rella kept her word. If not, anything done to Julep, Martha may as well have done herself.

She could not allow Mr. Sterling to ruin anyone else she loved. She had to keep him as far away from Larksong as possible.

"Will you let me care for you?" Kayus asked.

She nodded. She had chosen him, after all. As she had been told many times, it was better than the alternative of the Garden. Knowing that reality better than many, Nora willingly succumbed to degradation so Martha wouldn't. She had to make Nora's sacrifice mean something.

I'm sorry, Garrett.

Kayus wrapped her in his arms and she curled against him, serenaded by her tears and the terror of a now-silent circus.

28

FEBRUARY 1859
CHARLESTON, SOUTH CAROLINA

For Garrett, walking through the streets of Charleston was like encountering a youthful dalliance years later. Something so familiar yet no longer reflecting his adult life. He recalled every direction, passage, and curve with no desire to revisit them. Along Battery Street, his grandfather had built their "townhouse," more like a miniaturized plantation home with detached carriage house, slave quarters, and a dashing view of Charleston Harbor. Here his father stayed during weekend forays with investors, where the family wintered every social season, and retreated from malaria in the worst heat of childhood summers. Once the four younger brothers became overseers in the rice paddies, however, only Daniel and their father frequented the Charleston house. It was where the official plantation records were housed and the most valuable family mementos. Father always claimed that if he kept them in the main house, they were liable to be pilfered by their slaves' "ignorant hands."

Upon arrival, Lark House appeared as fastidious as ever; it hadn't aged at all, at least not from the outside. The classical white Georgian rose two stories above the cobblestone street and appeared to have been white washed recently. A pair of double stone staircases with black wrought-iron railings curved up to the front entrance, its grey door framed by two unlit gas lamps. Garrett observed his mother's lace curtains tied back at the first-floor windows, the glass panes' colonial leading like bars on a jail cell. A wooden sign hung from the front rail which read, *"Boarding House."* He wondered when that had happened and why.

"I never thought I'd come back," Cade said as they stared up at the house.

"Yeah. Can't say I'm happy we did."

"Me neither. At least it isn't the main house."

"Yeah, at least." All the worst things had happened to them at the plantation. Given Cade's fragile state, if he had to come face-to-face with those demons, he might not recover.

"Did you know Daniel was taking in boarders?" Garrett asked.

"No, he barely wrote us at all."

"So," Melvin cut in, arms folded. "You don't really even know this fella and he's our way outta here?

Garrett shot his mouth open, irritation rising, but Josiah spoke first. "He's good folk, Daniel is. He'll help us."

"What would you stake that on?"

Josiah's eyes met Melvin's. His hand rested on his shoulder, as he'd done so many times with the brothers. "I'da stake my life."

Bold words, thought Garrett. Even he wasn't willing to stake his life on Daniel's assistance. Unfortunately, it was all they had.

Melvin lifted a shoulder in a sideways shrug. "That's good enough, I suppose. Let's get to it then." He bounded up the stairs and, ignoring the brass knocker, pounded the door thrice.

Rolling his eyes, Garrett followed, elbowing the younger man out of the way. Clearly, it had been a while since Melvin had lived in the South and forgotten the way of things. Good, bad, or otherwise, there were some things a black man could not do, and slamming his fist against a white man's house was one of them. Did he want to set the neighbors down upon him?

"Let me do the talking," Garrett hissed. "You just..." He eyed Melvin's curled lip. "Stand there and say nothing."

"Like a slave," he muttered. "Thought I left the servitude behind."

Garrett rounded on him, snatching his shirt collar in one fist. "No, like a gump who doesn't understand when someone's trying to help him. We agreed to give you land in Washington, even though we don't know hardly anything about you. If you want to see that land, then stand back and shut up. Because, take my word, if I beat your face in right now, it isn't because you're black, it's because you're asking for it."

"That's true," said Cade. "He's beaten loads of white men, too."

"Cade!" Garrett hissed.

"Sorry."

With a light shove against the entry rail, Garrett released Melvin. "Do we understand one another?"

Melvin's scowl didn't lessen. Still, he nodded. "I ain't happy about it."

"I'm not either. Finally, something we agree on."

After another series of knocks, a call came from inside, "Mr. Lark, I think ya got folks on the stoop." A minute later, the door swung open, revealing their eldest brother. Daniel retained his well-polished air, tan hair cleanly cut and jawline shaven, charcoal jacket and trousers in tip-top shape, his usual silver pocket watch chain visible within his munition-grey waistcoat. He could easily pass at any of their father's clubs. Except the shadows beneath his eyes and the wrinkles about his brow spoke of hidden hardship. Could that be his motive for the boarding house? Alonzo Lark would have throttled his son for its development; therefore, Garrett rather liked the idea.

"Hello, Daniel," he said with a raised hand. "Remember us?"

His brother's jaw dropped. "Garrett? Cade? ... Josiah? Why are you here?" He looked past them. "Who's that?" Melvin still leaned against the stair rail, slender arms folded as he glared at the cobblestone walk.

"Melvin Whittle," Garrett explained. "He helped us escape."

"*Escape*? Were you in prison?"

"Of course, your first assumption *would* be prison."

"With you, yes, it would."

"We were, in a manner of speaking. May we come in?"

Garrett expected Daniel to pause in contemplation or to flat-out refuse and slam the door in their faces. Instead, he stepped back and waved them inside. "Yes, of course. Come in. It's wonderful to see you." After they exchanged a grip of the fist and were corralled into the sunlit entryway, he closed the door.

Everything was exactly as Garrett remembered. The curved central staircase with its straight white balusters and emerald patterned runner, the polished-oak-floor corridor, and the walnut side table with the metal mail tray Josiah would carry to Alonzo's chair. Their father's office doors were closed, but the matching parlor set stood open. Crackles emanated through the lit fireplace's swirled rosette screen and from out-of-sight corners, male voices engaged in low conversation. Boarders, most likely. As children, the Larks had rarely played in these rooms, always shut upstairs while their father entertained his associates and persuaded them to do his bidding. As the heir—and unGifted—only Daniel had ever been allowed access to those meetings.

"So, you run a boarding house now?" Cade asked the obvious.

Daniel flushed. "Uh, yes, for five years now. Opened right after Nancy left."

"Who's Nancy?" Garrett asked. *Please don't let her be someone I courted.*

If possible, his brother's embarrassment deepened. He glanced up the unoccupied staircase. "She was my fiancée for a time. None of you knew her—" He hurried on before any of them could retort. "—and it was extremely short-lived. A matter of weeks. I met her on a Thursday, proposed by the following Friday, and by two weeks after, she realized her grave mistake." He chuckled soberly. "She knew I had prestige, being who Father was. She didn't mind me having sold the plantation; she could accept a husband who didn't want to plant rice or cotton. What she couldn't accept was one who refused to own slaves when I had the means to do so. Once her father knew, everyone knew. The engagement ended and I was thoroughly ruined after that." He chuckled again. "My failure didn't seem appropriate for correspondence. Not when you had trials of your own, and clearly have still."

It surprised Garrett that he should realize little joy to hear of Daniel's misfortune. All those years at odds in their youth followed by their horrid final argument...he never thought he would find pity for his brother. Maybe some good had come from his time enslaved. He could recognize the toll Daniel's mishap had placed upon him; his defense of his beliefs had upended his life. Rejected by society, he hadn't invitations to clubs or parties or balls—all the environments where he thrived. Its dismantlement must leave him lonely. Garrett knew much of loneliness, especially now.

"I've rented your old rooms," Daniel told them, "but the attic quarters are currently empty, if you'd like to sleep there. You're most welcome, as well," he told Melvin. "Free of charge."

Mevin's sights finally peeled from the floor. "Free, you say? No payment at all?"

"Of course. You helped my brothers, so it's the least I can do. Now," he turned back to Garrett, either oblivious to or unconcerned with Melvin's astonishment. "How long do you plan to visit?"

"Only a day or two. Until we can devise a plan to head back west."

"Perhaps I can assist there. Let me show you to your rooms and then we'll meet in the office. We can talk there." He turned to Melvin again. "While you are welcome to stay as my guest, do understand that I must speak with my family in private."

Melvin nodded, still dumbfounded over Daniel's hospitality. "Of course. Had I any family, I'd want the same. My thanks for the room."

Once they had cleaned the travel dust from their necks and faces, they met in their father's office, sans Melvin. Like everything else in the house, the office remained practically the same—green trumpet vine wallpaper, diamond-beveled ceiling, chartreuse rug, and an oversized dark oak desk and cabinetry, both surely compensating for something. Its fireplace was an exact match to the parlor's right down to the screen's curled iron rosettes.

Garrett and Cade took opposite ends of the sofa while Josiah sidestepped the matching armchairs to stand near the far wall, the same place he had always waited on their father's instructions. It wasn't necessary—he was a free man now—but old habits died hard. Garrett gestured once to the armchair and upon Josiah's firm headshake, did not try again.

Yes, it was all the same except for one significant detail. Daniel had been the one who welcomed them into the room, Daniel owned the desk scattered with parchment and newspapers, and Daniel now headed for their father's liquor cabinet.

"You can't keep your servants, but you can manage to keep the refreshments flowing?" Garrett asked.

"If I recall, you spent rather a decent time flowing in refreshments yourself."

"That was a long time ago. I don't imbibe much anymore."

Daniel handed him a glass of amber liquid filled nearly to the brim. "Ah, but what is 'much'? Why don't you try it? It's the best I can afford."

Garrett sniffed it and finding its aroma sweet, took a tentative sip. "Hey!" he exclaimed. "This is tea."

His brother laughed, Cade right along with him. It was nice to see them smile again. "I told you it was the best I could afford." Daniel turned to distribute glasses to Cade and Josiah who, at the eldest brother's urging, reluctantly agreed to squeeze himself into an armchair.

Daniel butted against the desk; his nimble fingers folded around his tea glass. "Enough pleasantries. Tell me how I came to harbor fugitives."

"I made a deal with the devil and he played me like a fiddle," Garrett muttered.

Daniel's brows quirked. "I'm sorry. I don't understand."

Out then came the entire shameful truth. From the day they left Independence on the wagon train to Garrett's Gift sending him to San Francisco, to meeting Sterling, changing his ways, and then ruining his life and everyone else's. "I messed up," he lamented, his tea long gone, yet throat still parched from every word. "Tobias and Jamison expected me to mine a bundle of gold, maybe find another Gifted. Instead, I found fifty Gifted and lost everything." Daniel's wild eyes stared at him. "Aren't you going to tell me what a fool I am?"

His brother gripped the glass he hadn't once touched and finally took a sip. His eyes flicked between Garrett and Cade in an unspoken question, then finally settled on Josiah for the answer.

"It sounds like Ashley Sterling's become a powerful man."

Josiah shrugged. "He has his hands in ev'rything. Ya 'member how he could be."

"You know Sterling?" Garrett sputtered.

"I met him but twice. You did, too. At Father's funeral." Alonzo Lark's funeral had been an enormous affair. With the number of folks he had persuaded to do his bidding and the number of false friends made, nearly the entire city turned out for his funeral Mass. It wasn't surprising that Garrett couldn't remember Sterling, especially with eight years in between. A long complicated eight years at that.

Cade grimaced. He was probably thinking the same as Garrett. If they had known then what would happen, they could have put an end to it before it began.

"From what Father said—and what you've told me—Sterling isn't a man to be trifled with," Daniel continued. "How do you plan to convince him to give up Martha and Julep? It's unlikely you can."

His brother, ever the optimist.

"That's where we need ya help." Josiah gruffed. "Ya know I wouldn't ask it if I didn't need yas."

In silence, Daniel refilled his tea then sank into the wrinkled leather desk chair. He leaned back, his thumb tracing absently along the glass's bottom edge, lost in thought.

"Please, Daniel." Cade moved to perch on the desk beside him. "We're asking, not for us, but for Garrett's wife, my daughter, and Josiah's. I know we've had our differences over the years, but you are still a Lark. You belong with us, no matter what you've done. Yeah, you lost everything, but so have I, and that makes it even easier to start anew. Come to San Francisco, help us find Julep and Martha, and then we'll all go to Larksong together."

Another long pause followed where Daniel kept sights on his youngest brother, but seemed to stare straight through him, as though calculating which answer would be easiest to separate himself from their request. It made Garrett want to slide across the desk, tackle him, hogtie him, steal all his money, and drag him back to California, demanding his assistance.

Finally, "I can't involve myself in your problems, Cade."

"Why not, Daniel?"

His brother blinked. He stood, once again regaining the upper ground to the rest of them. "I don't belong in Larksong, I'll never have

Gifts like you do."

"Balderdash," Garrett argued. "Most of Larksong isn't Gifted."

"But they're not Larks. They're just normal folks and not part of the *Oblique*'s legacy. Larks are expected to lead."

"You've already lost your place here. What do you have to stay for?"

"Exactly. I never belonged in our family and obviously the life I'm living shows that. You succeeded where I've only failed. I need to pick up the pieces before I can ever think of joining you. Besides, there's talk of war coming, the southern states forming their own union. Maybe I'll join the army."

Garrett leapt from his seat. "To fight for *what*? The right to own slaves and treat them like garbage?" Sliding over that desk was sounding better and better.

"We never treated our slaves that way, and you know it. That was why we decided to become overseers as soon as we were old enough to ride."

"No, *I* decided to become an overseer. So did Tobias and Jamison and Cade. You were inside with Father keeping your porcelain skin from cracking under the sun. Then *you* sold all those folks *we* managed to keep safe for years. We might have treated them right, but whoever they went to likely didn't. Why couldn't you have given them to us and sold the land? You would have still made a profit and they would have proper lives in Washington."

"Is that what Tobias still thinks? His letters sounded rather different."

"Tobias would have done right by them," Cade said. "Our other colored residents have rich lives in Larksong."

Daniel gave a bitter exhale. "I don't doubt that, but what I've learned—what I think Tobias has and likely Jamison, too—is that you don't just walk out of Charleston with two hundred enslaved men and no way to care for them. You need free folks with years of a living wage, who can support themselves, until your new society bears fruit. Even then, someone would question you leading all those slaves across the South in a distinctly Northern direction. Might as well slap on a cap and call yourself conductor."

Garrett pressed his lips together.

"You may look on me like the devil," Daniel continued, "but the North wants to end the Southern livelihood, steal our economy, and leave us broken. This was your home too, Garrett. Do you want to see it collapse?"

"Yes, let it. The South would deserve it for what they've done to those people."

"It isn't that simple. Not everyone in the South owns slaves—there are many who don't—and many who treat their servants with kindness. Upending the slave trade overnight would plummet us all into depression and hurt the non-slave owners as well as the plantations. Prices would rise on everything. Inflation would send many innocent families into poverty. To say little of the impact on trade routes with the North and Europe. Would they be willing to pay more for Southern goods when they could obtain them at lower cost on their own soil? Profitability drives commerce. Freeing the slaves is the moral thing to do, but it cannot be done with the snap of a finger or the stroke of a pen. I see that now."

"Are you saying this because you lost everything when you became an abolitionist?"

"I was never an abolitionist, more of a gradualist, and I'm saying it because it's how it is, whether we like it or not."

"It isn't an easy thing, slavery," Tobias had told them once. *"Owning another man is wrong, but freedom is more complicated than just being free."*

It had always seemed that simple to Garrett, though. Men shouldn't be owned, and that was that. The trouble was that slavery came in many forms, some in concealed fashion like Sterling's performers and *Arletta*'s stokers, while others were clear as day. Owning another man was wrong, but Tobias still held papers to all the slaves they brought with them out west, including Martha. Didn't Garrett himself hold Josiah's slave papers back at the hotel? Or used to anyway. In a compassionate man's hands, those papers meant ongoing freedom and protection against the slave catchers. Slave papers held up stronger against the law than any freedman's papers. It wasn't fair, but it was the truth of it, whether they liked it or not.

For a minute, all was silent, four men lost in thought, until finally Josiah spoke. "Garrett, listen to your brother." He rose from the armchair, his robust shadow blocking much of the light brightening the window panes. "Some things canna be stopped, no matta how we try. We be fools to interfere where God has not." Crossing the room, he handed his half-empty glass to Daniel. "Thank ya for the room. We be outta ya way in the mornin'."

The door banged closed with his departure, leaving the three brothers to face one another in silence. Cade rubbed a palm along his forearm, his voice thick with despair. "Josiah's right, isn't he?" He stood, paced the room, and sat again on the sofa. Elbows went to knees, head into his open hands with a groan. "Slavery can't be stopped and neither can Sterling. I've lost Julep."

Garrett glared at Daniel. "Why'd you mention politics?"

"That's all anybody talks about anymore in Dixie."

"Well, we don't live 'in Dixie' any longer and I'm glad of that."

At his words, a simultaneous pain stabbed behind Garrett's eyes and within his gut, a pain that hadn't plagued him since his migraine in the lifeboat. Something was wrong. Something different than before.

Two fingers pressed against his temple as his eyes slid closed. He reached through his mind until he located Martha. She was still at Sterling's, although not in her usual bedroom. This wasn't a room he was familiar with. Not the show floor or the actors' courtyard, not Harvest Hill and—praise the Lord—not the brothel. Where did that leave and why?

He searched for Julep next and the tea glass fell from his hand, miraculously not shattering upon the rug. Its last amber dribbles soaked into the fibers.

Insistent fingers gripped his shoulder. "What is it?" Cade cried. "What do you see?"

"Julep." He opened his eyes. His brother's expression lay deathly pale. "She's in Larksong."

"*What*?" Cade scooted backward, his hand clamoring for the arm of the sofa and missing. He tumbled to the floor. "Julep's home? How? When?"

"I don't know. I can't see those things. All I know is she's there and Martha's still with Sterling. I have no idea how Julep could have escaped and made it back alone."

"Oh, thank you, Lord!" Tears streamed down Cade's cheeks, his hands clasped against his chest while he lay on his back and exhausted the heavens with his gratitude. Without a word, Daniel rose from the desk and left the room.

Garrett reached a hand down to pull Cade back to his feet, embracing him despite the ache in his head and fear for Martha in his heart. His brother grinned from ear to ear. "It looks like Sterling can be stopped after all."

Once again, Garrett pictured his wife in that unknown room. *Yes,* he thought, *but what had been the cost?*

29

That night, Garrett couldn't sleep. His mind rolled over everything and tortured him more and more. There were too many unknowns without clarity on who his Gift should search for. He kept reaching out to Martha and finding her in the same place as before. How had she ended up there? Who was she with? He knew it wasn't Sterling, but was another man sharing her bed? Is that how Julep escaped? Had Martha traded her body for her niece's release? It seemed like something his sweet wife would do, but how it filled him with rage.

He rolled over and punched the pillow, then slammed his face against the cotton and screamed. A low groan escaped his throat and he clenched the material, wanting to rip it to shreds and let feathers fly. This was all his fault. Why couldn't he have been a better man to begin with? Like Tobias, Jamison, or even Cade with his many insecurities. None of them would have led them into this disaster.

Stumbling from bed, he dressed in the dark, drawing on his borrowed boots and coat before slipping silently from the room. With cautious steps that seemed too loud, he descended the stairs and paused at the light flickering beneath the office door. Drawing near, he pressed his ear to the crack and heard no voices, but then noticed what sounded like the flip of a page. Daniel must be up reading, unable to sleep either.

Leaving his brother to it, he eased out the front door into the midnight streets, once so familiar and now so foreign. Without clear direction, he headed down the cobblestone past houses whose owners he once knew well. His father's favorite gentleman's lounge, The Bryson, winked at him from the corner, its patrons' silhouettes conversing business from within. A block over, a cacophony of entertainment filtered through tavern doors, a cloud of smoke hanging in the air above round wooden tables and quickly emptying glasses. Everything else was closed now, shutters latched, only darkness beyond. From one of the homes, a baby cried. A dog barked. A man shouted, "An' that's all yull get, an' like it!"

Near the corner of King and Broad, he passed the Welden Family's 1783 Colonial. He had courted their daughter Victoria for three weeks before moving on. She had been a nice girl and deserved for her first intimacies to be with someone who understood that. Instead, she had been with him.

Somehow, he found himself outside the Cathedral of St. John and St. Finbar, a brownstone church whose gothic spire rose into the stars above. This building hadn't been here when he last was. Back then, it had been but a small dwelling house, and he wondered when they'd expanded. The last time he set foot in a Carolina church—one nearer their plantation—he had been sixteen and enraged over his mother's supposed suicide. After he broke every candle and flung melted wax on every surface, he had screamed at Father Corbin until the priest banned him from the parish. Furious, he returned home and knocked his father unconscious across his office floor. It had been the shining moment of his young life, but he had known it wouldn't last. As soon as Alonzo woke mere minutes later, he locked his son in the attic for two days, alone except for the remnants of his mother's noose and the memory of her bruised neck and protruding eyes.

Her suicide couldn't be a sin, he had thought. It couldn't. Without their father's persuasion, she never would have done it on her own. Even so, she had still been denied a Christian burial. Did that mean she couldn't go to heaven?

He honestly still wasn't certain of the answer. Since returning to church last year, he had prayed for her soul at every Mass. He supposed that was all he could do.

When he tried the cathedral's door, it swung open under his touch. Glad to not be denied, he slipped in and walked the aisle, crossed himself and sat in the front pew. Silence melted over him in the darkness, save for the prayer votives, a few wall sconces, and the red tabernacle lamp. It had been too long since he experienced silence without sleep. San Francisco had been noisy and alive and never ceasing. His hotel, although a space all his own, kept him busy day and night. Even St. Mary's brick exterior could not cover the racket of the streets, and Mass contained more vocal prayer than quiet contemplation. Now the stillness overwhelmed him.

A tear trailed his cheek. He wiped it away. Another followed and he did the same. A third, a fourth, a fifth. By the seventh, he let them fall.

All his life, he had mocked his brothers over every little sensitivity. Especially Cade. But now he realized that what he had really wanted was to not be *himself.* Unable to connect with anything. Cut off from his emotions because life was too difficult to deal with. Yet, when he finally opened himself up to someone, she had been stolen from him.

"I don't know what to do, Lord. I...I've been lost most of my life. Angry with you and...haven't trusted you as I should. Honestly, I'm having a real tough time doing it now. I suppose you know that and maybe you've already cast your lots against me. Heck, I'd deserve it, I guess, but I'd sure like another chance to make things right."

No answer came, no rumbling in the clouds. Only the quiet and the still small glow of flickering flames.

"What did I expect? You've never answered when I wanted you to."

"But he does answer when we need him to." Cade stood beside the pew, an uneasy smile on his lips. "Mind if I join you?"

"I suppose you heard all that, then?"

Cade nodded.

"Then you might as well." Garrett scooted over, allowing room. Genuflecting, Cade crossed himself and slid into the pew.

For a minute, they both sat, staring at the altar and the crucifix and the little red flame indicating Christ in the golden tabernacle. The hour had to be after one a.m., but he felt as awake as if it were noontime. His mind raced. So much for tranquility.

"Go ahead and say what you're here for," he said finally. "You've got thoughts, I can tell. Call me a hypocrite and let's be done with it.

For once, please don't try to keep the peace."

"You think I'm going to rail on you in church?"

"Why not? I've done a lot worse than that in church. I should probably have gone up in flames the second I stepped through the door."

"The well don't need a physician. Only the sick do."

Garrett side-eyed his brother. "Huh?"

Cade shrugged. "It's something Jamison told me once. That Christ came for sinners because the sick need doctors, but the well don't. We're all sick, Garrett. Why would God throw us out of his hospital?"

"Why wouldn't God stop us from getting sick in the first place?"

"Because then we wouldn't be free to choose Him. You know what I've realized though? Satan has free will, too. Everyone always asks why didn't God do this or why didn't God stop that, but they never ask why the devil did this or stopped that. Because of evil, God is always working to correct the stupid ideas the devil suggests and we go along with. God's got good ideas too, better ideas, but He won't beat us into following Him. He isn't going to yell and scream. He wants us to freely choose Him and He weeps when we don't. But Satan will do *anything* to get us to choose him instead and so, it's harder to resist."

Garrett thought about that. He had always been the bad seed of the family—the liar, cheater, and debaucher—the one who got angry and destroyed the church sanctuary. It had always been easier to live a sordid life than walk the straight and narrow. Hundreds of times he had asked why God *didn't*; not once had he asked why the devil *did*.

"Cade, this is hard for me to say, but I misjudged you. When did you get to be so wise?"

"I'm not. Or at least not good at following my own advice. I'm afraid of everything, Garrett. I get these fits I can't explain—like the one in Brunswick—where it feels as though the walls are closing in, and most of the time, there aren't even any walls. Don't even ask me how many times I've lost faith and doubted and wondered if He cared."

"Like with Alice Ann?"

"Yeah. Especially with her." He huffed a breath that ruffled a strand of hair across his eyes. He shoved it back and folded his arms, slumping lower in the pew. "I know I just told you a lot of inspiration about God's ways, but I still wonder why He ever put her in my path."

"I wonder that, too. About her and about Martha. I've been with eighty-three women. Many who were highly respectable and would have made enviable *legal* wives. Why couldn't I have been taken with one of them? I don't regret marrying Martha, but God could have made it all so much easier."

Cade remained silent for several minutes and Garrett feared he'd said too much. Then finally, "Is eighty-three arbitrary or is that an exact number? And when you say been with, you mean—"

"Yes, Cade, I mean been with. And no, eighty-three isn't arbitrary."

"That's a high number."

"It is."

"Are you sorry?"

Certainly, he wished the past hadn't happened. Rarely had he dwelt over his feminine encounters before he turned his life around, but he'd sure thought a lot about them ever since.

"I think remembering how many women you were with means something," Cade said.

"That I'm depraved?"

"Maybe, but also that, in your heart, you don't want to be. You know love should mean more than just desires of the flesh. I would bet you still remember many of their names."

He did. He could name off the first thirty with no trouble. It became a little foggy after that and murkier still once he fell in league with the soiled doves of San Francisco. Some only fronted stage names like "Beauty" and "Euphoria." Others hadn't even offered one.

He should have never been with any of them. He should have treated them all like the beautiful treasure he had found in Martha, even when he knew they had no future together. Especially then.

"I am sorry, Cade. I've been selfish, and I don't think I realized how much."

His brother slung an arm around his shoulders and instead of decking him to the tile, Garrett let it linger. Men weren't supposed to need comfort, but sometimes, as hard as it was to admit, they still did.

When Cade spoke, his voice was soft, yet certain. "I think that's what happens when we truly love someone. There's no room for being selfish. We love them, one painful step at a time, and then we have to let them go. You can find people, Garrett, but only God can lead them home."

30

When Garrett and Cade returned to Lark House, all remained calm save the same flicker of light from beneath the office door. "You head upstairs," Garrett told him. "I'm going to check on Daniel before I head up."

"I could join you. Keep you from killing him." Cade gave a half-hearted smile which Garrett waved away toward the stairs.

"We'll be fine. Tonight's apparently a night for confessions and peacemaking, so it's about time I made peace with Daniel. This is something I need to do on my own."

Despite Cade's wary eye, he nodded. "Good night then. And Garrett? I'm glad we talked."

"Me, too, Cade. Try to get some sleep."

He waited until his brother's footsteps ascended to the third floor, then inhaled a few readying breaths. The last time he and Daniel stood alone face-to-face, he had been furious over his brother selling their slaves. He remembered telling Daniel he loathed him, that his brother was a good-for-nothing exactly like their father, how he was glad to be rid of him, and hoped never to meet again. Yet, here they were with only a door's separation.

"Lord, give me the words," he whispered as he turned the knob.

He walked into the room, assaulted by the pungent stench of burnt paper and ink. His brother bent over the blazing fireplace, tearing pages from a ledger, and tossing them into the flames.

"What are you doing?"

Daniel jolted upright, narrowly avoiding hitting his head against the mantel. Clutching the maimed ledger, he stared at his brother, jaw slack. "Why are you awake?"

"I couldn't sleep." Garrett stepped closer to the pile of ledgers stacked on the desktop. Keeping one eye on Daniel, he nudged the first few books to reveal the titles. Each one bore dates in sequence with the words "human property records" scrawled beneath. Opening the top cover, he found neat columns marked with slave names, sale dates, amounts, and purchasers. "These are Father's slave transactions." He looked back at his brother. "Why would you wait until now to burn them?"

"Housekeeping."

"At two in the morning?"

Daniel glanced at the flames and in that split second, Garrett recognized his intent. As his brother's hand shifted, he tackled him, sending them both into the desk and ledgers flying to the floor. He swept his foot across the carpet to kick the half-burnt book away from the flames, its bottom edge singed and smoking. When Daniel tried to fling another toward the fire, Garrett grabbed his wrist, twisted it, and shoved him against the desk.

"Tell me why you were burning these."

"Let me go and I'll tell you."

"Tell me and I'll let you go."

Daniel remained where he was, lips pursed in silence. He winced when Garrett twisted his arm further. "Tell me, Daniel!"

"Fine," his brother grunted. "It's because I'm as despicable as you and didn't want you to stumble upon the proof."

"What could you have possibly done? You were always the golden child."

"Father hated me."

"Only because you weren't Gifted. If you had been, being the dull boot-licker that you are, he would have let you rule the world."

"You might not feel so when you hear why I sold the slaves. It has nothing to do with economics or Southern liberty."

"Fine. Let's hear it."

"It's all in the ledgers."

Releasing him, Garrett stepped over the fallen ledgers and reached for the most recent one Daniel had tried to burn. He rolled his eyes up at his brother. "It's all in here?"

Without meeting his gaze, Daniel sank to the floor and began stacking the ledgers back into a neat pile. "You'll know as soon as you see it."

Steeling a breath, Garrett read the cover. Although blackened, he could make out the imprinted dates *1850-1851*, the years the last plantation slaves were sold, right before Tobias, Garrett, Jamison, and Cade had headed West. He opened to the first remaining page and skimmed the names and amounts. He recognized them as fieldhands from the rice paddies, some of the same paddies he himself had overseen. It wasn't difficult to recall their days spent together, harvesting rice to ensure the plantation's survival. He had always wondered what happened to those men, women, and children. Now he knew.

And the truth utterly revolted him.

While the children's names all showed various purchasers, the adults were sold to one person only—Mr. Ashley Sterling.

Garrett wanted to beat Daniel until he couldn't feel his fists anymore.

He braced a hand against the fireplace mantel, unable to so much as glance at his brother, or he really might dismember him. "You told me you only met Sterling twice," he ground out.

"I did. At Father's funeral and once when I was fourteen. I haven't seen him since, but everything about him made me believe he was not to be trifled with. He wanted sixty slaves, fifty women and ten men, for his new brothel. It had opened three years before and due to demand, needed an increased supply of workers. He knew I didn't want the plantation and knew I hated owning slaves. How he knew I'm not sure; Father must have told him. He was right, of course. I shuddered at the idea of continuing Father's legacy, but I also knew we couldn't afford to pay them all a wage. It tormented me every night trying to resolve what I wanted versus what was financially sound."

"You could have told him no."

"I couldn't have. If I didn't obey, he swore he would send his men after you and our brothers. He mentioned horrible torments I won't repeat, lest they haunt your dreams like they have mine. I've feared for you every day since you left."

Garrett's grip tightened on the mantel. He closed his eyes and still saw flames. "I would rather have kept those families together on our plantation, even as slaves, than to maintain my own safety."

"You were my brothers!" Daniel cried. "I knew I'd never belong with you, but I could do this one thing and save your lives."

"At what cost? It's too great to consider."

"And yet, I've thought of nothing else since."

When Garrett didn't respond, he heard footsteps shift and a thud as a pile of ledgers no doubt dropped upon the desk. The desk chair squeaked as Daniel sat and released a weary lament.

Something caught up to Garrett then, words his brother had said about the slaves sold to Sterling, that they were intended for the brothel. Those women he had harvested rice alongside, who had served under the wing of his protection, he had also unwittingly defiled. Even beneath his mask's anonymity, had they somehow been aware of who he was? He had paid for that depravity and paid dearly, with far more than the few measly coins he proffered.

"You should have let him kill me, Daniel. Everyone would have been better off."

"How can you say that?"

"If I'd never left Charleston, I would have never met Martha, never gone to San Francisco, and never ruined so many lives. To merely think of what could be happening to her...without me, she would have been safe and happy in Larksong."

"No, she wouldn't. If I didn't sell Sterling those slaves, all our brothers would be dead. There would be no wagon train, no new town. You might be content with your own demise, but could you be as such with theirs?"

The firelight danced off Daniel's features, seemingly aged decades over in only eight years. His lips pressed tight, a rigid line void of emotion. Hands clasped upon the desktop, back straight against the chair. Tan hair and trim beard, exactly like their father.

"You can't fight Sterling," Daniel said. "He always wins. Julep is safe in Larksong; be content with that."

"Is that how you would be? If your wife was imprisoned by a fiend, always at risk of selling her virtue or perhaps being killed? Would you leave her there, knowing you put her there?"

Daniel peered past him into the fire, where the pages burned. "No, but sometimes we have no choice."

"There is always a choice."

"Not when you're a slave."

"We're all slaves to something." Garrett laid the half-burnt ledger on top of the stack. "Go ahead and burn them. I wish I could erase the mistakes of my past so easily as you do yours."

He strode from the room and softly closed the door. No sense waking anyone who hadn't already heard their scuffle. Tears pricked again as he stared at the gilded ceiling. The elaborate mural washed like a watercolor through his vision. His mother had wanted to paint a rose trellis, surrounding an open blue sky. It was his father who insisted on the Versailles-inspired intricacy.

Had Alonzo Lark ever cared about anyone but himself? God gave him a family to love. He could have taught his sons to be someone good, even if they could not be politically great. In spite of that, Tobias and Jamison still ended up with loving marriages and beautiful children. Cade, at least, had Julep. Three out of five wasn't so terrible. It was better than his sisters. Thank the Lord they didn't live only to end up in Sterling's grasp.

His sisters... Conversations recalled in a series of supposedly unrelated details suddenly took on new meaning.

When Josiah said to Cade: *"They who love much, feel much. I's loved once, too. Ya never stop lookin' for it even after ya know it's gone."*

When Josiah reprimanded Garrett before his wedding: *"Love ain't somethin' ya do in a blast of stupidity... I've seen the pain of lovin' someone ya can never truly call yer own...Your mother. Her pain was great."*

When Sterling revealed his daughter's true parentage: *"Your father wanted to get rid of Clary and I didn't. Simple."*

And finally, when Daniel admitted: *"I only met Sterling twice. At*

Father's funeral and once when I was fourteen." The same year their last sister died.

Only once in Garrett's nearly thirty-five years had Josiah ever mentioned being in love. Now he knew why.

Taking the stairs two at a time, he skidded down the attic hallway and rapped on Josiah's door. Almost immediately, it opened followed by Cade and Melvin's. Apparently, no one could sleep tonight.

"What's wrong?" Cade asked. "Did something happen with Daniel?"

"Yes." But Garrett kept his attention focused on Josiah. The older man filled the doorway, hands slack at his sides, eyes moist in the dim lantern light, as though he knew exactly why he had come.

"When you told me it wasn't simple to marry someone like Martha, you meant you and my mother, didn't you?"

"Yes." Not a hesitation, not a blink.

"How long did you love her?"

"Every day since your father brought her home."

"Clary's my half-sister, isn't she?"

"Yes."

"Then whose child did we bury?"

"Ya father persuaded some doctor fer a white babe meant fer the potter's field. It hadta been left on the church step an' died hours later. After Clary's birth, ya father insisted ya mother be given laudanum. When she woke, he told her the babe had died."

"Did she know Clary was yours?"

Josiah nodded. "She begged me not to tell ya. 'Cause of how ya all admired me, she said. I didn'a feel worthy of that. An' it hurt me worse than death seein' how ya father treated her when I loved her more'n life."

"Did... Did Daniel know?" Garrett braced himself for the answer, that his brother had been the one to perform the exchange with Sterling. He released a sharp exhale when Josiah replied, "No. He mourned your sister, too. I always tried to protect ya boys from the day yous was born."

He extended his hands, palms up, pleading. "Can ya forgive me?" His eyes swept to Cade. "Ya, too? I shoulda never...with ya mother. I shoulda never done any'a it."

Without hesitation, Cade rushed across the hall, throwing his arms tight around Josiah's waist as though he were still a boy. Startled, the older man froze before slowly returning the embrace. "I'm glad our mother knew love," Cade whispered. "At least for a little while."

"Aye. That she did."

Garrett rested a gentle hand on the older man's arm, aware of Melvin's presence nearby. "We'll get Clary back, and Martha, and we're going to stop Sterling." Despite his confident tone, he had no idea how they would go about it, much less succeed.

Rather, Melvin voiced the question for him. "How? From the sounds of it, you stand no chance against him."

"But we should still try." They all turned at the sound of Daniel's voice from the shadows of the stairwell. Stepping into the corridor, anguish distorted his features. Red-rimmed eyes swept theirs, those of a man at battle with his inner self.

"Did you burn the ledgers?" Garrett asked.

"No." He met his brother's gaze. "I thought about what you said. We can't erase the past, but we can change its outcome. Our odds against Sterling are likely set for failure, but Julep escaped so maybe that means together, we can find a way."

"Then, you'll help us?" Cade cried. He released Josiah and gripped Daniel by the shoulders. "You're coming with us?"

Slowly, Daniel nodded. "I have a plan, but it will take time to prepare—"

"We don't have time," Garrett interrupted. "I told you, Martha's there and—"

"And she'll still be there a week or a month from now. You know your chances are better with numbers on your side, and numbers are not something you have. If Sterling's Gift is opportunity, then you must find a way to turn that on its head."

"And you know how to do that?" asked Cade.

"No, but Garrett does."

Four sets of eyes shot to Garrett who backed away, palms raised. How did they expect him to have the answer? So far, his plan involved them running into the circus, breaking into Harvest Hill, and pummeling Sterling until someone inevitably killed him, yet providing Martha enough time to escape. Garrett would survive *Arletta*'s furnaces and a lifeboat on a raging sea, wandering through Brunswick and confronting Daniel, only to die anyway.

"Sterling wins," he muttered. "He always wins."

Melvin's palm connected with Garrett's cheek, spinning his head sideways.

"Hey!" Garrett shouted. He raised his fists and Melvin clapped him over the ear, shoving him through Josiah's door and pinning him flat against the bed. He shoved his knee into Garrett's back and pinned both arms behind him. "Get off me! Why aren't you doing anything?" he yelled at Cade and Josiah who stood staring. Daniel closed the door behind them.

"Quiet down," he hissed. "The boarders will come questioning."

Melvin dug his knee in, causing Garrett to arch his back. He tried to buck the man off, but it was difficult with his face half-suffocated against the mattress. "You are a horrid excuse for a man," Melvin admonished. "This devil stole Julep and Martha. His man kidnapped some blind woman Cade told me about. You never knew your half-sister because of him. He tried to kill Josiah and you and Cade. He used you and your family to enslave people. You have a half dozen reasons to destroy him and you're about to quit? No. I only had one reason to escape Captain McCullen and I endured thirteen years for it. So, stop being chicken. Sterling can come quietly, or he can leave to the sound of a gunshot. Either way, he'll be taken care of."

These weren't words they expected from a man they barely knew. Melvin had no coin in the game. He was an angry man who hadn't been able to extract revenge on any of the oppressors in his life, so he was taking his vengeance wherever he could. Offering to murder someone and not batting an eye or shaking a limb.

"We should try to capture him alive," Cade said. "Final judgment isn't our call. We'll let the court decide."

Garrett exhaled through his nose. It was the Christian stance to spare him execution, unless the court deemed it, which he honestly didn't know if they would. Sterling had a hand in too many pockets in San Francisco and there was a chance they would let him run free. He had to hope that when the officials finally heard the truth, they would realize their mistakes in shaking Sterling's hand. Just as Garrett so deeply regretted it himself. The most important thing was that they stopped the circus and rescued all those imprisoned there.

"I'm with Cade," he said. "We capture Sterling and hand him over to the authorities. Everyone agree?" Daniel and Josiah affirmed their consent. "Melvin?"

"Fine," he huffed. Releasing Garrett, he tripped back off the bed and swung backward onto the corner chair. Garrett sat up, stretching out his muscles one side at a time. He rubbed his cheek, his jaw smarting from Melvin's palm. That was going to leave quite the mark tomorrow.

"Now, Daniel, how do you propose I turn the numbers in our favor?"

His brother paced to the window and propped himself on the sill, spine rigid against the frame. He watched the night, almost every house light in the city now extinguished except for entry lamps and the lantern on the small square table beside him. "You're the one who found Sterling's workers. You know who they are and where they're from. Most of their families are dead, but he doesn't have the power to remove entire towns. There are still people who remember those he took. Your Gift can find them. If I sell the house and most of my belongings, we can use that money to buy their trust. Don't worry; I won't leave the boarders high and dry."

"I's think I understand," Josiah said slowly. "Those found will come back with us. They's will be the numbers we need."

Daniel snapped his fingers. "Exactly. We'll intersperse with the circus crowd, all masked and in costume, and when the moment is right, during that final number, we'll have our day. Sterling'll be onstage surrounded by people who want nothing but his downfall."

It was a good plan, Garrett thought. If anyone would join them, it would be those who had personally known the victims. If they could manage to gather enough followers and stay low against the guards, it might actually work.

"There's a stagecoach that departs regularly from St. Louis," Daniel continued. "The route opened last September and can take us direct to San Francisco in twenty-five days. We'll send a letter ahead, Pony Express to Larksong, explaining what's happened and to meet us in California."

Garrett didn't really expect his brothers to come charging down to save the day, but he was desperate for a solution. Maybe Tobias and Jamison could get the Washington police involved. At least, if their plan failed, they would know how everyone met their demise.

"How do you know all this?" Cade asked.

Daniel ran a hand through his dirty-blond hair. "I've thought about joining you many times. Only made it as far as learning the pathway before I remembered what kept me here in the first place. But I think it's about time we put all this to bed."

Melvin released a loud yawn. "Speaking of beds, I'm goin' back to mine. Nicest one I've slept in in a while, so I thank ya, Mr. Lark." He tapped two fingers to his temple and swung off the chair, heading for the door. He paused before opening it. "So, we're clear, we start huntin' for folks in the morning?"

Garrett nodded. "Soon as Daniel sells the house, we're on our way to find them."

His pulse quickened and a sudden dread washed over him. Its slow ache crept beneath his skull as it had when he discovered Julep was back in Larksong. Before it grew worse, he relayed his goodnights and stole to his room. Closing himself in, he untied his boots, tossed off his frock coat, and sprawled across the bed, arms akimbo. A sliver of moonlight cast upon his stockinged feet and his brain chose that moment to remember the feeling of Martha's bare toes curled against him. Rolling onto his side, he crawled through his senses until he found her in Sterling's theater, in the same room as the last time. Always that same room, yet blind to all else. His Gift could find people, but there was no way to know what condition they were in.

Next, he searched for Clary. His half-sister was in another bedroom, closer to Harvest Hill. He recalled her wide brown eyes, surrounded by black lashes that swept her cheeks with each slow blink. What had Sterling done to her after their departure? Did she remain in his good graces or was her current location nothing more than a prison cell? All his life, he thought his sisters were dead. Would any of his brothers live long enough to know their newest sibling?

What if he failed at this like he had failed at so many things? He couldn't do this on his own.

The well don't need a physician. Only the sick do.

"Ok, Lord," he whispered. "Here I am. I ask nothing for my safety, only theirs. Keep them safe. Keep them safe. Keep them..." Finally, with sincerity upon his lips, he drifted off to sleep.

31

Sterling refused for Martha to rejoin the show until two weeks passed. That was fine by her. It had taken over a week to fully recover from her forgotten night with Kayus, especially when he insisted on performing regular intimacies. "We're newlyweds and Sterling expects it," he whispered into her hair once, which to her mind was the least romantic phrase ever uttered.

Not like how Garrett had spoken, with such lovely phrases of her worth: "You are the most beautiful woman I have ever seen." The smile on his face had been like a burst of sunshine on a stormy day. Even knowing he had seen a good *many* women, she still believed him. The lilt of his voice and the depth of appreciation in his gaze...everything he did left her feeling cherished and adored. "I can't believe this is our life," he had said. "I never knew I could be this happy." She hadn't known it either. They *had* been happy, too. For such a short time, they had foolishly believed they stood a chance.

I can't believe this is my life now, she thought. *I can't believe that happiness is gone.*

"Don't let those uneducated idiots dictate how we're going to live," he had said when she doubted. "Where is your confidence, Martha? Where is the woman who kept alive what little spirit I had all these years, who insisted I could do things I never thought myself capable of?"

She's dead, just as you are.

243

The name Bakhita might mean fortunate but neither of them had been. Every time she said *yes* to Kayus, she felt the weight of betrayal against Garrett and against God for giving herself to a man she didn't love. Every time she felt another piece of herself burn away and wondered why Sterling had given her the choice. Why hadn't he simply sent her to the Garden, as he had with Nora?

To add hurt to the heartache, June thoroughly despised her for stealing the one man she wanted. Every morning when Martha returned for breakfast, June called her horrible venomous names. At least Lissie still offered smiles and assurance, even if her kind words failed at their intended result. Nora's bed remained empty, an eternal reminder of their mutual grief.

Part of her needed to return to the show, simply to take her mind off everything else. Another greater part wanted her flaming batons to spiral down and set her ablaze.

Not that there was much point in performing. Since Moses's horse sabotage, the audience had become patchy, like an old man's thinning hair. Families, in particular, stayed away. The unsavory took their place. She watched more men enter the Garden doors than spend any time in the stands. Where the circus had failed, the brothel seemed to have not suffered at all.

The Monday before Martha's scheduled return, Clary arrived at her door, escorted by Kayus. She carried a silver tea tray complete with triangular meat pies in a flakey crust and a small plate of butter cookies. She smiled, which unnerved Martha more than Clary's usual scowl.

"I brought us a treat." She raised the tray as though Martha couldn't understand her words. "I've missed you in rehearsal. I thought we could talk while everyone else is on the show floor."

Martha's eyes flicked to Kayus. Was this his doing? Clary had never tried to befriend her before. Thankfully, he didn't smile, too, or she would have come wholly undone. "I escorted Clary to the kitchen and watched her make the pies," he said. "There's nothing in them that can harm you."

That wasn't what she had meant. Even so, she nodded. "Thank you, Kayus. You'll bring June and Lissie back after rehearsal?"

He nodded. "I will." Then he bent and whispered in her ear, "Don't let June bother ya none. Even if ya hadn't come around, I woulda never been matched with her anyway. Sterling's promised to put a stop to the gossip."

"It doesn't bother me none, honest. I don't want her in trouble." June may despise her, and Martha, in turn, been wounded, but she didn't want her roommate dropped into the Garden or matched with someone terrible. Suddenly, she felt so tired. "You'll come for me after the show?" she asked.

"It's Monday. No show tonight."

"Right, of course." She must be more tired than she thought, forgetting what day it was. "At seven then?"

"How's six?" he asked. "We could supper together."

"Oh." Was he implying something formal? Like a courtship? She hadn't even had that with Garrett. They wrote letters and then married without so much as more than a few evening talks beside the campfire or in his office when he proposed. Tears sprung to her eyes, again thinking of all they had missed.

She forced herself to nod woodenly. "Six will be fine."

"Perfect. Clary, I will return in two hours."

"Thank you, Kayus." Clary's bright expression remained until the door closed and they were finally alone. Then she swept across the room, clunked the tray onto the coffee table, and turned to grip Martha by the arms. "How are you, truly?"

Was that genuine concern she heard? "I..." *You're fine*, she told herself. *Tell her you're fine.* "I'm fine."

Clary's thick brows rose. "Are you sure because Kayus says you haven't been yourself lately."

Been herself? Of course not. Her entire life had been ravaged. Her husband was dead, and her replacement husband was nice enough, but not who she wanted. She slept in a prison across from three floors of ill-repute. At any time, Sterling could punish her for things she hadn't done and threaten her or worse.

She ought to wrench away and gobble down all the cookies in spite, but a weight dropped into her stomach at the thought. Her shoulders slumped forward. Moving ten feet to the sofa felt like a monumental achievement.

"I bet you're hungry." Clary released her and claimed a seat on the sofa, patting the other cushion before turning to pour the tea. "Come have a snack. Sterling doesn't like any of his girls to be too skinny."

"I'm not skinny. I think I've gained weight if anything." But who could tell? She hadn't bothered to fully dress since that night she woke in Kayus's quarters. Why bother? She had no one to impress with her appearance, no audience to entertain, and many nights spent undressed besides.

Somehow, she managed to drag her feet across the room. Her usual black dressing gown flowed around her ankles, its center tied low to show a flash of white nightdress. If she tried, she could almost imagine herself the lady of a grand estate—up north of course—able to lounge about in her underthings without a care to her attention. Except she rarely tried to imagine it anymore. Such wonderings never helped, for if she had been a lady, then there would also be a lord, and that lord should have been Garrett.

Settling onto the sofa, she drew her knees up and draped the knitted throw across them. The blanket had become her daily comfort during her weeks contained upstairs. Accepting a teacup from Clary, she thanked her and sipped the beverage, breathing in the delicious scent of black tea and lemon peel.

"How is the show?" she asked.

Clary peered at her from over the teacup's edge. "I see you watching from your room. You know how the show is."

"Your performance is still wonderful."

"They expect entertainment, and it's my job to entertain. I do what's asked of me."

"Do you always do what's asked of you?"

Clary glared at her and Martha pressed her lips together. Perhaps she'd gone too far. She should have accepted the brief branch of friendship and kept their conversation pleasant. After all, Julep was gone now and that had been her main concern. She must focus on prayer and give no more thought to her own escape or anyone else's. *This is your life*, she thought. *This is all our lives.*

Setting her teacup on the tray, she reached for a meat pie and nibbled the end, certain that her nervous stomach wouldn't keep anything settled. But its warm and gooey filling slipped over her tongue, so that she devoured its entirety and remained hungry for another. She took two cookies and ate them both.

"They never found the people who killed the horses," Clary said while Martha ate.

"I thought Moses did it."

"Moses admitted to it, but my father knows he couldn't have acted alone. Not to arrange such a simultaneous attack. So many of the stable hands ran to stop the horses that they were all spattered in blood by the end of it. No one could tell if they had been covered before. Father said it'll be another unfortunate loss."

Martha shoved the remaining cookie between her lips. "Good. There's nothing worth saving in this entire place."

Clary gripped her teacup, suddenly quiet. "There's always something worth saving, Martha."

"Who taught you that?"

"You did."

Martha swallowed hard. She wasn't that optimistic girl anymore. She was thirty-six—no, thirty-seven, she had missed her birthday— and she was old and she was tired. Her bones ached more than they used to and throwing the batons had sent her shoulder to places it shouldn't belong. Yes, she had saved Julep, and that was good and right. But what else was there to save? The other children? Of course, they were worth it. And the other performers would be worth helping, if they cared to go, except many didn't. Like June, they wanted to be here.

She blinked as Clary held out her open palm. There sat Martha's wedding rings, peach pearl against gold, still threaded upon the silver chain. She snatched them up, remembering the afternoon Garrett placed them on her finger and her devastation to wake and find them missing. "Clary, how? Where did you find them?"

"You handed them to me before your wedding to Kayus. You asked me to keep them safe, not to let anyone find them. Begged me, really."

"I-I did? I begged *you*?" Why Clary out of everyone? Why not Lissie or June? Why did she trust Sterling's own daughter to hide something so precious? "Did you take care of me after Kayus and I—when I woke up clean and clothed. Did you do that, too?"

Clary's smile wavered. She stirred her tea, the spoon clinking against the near empty cup. Slowly, she nodded. "You didn't deserve what happened, and it made me think that maybe...maybe, I didn't deserve what happened to me either. Do you think—" Her lower lip trembled, then she stole a breath and pressed on. "Do you think things would have been better with the Larks? If I'd been raised by Josiah, even though I'dve been a slave, do you think it would have been better than here?"

Lands, Clary, Martha wanted to say. *You* are *a slave.* But saying so wouldn't help. As deep as her hurt ran, for the first time since Nora left, she felt friendship again. With tears in her eyes, she did something she barely had the strength for. She handed the rings back. "Keep them," she said softly. "I can't wear them around Kayus, and I know you'll keep them safe."

The chandelier light reflected in the pearl, a small glowing orb of hope she wanted to feel but couldn't. Slowly, Clary's fingers curled around the chain and she dropped it in her skirt pocket. With that small but sure motion, Martha finally said goodbye.

Tears rolled down her cheekbones into her ears. She let them fall, her palms plastered flat upon her knees. "I miss him, Clary. It hurts so much, everything inside me."

"I know." Clary watched her thoughtfully for a moment. Then she set her cup down and scooted closer. She slid a tentative arm around Martha's shoulders. "I put the salt in the water."

"*You?*" For some reason, she didn't even care that Clary had let her take the blame. It served Mr. Sterling right to have his daughter turn on him. She rested her head on Clary's shoulder and thought how strange that a girl ten years younger was the one to do the comforting.

The fire tender didn't speak, but her presence said all that was needed. She had watched her birth father murdered. Just because she never knew him, didn't mean she didn't grieve.

Eventually, Martha's tears slowed and Clary eased her upright. Her wide brown eyes held hers. "There's always something worth saving, Martha. I need you to hold onto that belief when you hear what I'm about to say."

"You also put maggots in the food?"

"No, far worse than that. And far better." Yet, her expression implied more worse than better. She placed her hand over Martha's. "You're carrying Garrett's baby. I knew it the minute I changed your clothes."

32

"**Y**ou're having a baby."

Martha didn't reply at first, a cold dread flowing through her. She couldn't be bearing Garrett's child. Nearly five months had passed. She would know. Wouldn't she? It was imposs—

She stopped herself from thinking the rest. She hadn't experienced her courses since Julep went missing in May, and they had been sporadic for years before. Daily extremes could often make a woman miss, especially when she was well past her prime, as Martha was. Since coming to Sterling's, she had experienced a few stomach aches here or there, but nothing worrisome. Slight nausea, but no expulsion like Sarah or Coraline experienced. She had gained a few pounds, although again, nothing to be alarmed over. Jerking her hand from Clary's, she pressed both palms against her middle. What she found within was barely rounder than the natural curves developed by aging.

The chances were slight, but possible. The realization brought her no joy. Garrett was dead and no child deserved to be born into this. Was the baby even well to be so small?

Martha wrapped the knitted throw tightly about herself, shivering. The room blurred and she quickly dabbed the blanket's edge across each eye. She needed to be strong. This wasn't about her anymore. She must care for this child, the last piece of Garrett she had.

"What will I do?" she asked. "My husband is dead."

"No. Your husband is coming to collect you at six o'clock. You're having supper with him."

Martha's throat hitched, her tears turned to sand. She sprang from the sofa, the blanket bunching in her clenched fingers. "I cannot raise Garrett's child with him, Clary. I can't."

"You're right, so you have to make this baby Kayus's. My father feels betrayed by what Garrett did and he shows no mercy to those who betray him. Remember what he did to Josiah."

"No one will believe it. Not when I'm so far along—and what if the baby comes out white?"

"Find a way. Say someone violated you in the first few weeks; we're all masked, so you don't know who it was. Anything, but don't let Mr. Sterling or Kayus know the truth. If my father finds out, he'll force you to get rid of it. He won't care that it might be Gifted."

Get rid of it? She meant Mr. Sterling would kill it. Kill her baby. Kill Garrett's baby. The child they made *together*.

She rounded on Clary. "The minute he's born, you have to take him to St. Mary's. Isn't that what Rella did with the babies from the brothel?"

Clary nodded, but exhaustion overwhelmed her expression. "She did, but then she ran away. No one's allowed out anymore."

Kayus didn't take well to the news that Martha had been violated many months ago. He asked her a dozen questions: costume type, hair color, height, weight. Why didn't she pull his mask off? Why didn't she scream or tell Mr. Sterling after? Maybe he didn't actually believe her. Maybe he knew the child was Garrett's, but if so, he didn't reveal his suspicions. Instead, he told Mr. Sterling he had been the one who'd done it and received high approval on the coming addition. Martha, on the other hand, received only derision and scorn.

Although the circus never experienced another incident like the horse attacks, there were still frequent and unexplained occurrences of sabotage. Mr. Sterling continued to blame her, likely because he could. One night, he came to her room and, right in front of June and Lissie, shoved her against the wall, his hands around her neck until her vision started to darken. Then he dropped her on the floor and left. The bruises ringed her neck for a week. Whenever Kayus held her, sparks flared behind her eyes.

Now that he knew she was with child—and knew it couldn't be his—she found no solace in his arms. Night by night, the brief moments of tenderness faded until she wondered if she had imagined them. Her limbs were covered in bruises, her heart broken beyond repair. Every prayer held the safety of her child; not a one remained for her.

At least Julep was away. Rella, likewise, never returned. Martha must hope they were together and safe in Larksong. Still, she mourned the separation from the daughter of her heart.

"Mama," she would whisper through those dismal nights. "Remember the song we used to sing? I wish you were here to sing it again."

It was one of the few songs Martha hadn't sung aloud since leaving Charleston, but only in her head, the one about going up to freedom land. She had mentioned it to Sarah the night they ran from Hawthorn Ridge. Sarah had asked to hear part of the song, but Martha refused. She had wanted to keep what was her Mama's final song to herself. Now, she wished that she had shared it with someone else, so she wouldn't feel so alone.

Be as Christ to you, her mama would say.

So, she taught Clary the hymn and Lissie, too. June refused to join them, but Martha knew she heard their soft singing after breakfast each morning. Together, they prayed for Nora and all the others in the Garden. They prayed for each other and they prayed for themselves. For all the things worth saving and her deepest prayer, that her child would arrive healthy and be darker skinned than he was light.

In that way, the weeks passed. Possessions went missing and food rotted and too many people were punished without evidence. The audience dwindled, replaced with ruffians who spat tobacco and taunted the performers. Brawls broke out in the stands and Olo suffered twelve stitches from a thrown bottle. What once had some semblance of beauty and mystery behind the masks had been reduced to the ugly thing that it was.

She wondered why the police never interfered. Garrett told her there were laws. Why did no one enforce the laws?

She knew why. It was the same reason she could never leave.

Another month passed and then another. She sang her mother's lullabies and got down on her knees and prayed. To the God who brought her—and her child—into the world for a purpose she could not understand. To the One who worked things for good when she couldn't see how. To the Savior who rewarded the faithful, even if that reward was set for her in the next life. Slave or free, that God had never failed her and never would.

To Him, they were all worth saving.

"Ready?" Clary asked. She lit her baton and held open the show floor curtain. Martha caught Mr. Sterling watching from his usual place between the stands. Then, placing a protective hand over her unborn child, she and Clary walked out into the show lights together.

33

From the front row of Sterling's Theatrical, Garrett shifted in his seat, anxious for the performance to begin. Beneath him, the velvet-padded bench felt rigid as stone, as though nothing in the circus had changed, and yet everything had.

The audience contained no families now; those seats not filled by the men Garrett had found contained rough clods in stained clothing, some masked, some not. The line to the brothel marched out the main theater doors into the foyer. Something crashed upstairs, followed by a cry. He wondered if the voice belonged to one of their former servants, while simultaneously, not wishing to find out.

Self-conscious, he tightened the strings on his three-quarter face mask, even though they were already flush against his scalp, then checked the bowler tugged low to disguise his recently trimmed and oiled waves. All in order, save for the dust upon his ebony frock coat, navy waistcoat, and charcoal trousers. It had been a long thirty-two days on the Butterfield Overland Mail Stage and seven days longer than expected. Garrett, Cade, Daniel, Josiah, and Melvin all squashed together in a stage clearly not designed to carry five full-grown men, especially not one of Josiah's breadth. The coach jarred with every rut and its wheels caught upon each muddy crevice. Combined with the trail's tedium and the stench of unwashed bodies, he had found himself drowsing. He hadn't slept properly in months, even when cocooned by one of Mr. Spalderton's or Daniel's comfortable beds. Yet, somehow, sleep made sense when confined to a tiny wooden box.

Like a coffin. He shook his head, needing to banish that thought right now. He had his brothers and he had his men. This time, they would emerge the victors.

At least he had *some* men. Most of the farms they visited were either abandoned, burned, or being tended by new owners. News of the previous owners was grim with murder, supposed suicide, and suspicious accidents. He supposed he had inadvertently done that, too. By providing Sterling access to the Gifted, he had given access to those the circus-owner deemed dispensable. How many sins could Garrett pile onto his back? The priest would grow tired of hearing him confess them all.

All he needed was to add murder to the list. Under his frock coat, he carried a revolver on his hip and a knife strapped to his forearm, but, if it came to it, could he really kill Sterling? Wasn't the permanence of death for God to decide?

Not long ago, he wouldn't have even asked the question. He wouldn't have cared what God thought. Now, it bothered him to picture his soul—and likewise Sterling's—in jeopardy. Sometimes, he half-heartedly wished he'd remained in his depraved existence. Of the forty-two men they had gathered against Sterling, how many would face similar consequences?

"Ready?" Cade asked. Uncertainty peered out from beneath his mask's round eye holes, his dark curls hidden beneath a hooded cloak. "Because I'm not."

"All you need to do is help block the foyer doors. Leave Sterling to me."

The calliope ignited a fanciful tune, greeting the circus patrons as Ashley Sterling strode onto center stage. With a tip of his top hat and a toss of his tails, he extended his arms in greeting. As usual, no mask disguised his arrogant smile. "Welcome to Sterling's Theatrical! Have we got a show for you!"

Little does he know, we've got a show for him, too. If only they could pull it off.

Cream-colored mares charged around the show floor, while their acrobats flipped and flew, both in astonishingly fewer numbers than before. Kayus emerged, a cannonball in either hand. Lowering into a deep squat, he thrust the weights up and outward. They crashed mere feet from Sterling's polished boots, the sound like a muffled wave upon the shore. Betwixt it all, clown children danced with impish delight.

Garrett felt Martha's presence as soon as she neared the backstage curtain. Breath arduous, he watched as the crimson draperies parted for the trapeze acrobats, the juggler pair, and Clary with lit batons in hand. A stage hand followed wheeling the coal bin and then, finally, Martha stepped into the show lights.

Time reined to a halt as firelight danced across her features, and in particular, one very well-rounded feature. His labored breaths burned like flames within.

"Wait, is she...?" Cade whispered.

Yes, she was. Martha's expansive middle left no question as to what lay inside. Based on her size, the child couldn't have been conceived more than a month or two after he was enslaved on *Arletta*.

Maybe he *could* bring himself to kill Sterling. He sure wanted to.

"Garrett!" Daniel hissed from his opposite side. His brother's hand gripped his wrist, yanking him down from his half-standing position. "Stick to the plan."

"Someone violated my wife." He was about to rise again and storm the show floor, when Martha began to sing. Never had he heard her sing before, didn't know she could, and especially not with such enchantment. With grace and beauty, each note became breath to a dead man's lungs, her words stitches to his wounded soul.

"The sky may quickly darken. The earth begin to shake.
But still my Lord's love for me, nevermore will break.
We were called to freedom. Freedom, not for sin.
Called as one, to live as one, for eternal life with Him.
No one is my master. Except the Lord who calls me friend
Man may tie me tightly, but none steals my heart from Him."

From the shadows, Sterling's vision hardened; nevertheless, like a true ring master, he didn't interfere. He couldn't afford to play the fool in front of his patrons. The circus held his life. This show contained the epitome of his power. Everything here, rather literally, revolved around him.

Martha smiled as her voice broke through the din. Was that truly her voice that rose above the chandeliers? Did she even realize she had the capability to sing with such strength? Perhaps she *was* Gifted after all or perhaps God had simply granted her this one final blessing before the end.

"What happiness can equal mine? I've found the object of my love.
My Jesus dear, my King divine, is come to me from heav'n above!
He chose my heart for his abode. There he is my daily bread.
On me there flows his healing blood. With his flesh, my soul is fed.

I am my love's and He is mine. He dwells in me; in Him I live.
What greater gifts could love combine?
What greater then could heaven give?
I am the servant of the Lord. Let it be done to me as He will.
I am the servant of the Lord. And forever will be still."

Upon the final note, as applause raised and the audience whistled, she joined hands with Clary and together, they bowed. A smile passed between them in a glimmer of understanding. Were they...Garrett wondered...could they be...friends?

"That was beautiful," Daniel whispered. "I never considered servitude as a good thing."

"For most of my life, I didn't either," said Cade. "It was actually Martha who told me once that service doesn't have to be a trial. When one serves as Christ served, she said it can be a blessing."

Garrett couldn't speak. What he could do was stand.

Daniel yanked at his arm again. "Sit down. This isn't the plan." They were supposed to wait until the end of the show, assess the situation with the performers, most especially Martha and Clary, then wait until the regular audience departed to approach Sterling. But how could he wait a second longer when his wife—carrying someone else's child—was fifty feet in front of him? He wouldn't allow the beauty of that voice to be swallowed up.

"I'm changing the plan."

With a sigh, Daniel released him and stood, too, followed by Cade. After another few seconds, Tobias and Jamison joined them from the next section over. Garrett thanked God that Larksong had received their Pony Express correspondence as requested. For three days, he had waited at the rendezvous point, nearly ready to walk away when his middle brothers came riding over the hill. Their sincere smiles and heartfelt embraces became a statement of forgiveness he never expected. Nor would he forget his surprise when Rella dismounted beside them, sharing the tale of Julep's rescue and the uncertainty of Martha's fate. She had not, however, mentioned his wife being with child. Likely, she didn't want him to spiral out of control, as he considered doing now. She and Josiah now waited for them in Sterling's underground corridor, the same one Garrett had been led through to *Arletta*. The pair's presence in the theater would be too conspicuous, and they couldn't afford to reveal their hand before the proper time.

As the brothers strode onto the show floor, one by one they were joined by the other forty-two men set on Sterling's downfall. Martha and Clary faltered in their bows, backing away as the men created a semi-circle shoulder-to-shoulder. Garrett knew many also carried revolvers under their costumes, a few sporting knives or hatchets, and one a common work trowel. All with expressions that brokered no room for pity, excuses, or even mercy.

Sterling himself strode to center stage, Kayus directly on his heels, both their expressions livid. The rest of the audience murmured amongst themselves, some more loudly than others.

"Excuse me, gentlemen," Sterling nodded, "but you'll need to return to your seats or else leave the theater." Everyone standing remained silent, waiting on Garrett's cue as planned.

"Did you hear me?" Sterling shouted. "I said to get out."

"They heard you, but we're not leaving." Garrett broke the line, Cade and Daniel filling the gap he left behind. He moved to within five feet of Sterling, untied his mask, and removed his bowler. Martha audibly gasped, but he forced himself not to look at her. He couldn't, not yet, or he would fall to pieces. No matter how much he wanted to snatch her up in his arms and race away with her, he couldn't. They had a job to do, and it was bigger than her and him.

His once friend and trusted partner's eyes momentarily widened before thinning to slits. "Why, Mr. Lark, what gives you the audacity to interrupt my performance?"

Garrett met his hard stare. His lip twitched. "I wanted to show you something I learned during my time away." His fingers coiled into a fist.

He barely heard Daniel's muffled "Garrett, stick to the plan!" right before driving his fist into Sterling's ugly, evil, ever-lovin' face.

34

Martha's husband—her *real* husband—was alive. While she, his wife, had willingly agreed to be with another man. *Oh, God,* she lamented, *you spared his life, but could you not spare him this?*

As Garrett's fist drew back for a second blow, Kayus lurched forward, his own knuckles poised to strike. She knew they would be no match. He would slam his strongman's blow through her husband's skull and kill him. Throwing herself between them, she raised her arms to block Kayus, only barely aware of Garrett's shout, "Martha, no!"

Unable to stop his trajectory, Kayus halted a second too late. The misdirected force slammed her backward and her spine connected with the show floor, the force knocking her against the dirt. As pain pulsed down her sides, she instinctively covered her stomach for protection. Her head spun, chandelier lights blurring in her vision. She expected Garrett to rush forward—and he did—but Kayus reached her first, drawing her up and into him, placing his hands protectively against her back. "I'm sorry, Martha. You know I would never hurt you."

No, she didn't know that. He had promised to protect her and then hurt her nearly every night with his contempt. Had he known Garrett still lived? Surely Mr. Sterling had. When she twisted from Kayus's grip, he let her, instead moving his hands to rest upon her middle. The baby visibly tumbled within. "Did I hurt it?" he asked. She could almost believe he cared.

Laying her palm upon her stomach elicited another quiver of movement. "I think he'll be fine."

Her eyes tipped up, finally meeting Garrett's anguished expression. He had noticed everything—the baby, Kayus's tender embrace, and the obvious smirk upon the strongman's lips. Garrett no doubt believed that the very man who helped Mr. Sterling destroy their lives was also her baby's father. Perhaps he even believed they had entwined hearts as well as bodies. She shook her head. *No, never*, she mouthed. *I love you alone.*

Garrett tore his gaze away.

"...come into *my* theater," Sterling was saying, "frighten *my* performers, then assault me in front of them? It's hardly civilized behavior."

"From what our brother says, you aren't very civilized yourself." Four more figures broke from the circle, removing their masks simultaneously. Relief rushed through her at the sight of Tobias and Jamison, Cade alive beside them, and a fourth man whom she had never met but, by his similar features, she assumed to be Daniel. How they came to be together didn't matter so much as that they were here. Her family had come for her and brought an army, besides. Finally, this nightmare might come to an end.

"Ashley Sterling," Tobias said. "We're here to see you answer for your crimes."

"With this ragtag group? I hardly think they'd find reason. Honestly, fellows, how much did this man pay you to believe his lies? I can equally compensate. If you'll come with me..." Mr. Sterling started for the foyer doors, but the men maintained their human wall. Behind their masks, venomous eyes smoldered.

Garrett waved an arm to his followers. "These are the men whose friends and neighbors you kidnapped and murdered. It turns out they have plenty of reasons to seek revenge."

The remaining audience members' chatter fell to a low murmuring. *Murder*, they likely whispered. *This man? Surely not. He's a beloved staple in the community.*

"What about you?" Mr. Sterling scoffed. "You're the one who found them for me."

"Yes, and I've been making amends ever since. Probably will be until the day I die. Surprising as it seems, I think death would be too easy for you. Many of these men, however, do not agree."

Mr. Sterling's smile wavered, hardly at all, but enough that Martha noticed. Even in his times of fury, he had always worn a static arrogance, as he had known that, in the end, he always won. But now, slight cracks emerged in his assurance, a tiny spark of uncertainty she knew must be exploited.

"Hey!" someone yelled from the stands. "What's this? If it ain't part of the show, sit down and let's go." *Yes, precisely*, she thought. Guards framed every exit. They needed to separate Sterling from his men.

"Maybe you can come to an agreement," she told him. "Let the show proceed while you speak with the Larks in private."

At her suggestion, the tension in the ringmaster's chest seemed to ease. He smiled. "Sensible girl. I knew I chose well with you. Mr. Lark," he addressed Garrett, "you and I shall discuss terms in my office alone."

Garrett didn't budge. "Where I go, Martha goes. I'm not leaving her again."

"Where Martha goes, I go," Kayus replied. He helped her to her feet, his arm coming to rest possessively around her waist. She could tell Garrett wanted to throw punches again, but all he said was, "If your master receives his trusted second, then I'll have mine. Cade—"

"No," Mr. Sterling cut in. "You chose Martha. If you want a man, I choose for you. Daniel."

"Fine."

"And my daughter joins us."

It felt like a trick. It almost certainly was. His intentions couldn't be trusted. Garrett must know that, too, yet he nodded anyway.

"Excellent." Mr. Sterling turned back to the audience, his arms raised high again. "Sincere apologies, sirs, but I'm afraid an urgent matter has arisen. If you would be so kind as to exit the theater, you will all receive a free ticket at the front. And, of course, the Garden is always open for business."

262

35

Garrett had no misinterpretations that Sterling would renege on his word the first chance he found. He had no plan to negotiate with the man and no illusions that he could. The only negotiation would be whether Sterling would leave the premises on his own two feet, hogtied across the back of Garrett's horse, or buried six feet in the ground.

"Keep an eye on the guards," he told Tobias and Jamison before heading upstairs. "Stay to the plan, but have our men at the ready. Cade, Melvin, remain outside the office door in case I need you."

Tobias clapped his shoulder. "Be careful, brother."

"You, too."

Garrett turned to Martha, ready to extend his arm, only to find her already arm-in-arm with Clary, their hands clasped tightly together. Her eyes avoided his. He immediately thought, *Please, no, don't do this to me*, then instantly filled with remorse. Shouldn't he consider instead what had been done to *her*?

She hadn't meant for this to happen and hadn't wanted it; he must believe that. For months, the thought of her had kept him going, kept him alive, kept him sane. He pressed on because he knew she needed him. She still needed him, didn't she?

He felt her presence behind him the entire way up the white marble staircase, down the corridor, and into Harvest Hill. There, she and Clary parted, Martha finally moving to Garrett's side, although still not meeting his gaze. The situation felt too similar to that of months ago, except time had matured him in ways no man should experience. His newfound wisdom, however, meant he wouldn't be taken advantage of. Not this time.

Sterling removed his ringmaster's jacket, then laid it across his desktop. Beneath he wore a crimson waistcoat with a gold pocket chain and golden buttons. By one glance, it was clear the man wore neither pistol nor revolver. "Friends—" he began. *Ha, hardly*, Garrett inwardly seethed. "As you can see, Kayus and I are unarmed. You will accommodate me then, if I ask you to remove your own firearms. I find them so...distasteful."

"I find you distasteful, and yet here you remain."

He chuckled. "Such cheek, Mr. Lark. I thought you wished to play fair."

"I do. The way I see it, we're in your territory. It seems fair that Daniel and I receive an extra assurance of your hospitality."

Sterling's fingers flexed, a faint tick visible in his upper jaw. "You may have survived that ship, but if I go down, I will ensure you follow directly behind."

"Now who refuses to play fair?" He side-eyed Martha, her hands clasped upon her burgeoned middle. If he went to jail and Kayus didn't, would the other man care for her and their child? Would he give her everything she needed, cherish her like she deserved? Had his time with Martha changed his heart? Logic told him the law would not see Kayus free, but logic also told him that life often defied expectation.

No one made a move to sit, rather stiffly scattered throughout the room, Sterling nearest his desk, Kayus nearest the door, and everyone else in between. "Mr. Sterling," Daniel began. He stood before the hutch, its clock ticking each passing second. "A man should not be tried before all the evidence is procured. Therefore, we've asked Tobias and Jamison to perform a sweep of your theater and question your performers. We weren't here when everything occurred, nor will the police have been, so the more your employees contradict the accusations, the better it will find you. Does that not seem reasonable?"

"Reasonable enough." Sterling moved to the window, his back to them all. Even without looking, Garrett knew what he would find.

Closed stable doors and battened backstage curtains. Forty-two men plus his brothers questioning each performer and guard in turn. If the guards had intended to stop them, he would have already heard the commotion.

Ashley Sterling had become a powerful man, known by all and loved by none. So many missed opportunities to create something magnificent instead of something wretched. To offer intimacy filled with loveliness when it wasn't forced and bought and paid for. His soul had been sacrificed for his own desires. Love traded for greed.

Similar to the path Garrett nearly followed. He shuddered to think how close he had come.

"It's over," Clary said. "You know no one will defend you, not with those men to finally bring them hope. Before it ends, this place will be nothing but ash, and I, for one, am glad for my part in it."

"It was you who sabotaged the show?" Sterling whirled, murder in his eyes as he lifted the desk's ornamental globe paperweight. Then his attention flicked to Garrett, hand now on his holster, and he slammed the weight back to the desktop. "You helped kill my horses," he growled.

"I did not. I only added the salt and turned a blind eye when Martha tried to escape. Everything else was another performer out of spite." Her eyes flashed. "I wish I'd done it all. You murdered my father. You don't deserve to be rewarded for that."

Sterling sniffed. "He was only a negro."

"As am I."

"Only half," Daniel said softly. "Your mother was our mother, too."

Garrett had anticipated this moment, when Clary would discover the truth about her parentage. He fully expected her to draw inward as she had when her true paternity had been announced. To sit in shock as she tried to reconcile the pieces of her life. Either that or become enraged that she was related to a family that tore her own apart.

Rather, a single tear trailed her cheek until it caught upon the corner of her upturned lips. Without so much as a glance at her manipulative father, she ran to Daniel and threw herself against him, her head tucked close beneath his chin. His grip as fierce as hers, his cheeks as red as the blush her skin could not provide, he held her with a strength she had deserved all her life. "I cannot believe it," she murmured again and again. "I have family, true and good." She didn't know Daniel from Adam, yet she clung to him as though he had protected her all her life, and his solid grip now promised that he would.

"Did you know?" Martha asked Garrett, her first words to him since the circus floor. At last, her eyes rose to his. Such sadness lay within.

Whether her baby was Kayus's or not, he loved her. Had likely loved her since the Westward Trail. Always would. To return to her, he had braved fiery furnaces, stormy seas, stagecoaches, and Pernella's temptations. Throughout his life, he had made unconscionable mistakes, been with many women, and made deals with all the worst men. He didn't deserve a wife at all, much less her. But Jamison would tell him that none of them deserved God's graces. If He gave them what they deserved, they would all be burning.

If they survived this, he would do what he set out to eight months ago when she and Cade appeared in his hotel. He would love her with every muscle, sinew, and fiber, as a husband should. Together, they would build a life in Larksong. They may never be able to leave; the law likely would never change, but he could remain in one place forever if it meant being with her and their child.

Or Kayus's. It would take a while to overcome his feelings on that, but in time, he knew he could.

He eased his hand into hers. "I didn't know she was my half-sister. Not until recently."

"Enough!" Sterling's temple pulsed like he was about to explode. The flush of his cheeks rivaled *Arletta*'s furnace flames. "Your father and I had an agreement. Clary is mine! She cannot testify against me. She has no say. Who would believe her word?"

"I do." Martha spoke to Sterling; however, her gaze remained on Garrett. "I've seen everything. You blamed me for everything. You sent Nora to the Garden and left Hiram an orphan. You gave me no choice but to be with Kayus or join her there, and I am not the only one. There is not a single person here who respects you anymore."

"Your tainted skin is darker than my daughter's. Nora blacker still. No authority will listen to your lies." Sterling removed himself several paces, palms again braced against the window frame. "Besides, if you plan to throw stones, best you select some for your husband."

"What've I done?" Kayus asked. "I've always been loyal to you."

"I wasn't referring to you."

A tick twitched in the strongman's jaw while Garrett felt the same beat in his own. Martha had married Kayus in his absence? Not merely given herself to but actually *married*? Her fingers gripped his and he didn't know if he should jerk himself away. He felt so betrayed although he knew he had no reason. His wife loved him. She had undoubtedly thought herself a widow and well within moral grounds to remarry, especially when it saved her from the Garden. Yet, when she poured her heart out, his first instinct wanted to blame her.

That night at the Cathedral, Cade had told him, "Everyone always asks why didn't God do this or why didn't God stop that, but they never ask why the devil did this or stopped that. Satan will do anything to get us to choose him instead and so, it's harder to resist."

How devious, indeed.

As though the devil himself had heard, Sterling's wicked grin reflected in the window panes. "Each of you Larks have committed your own moral atrocities. What about all those slaves, Daniel? I remained forthright with my intentions. You knew what they were headed for when you sold them to me."

Clary's chin snapped to Daniel, her voice hardly more than a breath. "You sold him slaves?"

"I didn't want to. You have to believe me. He said he would kill my brothers if I didn't!"

"Poppycock," Sterling sniffed. "I love the Gifted. I've built my life on their talents. Why would I kill some of the most Gifted men I know?"

"Because we wouldn't join you," said Garrett. "Your life isn't built on the talents of the Gifted. It's built on control of them. Like our father, creating what you want, everyone else be hanged."

"That's all anyone ever does, Mr. Lark. Don't matter if he's Judas or Jesus."

"You're despicable."

Sterling laughed, low and cynical and...if Garrett had to find a word for it...evil. The circus master relished his malevolence.

"Despicable, am I? Who is more despicable, the man who sells a person's body or the one who buys her? The one who finds her so she can be bought? I earned more than a few dollars from you over the years, and that was long before we formed a partnership."

"Then that makes me despicable too. But I'm ready to right the wrong. I know what you did, and you can bet I will testify against you in the name of those who can't."

"Place your wager, Mr. Lark. I doubt you're willing to pay what it will cost."

Without warning, he snagged the paperweight and hurled it at his daughter. Daniel turned his body into her, however a second too late. The marble globe slammed into her bicep then to the floor with a sickening crunch, shards shattering in every direction. Even in Daniel's grip, she stumbled to her knees, her hand grasping at her shoulder with painful moans.

"Your own daughter?" Daniel shouted. "How could you do this?"

"Because he's a monster," Martha whispered, "and that's all he knows."

"Evil doesn't equal ignorance." Garrett lunged at Sterling, only to be side-tackled by Kayus midstream. They slammed into the sofa back with such force, it toppled forward against the coffee table. Kayus's arm, seemingly dense as a tree trunk and twice as heavy, pinned him against the sofa's underside, his legs flailing for anything they could reach.

His wife rushed forward, the strain evident as she braced one hand beneath her stomach, the other against her lower back.

"No, Martha! Stay away!" He grappled for his revolver, but his arms were pinned, also keeping his knife at bay. Swinging his foot around, his boot heel caught Kayus across the neck, and the larger man finally fell sidelong, unfortunately taking Garrett with him. They rolled into an armchair, Kayus gaining the upper hand once again.

Where was Daniel?

One glance found his brother cradling Clary as blood soaked

through the handkerchief pressed against her wound. Her eyes half lidded, her injured arm hung limp, fingers trailing the floor. Black marble shards shimmered around them like darkened diamonds.

Garrett jerked his head to the right a second before the strongman's fist slammed into the floor beside him, so close he felt the air whoosh against his ear.

"Kayus, don't!" He shifted again, narrowly avoiding a blow that would have surely cracked his jaw. "Help us fight him."

The other man's eyes burned bright. "He always wins."

"Interesting, because I don't intend to lose."

Martha's scream snapped both their attention around. Sterling had her by the arm, wrenching her behind the desk toward the inset wall cupboard. Juggling a key from his waistcoat pocket, he unlocked and opened the center door. *Well, I'll be...* he thought. It wasn't a cupboard, after all, but the entrance to another room.

She dug her heels in, leaning against Sterling's pull. "Move!" he shouted in her face. "Move if you have any care for your baby's life." That set her feet forward. She climbed into the cupboard, the circus master directly behind. *It's happening all over again*, Garrett thought. The two of them torn apart like before.

"Cade! Melvin!"

At the same time the door flew open, Kayus seized Garrett's revolver. A thunderous explosion rang through his ears, plaster and paint shattering as the bullet tunneled through its victim and into the wall beyond.

For a solid minute, the world muffled like water beneath the ocean waves. He struggled back to the surface as Melvin shoved Kayus off him with one determined boot kick. The strongman's corpse sprawled the floor, dark crimson tracing the white marble tiles to the hearth.

Melvin reached out a hand to Garrett, lifting him to his feet. A stream of blackpowder smoke drifted from the revolver in his opposite grip. "One down. One to go."

36

Moisture and wood rot emanated from the depths within Sterling's cupboard. Short and straight, its hidden corridor quickly shifted from wooden boards to a stone staircase. Martha descended the first step, Garrett's shouts fading with Mr. Sterling's closure of the cupboard door. Above them, amber gas lamps cast shadows along the rough-hewn walls, their silhouettes like elongated ghosts along the floor.

"Why are these lamps lit?" he muttered.

"Should they not be?"

Ignoring her question, his fist prodded into her back. "Get moving." Twelve more stairs and they reached a landing. Another staircase angled left, the amber lights continuing a downward path into a corridor which appeared to have been dug away rather than constructed. A mine shaft, perhaps? She didn't know; she had never seen one, only heard of them. At a fork in the path, Sterling pushed her right.

"You don't have to do this," she told him.

"People always say that when they have nothing else to bargain with. I could indeed 'not do this,' as you say, but here is what you fail to understand. I am willing to lose what I've built to gain something better."

"What of the Gifted? You said there aren't many left. You would abandon them? You would let the Larks claim your legacy?"

He wrenched her elbow back, jolting her to a stop. Spittle peppered her face while a distant *drip-drip-drip* assaulted her ears.

"You're such a stupid girl for such a pretty face. The Larks will claim nothing I haven't willingly allowed. Many of my performers are legitimately Gifted, but the rest, like you, are liars." His grip tightened as he drew her closer, the heft of her baby wedged between them. "You think I didn't know you made it up? Bringing the Gifted together was the start of my scheme, but it was never about that. It's so easy to convince people they're special, when they have nothing else to live for."

"You thought I had nothing else to live for?"

At the bottom of the staircase, stood Rella, one hand perfectly poised against the jagged rock wall, the other propped upon her holstered revolver. Braided chestnut waves draped her tan blouse, tucked into a simple skirt of gingham green. No rouge on her lips, no charcoal around her eyes. When she smiled, she became the woman from the westward trail, the way she could have been if Clinton Reed had never come along.

Martha ached to ask after Julep, except she couldn't let Sterling have the answer. If Rella had returned, she must believe Julep also was safe.

Rella released a puff of laughter. "You are so predictable, Ashley. So in love with the sound of your own voice."

Either forgetting he still grasped Martha's arm or not caring that he did, Mr. Sterling strode forward, dragging her along with him. He jabbed a finger under his wife's chin. "How dare you show your face here."

"You'd prefer it to be masked?"

All three jolted as a gunshot shattered the silence, echoing down the stairwell. "Garrett," Martha breathed. Had Kayus killed him? Had he killed Kayus? What of the others?

Please, Lord. I can't bear to lose any more of my family. There's still so much I haven't said.

As she finished her prayer, a door slammed open from above. "Sterling!" a man yelled. Cade, perhaps? A stampede hustled downward, or what echoed to produce such assumptions. Footsteps pounded closer with each passing second.

Rella casually lolled her chin toward the coming storm. Her tone

271

lay sweet as home-spun sugar. "Make a choice, Ashley. I guarantee they won't be as kind as I am."

What Martha had noticed before as a slight crack in Mr. Sterling's confidence now shattered before her. Even the amber light could not conceal his ashen pallor. It was true then; even the most confident—or the most vile—of men could still be shaken.

Releasing her, he shoved past the women and sprinted down the corridor, his shoe soles pounding his retreat. Rella puckered her lips after him. "Kiss, kiss, Ashley dear! Oh, I do hope I'll find something else to live for."

Mere minutes later, Cade and Melvin crashed down the stairs. The latter peered down the corridor with eyes black as night. "Where'd he go?"

"It doesn't matter," Martha cried. "We have to help the others." She gripped Cade's arm. "Who was shot? Is Garrett all right?"

"He's fine." He glanced over his shoulder. "Just a little short on air. That strongman flattened him then tried to kill him. It was Melvin's revolver you heard."

Martha blinked, gas lights swimming upon the face of the stranger who had saved her husband. Those hardened eyes...yet, as she examined them, they softened. A smile parted his lips, revealing a slight gap between his second and third teeth. Years ago, it had been wider. Large enough to ride a horse through, they had once joked.

She gasped and dropped Cade's arm. She knew those eyes, that crooked nose, that mouth. The rest of him she didn't recognize, but she still knew—she *knew*. Every day she had wondered what became of him. Every day, she hoped, she prayed, but could never bring herself to ask...and now...

"Lemuel?"

The little boy she knew peered out from behind those aged eyes. When he spoke, every word strained with emotion. "Ya, sis, it's...it's me."

More footfalls stampeded down the stairs. Garrett appeared, and his hands were on her arms, then his arms around her, whispering incomprehensible sentiments. She clung to him without words, none except her repeated prayer of thanksgiving.

"Cade, keep going," she thought she heard him say. "Stick to the plan." Was this part of the plan? Cade ran off, followed by Rella. All she could do was stare.

Lemuel reached for her, and Garrett relinquished her into his embrace. Her brother who had been wide-eyed and afraid, a mere stick of a thing, was now tall and strong and brave. He had saved her husband, the father of her child. His arms promised familial protection she hadn't experienced for so long. Once, it had been her way to care for him, but now he would care for her.

"But how?" she asked.

"Your husband. It seems he knew exactly where to look."

She thought she heard Garrett say, "If you're that surprised to see him, wait until you hear about Josiah."

"Josiah's alive?" How was this possible? None of this could be real. Everything began spinning, the amber lights and the rock walls swirling into a flood of gold and grey. "How is Clary?" she managed to ask.

"Jamison's with her now. He tore up the stairs when he heard the gunshot. Between him and Daniel, she's going to be just fine."

Martha smiled. "I'm so glad." Warmth enveloped her—*peace* enveloped her—and she welcomed it, surrounded by her husband and her brother, safe at last.

37

Ashley Sterling ran. For the first time in his life, he was outnumbered and outmatched. He knew when to count his losses, pack up and head out, at least, metaphorically so. He would be unable to physically pack his belongings, but hopefully there would still be time to secure his finances from the bank. Then he could start anew, on his terms, as he always did. His circus had gone to rot, so he would let it. He could fashion other opportunities elsewhere.

He pounded down the old mine shaft, the start of his dynasty before he had created his theatrical empire. The empire now crumbling around him. He could do better. He always did.

The pier lay just ahead. *Arletta* wouldn't return for several months, but his two-man schooner remained anchored as always. He could sail along the bay and dock inconspicuously among the other vessels. He would collect his money and be on his way.

At the entrance to the pier, however, as the dim lamps of the mine opened into moonlight, he discovered he was not the first to arrive. A negro monstrosity, skin black as sin, shoulders wide as a stallion's rump, stood at the water's edge. His shirt billowed in the breeze, hands fisted against his hips like a heinous pirate or a man who remembered this pier all too well.

Sterling stumbled backward, seeking shelter in the darkness. No, this could not be. He had seen that traitor stabbed, watched him bleed out upon the floor. How was he still alive?

He could accept one menace surviving, but all three?

274

Inconceivable.

Josiah's voice rumbled low. "Where's my dau-ter, Sterling?"

Ashley didn't have his revolver. Never carried it. Never needed to. He had the circus under his thumb. All his guards were perfectly loyal. His performers didn't admire but rather feared him. He had no need for weapons. His power was enough.

It would not be enough this time.

He pivoted away, down the opposite path, the one which led to the original entrance to the mine. Stumbling down another flight of stairs, he passed into the depths of forgotten gold dust, decay, and utter darkness. He clicked a knob along the wall and more gas lamps ignited, revealing another long tunnel with stone walls and a packed-earth floor. The lamps' amber globes sizzled away years of dust and neglect, their smoky scent whispering around him. Thinner paths jutted off like veins in an arm, each one having carried gold to the bloodline of his business. Many miners had died in those depths, but that had never concerned him. Their lives wouldn't have amounted to much anyway.

Up ahead, he heard noises. *The whispers of the cave*, he told himself. *Dripping water or bats*. But he knew they were not. Footsteps echoed against the rock, drawing closer by the second. Behind him more followed from the opposite path. "Sterling!" Tobias shouted. The footsteps slowed. "I know you're there."

Of course, he did. He had Garrett and Garrett knew where everyone was. Another massive disappointment found in that one. He could have amounted to so much. Garrett Lark could have been as spectacular as Sterling himself.

"It's over," Josiah called behind him. His steps, too, lessened. "You have nowhere lefta go."

Below the path, a wide crevice trailed into darkness and Sterling stilled, listening to the future close in. Josiah would kill him. If he had survived *Arletta*, he wouldn't care if he died now. He would kill Sterling, even if it killed him, too. If he failed at that, there were plenty of men in the theater waiting for Ashley's blood. Garrett might claim to offer a fair compromise, but that confounded Lark knew what he was. Vengeance lay right around the corner like a train which would never stop.

Well, Alonzo, it turns out we both lost. Only, unlike his friend, Ashley Sterling would decide when the game was over. He had built his legacy and he alone would end it. With a final breath, he stepped off into the ravine.

38

That night, in its darkest deadened hours, Garrett sat behind Sterling's desk in Harvest Hill, alone with his thoughts and all the ghosts of this place. And upon the desktop, a substantial stack of legal documents. In a strange twist, Sterling had left the circus to Alonzo. Since he was dead, however, it passed to Daniel, who of course, didn't want it. As Sterling's most recent business partner, that left Garrett to decide what to do with the most wicked place on Earth.

For the first time in almost two decades, the circus lay silent. All shows canceled; the Garden closed. Women and men seeing the outside, their eyes wide with the unfamiliar touch of moist ocean air. The performers had kindly taken in those from the Garden, offering them rooms within their own, providing them with bedding, food, and proper clothing. Caring for their physical ailments along with their emotional ones.

What was he to do with all these people? Some had chosen to return home, but there were over a hundred left without families, each suffering nightmares wrought by Sterling's hand. His Gift still couldn't locate the circus master, no matter how he tried. When Josiah and Tobias met up in the mine, they found a fresh set of prints in the dirt beside a ravine. Even with the gas lamps, it was too dark to observe the chasm, but logic said it was the only way Sterling could have gone without being seen. Had he fallen in or jumped? Either way, he had been swallowed up by his own pit of darkness and the irony was not lost on any of them.

To cross the T's and dot the I's, they summoned the police, but it seemed not a soul in town cared if Ashley Sterling had jumped to his death. With the briefest investigation, the police ruled it a suicide and called for a reading of the will.

By the time they returned to the theater, every one of the guards had fled, including Julio. That coward had disappeared even before their failed office negotiations. Whereto, Garrett knew well. If any of them had half a mind, they would travel far from here and never show their faces again.

He glanced at the clock on the hutch—a quarter to four in the morning. The great marble fireplace lay dark and cold. After the furnaces of *Arletta*, he had no desire to relight it. He knew fire was necessary to life—one couldn't cook, heat water, or mold metal without it—but for now, he could avoid the memories sure to come calling soon enough. So much guilt swelled inside him. He didn't know how to face that or how to begin to move on.

He pressed his thumbs to his eyelids and sighed. Martha would worry if she woke and he wasn't there. They had gone to sleep that night in silence, the baby wedged between them and her cheek against his shoulder as he stroked her hair. There was so much they needed to discuss, tears they both needed to cry, but neither was willing to offer their vulnerability to the other. Nothing felt safe between them yet.

But it would. One day, he was certain, everything would be wonderful again.

As she drifted off, she had whispered, "I love you, Garrett. Thank you for finding Lemuel and...and for coming back for me."

He had held her close, tears threatening. "You're welcome. I—I love you, too." He only wished he'd been able to bring her entire family home. What had happened to them, he didn't know. It had been shock enough when he searched for Lemuel and found him standing across the room.

Divine providence; it was the only way to explain it. How he should have trusted God first rather than trusting in everything else before Him.

Now, he was about to face a home he had never been to, a family he hadn't lived with in years, and a wife he barely knew. He was to be a father to a child born out of pain and regret and violation but who would be loved more than life itself. He didn't have the strength to raise this child as he should.

Nevertheless, it had also been his mistakes which inadvertently brought this child into being. He didn't regret that.

"They're coming home with us," he announced to the empty room. "Every person here will find a home in Larksong." He would sell the circus building and use the money to bring everyone back to Washington. Perhaps they would even create a new show, a place that was honest behind the scenes as well as on the show floor. It could be the type of career, home, and hearth his mother would have been proud to see her children pursue—all six of them.

Turning down the lamps, he locked the office and tiptoed back to Martha's room, the same suite she used to share with her three roommates. Lissie had chosen to return to Savannah with her parents, both surprisingly spared from Sterling's murderous tendencies. Nora, now freed from the Garden, slept with Hiram in the children's quarters. Meanwhile June, distraught over Kayus's death, had collected her things and left the circus without a backward glance.

Turning down the lamp in the sitting room, Garrett discarded his shoes and shirt and slipped into bed. His arms slipped around his wife's back to wrap her waist, right above her middle. Dipping his chin, he bent to kiss her neck, right where her wedding rings rested upon her clavicle. Clary had returned the silver chain after Jamison examined her, swathed her upper arm in medicinal-soaked strips, then declared it a clean break and thankfully, nothing more. It was too early, however, to say if her fire tending days were behind her.

Martha's eyelids fluttered open. "What is it? Is someone hurt? Did they find Mr. Sterling?"

"No. He's gone for good." He smiled with another kiss, this time to her cheek. "I have plans, Martha. So many wonderful plans for us. You, me, and—the baby." He shifted one palm to her stomach only to feel an assault from inside. Startled, he drew away, but she grabbed his wrist and splayed his fingers back upon her middle. Once more, joyous movement rippled against his palm. Tears threatened his masculine willpower and he reached to wipe them away.

"Don't." She took his opposite hand in hers and corded their fingers together. Ever so slowly, she lifted them to her lips and laid a kiss upon each knuckle. Her eyes studied him from beneath her own wet lashes. "He's yours, Garrett."

"The baby?"

She nodded. "Yours. Really and truly."

"But Rella didn't say anything—"

"She didn't know. I discovered I was with child after she left, and it had been long before Kayus and I ever—" Her forehead dropped, her tears warm as they fell upon their entangled fingers. She shifted sideways, her fingers slipping from his to reach for his cheek, gently caressing his beard as though such a simple action might regain hold of everything slipping away. "Oh, Garrett," she sobbed. "Won't you please forgive me?"

A cry ripped from his chest and he clutched her against him, drawing her as close as could be with their child between them. *Their* child, and he had almost lost them both. With every breath, agony tumbled from his heart and through his lips. His pain wasn't quiet, but no one would come running. The whole of the circus knew what they had endured.

Together, they wept for the days they could never regain. For the people Sterling stole who they couldn't save. For the family members they could never have back. They could start over, hopefully find happiness, but it could never restore that which never existed. With thankfulness, they wept for Julep, that she had not succumbed to a worse fate. Her innocence remained intact and one day, perhaps the past might be forgotten. Finally, they wept for all the nights Martha spent with Kayus while her heart belonged to Garrett and her soul cried out to God.

She shuddered within the circle of his arms. Her tears finally slowed and his lessened with them. "God was with me in every moment," she said softly. "Of that I'm certain. He held my hand while I suffered, then comforted me after all was done. Through all that pain, He brought about something greater, but oh, how I wish there had been another way."

Waves of emotion flooded through Garret. "I wish there had been. I should have never become involved with Sterling."

"Would you have ever wanted me if you hadn't?"

Through the blur, he felt her shift and peer up at him. The baby thrashed unexpectedly and kicked him in the stomach, temporarily knocking the wind out of them both. Together, they laughed. He lifted a lock of her hair and tucked it behind her ear. "I think I always wanted you."

"But would you have ever truly loved me? If Sterling hadn't come along, hadn't had the brothel, hadn't given you a chance to change, to be a better man, would you have?"

He turned away, heart thrumming with painful knowledge. It was similar to what Daniel had said, that if he never came west, Martha would still be enslaved in Hawthorn Ridge. "Maybe I would have, if I'd gone straight to Washington. If I had never been so obsessed over figuring out what my Gift wanted—

Gently, she tipped his chin back to face her. "Don't you see, Garrett? This *was* what your Gift wanted. Sterling had already set his mind long before you arrived in California. He would have done it either way. Had you not needed to return for me, he still would be. You saved so many."

"How can you see such beauty in such an ugly face? You ask me for forgiveness and I grant it freely, but can you truly do the same after all those women I took before you? How little I must have made them feel. I never rightly understood it before now."

She was still smiling. Why in the world was she still smiling?

Gently, she pressed her lips to his, letting them flutter like butterfly wings upon a flower. "Garrett, of course, I forgive you. You are the last person I want to lose. 'Above all, let your love for one another be intense, because love covers a multitude of sins.' King Solomon said that and he was with almost a thousand women."

Garrett choked. "*A thousand?* You're making me feel pretty good about my number now."

Martha laughed. "That only means that if God could use Solomon for his purpose after having all those wives and concubines, he can certainly use you."

"I think this is why I married you. You believe in me more than I deserve."

Teasing her fingers within his beard, she drew his lips to hers in a song lovelier than the one she sang at the circus. Together, their voices raised a new melody, sweet and supple, full of faith, hope, and the love that made two become one by the child held between them.

The Lord truly did work all things for good, for a good Father's work could only be based in love. The kind that offered forgiveness and understood pain; that sacrificed everything. The love that sailed around the world to save what it had lost.

The kind of earthly father Garrett never had.

The kind of husband and father he now trusted the Lord would teach him how to be.

39

Now that a "Permanently Closed" sign hung on the front gate of Sterling's Theatrical, Cade wanted nothing more than to return to Larksong, his daughter, and his recently completed fishing schooner. Assuming the boat hadn't been stolen, destroyed in a storm, or lost its anchor and floated away. That would be bad luck for business. But what, truly, were a few more hard times after all he'd been through? It was almost to be expected.

Unfortunately, his life in Washington would have to wait a little longer. Sterling's theater lights might be extinguished, but their work here was not. Garrett sat behind the circus master's massive desk, sorting through obscure files and burning most of them. Cade and Daniel, meanwhile, received the dreary task of packing Sterling's belongings into crates: either to leave behind, sell, donate, or take with them back to Washington. Cade would have preferred to toss everything into the chasm Sterling had supposedly fallen into, but respected Garrett's approach that doing so would be a waste.

Cade worked silently alongside his brother, separating literary volumes and countless knick-knacks from the bookshelves. Some would be useful back home, although most not. He threw a pair of charred fire batons into the "leave behind" pile and reached for a worn compass. Aiming it toward the window, the arrow didn't shift, the device clearly broken. Still, it reminded him of another time and a nearly-forgotten memory. Back when life was uncomplicated, before his mother died and he held another compass similar to this one, yet rather different.

At eight years old, he had been a typical curious boy, always wanting to be where his brothers were, always desiring to learn new things. One day, such curiosity led him to hide behind his father's office curtains, listening to Alonzo converse about things he couldn't yet understand. At the time, his father's associate had been a stranger. Only now did Cade recognize him for who he truly was.

"Sterling," his father had said. "I've amassed a fortune here. I have everything I want. I have no need to traipse to the frontier and risk everything I've built. You, too, have built a fair establishment."

"Indeed, my friend," Sterling replied, "but is that enough? Did our fathers not say our Gifts' origin lies in the west? Did not our grandfathers? We find that shipwreck and perhaps we find everything."

"Even if you do find it—unlikely—how do you intend to retrieve it? Unless you have the Gift of gills as well."

"I will find someone who can. Seven men returned from that ship; one must have a suitable heir. Someone who can sink down low or move the waters of the sea to allow me entrance. I have an acquaintance in Louisiana who has heard whisperings of a new theory, that humankind evolved from lesser beings. Why should we be surrounded by mere mortals when the Gifted are clearly the future of this world?"

"We are not God, Sterling. What you are suggesting is both blasphemy and likely treason. I rule the largest plantation in the South; I have no need to rule the world."

"You aim too low, Alonzo. I fear that will be your downfall."

"I fear the heights you reach for will be yours."

The men left soon after, and Cade raced from the room, certain his curiosity had gotten him into trouble at last. Frightened, he ran to his mother and spilled his confession amidst tears and apologies.

"What'd he mean, Mama?" he cried. "Papa sounded so angry. I thought it was good to be Gifted."

"It is," his mother said. "Of course, it is. You'll discover your Gift soon enough and then you'll know it's true."

"What if I don't? Daniel doesn't have one."

His mother had stared at him thoughtfully for the longest time, a sad smile on her lips, her porcelain white fingers holding Cade's tight. Then finally, she said, "Come with me."

Quietly, they moved through the house and slipped back into his father's empty office. Only a sliver of light crept between the window curtains and cut across the floor to the bookcase. From the top shelf, she reached on tiptoe for a plain wooden box, then from that box removed a compass and pressed it into Cade's empty hands.

Kneeling before him, she covered his hands with her own. Her words fell with unexpected gravity. "Hide this, my darling. Tell no one you carry it, not until your father is buried and you have gone far from this place. He will discover it missing tonight, and I will to take the blame. Don't you dare tell him otherwise." Her fingers tightened around his. "The compass is the key, Cade. I trust you to protect it."

"Mama, I can't." The tears were returning. How could she entrust him with this, to lie to his papa, to not tell his brothers? "I'm too afraid," he gasped.

She smiled. "You won't always be."

That night, he heard his parents fighting as he huddled in his bed, and come morning, Daniel cut their mother's lifeless body down from the attic rafters. The brothers knew their father's Gift had persuaded her to do it, but only Cade knew the real reason for her murder.

The compass is the key, Cade. Mama had died for that secret. Maybe it was time to finally figure out why.

Weeks later, when the circus folk finally rode into Larksong, Cade among them, Julep ran to meet him, her smile as wide as the sea. With tears freely flowing, he swung her up into his arms. So relieved was he that, for the moment, the compass was forgotten.

That night, however, as he tucked his daughter into bed, he noticed the worried crinkle of her brow. "Sleep easy, Julep," he whispered. "The bad man is gone. You needn't be afraid anymore."

Her wondering eyes stared up at him. "Everybody says so, but I came home and you weren't here. Rella said you would be here, but then you weren't. Papa, it scared me."

He stroked her dark curls, their shade an exact match to his own. Was this how his own fears and anxieties began? That day behind the curtains listening to his father and Sterling, only a few years older than Julep was now? He never wished that strife upon her—always wondering, always afraid, never trusting herself or her emotions.

"I know it scared you, Julep. I was frightened, too. But we're together now and I'm not going anywhere."

"But sometimes you do. You leave to sell the fish."

That was true. He couldn't allow his livelihood to disintegrate. "Then I will have to bring you with me. I think you're old enough to start learning the fish trade. Your mama would be proud." He said it without thinking and immediately bit his lip, wishing he could steal the words back from his daughter's ears. Alice Ann would have been proud, but she also wasn't here.

Julep's expression sagged. Her lids drooped to the rag doll clutched in her arms, then slowly raised to meet her father's gaze. "Is that why Mama left? 'Cause I couldn't fish? Do you think she'd come back if I promised to learn really well?"

If a heart could shatter, his did in that moment, but he couldn't afford to sit with the pieces scattered around him. He had to sweep them up, shove them in a box, and for Julep's sake, pretend he had everything figured out. "I'm sorry, sweetheart, but nothing you do will bring her back. You weren't the reason she left." *I was*, he thought, then shoved that aside, too. He had promised himself on *Arletta* that he wouldn't dwell on the past anymore. Alice Ann was gone. He and Julep would have a new start.

"Besides," he assured her, "I think your mama knew you still had your aunties, Martha and Sarah and Coraline. Then God blessed us with even more family since the circus people came to live with us. The town is twice as big. And soon enough, you'll have a new little cousin which means Auntie Martha will count on you to help her. Can you do that, be my big girl?" He pinched her cheek and she laughed, swatting his hand away with her rag doll.

"Oh, Daddy, I'm not big at all."

"No, but you will be soon enough." He gave a slow smile then bent and kissed her brow. "Goodnight, jewel. I love you."

"Love you, too, Papa."

He drew closed the hanging sheets separating the bedroom and living spaces and sucked in a breath to stem any emotion where it lay. With a determined exhale, he strode to his traveling trunk and extracted an iron key from the hidden panel in its side. Slipping the key in the lock, the latches popped along with a thin layer of dust.

He rifled through his belongings, removing them into a pile at his feet, until he found the second hidden compartment at the bottom. The place where his father's compass had lain undisturbed for the past nine years.

Or so he had thought.

The compartment now lay completely bare.

Only one person had been trusted with the trunk key's location. A woman he hadn't seen in four years. A woman he lost his heart to the day they met.

So much for allowing himself a new start.

Rejecting anymore consideration, he sought out his brother. "Alright, Garrett, you win. Help me find my wife."

Larksong Legacy continues with Cade and Alice Ann's story in *Stars in the Storm.*

AUTHOR'S NOTE

Like the characters in *Sparks Fly Upward*, anxiety, human trafficking (modern-day slavery), sexual assault, and sex addiction affect millions of people worldwide every day. If you, or someone you know, live with these conditions, you are not alone. Hope is only a call or click away.

Focus on the Family Christian Counselor Assistance
1-855-771-HELP (4357)
https://www.focusonthefamily.com/get-help/

Substance Abuse and Mental Health Services Administration
1-800-662-HELP (4357)
https://samhsa.gov/find-help/national-helpline

National Suicide Prevention Lifeline
1-800-273-8255 or Text "TALK" to 741741
https://suicidepreventionlifeline.org/

U.S. Department of State Trafficking Hotline
1-888-373-7888
https://humantraffickinghotline.org/en/

National Center for Sexual Exploitation
https://endsexualexploitation.org/

USCCB Sexual Addiction Resources
https://www.usccb.org/topics/marriage-and-family-life-ministries/help-for-those-struggling

There are many additional resources available in addition to those listed. While the organizations listed above are United States based, similar organizations are available in other countries.

Have faith. Have hope. You have beautiful purpose.

HISTORICAL NOTES

Thank you, reader, for seeing this novel through until the end. To date, this was by far my most difficult story to write both creatively and due to the subject matter. I always want my novels to have a happy ending, but what a way for us to get there. Authors often say that their characters do what they want, and it's so true. Ashley Sterling fought me at every turn. I had to constantly pull back on his desire to be, simply put, the epitome of evil. Unfortunately, there are real-life people who choose to embrace lifestyles far worse than the ones I have portrayed.

Human Trafficking—The Modern-Day Slavery:

"Slavery doesn't exist anymore." I can't tell you how many times I've heard and read that statement. Through human trafficking, slavery is unfortunately still very prominent throughout the world. It happens in every U.S. state, every country, to people of all races, all ages, to men, women, and children. According to the U.S. National Trafficking Hotline, they receive over 50,000 signals related to sex and labor trafficking per year. That's about 1 instance reported every 10 minutes.

Similar to Ashley Sterling, traffickers often gain their victims' trust by targeting those with unstable families, in economic hardship, or who feel the trafficker offers better options than their current situation. The trafficker often lies to coerce them into coming along willingly or uses drugs to bring them under submission. Once within the trafficker's "care," although the victims may despise their situation, they often feel as though they have no other options and no escape.

Sparks Fly Upward deals with three forms of slavery:

- Forced Labor – When people think of slavery, this is most often what they picture. This type of trafficking includes industries such as domestic work, agriculture, construction, hospitality, and housekeeping. In *Sparks Fly Upward*, this is represented by the circus performers and Southern slavery.

- Sexual Exploitation – In modern terms, this would include areas such as forced prostitution, pornography, and strip clubs. In *Sparks Fly Upward*, this is represented by the Garden workers and Sterling's arranged marriages.

- Shanghaiing – Most prominent in the late 1800s, men would be coerced onto or drugged and taken aboard ships often sailing for the East China Sea. They would then be forced into labor, usually never to return home. In *Sparks Fly Upward*, this is represented by *Arletta*.

In addition, the following character names were taken from real life victims of human trafficking:

- Martha's birth name, Bakhita is from St. Josephine Bakhita, the patron saint of human trafficking.

- Clary's name comes from an 1806 Virginia bill of sale for a "negro girl slave named Clary." Clary was purchased to be a Fancy Girl, a slave used primarily for her master's sexual fulfillment. Although I don't know what happened to the real-life Clary, I was glad to be able to give my character a happier ending.

The Best Brand of Babies:

Ashley Sterling's goal of matching up "ideal" partners to create perfectly Gifted babies was inspired by the Nazi Lebensborn Society. From 1935 to 1944, this program built maternity homes for arranged sexual encounters between specially-selected German women and SS Officers to create "racially-pure" babies. In other instances, they provided care to unwed mothers, then gave their children to high-ranking German officials. More than 7,000 children were born through one of these two methods. While many of the mothers were forced to comply, there were many who considered their selection to be a great honor. As the war progressed, the program also began to kidnap Aryan infants and toddlers from occupied countries, adopting them out to German families.

For a fictional account of the Lebensborn program, I recommend reading *Cradles of the Reich* by Jennifer Coburn, although please note that it is not a clean read.

All Aboard the Screeching Peach:

The abandoned ship, *Fly Felicity*, that the fictional Screeching Peach Hotel is built into is based on a real ship called the *Niantic*. During the Gold Rush era, ships flooded into San Francisco Bay, each filled with men wanting to try their hand at gold mining. Unfortunately, most of the crew wanted their chance too and abandoned ship. According to the 1858 San Francisco City Directory, there were 1,583 arrivals that year to only 848 departures, the other 735 ships left in the bay, stacked on top of each other, and taking up space. That doesn't even include all the ships left from 1848 to 1857.

To rectify the situation, the city decided to sink most of them, fill in the land, and build over the top of it. Some of the ships, however, like the *Niantic,* were beached, built onto, and turned into storehouses, shops, hotels, and saloons.

Likewise, the octagonal layout of Sterling's Theatrical is based on the 19th century craze of creating octagon houses. The thought was that having eight sides instead of four allowed more sunlight and fresh air to flow throughout the house, increasing overall health. Sterling, however, took such a design and created a dark prison, the exact opposite of its intent.

A Church for all Seasons:

As a Catholic, being able to write and research real-life Catholic customs is such a joy for me. Did you know that, although wedding rings were not regularly worn by American men until the 20th century, the Catholic Church has included a tradition of the groom's ring since the 12th century? Or that Catholicism is one of the few Christian denominations that does not include a bridal vow of obedience?

Garrett and Martha's wedding ceremony was taken from the Traditional Latin Nuptial Low Mass. Some portions of the Mass were condensed for the sake of the story's pace and were also translated from Latin to English to assist the reader with understanding. Most modern Catholic weddings are now said in the vernacular.

Both Old St. Mary's Cathedral in San Francisco and the Cathedral of St. John & St. Finbar in Charleston (now the Cathedral of St. John the Baptist) are still open and available for daily Mass. In my research, I could not find if the priests there performed interracial marriages; therefore, Father Bolin's character is entirely of my imagination. I have otherwise tried to portray their background and architecture as accurately as possible.

Acknowledgments

As always—and I can't say it enough—thank you to my readers! An extra special thank you to my newsletter subscribers who stayed with me through my social media departure and provided valuable story input, especially those who suggested names for the villains. Thank you to Erin L. for the name Ashley, Jodi W. for the name Sterling, and Lisa L. for the name Kayus.

To my husband, Scott, for your out-of-the-box story ideas and especially for figuring out Sterling's ending. Love you, honey!

To my children who support me even though "all I ever do is write." You are my best creation.

To my parents, Ken and Ruth, and my godmother, Mary, for your continued inspiration and, like Garrett, for showing me that a loving father (or mother)'s work is never done.

To my fellow historical fiction author friends: Jennifer Q. Hunt, Susan Laspe, Rhonda Ortiz, and Tanya E. Williams for indulging my random emails and texts asking for ideas and obscure information, which you almost always find. You amaze me. Thank you!

To my beta readers: Ann, Jennifer, Ken, Mary, Ruth, Sarah, Sharon, Susan, Tanya, and Tiffany. For your many comments, suggestions, and edits. Also, for insisting way back in *For a Noble Purpose* that there was more to Gabriella's story. Originally, I had decided she died on the trail, but you saw a better way.

To my advance reader team, the Catholic Writers Guild, and the Christian Mommy Writers group. Thank you for your advice, reviews, posts, interviews, and well wishes!

To the many organizations who helped make my historical information accurate and believable, especially the Missouri Historical Society, St. Charles City-County Library, St. Louis County Library, San Francisco Public Library, The Library of Congress, Old St. Mary's Cathedral - San Francisco, The Cathedral of St. John the Baptist - Charleston, The Museum of the City of San Francisco, The University of South Carolina, The Maritime Heritage Project, The Historical Charleston Foundation, The U.S. National Park Service, The Metropolitan Museum of Art, The National Gallery of Art, and all those whose historical stories were left behind. I hope you found the dreams you were searching for.

Most importantly, to my Lord and creator, Jesus Christ. Every good and perfect gift is from above. You use everything for good. Without You, none of this could be.

ABOUT THE AUTHOR

K elsey Gietl is the author of the early 1910s Over the Atlantic duology, the WWI War Across Waters duology, and the 1850s Larksong Legacy series. Combining faith, family, and lessons from our past, her books provide inspirational stories with a dose of romance and a dash of intrigue.

She holds a Bachelor of Fine Arts in Theatre Design and Graphic Design and has made a career in fields from event planning and proposal writing to product management and communications.

She lives in Missouri with her husband, two children, and two dogs. She is a member of the Daughters of the American Revolution and the Catholic Writers Guild.

You can connect with her online at:

kelseygietl.com

www.ingramcontent.com/pod-product-compliance
Lightning Source LLC
Chambersburg PA
CBHW022023240626
47154CB00007B/2235